BORN

DIFFER

Shared Experiences, Different Pathways

By

Michael Tinney

ISBN-13: 9781699670514

DEDICATION

Margaret Tucker (née Tinney),
a single woman whose strength inspired this book.

CONTENTS

CHAPTER 1

The Plan

30th June 2008

Tony woke with a start.

Shivering despite the warm sunshine, he looked around quickly, trying to clear his foggy mind as he lifted himself up onto his elbow to survey the landscape around him. The thick padded coat that he had acquired yesterday was damp from the morning dew, and his first action was to wrestle himself free of its confines and discard it on the grass.

The last 24 hours had taken their toll. Absconding from jail, he had travelled halfway across the country, before falling asleep in the open countryside. The sense of freedom yesterday was overwhelming, but today was different. Today his plans were about to become reality, and the very thought made his whole body shiver in the morning heat.

Hatred that had been eating away at him in jail was looking for a release. Tony needed to move on but his mind was in constant turmoil; with the explosion of colours and smells bombarding his senses it was impossible to concentrate. His jaw ached from the constant grinding of his teeth, and he felt stiff all over, more from sheer tension than the damp grass that had been his bed.

Time was already working against him. His absence would have set alarm bells ringing, and the authorities would be lumbering into action, with a full-scale manhunt likely to start in the next 24 hours.

No more delay – this was the time for action.

"One, two, three." He nodded as he whispered the final number and jumped a little unsteadily to his feet. He staggered forward and leant against the trunk of the tree that had provided overnight shelter. Raising a hand to his face he shook away the sleep and looked around, blinking, to take in the morning brightness.

Tony knew that now it was time to act without overthinking and deal with the consequences later. In any event the consequences could be no worse than his recent past. He had operated largely on instinct in prison, because it was the only way he could survive in there. Injustice was almost the code amongst inmates, and weakness was punished above everything else. Tony had survived, reacting to events but showing no emotion, no weakness. Now he needed to keep this up for just another few days, and then justice would be done and he could return to normality, if such a thing still existed.

He forcibly kicked the heavy coat away and wandered out from under the tree that had been his temporary shelter. Although now some 20 miles from where he had grown up, Tony knew this area well, and it was reassuring to see the familiar green of the countryside reinvigorating his dulled senses. After prison, the varied colours and diversity of the real world were almost straining his eyes.

The strict daily regime had really worn him down in the last few months, and for the first time in his life depression had started to set in. Everything was so grey and bland, from the food to the buildings to the repetitive daily cycles and associated noises, that it had gradually sapped away his enthusiasm for life, and numbed his mind. Hunger ate away at him daily, and sapped much of his strength or enthusiasm to do anything. The food when it came was always cold, and overcooked to the extent that he would close his eyes and be unable to guess what it was he was eating. His tastes were numbed as much as his other senses and this had brought back very distant memories of unhappy times in his early childhood, long before he had been adopted by Bob and Paula. He did not know if the memories were real or imagined; his past like so much of the present was a fog of unanswered questions and distorted truth.

Today it felt like he was coming out of a coma as the noises, smell and colour of his surroundings were bombarding his senses; even the air outside tasted sweeter. He could feel his brain sharpening as it lumbered back into life, ready to face the challenges ahead.

If it wasn't for the need to seek revenge he knew he would have buckled by now, but Tony had planned today for the last four years. Deep down he knew this was his one and only chance to avenge his brother's death and his own wasted years in prison.

There were so many thoughts to contend with, still so many unanswered questions, and yet the stunning beauty of the outside world on a bright spring morning was proving to be an unwelcome distraction. With a wry smile he walked down to the lone house in front of him, and took a bottle of milk from the front porch.

Tony had been only a few metres from the house for a full 12 hours now with no sign of life whatsoever, and the milk delivery was the first real indicator that someone was due home shortly. As he leant against the front porch drinking from the bottle the detail of the property was starting to sink in.

It was all red brick, built in a dormer bungalow style of about five bedrooms. The nearest corner was almost set into the hillside so that you could probably jump straight from the grassy bank onto the roof. A path ran around the entire property, but there were heavily padlocked gates on both sides. The only real approach to the property was from a single track road which all but ended at the house. It did carry on but was even more of a farm track from there on, with grass growing up between the wheel tracks. The lane appeared to lead to a picnic area and nature reserve, which bore a sign saying it was for public use but belonged to the junior school at the top of the lane.

After checking that no one was around he scaled the left side gate to get a better view at the back of the property. Every bit of knowledge would be important later, and he was not going to get any second chances. From the rear he had a perfect view of the downstairs rooms by looking through the long glazed conservatory that ran the whole length of the back of the property. In pride of place he saw the full-size snooker table in the front lounge, surrounded by cabinets full of trophies. His brother Graham had always been a better player than Mark; even when he was confined to the wheelchair for weeks at a time he could bounce back and win any tournament he entered. To him it was the only sport he had left where he could still compete and beat able-bodied players. Mark was obviously making up for lost time now on the local amateur circuit.

Losing his brother the way he did was still hard to comprehend, and it seemed to be part of a different reality. Mark's home would hopefully provide some answers. The house was immaculately laid out inside, with no expense spared on the furnishings or gadgets. No surprise there then, in fact he expected nothing less from Mark, but the high-level alarm, locked gates and barred windows showed a paranoia about security that was out of place.

After scouring the whole property for a good 45 minutes the frustrations were starting to grow. Tony needed defined answers to problems, and at the moment his master plan was anything but defined. He would need access to the property later if he was to confront Mark, and he wanted to keep the element of surprise as his advantage. That meant getting into the heavily secured building undetected.

Unfortunately there were no obvious entry points, and all he could do was sit on the front drive and think coolly about the options. On a warm day the upstairs windows might be left open later, and this could make the grassy bank the best route in, but it was really only half a plan. Muttering to himself to add clarity to his thinking, Tony went through his vague plans:

"Wait until Mark comes home and then be sure he is alone. Waiting for another day is not an option. After dark creep up to the house, and disable the telephone system." This was the most risky part of the operation because he had to act before the damaged lines were noticed, but he had seen at least three panic buttons in the house and he could not take chances. These were bound to be wired to the police.

Tony knew that he had made life difficult for himself whilst in prison, but even he was amazed at the lengths Mark had gone to. Three times the parole board had turned him down, and he should have been more intelligent from the outset. At first he refused to admit his guilt, and then kept on about seeking revenge against Mark whom he blamed for his brother's death even though Mark had never been either prosecuted or convicted.

Despite this, his time spent in prison seemed unjust for what was a relatively modest drugs conviction against which Tony still hoped to appeal in the long run. Even a few of the prison warders felt the system was working against him, or as they put it, his enemies on the outside knew the right people. Conspiracy theories were always rife in prison.

Mark had always been a nervous individual, but why the elaborate security in such a quiet rural retreat? Tony was only on a rehabilitation visit, and he should have returned to the prison yesterday. He was due for release in three weeks but the timing of his escape was crucial. No one expects you to abscond so close to release so the initiative was back with him. For the first time in years he was back in control of his life.

The loss of Graham had been a bigger shock than he had realised, and it had taken him nearly a year to start thinking straight again. Now he had to focus more than ever.

"After the alarm is disabled walk up to the front door," whispered Tony as he continued muttering the plan to himself. The roof option was by now all but dismissed. It was too noisy and too risky. "Keep the element of surprise and go in the front door. No forced entry, less to explain later."

Tony took a deep breath and thought of his options, he needed a mobile phone and the school run should provide the easiest opportunity to get one; 25 mothers collecting children from the local school probably wouldn't even miss the thing for a few days.

He also needed some protection. Mark had been an old friend, but first and foremost he was responsible for Graham's death, and he was going to be like a caged animal when confronted with his past. The whole point of today was to gain freedom and absolution, not a life sentence for a revenge killing. The question was, did he need an insurance policy, and would a weapon give him one?

He was so deep in private contemplation that he nearly missed the car that had stopped in the lane only about 50 metres away. It was the voices that startled him first, and he instinctively swung around to see a couple jump out of their car with a picnic hamper and blanket. They were an odd-looking pair to be out for a romantic lunch together in the country, and this was a suspiciously secluded place to choose for a romantic lunch. The man was about 40 years of age, balding with a middle spread that appeared to be the result more of business lunches than picnics. She was much younger, about 25 to 30, and extremely petite if not anorexic, with very long ginger hair almost reaching down to her waist.

Curiously it looked as though she had brought a pair of binoculars along for the meal, and both of them were struggling to hide their obvious guilt as they kept looking sheepishly around. Tony smirked to himself as he took in the scene, and imagined that they must be work colleagues out for an illicit meeting. He was tempted to follow to see what the binoculars would be used for, but was content in the end to just leave the possibilities up to his imagination.

Feeling a little conspicuous stood on the grassy lane, he didn't want to be there whilst they ate a prolonged lunch but his exit routes were blocked. The only solution was to bluff his way past them. He quickly broke into a gentle jog and nonchalantly passed the couple, acknowledging them with a simple, "Hello." They were deep in conversation with each other and scarcely paid him a second glance. As they walked along the grassy track Tony knew he had to get out of sight before they returned and silently skirted back up the small drive towards the house. He scrambled part way up the bank, and then dropped down onto the path behind the locked gate at the side of the house. As he did so he glanced back up to the top and he could have kicked himself for leaving his discarded coat up by the tree. Despite barely running 100 metres he could feel beads of sweat breaking out all over.

Before he could recover his composure though, he heard rushed footsteps as the overweight man suddenly jogged back, before stopping and nearly collapsing at the rear of his car, hands on his knees trying to get his breath back. Tony held his own breath, trying to stem the rising paranoia as he told himself that this had to be nothing more than strange coincidence, but even so he was immensely relieved when the man reached into the boot of the car and took out a bottle of water.

"Calm down, and focus," he whispered to himself for reassurance. Then he closed his eyes and lay back against the wall of the house. He had to stay out of sight from now on; at worst he may have his picture on the news, and the fewer people that saw him the better.

This was after all a quiet isolated track in the middle of nowhere, and there was no reason for him to be found out before he had the opportunity to confront Mark.

As he took in his new surroundings Tony conceded that it was certainly an impressive property, although the gardens looked somehow out of character with the rest of the house. Tony couldn't work out what looked wrong at first but as he kept looking from the lawn to the house it suddenly dawned on him. The lawns were uncut, and the weeds were starting to take over the flower borders whereas the house was absolutely immaculate in every detail. It was almost as though the occupiers were away or on holiday.

"No," Tony whispered to himself, forgetting that the picnic couple were still in such close proximity. Surely fate wasn't going to conspire against him again. As his frustration was starting to mount he remembered the milk that he had stolen earlier. Maybe the holiday was about to end, and what a return he had in store. He had a quick look around for other clues but there was nothing apparent. Tony sat for a while on a small wooden bench in the far corner of the garden, and even toyed with the idea of breaking into the shed, and mowing Mark's lawn for him. This was bound to unsettle him as soon as he arrived home. The very thought brought a smile to his face, but it was a silly idea that was bound to end in someone hearing him so he just relaxed and absorbed the morning sun.

After some 20 minutes he got up off the bench and carried on walking slowly around the house. As he reached the gate on the right he scaled the adjoining fence, and readied himself to jump down when another car turned off the main road into the lane, and continued on past the school. Tony had no option but to jump back down off the fence and hide behind the heavily padlocked gate.

The car pulled onto the drive and a young lady jumped out. As he peered through the gaps in the gate Tony recognised her at once, and the shock was so great he nearly called out. Tall and slim with shoulder-length dark hair, she was dressed immaculately as ever, but what on earth was Charlotte doing here? She never kept in touch with Mark, so how did she know where he lived? Had Tony told her in one of his many letters? Even so, why was she here, and why today?

Whatever it was she didn't intend staying long, as the engine on her car was left running whilst she ran to the front door and posted something through before jumping back in. The car crunched into reverse then paused for what seemed an eternity. Charlotte was staring at the gate, almost squinting, as Tony twisted so that his body was flat back against the property wall. Frozen to the spot, he could hardly even dare to breathe, and he could feel the blood pulsing through his body and throbbing in his head. So many questions were bouncing around, and his plans were now in complete turmoil. Why on earth would his oldest and best friend be here of all places, and why today? What was her relationship with Mark, and what had she put through the letterbox?

Suddenly new doubts started to creep into his mind. Over the years Tony had learnt to trust no one as much as Charlotte. Everyone else along the way had let him down. Promises to help free him had not been fulfilled, and if there was to be any point in his life at all he had to know why she was here. She was still staring at the gate, and Tony had his head twisted hard to the side so that he could see the back of the vehicle. Charlotte appeared to have a change of heart as she put the handbrake on and the white reversing lights went out as she started to open the driver's door.

Panic still froze him to the spot, and the beads of perspiration were stinging his eyes as they ran down his forehead. Still he could not move, even wiping the sweat away was too much and he barely winced at the pain. His mind was focused purely on what he could see, channelling his thoughts such that he was unaware of anything outside his tunnel of vision. Cramp was building in his legs as he was down on his haunches against the wall, clawing away at his calves every time they twitched, but his focus was elsewhere. His other senses were paralysed and although he could hear other people running in the distance his brain wouldn't register their significance and he continued staring ahead at Charlotte.

The footsteps were getting closer and his brain kept trying to alert him to the fresh danger. Then like the crack of a whip he finally registered the new threat. Unfortunately from his vantage point Tony could barely see the odd couple running but he knew they were getting closer. As they came into view through the narrow gap in the gate the man was struggling to run with the hamper, and both of them seemed agitated. Perhaps that is why they were apparently ending their lunch so suddenly. They stopped as their path was blocked by Charlotte's car and then the relief flowed through Tony's body, as she slumped back into the vehicle, put it back into reverse, turned around and sped off, flicking up some loose gravel as she went.

Now it was the turn of the couple to stare at the gate. *Is there a massive sign on the other side saying, "Hello, I'm hiding behind here"?* thought Tony.

It was only the briefest of moments before they looked back to each other, remembered that they were supposed to be somewhere else and carried on their way. The quiet tranquillity of the countryside returned but the adrenalin was still racing through his veins, and not for the first time Tony was starting to doubt his own nerve. He was the trespasser today, breaking the law probably for the first time in his life, and despite the wide-open countryside around him he felt like he was being watched.

He had to stay rational, knowing full well that no one was out there, apart from the couple who were now disappearing up the lane. Tony took several deep breaths, and waited, breathing deeply and trying to stay calm. As soon as it was all quiet, and the couple had driven off in their car, he wearily climbed up again and jumped over the fence.

Why, why, why? was racing through his thoughts, but most of all he wondered what was in that note from Charlotte. He approached the front door, knelt down and very gingerly lifted the flap on the letterbox to see if the letter had gone all the way in.

It was his lucky day after all. The bristles on the inside of letterbox were holding on to the last corner of the piece of paper, and it hadn't fallen through. Tony surveyed the situation for a few moments and let his knees fall to the floor so that his whole body was poised. He took a deep breath and moved two of his fingers towards the bit of paper, but they were shaking too much so he withdrew them quickly, and then clenched them with his other hand.

After a few minutes he opened the flap again and slowly moved his right hand forward, steady as a rock this time. Only the tiniest corner of the paper was visible; his fingers gently moved the bristles to one side so that he could get a better view, and then he edged toward the note. As his thick fingers gently eased the bristles away, it was suddenly too late, as he caught a glimpse of the paper fluttering to the floor through the glass of the door.

"Shit!" he screamed as he thumped the door in anger. He knew it was pointless, but after the tension of the last hour it felt good, so he hit it again and again, until he could see his knuckles starting to bleed. Frustrated and angry he sunk into a heap at the door and wondered what to do next. The last 36 hours seemed to take their toll as a wave of tiredness and anxiety filled his body. He knew that his body was demanding sleep and he had to give in if he was going to be able to function at all later on. Even so, his subconscious was still working and his mind was demanding answers. If Mark was away, then why was the note from Charlotte sat alone on the mat? Surely he would have had more post.

He forced the flap open again and held the bristles firmly apart so that he could clearly see into the hall for the first time. There was no sign of a neat pile of letters, prepared by a friendly neighbour, and yet the thin layer of dust over the ornaments did suggest no one was staying at home.

So why was the milk delivered today? Was it just a mistake, or was Mark due back? There were too many questions already, and he had only been out of prison for a short while. It had all seemed so easy when he sat in his cell planning what he would do, but that was before the unexpected quirks of reality. All too often his life had been disrupted by the actions of others, and usually sent into turmoil. Whilst in prison he had tried to make sense of events leading up to his arrest but to no avail. Conspiracy theories were rife, and Tony refused to let himself fall into that trap, knowing that he was above such trivial gossip and speculation but all the same he felt just like a pawn in a much bigger game.

He walked slowly back up the bank and settled down on top of his padded coat. His brain was trying to digest so much information that his skull felt too small, and Tony shuddered as he felt the frustration course through his whole body. To try and calm down he took some slow deep breaths and attempted to focus. He looked from his vantage point up to the school at the top of the lane, following the screams and shouts from the playground games. As he watched the children playing thoughts turned to his own childhood. With the sun warming his weary body his eyelids became increasingly heavy as his mind drifted back to his school days, where this whole sorry mess began.

With the warm gentle breeze adding to his physical comfort Tony allowed himself to drift off into an uneasy sleep.

CHAPTER 2

The Early Years

"Come on, Tony!" shouted Graham as he pulled the covers off his brother's bed. "Time to get up! It's BIG school tomorrow and this is your last day to prove yourself."

Tony tried to pull the duvet back on but it was no good. Graham was always first up. Their parents joked that he was hyperactive, and most teenagers only got up after eleven in the school holidays.

It was a strange sensation waking up with butterflies in his stomach, but the mere mention of BIG school was enough to set them off. The problem with a brother like Graham was that he was best at everything, and took his move to big school two years ago as just another day. Tony on the other hand was comfortable at his old junior school. They had only moved in with this family three years ago, and it had taken him longer to settle than his older brother. Now it was all change again, and half of his friends weren't even going to St Thomas Comprehensive.

As if all that wasn't enough, Graham and his best friend Mark had been on at him all holidays saying that he wasn't good enough to join their Warrior gang. Today was the initiation final, and Tony didn't have a clue about what was in store for him. He had hoped to finish the test weeks ago but they kept playing tricks on him, and changing the challenges. Tony was absolutely torn about whether to get up today at all or just forget the whole thing and face the consequences.

As he snuggled under the duvet memories of the last test came flooding back. The Warrior Challenge was apparently an essential for all year sevens who wanted to survive the first week and so it was that he had gone out with two other boys, James and Paul from his old class, led by Mark and Graham. The other two boys facing the challenge weren't particularly good friends with Tony or for that matter Graham and Mark, but they all knew how important it was to be accepted as part of the gang in the first term. They were the only three boys who lived in the village, so were determined to prove themselves fit for the challenge, as most of the other new pupils would be coming from bigger groups.

The five boys crossed fields and streams, scaled fences, and made makeshift bows from some old wood and string, which all seemed fun enough. Then Mark brought them back to the task with mention of the 'hollow tree shower challenge'. Graham said no at first but his objections lacked any real conviction and as ever Mark persuaded him.

After another couple of fields they all arrived and Mark explained the rules. He loved the power that he held over the three younger boys as they all sat transfixed. Privately they all called him Captain Stammer in reference to a slight stutter that only became apparent when he was either over-excited or nervous. At this moment, however, they were all too scared themselves to think of nicknames, and listened intently.

"All y-y-y-you…" Mark paused and took a deep breath. This may have calmed him but it only increased the tension amongst the others.

"All you have to do is to climb up the outside trunk of the tree, jump inside and put your hand out of the hole in the bottom to prove you have climbed all the way down."

It all looked relatively simple so Tony took the initiative and volunteered first, eager above anything to prove himself to the two older boys. The tree was only about five feet tall so he climbed up gingerly and before long was lowering himself down inside. Jumping down the last two feet and scrambling around in the mud looking for the hole, he felt sure some light would come through but he could see nothing so he shouted to the outside.

"Hello?" but there was no reply. "I am at the bottom but I cannot see the hole."

Silence.

"Hello?" he shouted as loud as he could this time.

"Hello," came the reply. "How far down have you got so far?"

Tony could hear the subdued giggles outside and knew this was all part of the challenge.

"I am at the bottom but I cannot see the hole."

A long pause followed, and just as he was about to shout again Mark spoke.

"We covered up the hole with leaves. It's all part of the challenge. Did I forget to tell you?"

It was obvious from the hysterical laughter outside that this was a new part of the challenge but Tony was unfazed and started prodding around the base with a stick he had found until suddenly it shot outwards and daylight seeped in.

"Okay," said Mark. "Now to prove you are all the way down inside hold your arm outside and count to fifty."

The older boys' laughter erupted from outside but Tony didn't care. He had done it and he would have the last laugh for once as he lay down on his side and pushed his right arm out. The joy was immense, he was in the club and now even Mark would respect him.

At first the sensation felt like his hand was being tickled, but then warm liquid started running down his arm, and Tony realised what they were doing. He tried to jump up but his arm wouldn't come out of the hole and he was stuck. He arched his back as he tried to get up and remove his arm in one go, but it was no use. The more he struggled the more it hurt, and the harder it became to extricate his arm. *Stay calm*, he told himself. *Breathe, relax, stay calm.* He relaxed his whole body, and stared up into the daylight at the top of the tree, but he still could not get his elbow out of the hole. Next moment even worse was to come as water flooded in from the top of the hollow tree, and Tony struggled to cover his face with his left arm, whilst still trying to free his right one. In sheer panic he wrenched as hard as he could and twisted round onto his knees as it came out and he pushed himself up against the far side of the trunk, kicking furiously at the puddle of foul-smelling urine that was starting to flood in through the hole. Scrabbling in the dirt with his feet, he scraped up enough mud to block the hole and sat quietly sobbing and listening to the exaggerated laughter from outside. He nervously sniffed at his left sleeve, and was relieved that it was covered in nothing more than water. In sheer anger he tore off his entire right sleeve and trampled it into the ground.

Feeling thoroughly miserable he didn't know what to do next, until his thoughts were broken by Graham's voice. "Sorry about that, Tony, I had the bottle of water up the tree but I didn't know what Mark was planning."

He stayed totally silent. He wasn't going to give them the satisfaction of a reply. After a few minutes Mark started, "Come on, T-T-Tony, it was only a bit of a piss take."

The exaggerated laughter started all over again.

"Climb out and join us, and we will make you a Warrior!" shouted Graham with a hint of sympathy in his voice. But Tony sat resolutely still and despite their pleas waited in near silence; he was swallowing his own tears but knew that he was controlling them enough not to be heard. His right arm was in agony, and the cuts were stinging like crazy. In the half-light he tried to pick the bits of encrusted twig off his skin. Eventually the pleading subsided and as it was starting to get dark he clambered up to look for ways out. Only then did the reality hit him. He was cold and damp, with fading light and he couldn't actually see a way to climb out. There were no obvious footholds and the trunk was too wide for him to push up against the sides. He tried from all angles but it was no good and with his right arm throbbing in pain there was nothing else he could do.

"Help!"

"Help!"

"I am in the tree! Help!"

He waited with his ears trying to pick out any sounds, but nothing.

"Help! Please, someone help!"

Still nothing, by now he felt so miserable that he just started sobbing uncontrollably and lay down again on the floor. He was starting to accept the inevitable, that this would be his bed for the night. He knew in his heart that crying wouldn't help, yet somehow, it was the only comfort that he had, and all he could muster was a pitiful, "Help," between sobs. As the last light was disappearing he gave up and just sat sniffling on the floor. The stupid bloody warriors. Charlotte was right, it was just a stupid boys' game. She was always right, and always bloody stuck up. Why did she have to be their neighbour, and in Tony's class again next year? It was strange to think of Charlotte now; she and Tony never got on, and he always thought of her when he was in a bad mood, and right now he couldn't be more upset, or in a worse mood. At least this thought brought a smile to his face.

Crack.

The sudden noise as something hit the outside of the tree trunk startled Tony, and sent his senses into overdrive. Adrenalin was coursing through his body as he sat bolt upright, not daring to breathe, listening intently for anything. He could feel the veins throbbing on the side of his neck as he tried to hear the next sound. Were the boys back? Should he shout, or just be quiet? He gingerly shuffled his feet around and listened intently, trying to breathe more slowly so that he could hear more. He remembered being told to stay out of the woods at night because a lot of old tramps used to doss in them. What if someone lived in this tree, and he was just getting home?

Tony knew the stupidity of his own thoughts but his heart and mind were racing too fast to be logical. Then he shuffled back in shock as a rough claw started scratching at the base.

"What is it, old girl? Where is your stick?" a voice shouted out.

Tony froze again now, and tried to think. What should he do?

Desperation took over.

"Hu-hu-hel…" he stuttered as he tried to say something.

Suddenly the dog went wild barking and clawing at the tree trunk.

"Quiet, girl, what was that noise? Quiet now. Down."

Tony waited for the barking to subside and tried his voice again.

"Help! I am stuck in this tree, can you get me out please?"

"What did you say? Speak up, will you? I am a bit hard of hearing."

Tony's heart sank again. How was some deaf old bloke going to get him out of here?

"I am stuck in the tree. Please help me to get out. My name is Tony."

"Is someone trying to play a trick on me? Here, listen, I may be old but I am not stupid, you know. Bloody trees don't talk, never did and never will, you know."

"It's not the tree, it's me, Tony, I am stuck inside."

"Stony the bloody duck, you say? I have never heard such rubbish, there are no ducks out here, and the noises are coming from this tree trunk."

"STUCK, STUCK, STUCK!"

"Now you mind your language, whoever you are. If I catch who is behind this I will tell your parents, using language like that."

Tony nearly gave up, unsure whether to laugh or cry. He knew though that this was his last chance and decided to give it one last try.

"PLEASE HELP ME, I AM STUCK INSIDE THE TREE!" he shouted as clearly as he possibly could.

"Stuck in the tree, you say? Well why didn't you say so first of all rather than trying to frighten me with all of your swearing? Leave it to me. I will go and get some help. I will leave Petra here with you for company and come back as soon as I can."

"THANK YOU!" cried Tony as the relief flowed through his body, and tears once again rolled down his cheeks.

Then within minutes he could hear another noise that sounded like a car approaching. Tony strained his ears to make sure he wasn't imagining things.

"You are in luck, sonny, looks like the search party has arrived."

At that point more light flooded in through the hole in the bottom of the tree and Tony could hear car doors slamming and people getting out. The relief he felt was immense as Charlotte's dad peered over the top of the tree with an outstretched arm for Tony to grab hold of.

"Come on, lad, you must be starving, and cold. We need to get you home," said Adam in a comforting tone.

*

Graham was grounded for a whole week after that, but everyone was going to know about the whole episode at St Thomas, because they had needed Charlotte's dad's Land Rover to get across the fields, and she had insisted on coming along for the ride. Apparently she had seen the other boys arrive home, and it was only her persistent nagging that had alerted the parents to what was going on. To cap it all Tony had to take round a box of chocolates the following morning and thank her. Ever since then she had just looked at Tony and smirked. Tomorrow was really going to be terrible, and his only hope now was to get through today's test with some honour. Mark said that his membership was cancelled because he had involved parents last time out. The Warriors were apparently very anti-parents.

Reluctantly he rolled out of the comfort of his warm bed, dressed and pulled on his trainers like a condemned man. He trudged downstairs to join Graham for breakfast and wondered just how bad the new challenge could be. Surely they wouldn't risk anything too stupid now. At ten o'clock the gang set off again with the party led by Mark. Tony slammed the front door behind him and dragged his heels as he walked slowly behind his brother.

"Bye. Look after Tony, won't you?" called Charlotte as they passed her front door. "Remember it's school tomorrow so he needs a good night's sleep."

That was all he needed; any more embarrassment today and he would never live it down for the rest of his life. Paul and James were just behind him and both sniggered, but rather than looking up he marched on with his head down, desperate to avoid eye contact with either Charlotte or the boys. The party went through to the end of the village and then across an old wooden stile across the fields. The farmers had all been busy of late with harvesting so the fields looked barren in every direction, but at least it meant they could go straight across the middle without walking all around the edges. After about half an hour they climbed up as far as the old Gorge, which had dried to all but a tiny trickle of water after the long hot summer. In winter the Gorge itself had anything up to three feet of water in it, filled by a torrent coming off the surrounding fields, and falling as a huge waterfall over the basin-like edge. Tony loved seeing the Gorge just after heavy rainfalls, and he would often come up here on his own just to survey the spectacle of the water pouring in. The noise was a steady rumble, and he could watch for hours as the dirty brown water flowed with occasional debris, from tree parts to old prams that had been picked up along the way. It was so destructive and yet paradoxically so calming at the same time. In a way it enabled him to relax and focus, with his mind caught up in the ever present burble of the flowing water.

Whenever there was a really heavy storm he would always make his way up to see just how much the rim of the Gorge had opened out due to the destructive force of the water pouring in. Strangely the shape retained the same sort of kidney profile, but as if by magic the Gorge crept a few more feet up the field every year. Today though, all was quiet, and the party of younger boys sat at the bottom barely acknowledging each other's existence, awaiting their instructions from Mark and Graham who had run to the top of the field alone. They were probably a mile from any road and in the growing heat even the birds seemed to be taking a rest, with only the odd wasp or fly causing any distraction at all.

"Re-re-ready then, first one to the top wins!" shouted Mark through cupped hands.

Easy, thought Tony. This was going to be a breeze after the last test, as he leapt to his feet and scrambled up the Gorge. Being taller and definitely more athletic than the other two, he ran on, pulling out a bigger lead all the time. Slowed a little by the loose shingle, he still made it to the top a full 20 seconds before the others. At the top he simply collapsed in a heap, and pumped his fist into the air in relief. The other two clambered up the last few feet and collapsed beside him, James first then Paul, trying to recover their breathing which wasn't easy in the midday heat.

"N-n-now," said Mark, "the challenge is as follows."

The words took a moment to register as Tony felt his anger rising. "What the hell? But you can't give us another challenge. You said first one to the top wins, and I clearly won!" shouted Tony indignantly.

"No," said Mark, apparently losing his stammer once he felt in control. "I said first one to the top wins the right to go first, but you all raced off so fast I expect you missed the last bit."

Graham, who was clearly enjoying the controversy, wandered over with an old wreck of a bike, and a long straight branch they had obviously brought up earlier in the week. Speaking for the first time, he gave the younger boys their task.

"Today we are going to play chicken run, and to make things easier you each have three runs. We will stick the stake in the ground six feet from the edge of the Gorge, and you have to cycle down from that tree over there in less than 20 seconds to pull the stake out. The winner will be the person with the fastest time, but remember to stop before you go over the edge."

"Forget it," said Tony, and turned away. "There is no way I am going to cycle full speed downhill towards the edge of the Gorge pick up the stake, and the then stop in six feet with only one hand on the brakes, on that old wreck of a bike."

"Chick-chick-chicken, that's why it's called chicken run." Tony wasn't sure if Mark was stammering again or not, and neither did he care, this was too risky, and after last time he would rather be ridiculed and face the consequences than start school with a broken leg and still be ridiculed. With that, he started walking away down the slope, looking to James and Paul for moral support.

"Come back!" shouted Graham as he and Mark huddled together in discussion. After a few moments they broke apart again and Graham spoke.

"We have decided to make things easier in that you don't actually have to pick the stake up, just put a leg or arm out and push it over. You can each check the bike over before your run, and if it gets too dangerous we promise to stop."

Everyone turned to Tony, who was now some six feet from the rest of the group, to see what his reaction would be. Faced with renewed pressure he had little option but to at least try, despite his gut instinct telling him to run a mile. After all, he supposed if any of them could do it then he felt sure he could.

"Okay, I will give it a go, but if I think it's too dangerous then that is it and you can all forget your silly gang."

"Glad to see my brother got some backbone after all, and don't worry, we will tell Charlotte how brave you have been if you succeed."

Tony blushed at the very mention of her name, he didn't even know why, but the more he tried to look normal the redder he felt his cheeks glowing.

"Right then," called Mark who was now clearly relishing the leadership role. "I will go to the top of the hill and check the bike over whilst Graham puts the stake in at the six-foot mark."

"You three go with Graham and check the position of the stake and then everyone come to the top of the hill, and I will go to the stake with my stopwatch to time you."

Everything seemed clear enough, though why Mark couldn't just let Graham have his stopwatch and do the timing was ridiculous. Tony knew him well enough by now, however, to realise that all the walking backwards and forwards was just his way of building up the tension even more. As he wandered up to the top of the hill, Tony couldn't help wondering just what his brother saw in his so-called best friend. Graham excelled at everything he did and Mark gained popularity by being so close to him. Together they were easily the best runners, swimmers, and footballers in their year, but Graham always had enough in reserve to beat his friend when it counted. If they hadn't been such good friends they were sure to have been rivals, so he could see the logic in them working together. Mark clearly knew this as well, and followed the old adage of 'If you can't beat them then join them'. Together they were a formidable force in school and out of it, but Tony resented the way Mark always tried to split the two brothers up, and undermine him.

A lot of the parents were also wary of Mark, for some trouble he had been in a while ago, but try as he might Tony had never got to the bottom of what actually happened. All he knew was that after they had been in the village a few months, and Mark started calling around, he heard a conversation between his new parents and Charlotte's dad warning them that he was not to be trusted.

Tony had seen how Mark always kept on the right side of Graham, but at the same time always looked out for himself first and foremost. He had let Graham take most of the blame after the hollow tree incident, although it was clear that Mark was the driving force behind it all. For now though, the challenge ahead was all that mattered so Tony put the other thoughts behind him, and looked at the long run downhill to the edge of the Gorge. Mark finished tinkering with the bike, put some rusty old tools back in the torn black bag hanging from the saddle and ran off downhill, shouting, "Wait for me to reach the edge and then come on down as fast as you can."

"What about the bike? I need time to check it out first, I need about ten minutes," queried Tony, in a deliberate ploy to avoid the actual ride for as long as possible.

Mark stopped midway down and turned. "I-I-I-I've done all that, just get on the bike and hurry up will you. If-if-if you take all the day the parents will come looking for you before we get a chance to finish."

"Bugger off, you said we could check the bike out, not you, so play fair." Tony was determined not to be undermined any more today. These stupid tests were humiliating enough without having to give up all pride.

"Chick-chick-chicken," taunted Mark, expecting the others to join in, but no one did.

"Give me the bloody bike for God's sake!" shouted Graham, angry at both of them for messing about, "This is only a simple task for you to show what you're worth for once. I am going to be so embarrassed when you join school."

At that, he snatched the bike off Tony, jumped on the saddle and started to pedal with all his might downhill. Mark, who had nearly reached the pole turned around as Graham set off and then ran waving his arms and shouting, "No! Stop! No! It's not your challenge. Stop!"

Graham pedalled furiously on, looking behind occasionally to show to the younger boys that he still had time to pose, but confident that he could complete the task in the allotted time. For Tony time was dragging, as he wished he had not made such a fuss. He had already resigned himself to at least trying the task so he should have just got on with it. As ever, Graham the super sportsman was about to show him up. Mark was clearly furious at the proceedings and even appeared to lunge at his best friend as he passed him midway down the course, trying to dislodge him off the bike. Graham was far too quick and simply pulled up the front wheel in the air as he passed him. All three younger boys were sat on the grass watching him go, as Mark looked at his watch and started calling out in slow staccato style.

"Fifteen, sixteen, seventeen."

Every second seemed to take an eternity. With Graham pedalling like fury, the enormity of what he still had to achieve hung like a black cloud in front of Tony.

"Eighteen." Despite his brother's super riding he was just approaching the pole as nineteen was called out.

In celebration he kicked it over and pulled up in another wheelie. At that moment time stopped. Tony sat transfixed like he was in a weird nightmare watching some terrifying things happen, but unable to act. He wanted to run on down the hill, but his whole body was frozen like a block of ice, yet from inside he almost felt like his heart was on fire as the heat built up within him. He blinked several times trying to clear his eyes. Unable to work his mouth, he couldn't shout or scream, much as his head was telling him to. He could feel the saliva building in his mouth but couldn't swallow and it started to dribble down his chin. Still he couldn't act. Blinking was the only reflex he had and the more he blinked the more he realised that this wasn't a dream but reality actually unfolding in front of him.

As Graham had pulled up the handlebars the front wheel seemed to take on a life of its own, and dropped away from the front forks. Seemingly free from the main frame it immediately gathered speed and rolled on over the edge of the Gorge in a sick premonition of what was about to unfold. No one could see the panic on Graham's face as he suddenly realised that the next six feet could be all that stood between him and death. With only seconds to go thoughts raced through his mind. The anger at Tony, which had pushed him on only seconds before, vanished, and he realised that his own bravado was putting his life in danger. As the front of the bike dropped the stupidity of the situation brought a grimace to Graham's face; he stiffened his whole body in preparation for what was to come, and held on to the handlebars with all his strength.

Tony was still unable to move as he saw the front forks, now minus the front wheel, hit the soft ground around the edge of the

Gorge and sink deep into the soil. The back of the bike arced high up into the air and he heard the audible grunt as Graham went over the handlebars. His back seemed strangely rigid as his feet swung over the top in a pendulum effect. *Let go,* thought Tony, but he couldn't shout and anyway it was no use.

Graham flipped full circle through the air and his whole body bounced off the edge of the Gorge with his spine and head taking the full force as another crunch could be heard on the otherwise still day. It was like he had landed on a trampoline as his upper body bounced over the edge and he tumbled head over heels out of sight. Silence followed and nothing moved. Waiting for any sign of life, Tony's brain was telling his body to act. Slowly he felt the numbness ebbing away, and he moved his right arm up to wipe the dribble off his chin. No one else was moving and with his legs still weak, he half ran half fell down the hill. With his knees unable to lock, they went out sideways at every step. Mark meanwhile was working backwards from where he sat in a crab-like motion, moving on his elbows and feet. James and Paul were both crying at the top of the hill, and offering no help at all.

"What are you doing moving backwards?" shouted Tony. "Get to the edge and check Graham."

"I-I-I...can't. Look, stop running, wait a second. We have to get this sorted. Don't tell the adults I checked the bike, okay. It was a silly accident, okay."

"You miserable bastard. Forget about that. You check Graham. Get to the edge quickly." Still running as fast as his legs would carry him, it was taking all his concentration just to stay upright.

Mark jumped up and body checked Tony as he approached in order to stop him. Mark was much bigger and heavier but the anger in Tony meant it was all he could do to hold him. Mark took a deep breath as Tony wriggled furiously, trying to break his vice-like grip.

"I will go to the edge, I just wanted to wait and see if he just recovered first. I hoped he might have just climbed back up. Wait here and let me check." Mark shouted the orders at the top of his voice, hoping to regain his authority. Tony wasn't sure but equally he didn't dare think about the consequences of that horrendous fall and stopped wriggling as Mark released his grip and ran to the edge. As he peered over he could make out the twisted form lying about halfway down. He raised his hand to stop Tony moving forward and then scrambled over the edge.

"Graham. Graham are you okay?" Mark desperately tried to stay calm, but the tears were welling up and his whole body was shaking involuntarily.

All he could get by way of response was a dull groan, and faint gurgling sound as Graham coughed up blood in front of him. Thoughts were racing through his head and he didn't know what to do. All the fun of the challenge from a few minutes ago had faded into this horror, and what about school tomorrow? Somewhere from the back of his mind he could hear voices telling him not move his friend, but he so wanted to pick him up and drag him back to the top. Help was all he could think of, and help was what he needed. Yes, that was it, they needed help, and fast. Mark scrambled back to the top ledge and barked out instructions.

"Tony, you have to get help and get it fast. Run back to the village and knock on the first door you get to and ask for an ambulance."

"What about Graham? How is he?" questioned Tony, trying to edge closer to see where his brother had landed.

Mark shrugged his shoulders, and replied as honestly as he could. "He looks rough, Tony, very rough, but we can't stand about arguing, he needs help now."

Tony looked uncertain but there was an air of unaccustomed sincerity about Mark's voice that convinced him to do as instructed, and after a moment's further hesitation he turned anyway and ran without saying a single word. As he watched him half run, and half stumble across the fields Mark's brain went into overdrive. The situation was pretty grave, and again he found himself in the middle of it all through no fault of his own. He knew how it would look to the adults and it was time for his self-preservation. The first thing he had to deal with was the other two boys. Mark had never cared for either of them much and only agreed they could join in to help spice the challenge up a bit, but it was never meant to end like this. Despite the seriousness of Graham's predicament, he also knew he had been in enough trouble this year already, and part of him was also desperate to do anything but face his crumpled friend again alone.

Damn, what were there bloody names?

Trying to sound confident and in control in spite of his inner turmoil he called over to them. "Y-y-y-you two stop crying and get here now. G-G-G-Graham needs your help. One of you needs to climb down and talk to him and keep him warm if he starts to get cold."

Slowly they got to their feet, still snivelling, and wandered over.

"Quick, for fuck's sake, this is the most trouble any of us has ever seen. RUN. RUN!"

As they reached the ledge they recoiled in horror at the sight of blood and the contorted body of Graham. It seemed like an eternity before either of them had the composure or strength of character to begin tentatively edging forward again. At the edge they both slipped down on their bottoms to where Graham was still twisting and moaning in agony. Mark quickly glanced around nervously, expecting an adult to walk over and reprimand him. Desperate in fact for some adult to take over regardless of the consequences that he was sure to face. It wasn't out of guilt, but he still bore the responsibility of having checked the bike over and knew full well how this would look.

He quickly ran over to the main frame and pulled the front forks out of the ground. There was no real damage to them but he had lost all rationale and despite the severity of his friend's injuries his focus was purely on repairing the bike. He knew that he had to get the front wheel back but as he approached the edge the sounds from below were getting worse, and try as he might it was impossible not to look. The two younger boys had stopped crying, but Graham now had a large patch of drying blood on his chin and down the front of his shirt. His breathing was laboured, and his chest was rasping like that of an old man on 60 a day.

Where was the help?

It seemed like hours had passed already, but the intense midday heat told him that in reality it was probably only a few minutes. The bike wheel had come to a rest in some undergrowth just to the right of Graham, and Mark scrambled down to retrieve it. Both front nuts were still on the spindle, and he couldn't explain what had happened, and how it all must look now. With the wheel in his hands he climbed back up and sat back on the ledge. His heart was thumping away and he could feel the blood pulsing behind his eyes as he squinted to block out the intense sunlight. He tried taking some deep breaths to steady himself, but his hands were trembling and sweat was running down his face. As he looked up he caught the eye of the younger of the two other boys, who immediately looked away, leaving Mark with a feeling of intense loneliness, and a strange shiver went through his body.

Was this the kind of reaction he would get everywhere in the street from now on? Would he be at school tomorrow with every one pointing and saying he is the one who killed Graham Park? Bloody school, why did it have to be tomorrow? This whole thing was such a mess, and it was just an accident but he was the eldest and he had checked the bike over. How could a bit of fun teasing the younger ones have turned so sour in the space of a few seconds? Why did life have to keep messing up like this? Mark took more deep breaths and tried again to steady himself. He picked up the wheel and climbed back up to the bike. As he approached it thoughts were now going too fast to even separate them but somehow he had to understand how this all happened. Knowing that his actions were completely illogical but not knowing what else to do he fumbled in the back carrier and found the spanners that he should have used properly earlier. By now tears were welling up inside as the enormity of the situation was increasingly taking over from the initial shock. Mark put the wheel back in place but the forks were splayed too far apart for both sides to screw on. He quickly tightened one side and then tried to lever the wheel and fork across to the other side to put the wheel back on. He lay on the ground with the front wheel attached on one side and the other fork clamped firmly between his legs. Then with his left arm he reached up and grabbed the handlebars, and pulled down in order to force the wheel far enough across to screw on the other nut. After several attempts the sweat was pouring off him, and on any other day Mark would have laughed at just how ridiculous he looked, but not today. With all his strength he was pulling down on the handlebar, whilst trying to control his breathing long enough to get the nut started on the thread. Eventually it started to catch on the thread and he could turn the nut on one, then another, then another thread. On the fourth full turn a sense of relief started to fill him, not because this solved anything but because he could manage it at all.

At that point the whole bike twisted and he could hear and feel the metal frame ripping across his shorts. Mark lay back on the grass and screamed out loud in frustration and pain. The tears were flowing now, and he pounded hard on the ground with both arms, until his hands felt numb. As his energy ran out he slumped back onto the ground and looked straight into the burning sun, forcing his eyes wide open despite the distortion of colours and images that resulted. When the pain in his eyes became unbearable he was forced to close them until it subsided and he was able to blink again and look on his surroundings, with a swirl of colours and lines blocking out his vision like droplets of oil in a rainy puddle. Gradually his focus came back but the real world looked worse than he had feared; the front fork that was attached had snapped off, causing the handlebars to twist, cutting across his leg, leaving a large gash that had started bleeding. In total despair he picked up the front wheel with the broken fork still attached and threw it back into the Gorge with all his might.

Then he looked down at his bleeding thigh, ripped off his T-shirt and wrapped it around. Tony was right. Sod the bloody consequences, Graham was all that really mattered right now, and he needed his friend. With his focus sharpening every moment he limped to the edge from where he could see that there was no real change. Graham looked desperately pale, and whilst the two other boys were doing their best to help they were clearly way out of their depth. Turning his attention to the village in the distance he thought he caught sight of flashing lights. Mark narrowed his eyes, still unable to focus properly since staring at the sun, and raised his hands to shield them as he looked across the fields. In the intense sunlight it was hard to see what was going on. Was the light playing tricks, or was that a blue flashing light approaching?

Yes, yes, he definitely saw blue lights. Then in the gentle breeze he caught the sound of sirens coming his way. Thank goodness, at last. Mark started to star jump in the air, waving his arms as vigorously as possible, ignoring the pain in his cut thigh.

"Over here. Over here!" he shouted at the top of his voice.

From the front seat of the police car Tony was able to pick out Mark jumping in the air to attract their attention as they sped across the fields. He hoped that they weren't too late and that Graham was still alive. The thought of losing his brother, and somehow being responsible, had forced Tony on when he ran across the fields. After the first 100 metres he felt a stitch build up in his side and from there things only got worse. His mouth was as dry as a bone and try as he might he couldn't seem to get enough air into his lungs. The first bit was downhill and then for the last two or three fields it was level, but each time he stopped for a gate or stile he wanted to just collapse on the floor and forget everything. He knew that this was all too real but hoped that it was just some bad dream that he was about to wake up from. As he ran on the stitch spread across his whole chest and his lungs seemed to be shrinking. Tony knew what to do and tried to slow down his breathing and take really deep breaths, but he could feel his ribs stretching as he inhaled, and a taste of blood was building in the back of his throat.

Sweat was running into his eyes making them sting, his nose was running and he could taste the combined effects on his top lip but it meant nothing. His clothes were sticking to his body making it even harder to run on and yet none of it mattered in the least. As Tony reached the last field he could see the houses on the other side of the road. By now he was stumbling more than running and the tracks in the field were making it almost impossible to keep in a straight line. His ankles were twisting with virtually every step, and where the crops had been harvested spiky little stems were trying to grab his ankles every time. He could see blood starting to cake with the dust from the field on his legs but Tony knew he just had to run on, and get help for Graham.

As he approached the old stile he saw the last person in the world that he wanted right now, and she was running towards him, almost as fast as he was running towards her. What was she doing here? Did she follow the boys everywhere, sticking her stuck up nose in, or was it just coincidence that she was always on hand to save the day?

CHAPTER 3

The Rescue

Charlotte had stayed in bed late that morning knowing that it was the last day before school started, and this was her last real chance for a lie in. Her parents knew that she was a bit apprehensive about her big day tomorrow as well, so they left her alone to do her own thing. After turning over several times and trying to force herself back to sleep she eventually gave up, showered, and wandered downstairs for breakfast. There was no one about, but her mum had left a brief note propped up against the neatly laid out kitchen table.

Hi darling.
Hope you slept well.
Gran and I have gone into town early to miss the rush.
Back about midday.
Dad is working away from home today.
Have a nice breakfast and spoil yourself.
Love Mum.

Short but sweet, and Charlotte knew how lucky she was to have such caring parents. It still amused her that her mum kept her notes so brief, and yet could talk the hind legs off any donkey when she was face to face with her. Being an only child she had both of her parents' undivided attention, but they had never allowed her to become spoilt or precocious. They were both strict but fair, and gave her as much time as they could. Dad worked hard as a farm manager for the big co-operative farm in the next village, and Mum worked part-time at the local village school that Charlotte had left last term. Part of her apprehension about tomorrow was going into school for the first time without her mum being there, and the rest was just about the fear of the unknown. Only three other children had left Aleton Primary this year and they were all boys. Deep down Charlotte knew things would be okay, but she wished her best friend Emma Williams was a few weeks older and then they would both be in the same year, instead of Emma having to wait another year to join her.

Still deep in thought she put the note down, and wandered through to the front door to get a fresh pint of milk from the doorstep. As she looked up the other three ex-Aleton boys were just trouping past the front gate. Her first instinct was to dive back inside and say nothing, but Charlotte so wanted to be friends with them, especially Tony, who after all only lived next door.

"Bye. Look after Tony, won't you? Remember it's school tomorrow so he needs a good night's sleep."

The words were out before she could even think what she was saying, and Charlotte was embarrassed almost as soon as they left her mouth. The last thing she wanted was to make Tony look stupid in front of the rest of his gang, because she knew how much it meant to him to be accepted. All she could manage was a silly smile, and then she did dive inside the door, and bit her bottom lip in frustration. It had been really nice of Tony to bring the chocolates after the tree incident, and Charlotte could see how embarrassed he was at the time and wished more than anything that he would have just stayed a while and chatted. Why was everything getting so complicated? Charlotte so wished she could stay in the comfortable little world of her old school where she knew everyone, and pretty much everything she had to. At the end of term Mr Linten, the headmaster, had given this speech about big fish leaving a small pond and moving up to a bigger pond where they were only little minnows. Apparently this was one of life's great challenges, and they would continue to face them throughout the rest of their lives. He told the leavers as well as the rest of the pupils that junior school was one of the most important building blocks in their lives. They would become unique and different people because of the way that the junior school teachers laid the foundation blocks for their futures.

It was a long and rambling speech when everyone just wanted to be on their way home, and of course the leavers had all heard it before over the last five years anyway. At the time Charlotte thought it was a silly idea and nothing since had changed her mind. After all, if moving up to bigger ponds was so great why had Mr Linten stayed teaching at the same school for 35 years? This thought had first struck her whilst she heard him rambling on at the leaving tea, and it still brought a smile to her face as she wandered aimlessly around the house.

With no one around and nothing much to do she wandered back upstairs to lie on her bed with a piece of toast and glass of orange. She would have to remember to take all the evidence downstairs before her parents were back, but in any case they would probably let her off just this once. Rules, after all, were made to be broken, as her dad was always telling her.

Ominously her new school uniform was hanging on the outside of her wardrobe all ready for the off tomorrow. Charlotte studied the clothes in detail, for want of anything better to do, and questioned if it really could make her look more grown up than her old uniform. That was what her mum and gran had said when they all went shopping together last month, but then every time she came out dressed in new outfits for PE, summer uniform and so on, they both kept crying. Charlotte couldn't see what all the fuss was about, but knowing they had been the same when she started Brownies and ballet, it was kind of expected.

Slowly with nothing of any consequence to occupy her mind she drifted off asleep again, only to wake with a rush of adrenalin when she heard someone coming in the front door. At first she sat up on the bed and froze; her heart was beating ridiculously fast inside her chest, and whilst conscious of it she was straining every sinew to listen out for another sound. There was no alarm clock in the room and Charlotte had left her watch on the kitchen table, but surely it wasn't midday already. Who else could it be in her house?

Without moving off the bed she leant nearer to the door and tried desperately to hear any tell-tale sounds, but none came, so she tried to crane her neck over further to see over into the landing area. Suddenly the door swung open, and Charlotte leapt back over the other side of the bed, only to be confronted by her mother's smiling face.

"Hi darling, have you woken up at last? Your gran met me in town and brought me back, so I got home earlier than I thought, she couldn't stay though, bridge group or something."

As usual her mum was rolling several sentences into one, but Charlotte got the idea.

"We had better move this glass and toast downstairs before your dad gets home as well, Miss. I got those new socks at last. In Marks of all places and they were reduced. I thought you were going to go for a walk across the fields this morning, still, if you need the sleep better today than tomorrow I suppose. Have you seen Tony today, why not ask him if you can walk to the bus together in the morning? I know you don't get on that well but you will both be nervous tomorrow."

Sometimes Charlotte was exhausted just listening to her mother. She managed to keep multiple trains of thought on the go at any one time, and talk constantly without losing track herself. Dad joked that he could never keep up, and in the end asked her to marry him just to catch her off guard and get a moment's silence. Apparently it worked for ten seconds and then she hadn't stopped since.

"Well what are your plans then, Miss?"

Where to start? thought Charlotte.

"I just dozed off to sleep, but I am going to go for a walk across the fields now if that's okay, and then I will be back for tea later."

"Yes of course, it is your day after all, if you don't want lunch that is. But with toast still in your hand from breakfast you are probably not hungry. But if you wait I will make you a picnic to take if you like. And why not ask Tony, and then you could ask about walking to the bus tomorrow, and your dad will be back at six, so we can have a cooked tea then," rambled her mother.

"Fine, I will eat later with you, and don't worry about a picnic, and what was the other bit?" frowned Charlotte in confusion.

"Tony," replied her mother, being unusually succinct for once.

33

"Oh yes, sorry, he went over the fields earlier with the Warriors gang so I might bump into him anyway, and we do get on, it's just that he plays with the boys always because he wants to be better than Graham at everything. Bye."

Charlotte loved giving her mother a taste of her own medicine, and ran downstairs with the toast and glass before her she could say anything more.

After a morning lazing around the bedroom the fresh air felt wonderful, and she just kept running in the direction that she had seen the boys leaving earlier. There was no doubt that they were trying to finish the Warrior Challenge, and from the way they were heading she was pretty sure that the challenge involved the Gorge. It was a boiling hot day and after a few hundred metres she slowed to a gentle jogging pace rather than the near sprint with which she had left the front door behind. Even so, it was only a matter of minutes before she could see the old stile, and as she approached it she was horrified to see Tony was running towards her in the opposite direction. Blood and sweat had combined with the loose ground to make his legs a dirty brown colour, and he was clearly struggling just to move.

"Come on!" she shouted in encouragement, not sure what his task was for today, but hopefully he was winning because no one else was in sight, and he looked like he was running for all that he was worth. Tony reached the stile and collapsed on the floor clutching his sides. As he rolled around on the ground his sweat-soaked clothes and body picked up the dust from the ground, turning him light brown all over. As she took in his dishevelled appearance and clear distress Charlotte was horrified. His ankles were covered in blood, and the sweat was literally pouring out of him.

"Get up, Tony, the challenge is never worth it, you look like a sausage now," she laughed, trying not to let him see how concerned she actually was at his appearance. Tony was gulping in huge amounts of air trying to tell her something.

"Police," he gasped. "Get help please. Graham at the Gorge. Quickly."

Charlotte could sense the urgency in his voice but what did he mean?

"Take a deep breath. You are not making any sense," she questioned, with her voice starting to waver as she feared for the answer.

He sat up as quickly as he could. In an effort to breathe more freely he was vigorously pinching his sides with his hands.

"Quick, please, Graham has fallen off his bike at the Gorge and he is badly hurt. We need police and an ambulance there as quickly as possible, please, please go now and get help. I will explain the rest later."

Charlotte knew from the tone of his voice that this was not the time to ask for detail. She simply turned around and ran to the nearest house as quickly as she could. Thoughts were racing through her head as she ran the few hundred metres. Big fish and little ponds meant nothing at times like this, and for the first time in her life Charlotte felt totally inadequate and out of control. Despite what Mr Linten had said a few weeks ago she already knew that it was moments like this that would define her life. As she approached the bungalow at the end of the lane Mrs Bennett got up from her deck chair and started to wave. Charlotte slowed for the last few metres to regain some composure and get her breath back.

"There has been an accident in the top field by the Gorge. One of the boys is badly hurt, can you please call for the police and an ambulance?"

"Oh, no, boys! Here, I brought my phone out into the garden with me. You phone for me it's the blue button then just dial the number 999."

Mrs Bennett stood with the phone in her hand slowly shaking her head from side to side, and tutting under her breath. Charlotte took the phone and spoke to the operator, passing on the few details that she knew at this stage.

"That's it, love, now press the red button to cut it off."

The two of them stood looking at each other and Mrs Bennett was the first to speak.

"Boys will be boys, my dear. Always have been and always will be. Ever since I was a young girl, and that is too long ago to talk about, boys have been getting themselves into scrapes and expecting us girls to get them out again. You had better get back. They generally go looking for danger if they haven't got one of us to keep them in line. I will call your mother later to make sure that everything is okay."

Charlotte liked Mrs Bennett, a friend of her gran, and would normally have stood talking for a while but not today. The operator had said to wait at the end of the lane by the road to help guide the police and ambulance to the scene, and she only hesitated for fear of finding out exactly what had happened to Graham. She made her excuses which were acknowledged by Mrs Bennett with a waving of her hand, and within minutes she was glad to hear the distant wail of the sirens. Whilst she waited for them she kept hopping from foot to foot, clapping her hands gently and looking all around, praying that Tony would meet her there, or another adult would come to her aid. It was no use though, the road was deserted, and for what seemed an eternity she had to wait as the sirens gradually increased in volume marking their approach. When she had left him Tony was clearly very frightened, and she was desperate to know more, yet frustrated that she had to stand like some guard on duty at the end of the road.

Suddenly the ambulance raced around the corner flanked by two police cars. Charlotte waved them down and passed on as much as she knew before the police officer invited her to jump in. They raced through the gate by the stile, and after a few hundred metres picked up Tony who was stumbling back up to the Gorge despite his obvious exhaustion. His legs were twisting with every step, and Charlotte knew that pure adrenalin could be all that was forcing him on. When the car pulled up alongside him he slumped onto the bonnet as he tried once more to gulp in oxygen, and get his breath back. One of the officers manhandled him into the front seat then took his place beside Charlotte in the back. They made slow but steady progress across the field, with all four occupants being thrown around due to the bumpy terrain. As they made their way the two policemen tried to find out what had happened and Charlotte listened intently to Tony's explanation.

At the mention of Mark's name, the driver interrupted, "Would that be Mark Richardson?"

"Yes, why?" whispered Tony, still fighting to get his breath back.

"No reason, just that I have come across the lad before, that's all."

This was enough to pacify Tony, but Charlotte couldn't help but notice the looks that the two policemen exchanged with each other in the rear view mirror. Clearly Mark was more than just known to them. As their car pulled to one side the ambulance shot past, and blocked Charlotte's view of Graham. She jumped out of the car and ran over to see what had happened, but pulled up abruptly like a racehorse meeting a fence it doesn't want to jump when she saw his twisted form and bloodied clothes. Tears welled up and she could not stop herself from crying. The ambulance men were assessing his injuries, and their whispered exchanges were not a good sign. After a few moments they signalled to the police for help, and slowly lifted Graham across to a stretcher. He was obviously in pain, but the screams she anticipated were strangely muted into dull groans, in between gurgling coughs from deep inside his chest. He was coughing blood in lumps and the ambulance man had to put his gloved finger into his mouth to clear the congealing mess.

All that Charlotte could do was offer her arm of support to Tony, and was relieved when he leant into her rather than recoiling away as she had anticipated. Neither of them spoke as the men put Graham into the ambulance then had a brief discussion with the police before setting off at a steady pace across the fields. Mark's leg was bound by one of the paramedics and he was loaded into one police car with the other two boys, then Charlotte and Tony were shepherded into the other. Progress to the hospital was very slow, and quiet.

Tony in particular said very little at first as the shock set in and he also tried to rationalise what he had seen. Everything at the Gorge had differed somewhat from the way it was when he had left to get help, in particular the position of the bike, and he couldn't work out how Mark had managed to cut his leg so badly. No one spoke on the way to the casualty ward, and surprisingly enough it was James who first broke the silence when they were all taken into a side room waiting for a doctor to arrive.

"Look, all of our parents have been called and I don't want anyone to mention the Warrior trials. After the last incident I said I would not get involved again, and I will be grounded forever if they find out the truth. Let's just say we were playing with an old bike and Graham fell over the edge. We start school again tomorrow and this has to stay quiet." He spoke with a calm authority that was in contrast to the snivelling child from earlier.

Mark took a deep breath, but avoided eye contact by looking to his feet as he slowly swung his good leg beneath him waiting for the others to respond first, but even he was impressed at how James was taking control.

"I agree with James," muttered Paul in a barely audible whisper. "It's my birthday in a fortnight, so I don't want any trouble or I won't get the new computer I've been promised."

Everyone turned to look at Tony, and he in turn looked around the room at each of the others individually. After a few seconds he spat in a harsh whisper, "Don't you realise my brother might die in this hospital, and you are worried about your bloody new computer, or being grounded for a while? You are all pathetic, and I am going to tell everyone what happened and whose fault it was."

With the final part of the sentence he turned and stared hard at Mark, making it perfectly clear who he thought was to blame, although Mark's refusal to make eye contact only made his anger rise. Silence descended once more until Charlotte spoke up.

"Look, I don't know the full facts—"

"Exactly, so stay out of it."

Now it was her to turn to stare some one out and this time it was Tony on the receiving end. The two friends locked eyes and everyone else waited with bated breath. Eventually Charlotte turned away.

"As I was saying, you all need to get some sleep and calm down and we need to see how bad Graham is first. This is all pretty serious, and everyone appreciates that, but if he is going to be okay then it is in everyone's best interests to limit the repercussions. I think that James is right and we should keep this as a secret between ourselves."

Clearly she had more to say on the subject but at that point two nurses and a doctor walked in, interrupting her mid-lecture.

"Now, I understand you lot have been overdoing it on the last day of your holidays, and you all need to be checked over by our already overstretched medical staff," laughed the doctor.

No one was taking this seriously enough for Tony's liking, and he was in no mood for exchanging pleasantries with the nursing staff.

"What about my brother?" he questioned.

"Ah, you must be Tony, the hero of the hour. Well we have only made initial checks at the moment but the good news is that he is not on the critical list. His recovery is likely to take some time, and beyond that it is probably best if you speak to your parents who are waiting to see you when you have been checked over."

Tony felt the relief hit the room as soon as the words 'not critical' were uttered, and no one seemed to listen to the rest. He also knew that getting everyone to give his version of events was going to be all but impossible in the circumstances. When the nurses had finished their checks they dressed the cuts on his ankles, and then took Mark away to stitch, clean and dress the cut on his leg. As the room fell silent again James stood up and faced Tony. "I know how you must be feeling but we have to agree to stick together on this. My reasons may appear selfish, but I know how parents see things and the full extent of this needs to be kept secret... agreed?"

Tony thought for a moment then nodded reluctantly.

"I will take that as a yes then. Let's all shake on it as a vow of silence."

As James offered his hand around everyone it seemed a little melodramatic to Tony, but strangely binding as well. For his part James felt empowered by his control of the situation, and as he retook his seat there was a definite air of closure about the room. Shortly afterwards the parents came in and took over proceedings. It was agreed that everyone had to get on with school the next day and with Graham still very ill, albeit not critical, Tony went home with Charlotte's parents to spend the night with them.

Adam, Charlotte's father, asked questions all the way home, much to his daughter's annoyance, as he tried to establish the full facts. Tony was pleased at last that someone was taking an interest, because both his foster parents and the police had told him to try and put today behind him and get a good sleep. He kept his word, however, and let none of the secret details out, preferring to keep his silence in case he could use the truth as a lever of some sort in the future, particularly against Mark.

Graham was conscious and had insisted that it was an accident, and he should not have ridden an old bike that he found in the field so close to the edge of the Gorge. Everyone seemed perfectly happy with this explanation, particularly when Mark and the others confirmed Graham's story.

"So how did the bike suddenly fall apart then?" asked Adam.

"Dad, leave it alone will you?"

"Charlotte, please, let Tony talk." Much as she hated being chastised by her father, especially in front of her friends, Charlotte knew better than to answer back.

"I don't really know, no one checked it I suppose, and Graham was just showing off trying to ride too close to the edge," Tony lied.

"Will you boys never learn your lesson?" questioned Adam, shaking his head with obvious annoyance. "It is about time you all started to take responsibility for your actions, you know."

"I know," replied Tony. Part of him was aching to tell the truth, and yet it was somehow easier to let the edited version run for the moment.

When they pulled into the drive Adam switched off the engine and sat still for a few moments.

"Well Tony, you probably think that I am as old fashioned and out of touch as my daughter does but let me give you a piece of advice."

A moment's silence followed.

"I know more about Mark Richardson than you do, and believe me he will get his due reward in time, not today, not tomorrow, but eventually his past will catch up with him. From what I understand Graham is going to be okay in the long run, and we all need to help him recover as quickly as possible. Keep what you know to yourself for now and watch his web of lies unfold in the future because it surely will. Now, Janet has made you both some supper so I suggest you have something to eat and get up to bed, to get a good night's sleep."

Tony felt embarrassed at the mention of lies, and was completely taken aback that his deception had apparently been so transparent, but he just sat in stunned silence and didn't say anything further. Adam had apparently said his piece, and was already stepping out of the car.

*

Charlotte put a reassuring hand onto his arm before leaning in and whispering, "Come on, let's go in. His bark is worse than his bite. Trust me." For the second time today he felt reassured by her support and tried to convey his gratefulness with a weak smile before opening his car door. They all went into the house and ate the bacon sandwiches as they were bombarded by further questions which they both managed to deflect before going up to Charlotte's bedroom where a camp bed had been made up on the floor.

"Goodnight, now you two get straight to sleep, lights out and no talking. I went over to your house, Tony, and got some pyjamas out, I hope they are the right ones. There is a brand new toothbrush in the bathroom so clean your teeth. I will wake you both up at seven o'clock... Goodnight. Oh, and you will need to get your school bags in the morning but don't worry, I have the key. Big school tomorrow, so it is time to put the excitement behind you both now... Goodnight," said Janet as she eventually took a breath, apparently oblivious to the fact that she had said goodnight three times in total.

"Night, Mum," shouted Charlotte as the door closed.

They took it in turns to traipse into the bathroom to get changed, wash and brush teeth then climb into bed.

"Night then," said Tony wearily.

"If I tell you a secret can you keep it to yourself forever?" said Charlotte in response.

"Pardon?"

"You heard me. Look, do you want to know why my dad has it in for Mark so much?"

Tony thought about the question for a moment. He really was past caring today and felt that they all had enough secrets to share for now, but Charlotte clearly wanted to get something off her chest as well.

"Okay then," he whispered back.

"Well, about three years ago a lot of the old people in the village started having things taken from their houses. You know what they are like, hardly any of them lock their doors properly, and most of them live alone. Well, a number of them reported money or jewellery going missing and then Mrs Bennett lost her husband's war medals. She actually caught the intruder in her dining room but he was too quick for her and bolted before she could get a proper look at him. After that they got more ambitious and the disappearances became much more frequent and the police were involved. Anyway, last year Dad discovered a den up at the farm and all the stuff was found inside, apart from a lot of the money which had obviously been spent. The police checked the site for fingerprints but couldn't pin it on anyone, and so they started to mount a watch on the place. That's when I found out about it because I overheard my mum telling your parents about it."

Tony still found it strange when Bob and Paula were referred to as his parents but he knew they didn't like being referred to as foster parents so he let it go without interruption.

"Anyway, after a couple of weeks guess who should be caught going into the den?" whispered Charlotte, her voice full of intrigue.

"I don't know," replied Tony, albeit half anticipating the reply.

"Tony. Who do you think this is all about?" The heavy hint of sarcasm in her voice showed that Charlotte was clearly losing patience as she had to explain every step. As the realisation struck him Tony sat bolt upright in bed.

"Mark."

"At last. You know you can be really hard work sometimes. Yes, of course Mark."

"So what happened? Why wasn't he arrested?"

"Well, they couldn't find his fingerprints on the stuff, because he obviously wore gloves, and he claimed he had never been there before. He said it was his test for the Warrior gang, and he even said Graham was going to meet him there later."

"And did he?"

"No, of course not, it was just a cover story, but even so they had no real evidence against him and so it was allowed to drop." Charlotte took a quick breath and clearly had loads more to tell but she was interrupted by a shout from downstairs.

"Quiet now, you two, and go to sleep, it's getting late, you can talk about today for the rest of your lives, now sleep," called Adam.

"Night, Tony. Sorry about Dad, he can be a bit of an old grump sometimes."

"Okay, but promise me you will tell me the rest tomorrow."

"Promise, but we had better go to sleep now. Night."

As they both tried to close their eyes they had a million questions racing through their minds, but equally felt a strange sense of ease despite the day's events. They were all much closer than before because of their shared experiences and secrets, but in particular Tony and Charlotte had started to find some common ground as the basis for their friendship.

CHAPTER 4

Back to School

The school term started the next day as expected and the schedules were hastily rearranged so that all four of the new pupils from Aleton were put into the same class. Originally they had all been split up into different tutor groups as was the practice at St Thomas Comprehensive to encourage them to integrate with new children from other schools, but it was agreed that they would be better off together in the circumstances. The new head teacher, a Mr Williams, took their first assembly and started by outlawing any gangs or groups at the school. Anyone who was found trying to involve other pupils in such an activity would apparently be put on immediate detention with no questions asked.

All of the assembled children sat in complete silence listening to their head, with occasional glances in the direction of the Aleton Four, as they jokingly called themselves over the next few weeks. For the first day and a half everyone else in the school pretty much left them alone, but eventually curiosity won the day and the questions started to come thick and fast. By this stage the rumour mill was also working at full steam and grossly exaggerating the full extent of the injuries to Graham.

"Is it true your brother was riding a motorbike, and he went over the edge of a cliff?"

"Did your brother really get decapitated by some old tramp when he was riding his bike in the fields?"

"Is Graham coming back to school now that he's lost both his arms and his legs?"

As time went on the stories became even more ridiculous. Fortunately Mr Williams decided to intervene after hearing one of the Year Sevens asking Mark if it was true that only Graham's brain had survived the accident, and it was to be put on display in the school hall to motivate the pupils during their exams. At assembly the following morning it was announced that Graham was leaving hospital over the weekend, and would be returning to school after the autumn half-term week. He was likely to spend several more months in a wheelchair, but would eventually recover and lead a perfectly normal life.

The words 'perfectly normal' seemed to take all of the intrigue out of the story, and by the Monday morning of the following week the playgrounds were again dominated by usual topic of the weekends sport, flirtations, and general gossip.

Mark was a great help throughout this period, as he had been assigned to look after the others, and Charlotte thought that Tony should give him another chance, but he was having none of it. He did change his opinion of Paul and James, who he had seen as nothing more than classmates beforehand, but gradually the four of them built a unique friendship. Over the next few years the six children who had been involved in the incident moved on, made new friends, got into new scrapes but all stayed very closely together.

They rarely talked about the accident, but on the last days of the summer holidays it became an annual pilgrimage to visit the old Gorge together. At first the younger ones were more reluctant, but with each passing year they increasingly took responsibility for the organising. It began to form a kind of purpose for the bond that held them all, and with increasing vigour they started to take over the organising, sorting out food, and drink, exact dates and so on, to the point where Tony and James decided to mock up an invitation ahead of what they all anticipated would be the final anniversary. It wasn't definitely going to be the final one, but Graham and Mark were sitting A Levels at the end of this school year, and were already planning a long summer holiday abroad before going to university. After that they would be in the big wide world, and the events at the

Gorge would surely be forgotten.

With the end of the holidays fast approaching he knew he would soon have to break this habit but even so, Tony reached up and hit the snooze button on his alarm clock for the fifth time. He was trying to avoid waking up at all, hoping to stay in bed late, and so far it was working. Graham hadn't been in to give him hassle, and what's more Paula hadn't shouted up the stairs either, telling him that he was wasting the best years of his life in bed. Another nine minutes passed and the music started again, up went his arm and hit the snooze button.

Six times! thought Tony. He had only been allowed to do this once before when he was off school ill, and he knew that at some point the music stayed off for good, but he wasn't sure if it was after eight or nine snoozes. It was now his ambition to find out today, but at the same time he wanted to know why no one else was shouting at him to get up.

Despite his best efforts he found it increasingly difficult to sleep, and eventually threw the covers off in frustration. As he opened his eyes he saw the card propped up against the mirror in his bedroom. As he read the words it brought a smile to his face again. He had worked on the wording for hours yesterday but they had certainly got it right in the end.

Please join us one and all for the Aleton Gorge fest.

Bring all the food you can carry.

All the cans you can drink.

It starts when the night sky is starry,

And ends when the horizon turns pink.

Help us one and all to make this one the best.

They had delivered the invitations yesterday, and the party was planned for tonight.

"Come on, Tony now, it is quarter past nine, don't waste the best years of your life in bed." The interruption from Paula was actually quite welcome. Tony was ready to get up and really just waiting for some motivation to do so. He quickly showered and changed then headed downstairs.

"Sit down, love, and then help yourself to some cereal." As Tony leant over the kitchen table Paula continued. "What are your plans today then?"

"Oh, nothing much, just sorting out the Gorge fest for tonight. I am going over to James' house in a bit. Charlotte and Paul are meeting us there. Then we will get our tent out ready for tonight."

"I don't know why you all want to make such a big deal about this Gorge fest, you know. We nearly lost your brother that day, and it has never been a day to celebrate in my book."

"Oh, it's only an excuse for a night out, nothing more than that. You know we won't come to any harm." Despite his assurances Tony understood Paula's anxiety, but the Gorge had a strange draw for them all. It represented such a focal point in all of their lives, and in a way it was central to their friendship. For Tony it also marked the point in his life when he stopped blindly following Graham, saw his brother's own fallibility and struck out on his own for the first time.

"No alcohol though, you younger ones are still only 15. I'll find out if any of you have taken any drink up there."

"We won't. Like I said, it's only a bit of fun," laughed Tony, although even he knew it sounded less than convincing.

In truth he hadn't actually thought of it before but maybe one bottle wouldn't hurt. He made a mental note to mention it at James' house later to see what everyone else thought.

*

Charlotte loved to wake in the mornings with the sunshine streaming through her windows; and as a treat to herself she always went to bed with the curtains open during the summer holidays. The brightness gradually built from about 5.15 each morning and she would slowly drift in and out of sleep over the next few hours. Sometimes the bright sun meant that she squinted at first, but the feeling of the warm morning rays was unbeatable, and set her up for the whole day. The end of the school holidays meant that winter was approaching, and apart from Christmas winter held no attraction for her at all. The long, cold, dark days failed to motivate anyone, and most of the adults she knew seemed as grey and miserable as the weather. Today though was still summer, and the only difference to the usual routine tonight would be sleeping out in a tent, and hopefully sensing the growing warmth from the dawn break through the canvas. By seven o'clock the sun was already at full strength, and Charlotte was sat up in bed reading a book when the usual tap came on her bedroom door.

"Come in, Mum."

"Good morning, darling. I thought you might like a cup of tea in bed as a treat. Dad had a problem at the farm again last night and didn't get home at all. I do worry about him, you know, he works so hard to support us both, so selflessly... Oh I do love your room on a summer morning, all the lovely sunshine streaming in through your window like that, though I don't know how you sleep with your curtains open at night. I said to your dad only the other day how I love this room. When you move out I think we will sleep in here, you know, not that we want you to leave of course, but I'm sure you will leave your old mum and dad for university soon enough, and it only seems like yesterday you were born, you know."

"Thanks for the tea." Charlotte knew she had to jump in as soon as there was the briefest of pauses. "I am getting up in just a minute anyway, just as soon as I finish the last two pages in this chapter."

"That's nice. We will be able to have a leisurely breakfast together if you like. Only normally it's such a rush on school mornings, that we hardly get chance to talk. And at the weekends I am rushing off to do the flowers at church for weddings or whatever. Did I tell you last night that Mrs Bennett had a bad fall yesterday, and she had to spend the night in hospital? Apparently she might have broken her hip. It makes me worry about your gran, you know, still in that house on her own and all."

"That's awful. How did it happen?"

"Well I don't really know, to be honest. Your dad went over after he heard about it and I went with her to the hospital but she is getting so frail and confused now that it is hard to make sense of it. She is more afraid that her family will put her into a home than anything. She mentioned someone breaking into her house again, even said it was the same boy as last time."

"Well was it?" questioned Charlotte, trying hard not to show too much interest.

"I can't really say. I don't know if anyone broke in or not, and your dad couldn't find anything missing. Possibly some money but none of her jewellery and that was all out on the sideboard plain as you like. And anyway, I was around at Carole Richardson's house at the time sorting out the parish meeting agenda for next Friday."

"And where was Mark?"

"Well when I arrived he was just having lunch with his mother then he went upstairs to his room and I heard him playing his music all afternoon until I left. Then I went past Mrs Bennett's house, and I don't really know why I went up to the door, but it is just as well I did because that is when I heard her cries from the hallway."

"So it couldn't have been Mark then, and we don't really know for sure if it was him before," asserted Charlotte.

Her mum took a moment to think before responding, as though she was trying to gently break some bad news to a young child. "I know he seems like a nice lad, and he always looks out for the rest of you, but your dad has good instincts about these things and he doesn't trust him to this day. Reckons I am too trusting and Mark could have easily left his music on and slipped out for the whole afternoon. He said that once I started World War Three could have been and gone by the time I took my first breath."

Charlotte tried not to giggle but couldn't help herself.

"Well, you pair can laugh all you like but I am not as daft as you both seem to think, and I am sure he was up there all afternoon. Anyway, I will put some toast on and see you when you are ready."

The giggles returned, and Charlotte quickly finished the last two pages with one hand over her mouth so that her mum wouldn't hear them. Then she showered, dressed and went downstairs for breakfast. They chatted away about plans for the Gorge fest and discussed Mrs Bennett some more before her mum wandered into the utility room and came out with a huge hamper.

"I prepared this for you for tonight. There is plenty of food and I put a bottle of wine in there as well for you all to share. But I don't want you taking loads more up there, just the one bottle for the four of you. The older lads will no doubt take their own drink, after all they are 18 soon but I am only allowing you this one because I know I can trust you."

"Thanks Mum, and I will make sure that they don't all get drunk. Anyway, more to the point, I don't know how we will get that massive hamper up to the Gorge."

"That James is a big strong lad, you will have to ask him. You know I saw him in town last week and he towers over his poor mother. I said to her at the time, I hope you don't have to tell him off very often, because I bet she couldn't even reach up to clip his ear."

They chatted away for an hour or more over their leisurely breakfast, and then they washed the dishes before Charlotte checked the time and was just putting her shoes on when the front doorbell went.

"That is probably Tony, he said he would call before he left to go to James' house. I will see you later."

"Don't forget the hamper."

"I won't. I will be back later anyway. Bye," called Charlotte.

Tony was at the door smiling broadly in anticipation of the day ahead.

"Ready?"

"Yes, and Mum has prepared a massive hamper for us all so we don't we need to worry about food, and she has even included a bottle of red wine for the four of us to share."

"What about Mark and Graham?" quizzed Tony, almost defensively.

"Don't worry, I am sure they will get their own provisions."

"I hope so, only they were moaning yesterday that they had no money for any."

"There is more than enough food, and I bet they at least get a bottle of cider to share, after all they did last year and then said we were all too young to have any. Remember?" challenged Charlotte.

Tony did remember. "Still, your mum is pretty cool packing some wine, because Paula just gave me a lecture about not drinking."

"Well she knows that girls are so much more mature than boys." As she finished the sentence Charlotte started running. They were only metres from James' front door, and she knew she had to get there before Tony realised what she had just said. She beat him by a good fifteen seconds as he was in no mood to react and just laughed at her comments.

"Ah well, at least Swotty Lotty is useful for some things."

Charlotte hated the term 'Swotty Lotty', which was an unfortunate nickname that she had picked up at school because she usually came top in everything. Normally her closest friends defended her when it was used, but they also knew that it was the ultimate put-down when they couldn't think of anything else.

"Ring the bell then, James may have many talents but I don't think he is telepathic," teased Tony.

"I have already rung it like 14 times actually, I cannot believe how slow you are today," replied Charlotte.

"I am sorry, but I only heard you the once," said Julie as she opened the door.

"No, not you, I was only joking with Tony." Charlotte's cheeks, already pink from the brief sprint to the front door were now positively aglow with embarrassment.

"I know, I saw you beating him. Come on in. James is just finishing a late breakfast in the dining room."

Paul had obviously arrived earlier but he was sat glued to the television with a PlayStation controller in his hands, feverishly hitting the buttons. "Hi guys, I am nearly beating James' score, then I will be with you."

James motioned them both to sit down, with his mouth obviously full of breakfast cereal.

"Have you two eaten already or can I get you something?" called Julie from the kitchen. James mother was of Jamaican descent and basically insisted on feeding everyone all day long. The food was amazing, and her hospitality was legendary, but it was impossible to keep up with the conveyor belt of food that was constantly on offer.

"No, I'm okay," answered Tony.

"I've eaten already, thank you Mrs Alan," chorused Charlotte.

"Ooh, I've eaten already, thank you Mrs Alan," whispered Tony in a mocking voice.

James started giggling and had to put his hand up to stop him spraying everyone with the contents of his mouth. He quickly swallowed what he could and whispered back, "You two really are like an old married couple the way you act sometimes."

"What about tea or coffee? I am just making James a cup of coffee so it's no trouble."

"Coffee would be lovely, Mrs Alan, and I am sure Charlotte will have the same but please don't go to too much trouble for us." Tony jumped in first before Charlotte could say a word.

"Like I say, an old married couple, you even answer for each other," continued James.

The four friends hung around the house for a few hours and then went out in the garden to plan for the night ahead. Once everyone heard about the massive hamper they were impressed and the boys turned the conversation to the Games that were on Saturday at school. Ever since Graham's accident the four big local secondary schools had organised a fun day of games on the last Saturday before term started. The idea was to provide some focus for the pupils as the school holidays were reaching their natural conclusion. It also served to bring all of the pupils from the first year together for the first time, and gave them their first opportunity to support their new school. Over the years St Thomas had done well especially in hockey, but despite reaching two football finals they had never won this title. James and Tony were both convinced that this was all about to change, and they had been helping to coach a lot of the younger boys in an effort to ensure they made the final at least. Mark was a good sportsman, and he had worked well with the other sixth formers to really bring on their fitness ahead of the long holidays. He had even drawn up an exercise routine for them all to follow, and with his captaincy they would surely do well, if they were allowed to compete in the final.

He had played for the lower sixth form last year, and nearly won the game for them, but in the end they had to settle for a 2-1 defeat to their arch-rivals Chiselton School. Charlotte was to play in two matches, but despite her natural athleticism had little interest in the Games, so as the boys discussed tactics she lay in the sun trying to improve her tan a little. Paul was no sportsman, but was on the substitute bench for two matches and James had been made Year 11 team captain. He had promised that everyone who volunteered was to get at least ten minutes of play during the day.

"Do you think you will be fit enough to play in all three of matches then, or will you substitute yourself if we are losing and you are tired?" asked Paul.

"I will step down if needed, but our year is strong, and we should win all three of our matches. We are unbeaten in the interschool's cup this year, and I phoned around yesterday to make sure everyone is fit," replied James.

"Who will you put in as captain if you do come off?" asked Tony.

"You, of course, and that's why you have to play in the last two games, and not the first two! That way if I am knackered you should always be in better shape."

"What about the final though? Do you think Mark is up to the job?" continued Tony.

"Y-y-y-yes, of course he is," replied James in a half-hearted imitation, at which point the three boys all burst out laughing.

When the giggling finally ended he tried to justify his comments.

"If he motivates the team then he can definitely win it, but you know what he is like, if they go behind he tries to take the world on single-handed. It's definitely down to how well he plays as part of the team on the day. If he has a bad day they are no way good enough to carry him."

"It's such a shame Graham cannot play, he was a fantastic player before the accident, and I still reckon that Mark is like he is because he tries to compensate for Graham not being part of the team," interrupted Paul.

This was a common topic of conversation when they discussed sport, and Charlotte had heard it all before several times.

"Next thing you will start the one about how intimidated you all used to be about Mark, and how now you cannot believe that he is actually smaller than you both." Charlotte feigned an exaggerated yawn with her hand over her mouth as she finished the sentence. The three boys looked at each other and James gestured towards the half-full watering can that was sitting beside his chair. Tony didn't need any further provocation; this was the second time today that Charlotte had put him down, and he quietly stood up and picked up the can. Charlotte was lying flat out on a sun lounger with her eyes closed behind dark glasses. Tony lifted the can high above her head and tipped it forward. At first a gentle spray came out, but then the rose came off the end of the spout and the remaining water gushed out in a torrent, absolutely soaking her. Everyone stood still for a moment waiting for a reaction then Charlotte jumped up in horror at what Tony had just done. Her soaking T-shirt was now almost see-through and for the first time Tony realised she wasn't wearing a bra underneath it. They all stared at each other, in complete silence, broken eventually by Charlotte screaming at them.

"Stop looking at my chest, you perverts!"

All three boys went bright pink and looked away then Charlotte ran into the house in tears. A few moments later Julie came out with a face like thunder. "You three had better be ready to start grovelling to me first and then that beautiful young lady. You don't deserve a friend like that, and you Tony, I am frankly amazed at you."

Everyone was now looking at Tony, who swallowed hard and issued a faint, "Sorry, it was only a joke."

"Don't say sorry to me, it's Charlotte who you reduced to tears, now go and apologise to her. And you, James Alan, don't think you are too big for me to clip you around the ear. Now take that silly smirk off your face. Your friends wouldn't think you were such a big lad if I told them how old you were when you stopped wetting the bed."

Charlotte had already changed into one of James' shirts and was stood in the doorway drying her hair with a towel. Her tears had stopped but the tell-tale red rings were still around her eyes. At the mention of bed wetting, however, she burst into laughter, but surprisingly she was the only one who found it at all amusing.

"Are you okay there? I am sorry but it's a lesson you will have to learn that boys always let you down just when you think they have grown up a bit. Anyway, it's not my place to apologise for this lot.

You all wait there a second whilst I help Charlotte sort herself out." Julie walked over and in an apparent show of solidarity put a comforting arm around her shoulder before they both disappeared into the house.

The three boys looked at each other somewhat bemused as the ladies went in, closing the door behind them. They waited for what seemed like an eternity, not sure how much trouble they were really in, but that question was answered soon enough as they heard the upstairs window open and all looked up as the two buckets of cold water descended down on them. Apparently now it was hilarious and not a bit immature. As Tony James and Paul squelched up to the back door all soaked through to the skin, James reached out for the handle only to find that they had locked them out. Charlotte and Julie reappeared behind the glass panel in fits of giggles.

"I am going to go home and get changed, and don't forget the food hamper is at my house. So call for me around four o'clock and I will be ready to walk up with you. Bye, little boys!" shouted Charlotte through the glass. At that she turned and ran back inside the house and out of sight. The three of them dragged their respective deck chairs into the middle of the lawn, out of harm's way, and settled down to dry out.

"Well that was definitely worth getting wet for," mused James.

Tony and Paul knew full well what he meant, but were too embarrassed to discuss it.

"Oh come on, you cannot tell me that you didn't notice Swotty Lotty is developing into a swell young lady these days."

"Two swell if you asked me," continued Paul, before laughing almost hysterically at his own joke. Tony didn't know why he could feel the red flush filling his cheeks, but he felt uneasy, and wanted desperately to change the topic of conversation.

"Do you think we should buy her some flowers or something? We don't want to ruin everything for tonight, do we?" ventured James when he eventually got over his own fit of giggles.

"Listen to Mr Romeo. You had better watch out, Tony, or he will be stealing your girlfriend from under your nose before you even realise it."

"I have made you all some lunch, though I don't think you deserve it, and I think you should all go to the post office this afternoon and get something for Charlotte to apologise properly," interrupted Julie from the back door.

It was always the same at James' house; they barely put the dishes away from one meal before his mum had prepared the next. The mood was still a little subdued as she brought out plate after plate of nibbles and salad.

"There may be a bit much but I was expecting all four of you to be here." There was a deliberate hint of sarcasm in Julie's voice that everyone chose to ignore.

They ate in silence for a few minutes then talk turned to some form of apology. After a brief discussion they decided that maybe the classic failsafe of chocolate was a good idea and after lunch reluctantly headed to the post office. At four o'clock they made their way to Charlotte's house weighed down with a heavy tent and small box of chocolates from the pennies they had managed to scrape together between them. Paul and James dropped their heavy bags by the front gates and sat down, leaving Tony to wander up the path with the chocolates and knock on the front door. He felt a certain sense of déjà vu walking up the short pathway, and a sense of duty over reason bearing heavily on his shoulders. He rang the bell and as he waited couldn't help but think how pathetic and inadequate the present looked as he turned it over in his hand. After a short wait Janet opened the door.

"Hello Tony, I don't think you are the most popular of people today. Don't worry," she continued with a smile, "I think you will be forgiven soon enough, and the chocolates are always a good idea. Come in."

They both wandered through to the rear of the house, where they found Charlotte sat at the table with a glass of orange squash.

"Hi, erm, sorry about earlier. We bought you these," muttered Tony.

"Thank you. I suppose the thought was there." Charlotte took the chocolates without looking directly at him.

It was a start, at least they were talking.

"Come on then, you two, grab a handle each and off you go. Enjoy yourselves up at the Gorge tonight, and I hope to see you all talking as usual in the morning when you get back. Now come on, give us a kiss and off you go." Janet had a determined look on her face that meant neither of them had room to negotiate. So with a shrug of submission they said their goodbyes, grabbed a handle each on the large hamper and wandered out to meet the others.

*

As soon as the four of them set off they forgot their differences from earlier. Normal conversation was easily resumed, but all the same Tony was a little surprised when Paul moved across to Charlotte and took her side of the hamper from her.

"Here, let me, it isn't fair on you having to lug this heavy thing across these fields."

"Don't worry Paul, I can manage just as well as any of you lot," replied Charlotte tersely.

"Please let me take it, not because you are a lady, but because I am trying to be a gentleman. Seeing you earlier, when Tony soaked you, made me realise that you are a beautiful lady these days, and we shouldn't take you for granted."

Tony stood still open mouthed expecting Paul to receive a swift slap in the face, but surprisingly Charlotte seemed to be taking the compliment well. "Thank you, Paul," she replied. "I never knew you cared."

"Like I said, we all have to stop taking you for granted, and see you as the gorgeous lady you are now rather than one of the lads. You will always be one of us, but… I am sorry about earlier, that's all."

"Thank you, Paul, that was really kind of you. Here, I shouldn't be so stubborn, you can take the weight if you like, but let me have your bag in exchange," replied Charlotte with the normal warmth they expected from her. Tony felt like his half-hearted apology from earlier was even more inadequate now, and James only compounded this when he started.

"Paul is right, and I am sorry for my part in soaking you." He hesitated for a moment as if to summon the courage from somewhere before continuing, "Mind you, that is a lovely figure that you keep hidden under those baggy clothes, you will have to ignore me if I can't take my eyes off you in the future." Again Tony expected swift retribution from the back of Charlotte's hand, but instead she moved over and threw her arms around James, before giving him a playful peck on the cheeks. Then she moved over to Paul, and after a brief cuddle motioned towards Tony.

He felt ridiculously uneasy as he also gave Charlotte a brief cuddle, and he could feel the burning fire in his cheeks which he knew must be radiating like a glowing beacon for all to see. This time it was Charlotte who had the apology to offer as she spoke. "I am sorry if I was a bit off to you lot, only it is not the best time of the month, if you know what I mean, and I was embarrassed at you lot seeing me like that, but the compliments were very welcome, and I do forgive you all."

Tony didn't know what to say, it was like they had all been transported to some strange land and the conversation was in a foreign language. These were his oldest friends, but they seemed to be moving ahead of him, and talk of monthly problems was definitely somewhere he didn't feel comfortable going right now.

"Come on, Tony, I cannot manage this alone. Stop daydreaming, will you? The T-shirt has dried now," laughed Paul as he grabbed the other side of the hamper and hoisted it up.

Suddenly awoken by the rebuke from Paul, he was even more embarrassed now that James and Charlotte also joined in the giggling. Still lost for words he had no option other than to pick up the handle and walk on. They continued their leisurely stroll across the fields, and the conversation went on in much the same vein as before.

"So how are you and Katy Davis getting on then?" quizzed Charlotte.

"Fine, thank you," replied James. "Why do you ask?"

"No reason, just interested to know how it is going, that is all."

"I thought you girls all gossiped away between yourselves about us men," interrupted Paul.

"Men now are you?" laughed Charlotte before quickening her

pace to stay just ahead of him. "When did that happen? I must have missed it."

"Perhaps I will show you one day if you get lucky," he teased in reply.

"Promises, promises, but I hope I won't be disappointed," giggled Charlotte.

"You won't," confirmed Paul.

As they made their way up to the Gorge Tony said very little, and was surprised at the conversation going on around him. Despite knowing Charlotte for so long he didn't have the confidence to talk to her like Paul was, and he felt strangely uneasy and insecure. They were all growing up, and the focus of their lives was changing, but sometimes he wished the status quo would just remain the same. The thought of girlfriends quite frankly scared the life out of him right now, and he always felt uneasy in these situations even with the closest of friends. Despite this he was even more surprised at the growing confidence in Paul, who continued flirting with Charlotte for the rest of the walk. It felt to Tony as though the events earlier had unleashed some new driving force in him that he hadn't seen before.

When they eventually arrived there was a lot of confusion with poles and guide ropes but the tent was up by six o'clock. Graham and Mark had arrived much earlier, erected their own tent and sat drinking cider and laughing at the attempts of their friends without volunteering them any help or support at all. As soon as the massive hamper was opened though they dived in and helped devour the sandwiches, crisps, and snacks that had been prepared for them. After filling their stomachs everyone sat around too full to move, and as happened every year the conversation moved back to the day of the bike accident.

This was followed by everyone listing all of the accidents that had followed over the years, usually in as much graphic detail as they could muster. Graham showed off the scars on his back from the surgery to repair the damage to his spine. Mark showed the scars on his shin from the break that had required a plate to be screwed in his leg, following a football accident. James still had the marks on his foot from the nail that had gone into his sole and came out the top when he had jumped off the woodpile at his house and landed on a discarded plank.

Paul had the remnants of a burn on his chest from running into a barbecue at his own tenth birthday party and knocking the whole thing over before falling on top of the burning coals. Even Charlotte could tell the others about the time that she was on holiday and a horse at a trekking centre had reared up, throwing her off and breaking her arm. The break required surgery to straighten it out before it set and she had a long red line down her forearm as a result. For the second time today Tony felt left out of the very group he was sat in because he had pretty much always stayed out of danger.

"Surely something has happened to you at some time," joked James as he tried to bring his friend into the conversation. "How are you ever going to get a girlfriend if you cannot tell her how brave you were in the face of danger?"

"So that's your plan then, is it James, to get your smelly foot out on your first date to impress the girls? I don't think so somehow," laughed Charlotte.

"Well Miss Charlotte, it worked for Katy Davies."

"Ugh, that's disgusting, I never could understand why she wanted to go out with you."

"You are only jealous of her. Look, if you like I can show you a bit closer, not many girls have been lucky enough to see my scars yet, so you will be able to say you were one of the first," continued James as he proceeded to remove his boot before swinging around on his bottom with his leg hovering over Charlotte's head.

"Ugh, I think I am going to be sick."

Paul, who had been full of chat all afternoon, then interrupted. "If you had gone first on the Warrior Challenge then you would have the scars to show for it, Tony. Perhaps you are just more sensible when it comes to seeing danger."

"More sensible! You must be joking. More boring... You lot forget he has always been wet nursed by me all his life and it's because I have always looked after him that he has never been in danger. I even used to steal food for him to keep him from starving when he was only tiny." With that, Graham turned away to take another swig of cider, but he sensed immediately that the seed of curiosity had been sown, and he waited to milk it for all he could.

"What are you on about now? You've had too much to drink," laughed Tony a little nervously.

"Oh, it was nothing important. Don't worry about it."

Tony was actually quite happy to leave it, but unfortunately Mark spoke next.

"D-d-don't leave us all in suspense, mate. Tell us a story." He rolled over laughing as he finished, clearly enjoying the effects of the many discarded cider bottles scattered around him.

"No, I am sure you lot have better things to discuss than me almost saving my little brother's life," replied Graham, who then paused before adding an exaggerated, "again."

Charlotte, Paul, Tony and James couldn't agree more, but before any one of them mustered up the courage to say so Mark interrupted again.

"T-t-tell us the story, mate. We are all intrigued now. You are just a big shy hero at heart aren't you?" Mark playfully poked at his friend with the top of the bottle as he spoke.

"Hardly," muttered Tony under his breath, but unfortunately his brother heard it and it seemed to provide the inspiration he needed to tell all. After shooting a harsh stare across Graham deliberately cleared his throat as if for dramatic effect and began.

"You are probably too young to remember but before we went to Bob and Paula, we lived with Mum's Great Aunt Mary after the car accident."

The car accident was the one that killed Graham and Tony's parents. No one had ever really discussed the details, and the brothers very rarely talked about it so the others knew better than to interrupt.

"She was an old woman, probably about 70 at the time of the accident I suppose, and didn't really want us but she was our only remaining family, and I suppose felt duty bound to take us in. You were only two when Mum and Dad died and everything seemed fine at first but after a couple of months as she got older it all went downhill. I used to take money from her purse every day just to buy food for us, and I would climb out of the window at night, and go to the shops."

He paused for a minute and took another sip from his bottle of cider. Everyone, including Tony, was transfixed and no one dared say a word.

"This went on for about a year. Everyone knew she was getting forgetful, and struggling to cope with two young children, so the people in the village shop just turned a blind eye when this six-year-old child came in at eight or nine o'clock each day for provisions."

Another sip of cider, and the pause seemed to go on forever.

"And?" questioned Tony eventually.

"Well the school was getting a bit worried about my appearance and so on, but I always told them that it was all okay and so no one took it any further. Then things started to get even harder because apparently she was losing her mind a bit and getting more confused day by day. Anyway, because the cupboards always had plenty of food in them without her ever going to the shop she thought that the elves were helping her each night, and doing the shopping for us."

Everyone knew how serious this was, but by this time Mark had already had several bottles of cider and couldn't hold back. He got unsteadily to his feet and started to mock in a high-pitched voice, "Come along now, little elves, don't wake those little children upstairs in bed. Did you get all my shopping today? If I leave my ironing out tonight would you be loves and put that away as well. N-n-now look here, I am putting my false teeth down here."

Mark made an exaggerated motion to lay something on the side. "Now I need them in the morning so don't take them away and leave me a pound instead, will you?"

Graham was clearly unhappy at this intrusion into "his moment", but he waited to see what effect Mark's antics would have on the others.

"That's the tooth fairy, not the elves, you fool!" shouted James, with tears of laughter rolling down his cheeks. Graham went to speak in reply but by this stage everyone was rolling around on the floor laughing.

It took them ages to settle, because every time the laughter subsided Mark would come up with another line: "To your elve, mate," lifting his bottle up to Graham's, or, "Elve me clear up all these plates, will you? We don't want the farmer thinking we are a messy lot."

"Elves is alive."

"You mean Elvis," replied Graham, forcing a very obviously put on laugh as he was desperate to get back on track and finish the story.

"What? He was helping your auntie as well, was he? The old hound dog."

It took them ages to settle but eventually everyone had exhausted all of their Elvis and elves jokes and, apart from Mark, they all wanted to know what happened next. Mark was quite content to go on making fun all night with just the occasional trip back to his tent for some more cider. Tony eventually came to his brother's aid.

"So you said things got more serious at that stage. What actually happened?"

"Well you obviously don't remember but the food ran out and although it only went on for a few days we were starving. She didn't bother going to the post office, not even to get her pension, and the money quickly ran out as a result."

Graham took some more cider and sat once again in silence.

"And?" begged Tony again. He wasn't sure how much the story was being embellished for dramatic effect but some of it rang true, and it did account for some of his brother's controlling and sometimes protective personality.

"Well I did the only thing I could to look after us both and stole as much food or money as I could to survive. Each night when you went to bed I would slip out and go round the houses in the village. It was summertime fortunately and I would pick two or three places different places to call on each night. Most people would leave their kitchen doors open until they went to bed and I would nip into their houses, grab what I could and run out again." As he finished Graham stared straight ahead, and whether this was done for effect or not it looked very poignant.

"So how long did this go on for?" Tony was intrigued not least because this was the first he had ever heard of it, and it was so rare for Graham to open up like this. He usually liked to be the big brother and just dismissed Tony whenever he tried to find out any details of their past or indeed their parents. Graham enjoyed having power over others, especially Tony, and whether he knew anything or not used his perceived knowledge to his own advantage. Tony did know that his parents were killed in a fatal car crash involving a drunk driver, but that was about it.

After another long, almost painful silence Graham continued. "Well, it was only about two weeks in total, but the problem was that very often there was no food around that I could pick up quickly. So I started to take more money and use this the next day to buy food."

"And I suppose that is how you were caught?"

"Yes, I am afraid so. I was okay for the first couple of days but there was this one house where the man always left his wallet on the kitchen table, and it was always full of cash. At first I would just take say five pounds but then I thought if I took more it would be safer because I wouldn't have to go to any other houses. Anyway, they eventually worked it out and lay in wait for me, so when I came out the back door they grabbed me."

Charlotte gasped in shock. "My god, you must have been so scared. How old did you say you were you at the time?"

It seemed like the first time that she had spoken all evening, and Graham turned to face her.

"Well I suppose I was about six or seven, and I didn't know what to do. The really stupid thing is that I still remember the fear of those few seconds to this day. The man was in his fifties with a beard, and I thought he looked like Fagin, and he was going to make me work for him stealing every night. I tried to struggle and get away but it was no good, and then his wife came out and she recognised me from the village. Anyway, the police and social services were called and then we were moved around and eventually ended up here with Bob and Paula."

"A-a-and damned spiffing it is that you came into our lives, old boy, they wouldn't be the same without you. What with elves, Fagin, Elvis and poor auld Aunt Mary you can certainly tell a damned fine bedtime story. Whose turn is it next?" Mark was clearly drunk by now and everyone else was starting to tire of his constant interruptions, particularly as he slurred his words and took ages over each sentence.

There was a long silence that followed as everyone was left alone with their thoughts. Charlotte wondered why Mark and Graham had brought so much cider, and although she quite liked Mark normally, thought he was being a prat tonight. Tony was surprised that Graham was talking to them all on his level for once, rather than talking down to them, and although he found Mark's outburst really funny he didn't want Graham to get side-tracked if there was more to come. Paul was amazed at the story so far and couldn't believe what he heard. He had never really been in trouble in his life, in fact he had never really done anything at all his whole life, but he had always looked up to both Mark and Graham, almost hero worshipped them at times. For anyone to steal at the age of six or seven, just in order to live, was quite unbelievable, and definitely worthy of his respect.

James had listened to the story and taken it all in but his mind had wandered off and he was concentrating on the games that were due to start in less than thirty-six hours. He had shared the bottle of wine with the other three, and enjoyed it, but he knew that he had to look after himself for Saturday. The games were a must-win this year and Mark was the most vital element of their success. He knew that the rest of the school could deliver but both finals depended on him inspiring the sixth form teams to victory.

James could see a confrontation coming as Mark staggered off into the tent for another refill, when he should really be more interested in getting a good night's sleep. After a few moments he staggered back without any cider and James breathed a sigh of relief as soon as he spoke.

"Well, tha-tha-tha that's all the cider gone, so I guess it's about time we all called it a night."

Graham looked around slowly at the assembled group and asked, "What about the other stuff I thought you said you brought it with you?"

"D-d-d-d-don't worry, I did, but not in front of the children, dear. They are all at an impressionable age." Mark was staggering around now trying not to fall over as he was bent almost double and wagging his finger in their faces. He had clearly lost most of the control in his legs and as he swayed wildly it was all he could manage to stay upright.

James couldn't contain himself any longer. "Look, Mark, I don't know what your problem is but you are the best chance we have of winning the games so why don't you give the alcohol a rest and get some sleep? You have got to be fit for Saturday."

"Yes, Mummy dear. You won't mind if I have just the one cigarette before I go to my bed though, will you?"

James sat silently, not realising that he smoked.

Mark pulled a cigarette packet from his top pocket and flipped the top to reveal a number of hand-rolled fags that he had obviously prepared earlier. He took one out and lit up, drawing deeply and exhaling with an exaggerated, "Ahhhh."

Graham leant over and took another one from the open packet that was being offered to him from his best friend.

"Anyone else like to unwind with one of Columbia's finest?" he questioned.

Furtive glances were exchanged between the other four with only Paul showing any interest. He was fed up with his goody-two-shoes image, and wanted to live a little. Anyway, everyone did drugs at some point so why not tonight, and he knew that Mark and Graham were sensible enough.

"Go on then, I will please," he replied a little nervously.

"Well, well, well, the Gorge throws up another surprise for us, Graham. Another member for the Warrior gang," giggled Mark.

Graham looked over to Paul. "It's up to you, you don't have to."

"I want to, I know what I am doing, you know," shrugged Paul, as he leant forward to take the joint on offer.

"If you have any of that stuff you won't be playing on Saturday, Paul, because I won't let you." James knew that it was a lame threat but he also felt some responsibility for his friend.

"Yeah, right. You were only going to pick me out of pity, and you are more likely to win without me anyway." With that, Paul lit up before taking a short puff and starting to cough.

"Take it steady, young Warrior. Breathe in, take some water and try again." Mark was assuming control despite his own state of intoxication as he handed over a bottle of water.

"I am going into the tent, is anyone else coming?" interrupted Charlotte, clearly unimpressed with proceedings.

"L-l-look boys, the lady is tired and wants you two to take her to bed. Off you both go," continued Mark in a sarcastic voice.

Tony and James weren't in the mood for any more of Mark's taunts but at the same time they didn't want him to think he had won.

"I will only be five minutes," replied Tony.

"Me too," said James.

Silence took over the camp again after Charlotte left, interrupted only by occasional coughs from the three boys who were all obviously equally unaccustomed to smoking. James tried to restart conversation but no one else seemed to have any appetite for it. After a quarter of an hour he jumped up, offered a hand to Tony who he pulled up with him and wandered over to the tent just as the other three were lighting a second and final joint from the packet.

"Are you asleep?" whispered Tony after he had snuggled down in his sleeping bag.

"Yes," came the hushed replies from both Charlotte and James.

"What do you think about that then?" he continued.

"Go to sleep, Tony. They may be idiots but that is their problem. And Paul looks up to them too much but he will learn one day," answered Charlotte before James could say anything.

"Yes I know, but where do you think all the money came from for all the cider, and cigarettes, and dope that they said was in them? Remember Mrs Bennett was robbed earlier this week." Tony could barely hide the accusing tone of his voice.

Charlotte thought for a moment. "You might have a point, but all the evidence is gone now isn't it? Anyway, it's late and I want to sleep so goodnight."

"Do you think Mark and Graham robbed Mrs Bennett then, Tony?" questioned James as he joined in.

"No, just Mark of course. He had the booze and fags and where else would he get the money from?" answered Tony indignantly.

"Night," replied Charlotte with a heavy sigh.

Before anyone could speak again they were interrupted by Paul falling heavily into the tent, gasping for air.

"My inhaler. It's in the bag. I need my inhaler," he wheezed, clearly in a great deal of discomfort.

"You bloody idiot, Paul. I told you to leave them alone," shouted Charlotte as she sat upright and started to rummage around.

"Quick, my inhaler."

Everyone grabbed their torches and tipped over any bag they could find in an effort to find the inhaler. Paul was kneeling in the doorway gasping for air and coughing in between when James found it and tossed it across the tent. His friend pressed the top and took several deep breaths. This settled him for a minute before he turned and threw up outside the tent. Graham and Mark burst out laughing and James jumped up ready to go and confront them both.

Charlotte reached across and grabbed his arm. "Leave it, they are not worth it. Please just look after Paul."

James reluctantly sat down again and put an arm around Paul's shoulder. "I guess that's the last time you try and smoke then?" Paul just looked at his friend and nodded.

"Are you going to be sick again?" James continued. "Because if you are then we had better sleep outside, and leave Tony and Charlotte in here. I don't want sick inside the tent."

"I think I will be okay. I will just sleep here by the door though."

Charlotte passed his sleeping bag across and Paul wriggled down inside before lying down and falling asleep almost in an instant. The other three shook their heads simultaneously, turned out the torches and all lay down to sleep.

Dawn came around all too quickly, but there was no activity from Graham and Mark's tent. The others got up, talked only in whispers so as not to wake them up and packed everything away as quietly as possible. They weren't exactly being kind, it was more a case of preferring each other's company than Graham and Mark's. Within half an hour they left for the fry up that Julie had promised the day before. As they were leaving James and Tony slackened off the guy ropes so that the other tent collapsed, but the loud snoring continued and there was no other reaction from inside.

CHAPTER 5

The Games

Nine o'clock Saturday morning soon came around and by that time James had already been at the school for an hour sorting all the teams out, checking that full-strength squads were available for every year. By midday things were going well with six games won so far out of eight played, but James was still anxious because he hadn't seen Mark, and they even wondered if he was still up at the Gorge asleep in the tent.

Charlotte and Tony were helping with the overall organisation, making sure that all of the teams were in the right place at the right time. The sense of expectation was really high amongst all of the St Thomas teams, and everyone knew that if they did their bit then surely for the first time both the boys and girls could be overall winners. James kept a running tally of the scores all afternoon, and by three o'clock they had already done enough to reach the finals. This was a fantastic achievement, and the whole school was buzzing with excitement, but no one had seen Mark.

"Charlotte, you and Tony go and have another look for Mark, he should have been here hours ago. His team are all assembled but they are lost without him," said James anxiously.

They had both been looking all afternoon, but there was simply no sign of him.

"I can't, mate, I am due to play my first game in a minute. Look, we are in the finals so why not give Paul a chance and you go find him with Charlotte?" replied Tony.

Normally James would have given anything to keep playing but he knew the importance of finding Mark was far greater right now.

"Okay, you take my captain's arm band, and no excuses, we still have to win our last two games. Paul, you can play in my place."

Paul had brought his kit despite James' threats at the Gorge, and he was eager to do his bit. The first game was an easy win 4-0, and then as events were over running they only had a five-minute break before the final match. As they wandered over to start the final match James ran over, and pulled all of his team into a huddle. "Look, I know we are through but you must win this game, to keep Chiselton out of the final. I have looked at the scores and they will still go through if you lose this match."

"Have you found Mark yet?" asked Tony.

"Yes, just and he is an awful state, he stayed up the Gorge again last night with Graham smoking and they both look dreadful," replied James.

"Shit! They both know how important today is!" shouted Tony in amazement.

"I know but they are just laughing about it, and saying we are taking it all too seriously. I have a good mind to tell Mr Williams what they have been up to and get Mark taken off. I have only played one match and could easily do a better job than him." James could barely contain the anger in himself as he shook his head in frustration.

Charlotte ran over to join them. "Your last group match is ready to kick off in one minute, and I have just found Mark and he looks dreadful."

"We know," they both chorused.

The first half of the match was a real struggle. Chiselton wanted the win as badly as St Thomas wanted to deny them. Paul slipped in defence and allowed their striker an easy run at goal to put Chiselton 1-0 up after just three minutes. Another defensive error five minutes later and it was 2-0 up, with a quarter of the match gone. Tony knew that they had to pull together better but it was the end of a long day for many of the players and they were tiring fast. The match settled for a while until the 18th minute, when St Thomas managed to drag one back, but in the last minute they conceded another to bring things back to 3-1 at the interval.

James ran on to do his team talk at half-time and try to inspire his side, but their heads were down and it was clearly having little effect. Word had gone around that Mark was looking decidedly the worse for wear and the point of winning this game was lost on most of the players. Surprisingly Charlotte provided the motivation that everyone was looking for. "Why don't you play in this match, James, and replace one of the more tired players?"

"That's okay, I don't mind coming off." Paul accepted the inevitable as the rest of the team looked immediately in his direction at the mention of tired players.

"Sorry, I didn't mean you necessarily," said Charlotte, shrugging her shoulders.

" It's okay, I have played more than I expected already," smiled Paul.

Chiselton knew straight away that this was a different match when they saw James take the captain's arm band for the second half. He was as well known amongst schoolboy teams in the county for his individual skills as his leadership. The whole of the St Thomas team took on a new complexion. Within three minutes they scored again to make it 3-2, then the equaliser came six minutes later. All of the other matches had finished by now and the biggest crowd of the day so far was watching and cheering on their side.

There was an enormous cheer on 18 minutes when James scored again to take them 4-3 up, putting them into the lead for the first time. Everyone on the side-lines was checking their watches and after 19 minutes the whistles from the crowd started urging the ref to blow for full time. With just 10 seconds to go Chiselton took the ball and started to move up field towards their opponent's goal. James was running as fast as he could from the halfway line urging his side not to do anything stupid or concede another goal. The two St Thomas defenders had thought it was all over, and were caught unawares. They both ran forwards and lunged dangerously at their opponent as he struck for goal. The ref was right on the ball and blew for a penalty even before the Chiselton player dramatically fell to the floor clutching his right shin and rolling around.

As soon as the ball was back on the pitch he managed to regain the use of his leg and scored easily from the penalty spot. A draw was no consolation for James, who knew that with Mark only at half his usual best Chiselton would be too good for them in the final.

True to form the girls easily won the hockey 3-0, and then everyone lined up in eager anticipation for the final. James and Tony knew what was to come, and wanted to leave before the kick-off but felt duty bound to stay and watch. Mark trudged onto the pitch, and his feeble commands were hardly audible above the noise of the crowd. When the ref heard the Chiselton team captain giving his own orders with a mock stammer he called them both to one side and asked for a fair, clean match. He stressed that this was supposed to be a fun day, and he didn't want the final to ruin an otherwise excellent event. Both captains nodded in agreement, shook hands and took their positions. Graham, James, Tony, Paul and Charlotte were all behind their team's goal as three excellent goals meant they went into half time 3-0 down.

James was furious after all his efforts, and he wanted to blame everyone around him, but in particular Graham. "Why did you let him get in this state? You know how much we want the cup this year."

"It's not my fault, he should be able to cope better. Look at me, I'm fine," laughed Graham.

"You don't look it," replied Charlotte with a look of disgust.

"Yes but if I could I would do a better job than Mark is out there."

"I don't understand you, Graham. You have caused this situation deliberately. You can do what you like to yourself but why do you have to bring other people down with you all the time?" said James in near desperation at the events unfolding in front of him.

"It's not my problem. If they can't win they aren't good enough, are they? It's only a game," laughed Graham.

"You have done this on purpose, haven't you? Just because you cannot play and have all the glory you don't want Mark to get it either. Can't you at least admit that?" continued James, shouting above the noise of the crowd.

Everyone stayed silent for a moment and then Charlotte was left to pick up the pieces. "Look, calm down will you both? It's no one's fault, okay. Let's just see how this next half goes. Mark is coming over so stop bickering for a moment."

"God, I feel rough. I-I-I-I-I told you we shouldn't have drunk all that cider you bought."

"You didn't have to drink it, anyway I'm fine," answered Graham.

"Only because you kept b-b-b-b-bloody winning. I still reckon you were cheating. Anyway they are calling us back on. I cannot believe it is three bloody nil already." Mark shook his head as he trudged back over.

Graham went bright red as the others glowered at him. James went to speak, but Tony put his hand up to stop him.

"If this is some sick way of getting revenge you really are pathetic."

"Bugger off, all of you." Graham didn't wait for a reply but simply turned, pushed roughly past James and walked off. He was soon lost in the crowd and everyone turned back to the game.

Chiselton scored again before they relaxed a little and the final score finished a slightly more respectable 4-2.

"Ah well, boys, just think, it is all up to you three now to break the jinx and win it for the next two years when you are in the final." Charlotte's words were scant consolation as they stood for the final prize-giving ceremony, but in their hearts they all knew she was right, and they were already looking forward to the challenge.

*

School resumed the following week and for once there was none of the slow build in the first few days. Talk of the Games was rife before the first bell, with James vowing to avenge the defeat when he represented the sixth formers next summer. The summer had been long and hot, and everyone had stories to recount so when they went into registration the room was positively buzzing. Mr Peterson stood at the front of the class and after a few moments lifted his hand to indicate that he wanted silence.

Being respected amongst the pupils and renowned for his strictness, the volume reduced immediately, and everyone sat looking curiously around as he paced up and down the room. He cleared his throat after a few moments and began.

"It has been my distinct pleasure to follow most of you from your first days in this school, and in the main it has been a pleasurable experience. Today marks a crossroads for all of you. You have two choices, either you start to work, and I mean work like you have never worked before, and you will make the best attempt possible at your exams in the summer. Alternatively you can be tempted by the distractions of television, your friends, the opposite sex, and you will probably do enough to get by, but in the long term you will live to regret it."

He paused for several minutes in a rather dramatic style and let his first words sink in.

Charlotte had always liked their form tutor, and was already planning her daily revision schedules in her mind. So what if she was called 'Swotty Lotty'? She had thought a lot about her future over the summer holidays and was determined to get through her GCSE exams, A Levels, and university to become a doctor. She hadn't actually told anyone else of her plans as yet, least of all her mum and dad, but she knew they would be supportive and proud of her decision.

James was also reflecting on what was necessary, aiming to work as hard as he could at his exams, even committing every spare minute to his school work. The problem was he knew this would have to be balanced against rugby and football practice as well as Katy Davis who gently kicked the back of his chair at the mention of the opposite sex. Paul meanwhile had already started his revision in the summer holidays, reading as many books on maths and the sciences as he could find. He knew that this year was all about doing well enough to get into the sixth form when he could concentrate on three or four important subjects. He had no interest for languages, geography, history and the like but the school had refused to let him drop them when he went into Year 10. The bit about doing enough to get by definitely struck a chord, but he reasoned in his own mind that if he put double the effort into the subjects he liked then no one could ask for more.

Tony listened to the opening speech from Mr Peterson with increasing anxiety. He knew he was a reasonably capable student, but he had never really had to work hard before and even now doubted whether he had it in him to do the work necessary. His mind was thinking ahead to the results day, and he remembered the way that Graham had been really worked up last summer before getting his. As expected Graham and Mark had done well, getting a mix of the top three grades in eight subjects. Tony's predicted results according to his mock exams last term were similar, but what if he failed? His worst fear was failing the lot and having to go back and re-do this year of school. As he thought of the possibilities he didn't even notice that he was subconsciously twisting the ruler in his hand at ninety degrees. Suddenly a loud bang broke the silence as bits of the ruler flew in all directions. Everyone looked around and Tony could feel the burning sensation in his cheeks behind their bright red glow.

Instinctively he pushed his chair back in an effort to get the bits.

"Leave it." The two words were uttered in a hushed tone From Mr Peterson before he continued as if nothing had happened.

Tony sat back into his seat as he could feel the sweat building in his hands, and his heart bursting out of his chest.

"As I was saying, I have known you all now for a long time, and I already know that you all have it in you to do well next summer. You must not let the pressure get too much for you."

He paused again and Tony stared blankly ahead feeling that everyone else was staring at him.

"This is by far the most important stage of your lives so far, and I stress the words so far. Because in years to come when you face the challenges of A Levels, degrees, marriage, divorce, parenthood, work, sickness, wealth and health you will hopefully view these exams as just another small stepping stone. For now, however, they are a giant leap for all of you, and they require your 100% commitment."

It was a well-rehearsed speech, reflecting many years as a teacher, and it had the desired effect on the whole class. The bell went within seconds of his final word and so the year started. From then on it was a whirlwind of coursework deadlines, revision, mock exams, elation and frustration.

Half terms, Christmas, and then Easter came and went, and before they knew what had hit them Charlotte, Tony, James and Paul were lying on the school playing field after their final English literature exam. Everyone was exhausted from the intensive year of study, and more importantly the three long weeks of non-stop examinations. James was first to sit up and address the others. "Well I cannot believe that it is all finally over. Just think, if I wanted to I could leave school now."

"You aren't going to though, are you?" replied Charlotte as she sat up and leant against her elbows on the grass.

"No, Miss Charlotte, I will still be there for you next year, don't worry, but I am not going to think about school now until my results come out."

"Me neither," chorused Paul and Tony, without lifting themselves up off the ground.

"You are coming to the ball though on Friday, aren't you? Katy told me that her mum was making her a ball gown." Charlotte was absently picking at the grass as she spoke.

"Yes I know, and yes of course we will all be there, won't we? Has Tony asked you to escort him yet?" laughed James.

Tony didn't react but sat twisting at the grass beneath his fingers. He had been going to ask Charlotte for weeks now but the time was never right, and anyway the exams were top priority until now. Still, he knew no one else in his year was going to ask her. Apart from the final week of exams, and the penultimate Games for everyone in Year 11 it had been the main topic of conversation at football practice on Saturday mornings.

It was a tradition at the end of training each week to discuss who fancied who, and whenever the matches were called off they would usually spend the morning drawing up a secret chart putting all the girls into their list. They kept an empty ice cream container hidden in one of the lockers with all of the girls' names on it and their pairings.

Even on weeks when James was away Katy Davies was usually voted as most beautiful girl in the year, with Charlotte normally just in or out of the top ten. Had she known about this she would have been secretly quite proud of it, but the St Thomas Top Totty chart as it was known was a very closely guarded secret. After the last session on Saturday morning James made everyone put their top three choices for the ball on a piece of paper, and then they had to pass the paper on to the person next to them who read it out. This was meant to avoid any conflicts in the year, and gave everyone the chance of going to the ball with the girl at the top of their lists. No one even considered the prospect that the girls themselves would have their own opinion on who should accompany them.

Almost every boy in the year attended because it was the last chance to train together ahead of the Games in a couple of months, and after the drudge of endless revision everyone really enjoyed the mornings. Morale was high on the final session as they all left knowing not only that their choices were safe for the ball, but that they could be the first team to beat Chiselton and win the Games outright.

The few conflicts where the same girl was chosen twice had been easily resolved, and just the memory of the whole morning brought a smile to Tony's face as he twisted around and sat up. James and Paul both noticed the smile, and knew exactly what was on his mind. They both looked to the ground and tried to hide any giggles from Charlotte, but she knew something was going on.

"What is amusing the little boys now then?" she asked.

Silence apart from the sound of suppressed giggles.

"Well if you must know I have already accepted the head boy's invitation to the ball, and he is picking me up in his car at 7.30pm." Charlotte deliberately emphasised the head boy to drive her point home.

"Mark?" spluttered all three boys in total disbelief.

"Yes," nodded Charlotte, looking at each of the three boys in turn.

"Why does M-M-M-M-Mark want to take you to the ball?" asked Paul incredulously.

Both Tony and James had to laugh as he mocked Mark.

"Probably because he knows that no one in my year is mature enough to notice a real lady when they see one, and I think even Katy was jealous when I told her earlier. Anyway, I have to go shopping for my dress with my mum this afternoon so you boys play nicely and I will see you on Friday." With that, Charlotte jumped up, pulled her bag over her shoulder and wandered off.

"I think you have blown it, mate," said James in mock surprise. "She may be bluffing, but somehow I don't think she is."

"Ah well, plenty more fish in the sea as they say." Tony was putting a brave face on it but secretly he was gutted that Charlotte was going with someone else, let alone Mark of all people.

To make matters worse Mark was at his house when he got home, and couldn't wait to rub it in.

"A-a-alright then, mate. Do you want a lift to the ball on Friday? My car seats five so I have g-g-got room for one singleton, assuming you will be on your own." Mark and Graham fell about in exaggerated laughter, and Tony desperately tried to think of a suitably witty riposte but nothing came to mind.

"Don't worry, little brother, I will look after you, and make sure that you are not too lonely. I could ask Janice to ask Jackie Tripe for you if you like."

Tony didn't know who his brother was even talking about but whenever Janice came round she always referred to Tony as Graham's baby brother, and the thought of her involvement didn't give him any comfort at all.

"No thanks, I can sort myself out thank you very much," answered Tony.

"What about them elves your family keeps? Have you still got one that Tony could take?" joked Mark as both of the older boys fell about laughing again. Tony meanwhile just shook his head as he tried to rise above their taunts.

Paula, knocking gently on the half-open door, interrupted them. "Did you want to stay for something to eat, Mark? Only Tony and Graham have promised to stay in tonight because we have to discuss some things with them."

"No, I am okay, thanks. My tea will be ready in ten minutes so I am just about to go, thank you."

Tony was always amused at how polite Mark could be to adults, when every comment to him was an insult of some sort or another.

"Okay then, well ten minutes it is, Bob is due back now so I will get tea ready," continued Paula as she went back downstairs.

They waited for her footsteps to fade away before saying anything else.

"Th-th-that's going to be a waste then, in the circumstances," whispered Mark.

"What is?" Tony knew as soon as he asked that he should have stayed quiet and just let the comment go over his head.

"Well, i-i-it sounds like you are going to be told the facts of life from good old Bob tonight, and it will be a bit early for you, won't it? Perhaps he should go next door and t-t-tell Charlotte."

Tony had enough at this stage and jumped straight onto Mark, rolling him off the bed. Graham joined in and all three rolled around on the floor. Eventually Mark managed to get himself on top of Tony and sat across his chest, whilst Graham held his arms out in front of his head and sat on them.

"N-n-now now you won't ever get Charlotte by fighting, I think your brother needs to say sorry, don't you Graham?" said Mark through gritted teeth as it took most of his strength to stop Tony wriggling beneath him.

"Yes I do, or accept the punishment." Graham quickly looked around for something to punish Tony with and saw a half empty bottle of aftershave on the bedside table.

"Here!" he shouted as he picked up the bottle and threw it to Mark.

Mark twisted off the cap and tipped the bottle sideways until it was about to spill then with his other hand he grabbed Tony's nose.

"S-s-say sorry to Uncle Mark, or drink the juice."

"Piss off," was all Tony could say as he grabbed a quick breath and clamped his lips together again.

"Tut, tut. Fighting and swearing, that's two apologies we need." Mark was absolutely revelling in the power he had over Tony.

Graham just smirked and shifted his weight, causing his knees to send shooting pains through Tony's arms. He still kept his lips tight shut, but he was running out of breath fast with all of the physical exertion. All three boys stared at each other to see who would break first but eventually Tony had to breathe and Mark instantly poured about half of the contents out. Tony coughed and spluttered but clamped his lips tight again.

The taste wasn't as bad as he had imagined, but his lips were stinging as though it were acid in the bottle, and his eyes were nearly as bad where a few drops had reached them.

"Tha-that will do for one. Now is it to be another drink or an apology?"

This time Tony didn't wait until he was gasping for air but opened his mouth slowly and quick as a flash Mark poured in another slug of aftershave. Graham laughed and jumped off his arms.

Tony quickly raised himself up on his elbows and spat the contents that he had retained in his mouth out in Mark's face.

"Aaaggh!"

"Sorry, boys!" he shouted as he vaulted over the bed and made for the door before they could collect themselves.

"Tea's ready, come on," came the simultaneous shout from downstairs.

Without stopping to see what had happened Tony ran downstairs taking the steps three at a time.

"What's that horrible smell? Aren't you all getting ready for the ball a bit early?" asked Bob.

"Remind me to get you some more aftershave tomorrow. That smells disgusting," said Paula as she pulled a twisted face to show her disgust.

"No, it's okay, Paula, I was just messing with the bottle in Graham's room and the lid came off by accident, that's all." Tony pulled out the chair and sat down. He could hear the sink being filled in the bathroom and after about five minutes footsteps as the other two came downstairs. Mark was clearly rubbing his eyes as he shouted goodbye and went out of the front door. Graham was unfazed by the incident upstairs and the usual family banter continued around the meal table. Paula cleared everything away, and then they all sat at the kitchen table waiting for Bob to speak.

"I am sure that you are both wondering what you are here for, and it's neither to talk about your exams or the facts of life. In fact I am sure you could probably both teach us a thing or two already," he laughed a little uncertainly.

Everyone smiled around the table. Bob was a good, decent man often of few words who had always done the very best he could for his wife and adopted family. They had very few rules in the house, and this had been rewarded with very little trouble between everyone over the years.

"The fact is that Graham is already 18, and therefore an adult in the eyes of the law, with you, Tony, only a couple of years behind. We have been extremely proud of your achievements to date and hope that as you move into adulthood you will continue to involve us in all aspects of your lives like normal parents."

Graham and Tony looked across at each other and nodded in approval, knowing that nothing else was needed, but wondering where the conversation was going.

"Well, when your parents died they had written a will leaving you both a sum of money that was to be your inheritance on your 20th birthdays. Paula and I don't handle any of it, but we will give you details of the solicitors involved."

This was a total surprise, and the burning question in both of their minds was how much?

"I am sure that you are both wondering how much."

They both shook their heads. "No."

Bob smiled for the first time. "Yes you are. Don't forget I know you both by now. Anyway the sum is currently about £80,000 to be split equally between you."

He paused for a minute as the news sank in. £40,000 each when they were 20, which seemed like an absolute fortune.

"Now believe me, this may sound like a lot of money." Bob was almost mind reading as the conversation went on.

"It does," interrupted Tony with a broad grin on his face.

"Well believe me, it won't go that far so use it wisely. This is a legacy from your parents and not one to be wasted." The serious note in Bob's voice told them both that this was not the time for wise cracks.

As the conversation continued for another hour or more the earlier squabbles with Mark were forgotten, and when the boys went up to bed they both sat in Graham's room discussing their good fortune and making lavish plans for their 20th birthdays.

CHAPTER 6

The Ball

Friday came around in an instant and everyone was buzzing with excitement. In the event only half of the boys in Tony's year had either been accepted or mustered the courage to do anything about it so he was not alone in being alone. On the day he was actually quite glad to be going with Paul, and a couple of other mates, and he was sure that James would be around most of the evening as well. Paul's mum picked him up at seven, and the single lads all congregated outside the entrance to the school hall in a big huddle discussing the various outfits and dresses on display as everyone else arrived.

James and Katy were one of the first couples to arrive, and they were greeted by loud cheers, wolf whistles and clapping. As they walked up to the steps Paul jumped in front of them, held the door open and feigned a slow bow. Everyone's spirits were high as more and more pupils arrived mostly dropped off by admiring parents, but some arriving in their own cars. Mark pulled up at quarter to eight, and proudly walked by the assembled crowds of both single boys and girls to the front door. After greeting James so courteously Paul had felt duty bound to stay on as doorman, and as every couple arrived he shouted an introduction for them.

"Ladies and gentlemen, we are now pleased to welcome our very own head boy Mr Mark Richardson, accompanied by Miss Charlotte McArthur of Year 11."

When they reached the top step Mark stopped and turned, waited for the cheering to die down then turned again and went in. At the stroke of eight o'clock the music in the hall fell silent and Mr Williams came out to the main door.

"Thank you Paul, you have done an excellent job. Now we would like everyone inside please, so choose your partner, line up, and we will begin."

As Paul reached the bottom step Harriet Miles walked up to him and without saying a word they linked arms together and formed the start of the queue. Everyone else was slowly pairing off and suddenly Tony found himself looking around for a potential partner. His best friends were all sorted, and without them he felt lost and isolated. He swung around slowly, as everyone else seemed to be rushing this way or that to link up, when he spotted Julie Woods similarly isolated on the other side of the crowd. She smiled as his eye caught hers and he decided in a flash to move over in her direction.

"Would you—" But that was as far as he got.

Suddenly one of the lower sixth boys grabbed her arm.

"Come on then Julie, I couldn't find you. Sorry I am late."

And in an instant they too had joined the queue. From the back of the line Julie turned and shouted, "Tony, quick, Mel is over here on her own."

Mel Clarke was hardly his first choice, in fact she hadn't ever made so much as number three on his list, but there didn't appear to be anyone else around.

"Hi Mel, would you like to come into the ball with me?" he asked rather timidly, although trying desperately to hide the waver in his voice.

"Yes, there doesn't look to be much choice does there?" With that she stretched out her hand and Tony grasped it and joined the back of the queue. Julie turned around and smiled at them both, and Tony kicked himself for the missed opportunity.

Julie regularly featured at number two on his list, and would be promoted to top spot whenever Charlotte really annoyed him, and yet here he was with Miss Never Been On Anyone's List Mel Clarke. The line of students slowly marched into the hall, and then at Mr

Williams' request stayed with their chosen partner for the first dance, before splitting off and slowly congregating in their usual group of friends. It was a good hour before Charlotte joined them, and she walked over with Katy, and Julie.

"Hi Tony. Sorry I missed you earlier, that boy is a bit of a creep but I promised to go with him in the week. Would you may be like a dance later?" asked Julie with the same friendly smile that she had earlier. Everyone else seemed to have suddenly fallen quiet, and they were all looking at Tony awaiting his reply.

"Yeah, that would be nice," he replied, hoping that no one else could see his embarrassment in the half-light of the hall. He refused to glance around as he kicked himself for saying 'nice'. Why did his vocabulary always let him down when he most needed it? Fortunately no one else seemed to notice and the evening moved on quickly. A few people asked Charlotte where Mark was, but he was nowhere to be seen until about eleven o'clock when he made a point of coming up in front of Tony and asking for the next dance. Graham was with him and they were both in very high spirits.

"G-g-got your lovely aftershave on for the girls today then, Tony?"

"No," came the curt reply from Tony.

"Come on, Mark, I want that dance then please," interrupted Charlotte in a vain effort to change the subject.

"Yes, Graham and me. Where have you been all evening anyway?" Janice was clearly not happy at being left to her own devices so far, and she pulled Graham with a determination that told him she meant business.

"I was just having a laugh with Mark and the others."

He hesitated for a moment then added more light heartedly, "Here, pass me your handbag and I will put it on the side unless you want to dance around it."

"No, it has my things in and someone may take it." Janice was clearly in a bit of a sulk, and unlike Graham she couldn't care less what the others thought.

"Look, no one else is dancing with their handbags, are they?"

Janice looked around then thrust out her arm, clearly not amused, and Graham took the bag. As he walked over to the side wall he slipped, dropped the bag and sent the contents flying. Tony smirked to himself, and looked at Janice. She stared back, but said nothing.

Graham gathered the contents then carefully and deliberately slid the bag between two chairs stacked in a pile at the back of the hall, before returning to take Janice's hand and join the others. This left Tony alone again with Julie beside him. She smiled as he looked across, and whilst Tony was still looking for the right words she motioned towards the dance floor. "Come on then, let's dance."

He was relieved not to have to do the asking and enjoyed the next couple of dances with Julie before suddenly the evening was brought to an unexpected stop. Whilst dancing they were aware of a lot of activity just outside the hall.

Both Mark and Graham had slipped away from the rest of the group to investigate. They returned as soon as they had seen what was happening then grabbed their partners tightly around the waist and carried on dancing. Whispers were echoing around the hall, and Tony listened as intently as he could to hear what was being said. He picked up the odd bits.

"What's happening? Police, Year 6 boys, drinking, smoking, Mr Williams, teachers, fighting."

Suddenly the lights came on, and the music was abruptly halted. Mr Williams walked into the hall with a face like thunder and he had two policemen with him.

"Hey, it's the strippers!" someone shouted, but the laughter was short-lived as Mr Williams was clearly not amused.

"I am very sorry to say that this evening's ball is over. There has been some fighting outside involving some ex-pupils and I have had to call in the police to sort matters out. Regrettably they have found a small amount of drugs on those involved and I have asked them to prosecute the offenders. As a matter of course they have to check everyone else here so please form two orderly queues by the main doors, one male, one female, and an officer will check you as you leave."

Janice went to retrieve her handbag, but Graham grabbed her arm. "Leave it, I will get it later."

"No, I need it to be searched," replied Janice through gritted teeth as Graham's attitude all evening was clearly starting to grate.

"Janice, listen to me. It looks a bit suspicious being hidden. I will get it later." There was a finality about his tone that said the subject was now closed.

"He is right, Janice, if Graham has to go searching amongst all those chairs it will look a bit odd." Tony didn't know why he was interfering but he was nervous of the police and knew it was not the time to start acting suspiciously. It took a good 40 minutes for everyone to file out and fortunately for all of them nothing more was found. People were gradually walking off and parents were starting to arrive when Mr Williams came again to the top of the steps.

"Mark Richardson, Graham Alford, over here please."

Tony thought his heart had actually stopped.

Charlotte, who was stood right next to Mark holding his hand, felt him tense at the mention of his name. The two boys looked at each other, nodded and went forward.

"You may have left this school officially but you are still the most senior two here so can you grab some of the others to come in and help me pack the chairs away before we go?" Mr Williams seemed oblivious to the relief that suddenly swept through the small assembled crowd.

"Y-y-y-yes, of course Mr Williams."

The two boys turned with massive smiles of relief on their faces and motioned across. "Come on James, Tony, Charlotte, Julie, Paul, Katy. Mr Williams has asked us to help pack away," shouted Graham.

With that everyone went into the hall, and started to tidy up. Tony noticed Graham retrieve the handbag who in turn passed it to Mark. This seemed a bit odd but maybe Graham and Janice weren't talking. After all, that was by no means unusual. His thoughts were interrupted as Julie came over. "Thanks for the dance. I did enjoy this evening, well, apart from the end."

"Yes, me too." Tony didn't know what else to say.

"My mum is here now so I am off. Here is my number, phone me if you would like to meet up during the holidays and you can come over." With that, she turned and left.

Tony was left unsure about what to do next. He had the torn scrap of paper in his hand, on which Julie had written her name, phone number and a small cross. Everyone else around him was busy so he quickly stuffed the note in his pocket and carried on with the chairs. Katy's mum picked her up next, then when all of the stacking and tidying was done James Paul and Tony said their goodbyes and wandered outside together. It was only two miles back to the village, and rather than get the parents over they had agreed in advance to walk back together.

"Whose idea was this?" asked James with a half laugh.

"Er, yours I do believe," answered Paul.

"Yes it was. I was going to get Bob to pick us all up," confirmed Tony.

"I know but it wasn't fair because your parents picked us up last time. And my dad is away on business until tomorrow, and Paul's mum has already driven," countered James in reply.

"They offered though." Then as if to emphasise his frustration Tony kicked at a loose can in the car park.

"Ah well, the exercise will do you both good and get you ready for the Games. Come on, race you to the school gates," continued James, as he chased the can and rolled it away in front of him. As they knocked it between each other across the car park they became aware of raised voices in the distance, arguing. Before they were near enough to see who was involved James put an arm out both ways as he slowed down, forcing Paul and Tony to stop as well. The can rattled on a little way further, encouraged by the slight downhill slope to the car park before coming to a rest over a drain.

"Shh, it's Charlotte and Mark," whispered James.

"No way, Mark, why do you always have to be a prat and spoil things? I am not getting in the car with you if you have been drinking." They could all hear now and it was clear that Charlotte was not impressed. They all knew that she could more than hold her own though, and for a moment they were quite happy to listen as she cut Mark down to size.

"Come on, Charlotte, he only had one. Janice is fine with it. It's getting cold, and it's only two miles to home. He could do it blindfolded." Graham's voice was slightly muffled, and the others were straining their eyes against the dark and cold to see what was going on.

James moved forward out of the shadows with Tony and Paul at his sides. "What is going on?"

"Mark and Graham have only been drinking, haven't they? I walked over here with Janice to go home and they were both drinking cider and smoking." As she finished Charlotte moved away from the car so that she was stood just in front of James, Paul and Tony.

"Walk back with us, Charlotte, we have all had enough trouble tonight," said Tony, taking strength from their greater number. "And you, Graham. Come on, it's only a short walk."

"Don't worry about me, little brother, I am staying in the warm car, thanks." Then as if to prove a point he pulled the door shut and waved sarcastically from inside.

Charlotte looked back at Mark who just shook his head and jumped in the driver's seat. "Sorry Mark, but I am not going anywhere with you after you have been drinking."

With that, he started the engine, turned on the lights and sped away. The remaining four looked at each other, shrugged their shoulders and set off towards home. The mood soon lifted when the car lights disappeared into the distance and as they walked along they all linked arms together and discussed the evening on the way.

"So are you going to use that bit of paper and phone Julie then?" asked James which brought the line of them to a sudden stop.

"Did Julie give you her number?" asked Charlotte in surprise.

"Maybe," said Tony as he moved forward, dragging the rest of them on again.

"Maybe… Duh… of course she did, she fancies you," laughed James.

"Rubbish." Clearly frustrated that they wouldn't walk faster, Tony broke the line and marched ahead.

"James is right, she always puts you near the top of her dream guy list," laughed Charlotte with an obvious hint of mischievousness in her voice. This stopped the boys in their tracks so abruptly you could almost hear the screech of their shoes on the tarmac. Charlotte could sense what impact her words had, but she carried on a few more feet to what she considered to be a safe distance before she turned and smiled at them.

Paul spoke first. "You mean to say you girls draw up lists of guys you fancy?"

"Paul, my dear, what do you take us for? We are young ladies, you know," said Charlotte rather coyly.

"But that's degrading and sick," he continued in clear disgust at the startling revelation.

"Yeah, Paul's right, you wouldn't like it if we made lists about you girls, would you?" agreed James, also clearly bemused by what he had heard.

"It's not just about you boys, James, it's about any man. We can even make a man up if we like, you know, Paul's legs, your eyes, Tony for the body and so on… Well probably not Tony for the body but you get the idea." Charlotte was edging back all the time, waiting for it all to sink in.

"But that's even more stupid, and fancy calling it the dream guy list," sneered Paul.

"Well that's better than the St Thomas Top Totty list." Charlotte's words brought a stunned silence. The three boys looked to each other, trying to suppress their smirks, and unable to take in what Charlotte had just said.

"I'm sorry?" questioned James.

"Oh, don't be sorry James, it's okay, we know it wasn't just you," replied Charlotte.

"No, I mean I am sorry I didn't quite catch what you said." He cupped his hand up to his ear as he feigned deafness.

"Aaagh, losing your hearing as well now, are you? Ah, well, none of you will ever catch this St Thomas top totty anyway. Bye." With that, Charlotte picked up the hem of her dress and ran on ahead. For a moment the boys stood watching her run off into the distance then they decided to give chase. Even in an evening dress Charlotte was quick, and she took some catching. Tony caught up with her first and grabbed her by the arm. "Hold on a bit, wait for the others."

Charlotte stopped to take a breath in between fits of giggles. "Need your friends here to help, do you? You boys are all the same, you only find strength in numbers."

James and Paul caught the last bit as they arrived, but both were out of breath.

"So how come no one has ever mentioned this so-called list before then?" questioned Tony.

Charlotte was still in fits of giggles, and the others were finding it hard not to join her. "Are all of your egos a bit hurt, boys?"

James had just about recovered his breath by now, and joined in "Leave it, Tony, I think Miss Charlotte here is fishing for information and knows nothing."

"Well I know a lot more now, don't I?" she smiled broadly back, clearly loving being in control.

"Not as much as you think, and I think we should change the subject to say, the Games now, don't you lads?" James was desperate to take charge, but Charlotte was a hard act to beat.

"Lads, is only a grown-up name for boys, isn't it? Because we all know that boys never actually grow up, don't we?" Charlotte knew she was outnumbered but she wasn't going to let that bother her.

"My, we are in a mischievous mood tonight aren't we?" With that, James moved forward and before she realised what was happening had picked Charlotte up and was carrying her on his shoulder. Charlotte pretended to scream, and kept beating James on his back with her fists. "Put me down, you brute. I don't know what Katy sees in you, all brawn and no brain."

"Right lads, shall we dump the witch in the village pond?" Despite the gentle blows on his back James marched on ahead carrying Charlotte with him. Eventually as he began to tire he offered a truce and gently lowered her to the floor. Still laughing and joking they walked the last few hundred yards to the start of the village where they reached Paul's house.

"Right then, that's me home, see you all in the next few days."

Paul shook hands with Tony and James then offered his hand to Charlotte. She reached forward and gave him a peck on the cheek.

"Thanks for tonight, it has been good." Despite the recent banter there was obvious sincerity in Charlotte's voice.

Paul turned then asked jokingly, "So was I top of the dream guy list?"

"Kind of."

"Really?" Even he knew his last remark sounded a little too desperate.

"Yes, Mark was top but we decided he would be better with your voice." Charlotte shrugged her shoulders as she finished.

"Great... Now I will really sleep better... see you all tomorrow," and with that Paul disappeared inside his house.

"What is it with you girls and Mark? He is just an idiot." Tony shook his head in obvious disgust as he finished.

"Sometimes, Tony, but he does have dreamy eyes and a hunky body." Charlotte sighed heavily to emphasise her appreciation.

"Trust me, mate, you are better off leaving it. I tried to have this conversation with Katy, and she still thinks Mark is the best looking guy in school," added James.

"Oh, so she does have some good taste then." Charlotte was enjoying herself, knowing that for once she had the upper hand, and with Paul gone the odds against her were reduced still further.

"But I still find it—"

"Shhh," James interrupted Tony mid flow. "Down there outside my house, is that police or an ambulance?"

Charlotte gave the answer, but they could all see for themselves what was going on. "It's both, James, and that looks like someone on a stretcher."

James missed the last bit as he was already sprinting off down the road. Tony turned to Charlotte. "Shit, what's going on now? Come on, let's get after him."

As James approached the house Julie jumped from the back of the ambulance and ran over to her son. She had obviously been crying, and as James put his massive arms around her she looked very frail and weak. Her personality normally meant that the way her son towered over her went unnoticed, but tonight she just looked vulnerable and frightened. She composed herself as Tony and Charlotte caught up, and pushed gently away from James.

"Thank goodness you are all safe, I was starting to get a bit worried about you all."

"Mum, forget about us, why is Dad on that stretcher?" The joy in his voice from a few moments earlier had now been replaced by fear, and he didn't dare wait for a reply before continuing. "Mum, what's happening? I didn't think Dad was due home until tomorrow."

"No, he wasn't, but he phoned this afternoon and said he was feeling unwell so he decided to drive back early. I'm sorry, I should have told you but I didn't want to spoil your evening, and Katy looked so beautiful in her dress." Julie always seemed so vibrant, but tonight she had suddenly aged by about 20 years.

James put his reassuring arm around her shoulder again. "It's okay. What happened?"

"Can you come now, Mrs Alan? We really have to get your husband to the hospital as soon as possible."

The paramedic was closing the door as he spoke, ushering her inside.

"Please, just a second. This is my son, I have to just explain," she pleaded.

"Okay but quick as you can please," he added with real urgency in his manner.

"When he got home he sat in his chair and fell asleep for a good hour. Then I got a snack ready and called him, but when he got up he felt giddy and sick and collapsed which is when I called for the ambulance. They think he has had a heart attack. They have been here for over an hour trying to stabilise him, and now they are taking him to the hospital." As she finished Julie couldn't help but look inside the ambulance at the grey form lying just to her side.

"Oh my god." James wanted to say more but physically couldn't as a lump stuck in his throat.

"It's okay James. Look, Janet and Adam are in the house so you can all stay here tonight or go back with them to Charlotte's house. I have to go to the hospital and I will phone you as soon as I know anything."

"I will come with you."

"Please James, don't argue, stay here. I will let you know as soon as I know anything. We both love you."

"You too."

James felt the tears rolling down his cheek, and wanted them to stop but couldn't. Charlotte put a comforting arm around his waist and half dragged him to the front door where they were greeted by her parents.

"Oh, thank goodness you three are here. I was about to send Adam out looking for you all. We saw Mark driving through the village nearly an hour ago, but we guessed you three would stick together. I am sorry about your dad, James, but these things so often seem worse at the time. Look, all of you come in I have just put the kettle on. Coffee or tea?"

Janet was talking in a half whisper and no one really took in a word she had said.

Everyone trudged through to the kitchen, and sat at the table. Janet then joined them, sitting in silence for several minutes, before standing up to make her way across to the kettle.

"James, I am sorry to be a nuisance, what with being here to help, but I don't want to go through your mum's cupboards."

"Mum, it's okay," said Charlotte as she got up. "I know where everything is. Just sit down, and let me make the coffees."

"Okay darling."

Silence prevailed until the coffees were on the table, and Charlotte sat down again.

"Do Bob and Paula know that I might be late?" asked Tony, knowing that it sounded a bit pathetic, but wanting to break the uncomfortable silence.

"Yes, we phoned them just when we saw you coming down the road to let them know what was happening. They are waiting up, and we promised to get you there as soon as we can, lad." Adam had joined them in the kitchen and unlike his wife he was usually succinct and to the point.

What little conversation followed was very stilted, with everyone taking regular small sips of their hot drinks to pass away the time. James remained silent throughout. Charlotte tried to put herself in James' shoes right now. She couldn't stand the thought of one of her parents being taken away in an ambulance, and she so wanted to say something supportive. The whole evening had been a roller coaster of emotions, and her heart was thumping away in her chest like a drum beat. She noticed from the clock on the cooker that it was now quarter past one but with her mind racing tiredness wasn't even starting to creep up on her.

Tony was very uneasy with the whole situation as well. He never really knew his own parents, but he knew the massive impact that their premature deaths had on his life, and that of Graham. He knew also that words of consolation meant little at this stage, and he secretly held his hands together under the table praying that James' dad would be okay. He wasn't particularly religious but at times like this he knew it had to be worth a try. The phone interrupted the silence, and everyone at the table jumped. James pushed his chair back and ran to the living room.

"Hello," he whispered into the handset, as though he was afraid to wake anyone due to the late hour.

Beep, beep, beep.

"Quick, put the money in," he whispered again to himself, knowing it was his mum struggling with the hospital payphone.

"James, is that you?" came the distant voice from the receiver.

"Yes."

"I think you need to come to the hospital. Your dad is stable at the moment but he had another attack in the ambulance on the way here. Ask Adam to bring you in. My money—"

Beep. Beep. Beep. Brrrrrrrrrr.

James held the handset against his chin for a moment. He was aware that someone else had come into the room after him, but was too absorbed in his own thoughts to even acknowledge them. Charlotte spoke first. "James, is everything okay?" She winced at her own stupidity as the words left her mouth, knowing of course that things were far from okay. Rather than compounding things she allowed her friend time to compose himself.

"Yes, well no. I don't really know, but Mum wants me to go to the hospital if your dad will take me."

"Yes, of course. Wait a second, I will get him." As she ran out of the living room, she could feel the tears welling up inside her, and her chin quivering in fear. She stopped momentarily in the hall trying to compose herself and took a deep breath before walking into the kitchen.

"Dad, James has to go to the hospital. Can you take him?"

"Yes, of course, just give me a minute. Go and see he is alright. I will be there." With that Adam looked around for his keys, and coat. James was happy to let Charlotte do the organising for once and just slumped onto the sofa oblivious to the plans being made around him. After a few minutes Adam walked in.

"Okay lad, are you ready?"

"Yes." James deliberately avoided eye contact with everyone as he shuffled out to the car. He knew everyone meant well, but he also knew they were all bottling up their fears, and he was afraid of what he might see in their eyes. They watched the car leave and returned to the kitchen, where Janet quickly washed the dishes in the sink.

"Right, you two both need to get to your beds. James will need you to support him tomorrow and you won't be any good if you are worn out as well. So come on, get your things and let's walk back. Bob and Paula are no doubt wondering what is happening, and they will want to get into their beds as well. I have a spare key so come on, let's lock up and walk back home."

Not knowing what else to do for the best, they both reluctantly followed Janet's instructions.

*

Tony had a restless night's sleep, and woke several times with his heart beating furiously in his chest. The recent memories of the ball, along with long-forgotten thoughts about his own parents kept his mind too active to sleep well. Graham had dumped his fully packed rucksack in Tony's room as well, in readiness for his trek around

Europe that he was due to embark on with Mark the following day. It would be strange going through the summer holidays without Graham and Mark around, but they were due to go to university in October so it was a feeling he would have to get used to.

As Tony opened his eyes for the fifth or sixth time that morning he could see the bright green digital numbers on his alarm clock read 6.45. He lay with his head on the pillow staring at the display as the minutes slowly ticked by. There was no purpose to it but Tony started counting the seconds trying to guess the exact point at which the numbers would change again.

At 6.59 he pulled his arm from under the covers and left it hovering over the snooze button. He had set it to alarm rather than radio when he went to bed because he had wanted to be first up, but now he wanted just another nine minutes of snoozing.

"Forty-nine, fifty, fifty-one, fifty-two," he whispered to himself, knowing full well that he could turn the whole thing off if he really wanted but that would have meant sitting up in bed to turn the alarm clock over. Instead he stayed snuggled in bed with just his left hand hovering over the snooze button.

"Fifty-nine, sixty, sixty-one."

Beep, beep.

Tony smiled at the accuracy of his counting and tapped the snooze bar.

Beep, beep.

He tapped again, but harder this time.

Beep, beep.

He could hear someone else moving around the house so he sat up and pulled the plug out of the wall.

Beep.

Just as the numbers faded away Tony realised it had been the phone ringing, not his alarm clock, and he could just make out Paula talking in the hallway.

"Hello."

"Hello Adam, thanks for ringing us. How are things?"

Another brief pause.

"That's terrible. It makes you think though, doesn't it? How old was he?"

Silence again.

"Sixty-four, that's no age, is it? I will tell Bob and the boys, give my love to Julie and James, tell them I will pop around later."

Tony knew from the half conversation what was being said and all of a sudden a cold shiver went through him. Only moments before he was comfortably slumbering in the warmth of his duvet, but now his whole body felt ice cold, and yet his feet and hands were clammy and hot. His mouth felt so dry and he could not focus his mind. Paula was sure to come up the stairs any second, and he wanted the ground to just swallow him up so that he didn't have to face her.

He had met James' dad several times, but he was usually away working so he didn't know him particularly well, and somehow this made the intrusion that was about to shatter his life even less welcome. Tony knew that his thought pattern was totally irrational, but he hated the way life changed so dramatically. They had all been so happy last night as they made their way home, and now outside influences were going to intrude on the comfortable world where he preferred to live his life.

Ever since he was a young child Tony liked to build friends around him and live almost in a bubble of security and happiness. Above all he didn't like change. At times like these he always felt vulnerable and threatened. It was the same when he went to new families as a child or moved schools. He didn't see positives in new things for a long time. He hadn't really experienced a death like this before but he was afraid of what changes it might bring. Would James and his mother be able to keep that big house on, or would they move away? Would James look to Tony for support, or would it be Katy who would help him through?

At the back of his mind Tony knew he was being selfish, but he hated these things happening and had a right to feel sorry for himself. Paula knocking gently on his door interrupted his thoughts.

"Come in," he whispered. It wasn't intentional but his mouth was so dry he could barely make himself heard.

Paula walked in and sat on the edge of his bed.

"How are you, love? Did you sleep well?" she asked.

"I heard you on the telephone. He has died, hasn't he?" Tony looked straight into her eyes as he spoke, and he could see the truth and sadness deep within her even before she spoke.

"Yes." She nodded slowly. "He never recovered from the second heart attack, and he passed away this morning."

Tears were welling up in her eyes, and Tony found himself fighting the natural inclination to cry. Despite the fact that his whole body was trembling within he gently took Paula's hand and squeezed it. She shuffled up the bed and gave Tony a hug. He had never felt her trembling before and in his arms she suddenly felt so frail. This strong woman had nurtured him since he was a young boy, but suddenly she needed the protection he offered through his strong hold.

"Life is too short, I am afraid, and these things bring it all home. Bob is only six years younger than Phillip you know." She was trying hard to retain some composure, and give back strength to Tony, but neither knew what to say and a welcome silence followed.

Neither of them was aware of anyone else in the world let alone the house until suddenly the bedroom door swung back and Graham jumped on the bed singing at the top of his voice, "We're all going on a summer holiday, no more working for a week or..."

He stopped mid-sentence and surveyed the situation for a moment or two.

"Don't tell me you two are missing me already, and don't cry Paula, no one has died. I will only be away for a few weeks." His laughter faded almost comically as the gravity of the situation he had intruded on began to dawn on him.

"Graham don't you ever think of anyone else except yourself?" said Tony with obvious exasperation.

"Give over, little brother, you will be able to have a little cuddle every morning without me seeing from now on if you like." He knew something was seriously amiss, but as always he went on the attack to defend his own vulnerability.

"Get lost, and don't rush back on my account." Without meaning to Tony almost spat the words out.

"Both of you stop it. Tony, your brother doesn't know what has happened so calm down. Graham, try to be a bit more sensitive, and both of you remember you only have each other as real family." Paula's face was bright red with fury at them both, her parental power now fully restored. For a few moments the two boys sat looking awkwardly at each other.

"Now for your information, Graham, James' dad died last night, so please show a bit of respect today." Paula spoke quietly and calmly.

"Bloody hell, how was I to know that? Shit. Shit. Shit, I am sorry." Graham appeared visibly shaken.

"Language," Paula tutted.

"Sorry," came the feeblest of replies, but even Graham knew when to act with humility.

"Okay, well I am getting breakfast ready and then Charlotte is coming over to go up to James' house with Tony, so I will see you both downstairs in a few minutes."

At the mention of going up to James' house Tony felt his heartbeat race again. He wasn't sure if he was ready for that as yet, and as he showered and wandered downstairs he was desperately trying to think of excuses.

*

As Charlotte woke she felt the warmth of the sun on her body and hoped that this was a good sign for the day ahead. She had slept well in short bursts, exhausted by the evening's activities, and long walk home, but her mind was too preoccupied to really sink into a deep sleep. When she had eventually reached her room the night before, the bed had never looked more inviting. Even so, she took time to look at herself in the long mirror before carefully hanging her dress up and getting her pyjamas on. It was the first time she had worn such a beautiful dress, and she had felt so proud walking up to the door as Paul ceremoniously introduced her and Mark. No one had called her Swotty Lotty all night, in fact she hadn't heard it ever since the other girls found out who had invited her to the ball.

The end of the evening was a real shock but Charlotte wasn't going to let that ruin her memories of the night. It was only half past six when the phone rang and she knew that it couldn't be a good sign, so she jumped out of bed, pulled on a dressing gown and ran downstairs. As she entered the kitchen Janet was replacing the receiver and she stood for a few moments with her back to Charlotte.

"Is everything okay Mum?"

Startled Janet swung around and faced her daughter. "No. I am sorry for your friend James, but it seems as though he has lost his father, and poor Julie, I don't know how she will cope on her own. I know he is a good lad. You are all good children, but it never seems fair. And he was due to retire this summer after 34 years with one company, and now what will happen to poor Julie? I don't know. I just don't know."

Charlotte walked over and embraced her mother. They were both crying, silent tears, reflecting on what it all meant to them. As they continued to hug one another there was no sound, but the tears rolled gently down their cheeks. Eventually Janet moved away, wiped her cheeks with the back of her hand, sniffed and cleared her throat.

"Your friend is too young to have to deal with all this, and I don't know how he will react but I know you will support him. I am afraid that this is something you will deal with more than once in your life, but it never gets easier, and it never seems to be fair. Life has a habit of biting back at you just when you let your guard down." Janet never liked to preach to her daughter but she felt desperately sad and emotion was getting the better of her.

"I know, Mum, it's okay," replied Charlotte.

"No darling, it's not okay. I was so proud of you last night in your lovely evening dress, and I was dreaming of all the times we would have together in the future, and I was even thinking of what you would look like in your wedding dress when Julie phoned. Your dad answered for me, and I was angry at first that we had to go up to their house and ruin all of my daydreams. I know it's selfish now but at the time I was so proud and so happy." As she finished Janet turned away and wiped away the tears that were refusing to stay in.

Charlotte moved across and embraced her mother again. "It's okay, Mum, you are the least selfish person in the whole world."

As they stood together Charlotte felt uneasy at the sudden role reversal. She knew that she was more in control of the whole situation than her mother, and for the first time ever she even felt like she was acting more like a parent than a child. Suddenly Janet pulled away and looked her daughter straight in the eye.

"Promise you won't say anything but your father is going in for tests on his heart next month and I was worried sick even before last night. We weren't going to tell you, and I shouldn't have really but I know you are strong enough to deal with it, and anyway it might still be nothing. I suppose that I just want you to know why I am in such a mess, especially when I didn't even really know Phillip."

Charlotte could do nothing more than stare back at her mother in disbelief. After what seemed like an eternity she eventually blinked and both of them broke the stare and looked away.

"Why on earth haven't you told me about this before?" questioned Charlotte indignantly.

"You had your exams, Charlotte, and before last night I thought it was just routine and I didn't want to bother you."

"And now?"

"And now I don't know anything anymore, but we have to hope it will all be okay. The only thing I do know is that worrying about it won't change the outcome or help anyone. Now look, your breakfast is ready, I have made porridge, and the kettle is boiled. Would you like tea or coffee? Why don't you get showered and dressed properly and I will have everything ready. Then I have said you would call around and pick up Tony on the way to James' house." Janet was nearly back up to speed, though more from obvious fear than any sense of normality.

Charlotte blinked again and shook her head as she suddenly realised that Janet was back in control. "Er, coffee please. Yes, I will get a shower and be back down in ten minutes."

As she walked upstairs she was thinking over in her head about ways that she could help. Above all she didn't want to get in the way, and she knew that Katy and Tony would offer James the best support, but she really wanted to do her bit. These thoughts were still uppermost in her mind an hour later as she sat at the table in Tony's house waiting for him to come down the stairs. Bob and Paula were trying to keep the conversation going, asking all about the ball, but inevitably it was all unusually disjointed. Eventually Tony sauntered in and sat himself down opposite. Very little was said as he slowly ate breakfast and eventually they found themselves walking up to James' front door.

Neither of them wanted to ring the bell, and as they were on the step arguing about who would do it Julie suddenly opened the front door. Oh, hello you two, I am glad you came, I thought that I heard voices." Despite all the thought and preparation from both of them it all now seemed so much more real. Neither had expected to see Julie at the house let alone opening the door.

Charlotte took a deep breath and spoke first. "I am really sorry about Mr Alan."

"Thank you, love, it means more than anything to me that James has the support of his friends at times like these. Katy came over about an hour ago and they are both out in the garden at the moment, just wander through, you both know the way."

Tony didn't say anything as he walked past, but he managed a half smile as he made eye contact with James' mother. As soon as they reached the back door James stood up and beckoned them over. The conversation was punctuated with long bouts of silence, when everyone simply stared at the ground, but the day soon passed, and from then on it became a little easier to face with each subsequent day.

The whole of the summer holidays seemed to pass with even more speed than usual. Everyone felt the impact of Phillip's death, not least at the funeral a couple of days later, but as the weeks passed they all gradually put it behind them and moved on. It was a wet summer, and this added to the general feeling of despondency at times but Charlotte, Tony, Paul, and increasingly Katy were at the side of their friend to help him through.

The arrival of exam results in mid-summer almost caught everyone by surprise. They knew it was coming but had been happy to dismiss the date from their minds. Paul mentioned it first just before he went away with his parents on a fortnight's holiday.

"Do you lot realise that we all have to go and get our results the day after I arrive back from my holiday?"

"I know but I wasn't going to mention it. Anyway, Graham has asked me to pick his A Levels up from school the week before and keep them hidden until he gets back," answered Tony, hoping that no one else would pick up on it and the conversation would quickly move on to something else.

"You are joking. You will open them though, won't you?" enquired James.

"I am not sure but I thought I could tell him that I have opened them and tell him he failed everything," laughed Tony.

"No because then he would come back with M-M-M-Mark, and that is all we need to ruin this crap summer completely," added Paul.

The three boys all burst out laughing whilst Charlotte and Katy jumped to Mark's defence.

"Mark is all right, and so is Graham for that matter," said Charlotte almost too defensively.

"Yes, you little boys are just jealous because they can drive, drink, and go on holiday without their mummy and daddy." Katy hadn't meant to direct the comment at Paul, but he went bright red anyway, and so she ran over and put a comforting arm around him. "I am sorry, I didn't mean that."

"It's okay, but either way at least I get a holiday before the dreaded exam results," he answered a little uncertainly.

In the end the results were pretty much as expected. Charlotte picked up ten straight As. James and Katy had an identical mix of five As, although Katy had an A star in biology, three Bs and two Cs. Tony had a mix of Bs and Cs whilst Paul excelled with A stars in maths, physics and chemistry, achieved grade Cs in history, English, politics, and geography, but could only manage Ds in French, German and biology.

With results out of the way talk finally turned towards the Games, and although James found it hard to feel his usual enthusiasm he desperately wanted to win both of his final years in the competition. Everyone knew how much winning meant to James, and did all that they could to be supportive.

When the day itself arrived it came in a blaze of early morning sunshine, and Charlotte called for Tony as agreed at eight o'clock. On the way up to James' house they could both feel the butterflies starting to build.

"I cannot believe that you boys have got me so worked up about these stupid Games. I am even feeling nervous, and I could hardly sleep last night," said Charlotte.

"But it is important, especially to James, I just wish his dad could have been here tonight when he brings the cup home," answered Tony.

"If, you mean," said Charlotte, trying to be a bit more rational.

"No, I do mean WHEN. We will win, don't worry. We have easily the best team in the tournament." Tony was adamant and it came through in the unusually forceful tone of his voice.

Charlotte knew better than to argue, and secretly had been praying all week that both the hockey and football finals would go to their teams.

"Come on then, show me how good you are, race you to the door." Even before she finished the sentence Tony had raced off ahead, and by the time she caught him up he had already rung the bell and was waiting for James to answer the door. As they stood on the porch they could hear the bolts being undone, and opened.

"Morning," smiled Katy as she beckoned them both in.

They stood still for a moment.

"Bloody hell, you must have got up early this morning to be around here already. Did Julie ask you to come over and wake James up because she was going away?" with almost naive innocence.

Katy went bright pink and looked to Charlotte for support. She said nothing but kicked Tony sharply on the ankle.

"Ouch, what?" Still blissfully unaware of what was wrong, he hobbled into the hall. As Tony stood hopping around on one leg the two girls linked arms and wandered up the hallway to the dining room.

"I have just cooked James breakfast and there might even be some left if you are quick," shouted Katy.

After vigorously rubbing his ankle for a few seconds Tony walked into the hall, and slowly turned to close the front door. The realisation that Katy had stayed the night came as a bit of a shock, and he wasn't even absolutely sure why, let alone how he was supposed to react to the news. James had been going out seriously with Katy for a good year now, but it had never crossed Tony's mind that they would be sleeping together, and although everyone talked about it he didn't think any one of his year was actually doing it. When he reached the door to the dining room everyone else was sat down eating bacon rolls, chatting about the day's games ahead.

Tony just stood in the doorway shifting his gaze back and forth between James and Katy. They didn't look any different, and neither looked any older or more mature. If anything Charlotte still looked the most grown up by far, and she hadn't slept with anyone, at least as far as he knew. As he continued looking at his three friends James looked across and caught his eye.

"Come on in and sit down or these bacon rolls will have all gone. The tea in the pot is still hot if you want some."

"Sorry, I was just daydreaming," replied Tony as he pulled up a chair and sat down.

Charlotte leant across and held his hand in a mock sign of support. "Don't worry, your time will come one day. There is someone out there for all of us." She could hardly contain the giggles as she finished and then looked at Katy who also burst out laughing.

James looked across at the other three with a questioning glance and despite a mouth full of bacon roll, asked, "What?"

"Don't worry, mate, it's just girls' stuff. They both need to grow up a bit if you ask me," replied Tony with an unconvincing laugh.

James washed the last bit of roll down with a swig of tea, before he spoke just as the giggles were subsiding. "Little things, eh, please little minds don't they?"

Charlotte and Katy just looked at each other and burst into another spontaneous fit of giggles.

"Now what have I said?"

"Nothing," chorused the other three.

The remaining breakfast was rushed as they all realised it was already 8.30, and they left the dining room in a complete mess as they rushed out of the door towards school.

After a brisk half walk, half run they arrived at the school gates by 9.00 to be greeted by Mr Williams.

"Morning to you all and I am glad to see that my new sixth year students are all so punctual. Let's hope that you keep it up all year."

"Yes sir, and it looks like we have better weather for the games after the rain we have had lately."

"Yes James but I am afraid that the sports pitches are all very wet, and there are some ominous rain clouds over behind you."

"Don't worry, sir, we can win despite the weather," continued James with a cautionary glance up at the clouds.

"I hope you are right, but in the meantime can you four please check with the year captains to ensure we have a good turnout and liaise with me during the day to ensure everything runs smoothly. You should all know the set-up by now."

"Yes sir, see you around ten for the first kick-off."

They all split up for the next hour but were reassembled with Paul and a few others on the touchline for the start of the first hockey and football matches, just as the first spots of rain fell. The results went well all morning, in spite of the weather, and when they walked into the main hall at lunchtime Mr Peterson who as official record keeper was smiling broadly for the first time that any of them could remember.

"Good to see all of my star pupils together. Congratulations on your exams."

"Thank you," chorused the assembled group.

"I know that some of my colleagues obviously had some input, but as your form tutor who has nurtured you all through thick and thin I hope that my inspirational speeches actually worked for once."

Mr Peterson was never this happy, and Tony assumed he had already started to celebrate their early success on the sports pitch with a drink or two. Everyone was a little taken aback by his jolly demeanour but as usual it was James who found his voice first.

"So are those results right? We have only lost one game all morning."

"Mr Alan, after all the praise that I have heaped on you, you still have the audacity to question me." Whether in jest or not the broad smile on Mr Peterson's face had been quickly replaced with one of seniority.

"Sorry sir but they are quite incredible results aren't they?" answered James defensively.

"They certainly are, and I have a very good feeling about today."

The nerves were buzzing around the group, and Tony's heart missed a beat altogether as Julie ran over and whispered in his ear.

"Hi, missed you. You didn't phone me all holiday and you promised."

He felt his face go bright red, and the rest of the group just stood staring unable to hear what was being whispered into his ear.

"I am sorry but it has been a hectic summer," he replied rather lamely.

Julie smiled back and put a finger to Tony's lips. "It's okay, I will give you a second chance."

Then turning to James: "I was really sorry to hear about your dad, I can't imagine what it is like, and I don't mean to bring it up today but I have been unable to say anything before."

James simply acknowledged her with a nod then leant forward as she put a comforting arm around his neck. The moment seemed almost frozen until Mr Williams came running up in an obvious state of panic.

"Mr Peterson, I need your help please in the staff room now. The Head of Chiselton is calling for the games to be called off because of the conditions and the state of the pitches. Two representatives are required for each school to take a majority vote."

"No way, that old slime ball MaCauley was in my tutor group at uni. and he was a cowardly little sod then as well." Then with a quick look at the shocked faces around him Mr Peterson added, "Apologies, ladies."

The unfolding news was a bigger shock than their teacher's language, and everyone just stood around in disbelief, as they wandered off to the staff room.

"They cannot do this just because we are nearly through. Look at the tables. Chiselton have to win every game from now on to make the finals, that's why they want out." James was trying to contain the anger within him as he gesticulated to the others around him.

"You have to admit it is pretty wet, James," ventured Paul rather lamely.

"And!" shouted James in utter disbelief.

"Well it's wet, that's all I am saying, and some of the younger ones might not like playing in the rain." Paul looked around the others for moral support but they all avoided his gaze.

"Crap, it's a cop-out," continued James as he turned back to stare once more at the tables above.

The debate continued for the next ten minutes until Mr Williams walked back in and purposefully strode towards the main stage.

"Attention please. Everyone."

The background noise quickly subsided and everyone stood facing the front.

"You will all be aware that the worsening conditions are making continuation of the games this year very difficult, and a number of parents have contacted the school expressing concern. We have decided therefore after a brief meeting to continue for the moment but review matters by committee in one hour."

A small cheer went up from the assembled pupils and James wandered over to talk to Mr Peterson.

"So you managed to outvote Mr MaCauley then, sir?"

"No, James, and he wasn't a politics student for nothing. I think he has just outflanked a dumb old historian."

"Why? The games are continuing, aren't they?"

"Yes, young man, but it is all about playing the intelligent game in this world as you will one day realise. I went in that staff room all guns blazing and tore into the people who wanted to call off the games, and our friend Mr MaCauley actually supported me, and the others then followed suit." Mr Peterson was staring into the distance as he finished, clearly eyeing up his adversary.

"That's great, sir, so what is the problem?" quizzed James, unable to see any possible hidden agenda.

"Well he now knows that the others will follow him now when he changes his mind at the next meeting and asks for the games to stop on some spurious grounds like worsening conditions."

"But they might also support you."

"No, because he provoked me into an irrational rant about keeping the games on regardless, and now he is going to look the more level-headed and sensible of the two of us. Believe me, if you are going to win an argument you have to remain rational above all else." Mr Peterson shook his head as he finished, emphasising his annoyance at himself.

"But," interrupted James, still certain that his teacher had done the right thing.

"No more buts, Mr Alan, I may have blown your chances of success for which I apologise, but let's get out there and play on for the moment, and pray for better weather."

When they re-emerged it was surprisingly to bright sunshine, and everyone quickly assembled either on the pitches or around them as spectators. Charlotte watched the start of the Year 4 hockey before she ventured over to join the rest of the group.

"We are 1-0 up already with a goal in only 42 seconds," she whispered as she raised her hand to show crossed fingers.

"It may not be enough though from what Mr Peterson was saying, particularly if Chiselton lose both their games and they are already 1-0 down in the hockey," replied James. He was trying, but failing miserably, to sound upbeat.

"Come on, James, you will get your moment of glory." It was Tony who was trying to raise the mood this time. "Let's just watch this match and see what happens."

"Yes James, Tony is right, I am going back to watch the hockey. See you all at half time."

The three boys watched Charlotte, Julie and Katy run back across the field then turned to watch their game. All was quiet for a few moments until Paul broke the silence. "Julie seems keen, mate, are you going to ask her out?"

"Don't know," answered Tony without acknowledging his friend. Instead he just stared fixedly ahead.

"Go for it, mate, you have nothing to lose and like Paul says she seems keen enough," said James as he winced in acknowledgement of a heavy tackle on the field.

"Yeah I will," continued Tony, still staring stoically ahead.

"When?"

"When I am ready! Anyway what about you and Harriet? I haven't seen her around much today," snapped Tony, barely able to disguise his obvious annoyance at the constant barrage of questions.

"No we had a row, and she said I was a nerdy geek," laughed Paul, trying hard to seem unconcerned.

Both James and Tony tried hard to contain their laughter. "Why?"

"I don't know exactly, I called round after the exam results to take her a present I bought her on holiday, and she got all funny."

"Why exactly?" asked James, who was now also losing his focus on the game.

"You know women, can't live with, can't shoot them as my dad would say," laughed Paul.

"Come on, tell us the whole story, what exactly happened?" continued James, trying to show genuine concern.

"Well I gave her the present, this T-shirt I had bought for her, and she went to put it on."

"Good so far. I hope you are listening, Tony you may get some good tips here as well."

"Well whilst I was waiting for her to change I started talking to her parents, and her dad had just bought a DVD collection of Star Trek series one and two," replied Paul, seemingly oblivious to the reaction from the other two. Tony and James looked at each other and burst out laughing.

"Don't tell us you sat and watched the whole lot with her dad." James was wiping tears from his eyes as he leant on Tony trying hard to stop laughing.

"No, of course not," continued Paul as soon as he had a moment of silence, "I waited for Hattie to come downstairs and told her she looked really pretty, which she did, then we watched just the first four episodes."

"Four episodes. You are joking, what did she want you to do?" asked Tony in utter disbelief.

"Oh, she went back up to her room and listened to music."

"Paul. Paul. Paul, I may not know much but if her parents are happy for you to go up to their daughter's bedroom and listen to music you go. You do not sit and watch Star Trek," said Tony as he shook his head.

"You may laugh, but her dad has leant me the rest of series one, and I can have series two when I have watched them, so it wasn't a wasted evening."

Even Paul could see the funny side of it all by now, and their laughter was interrupted as Julie ran back over and covered Tony's eyes with her hands. "Guess who?"

Her reached out behind to grab at whoever it was but she jumped back.

"Charlotte?"

"Wrong answer! Try again." Julie removed one hand and playfully tapped him on the back of the head at the mention of Charlotte's name.

"Julie," he whispered, thankful that she couldn't feel the heat now burning his cheeks.

"Well done. I don't know. What does a girl have to do around here to be number one choice? I am going to have to ask Katy how she does it."

Tony shifted uneasily on his feet. He had known it wasn't Charlotte, and saying her name had been an almost instinctive reaction. The uncomfortable silence was now ringing in his ears and he was desperate to change the subject. "So what is the score in the hockey?" he eventually asked rather weakly.

"Three-nil so far, and Chisleton are only just managing to contain it at that. Apparently a lot of parents picked up their children earlier and they are struggling to make up a full team."

"Yes!" shouted James as a rather belated whistle blew to signify nil-nil at half time in the football.

The five-minute break passed quickly and Julie ran back to the

113

hockey as they resumed.

"She has definitely got the hots for you mate, and if you don't do something about it someone else is definitely going to step in there." For James it was only a throwaway comment, and he didn't even expect a reply, but as Tony watched Julie run back he could only agree. She seemed to have grown taller over the last six weeks and was now only an inch or two shorter than his own six foot. She had very long legs, a slim figure, and shoulder-length hair that had gone much lighter over the summer. Tony didn't really have a perfect woman, but he knew that few blokes would turn Julie away, and yet he still lacked the confidence to make a move. He was so scared that she was just playing with him, and yet he knew that the evidence to the contrary was clear enough. The problem was he couldn't see what she could find attractive in him, and he was afraid she would discover the true person if they did go out and be disappointed.

After the ball he had sat thinking about phoning for hours but he wasn't sure how she really felt, or indeed what he would do if she agreed to go out. Today things didn't seem to be much clearer. He felt this all-consuming warmth inside every time Julie was around. It was an unusual feeling that he almost struggled to understand or contain at times, and he was conscious that it seemed to remove his ability to make normal conversation. He really wanted to be away from everyone else to talk to her properly, but at the same time wondered how she seemed so natural and relaxed about it all.

Tony felt similarly uncomfortable around James and Katy when they first started to go out, mainly because he knew he wasn't ready for such a relationship at that time, and felt somehow inadequate next to them. He continued daydreaming and his mind drifted back to his first memories of James and Paul. He had felt so superior back then, but over the years James in particular had moved on to be easily the most mature person in his year. They all got on well, but Tony knew he lacked the confidence of his friends, and felt he always had to push himself to be more outgoing than he naturally was if he was going to get on.

"Look at him daydreaming about the woman of his dreams. You won't see the football that way mate you have to turn around," chided James.

The score was still nil-nil, and it was becoming a very scrappy contest, with poor playing conditions, and at this late stage in the qualifying rounds every point mattered. Suddenly with the ref's whistle already in his mouth, the Chiselton striker had the ball and a free run at goal. This was obviously going to be the last kick of the ball, and as the goalie rushed forward to meet his opponent he swung out wildly with his left leg. His mistimed kick put him off balance and he slid forward in the mud, causing the two boys' shins to meet with a sickening thud. Everyone around the pitch gasped then stood still waiting for a reaction. The ref's whistle couldn't drown out the screams of agony from both players who were clutching their legs and rolling around in the mud.

Several teachers and concerned parents ran onto the pitch, and between them and the attendant St John's Ambulance helpers they carried the boys into the school buildings. It was quickly apparent that only the goalie's leg was broken, but the clamour to call off the games grew ever stronger.

Mr Williams climbed up on the stage again.

"If I could have your attention please." After a brief moment the clamour died down and silence prevailed. "The injury to Mr Peter Jenkins is quite serious, and a number of parents and head teachers have rightfully requested that we review the decision to continue again. I will now hold a brief meeting in the staff room, and we will announce our decision in five minutes' time. In the meantime please could I ask that everyone stays here?"

When it came the decision was hardly unexpected but after months of expectation it was as a huge disappointment.

"Ladies and gentlemen, your attention again please. We have reviewed matters and I regret to inform you that we have decided to call off the Games. The trophies will be shared amongst the four competing schools evenly during the year and all I can do is say a massive thank you to all the pupils who have participated and ask you to pray for a drier summer next year."

Everyone helped to pack away the equipment but what little conversation took place was rather subdued. Only Paul seemed at all pleased with the outcome. Hattie had turned up hoping to take part in the final, only to be told the bad news. Paul was obviously wary of her when she walked in but James had broken the ice between them by making light of what had happened and she quickly appeared to forgive him.

"Well if I am not needed to play this afternoon I am going home. Do you want to come and listen to that music you missed last week Paul?"

"I am forgiven then?"

"Maybe, just don't get any of my dad's DVDs out," she smiled as she linked arms and dragged him away.

As they left everyone else stood around uncertain as to what was the best plan of action. Julie broke the silence as she turned to Tony. "My house is only over the back of the playing fields. Why don't you come around for coffee?"

Taken aback, he immediately thought of an excuse. "Well I should really be getting back." As soon as the words left his mouth he was regretting them, and kicking himself. Of course he didn't have to rush home, so why not go around to Julie's?

"Oh well, the rest of you are still coming aren't you?" she replied, seemingly unfazed at Tony's rejection.

A chorus of, "Yes," went up from the rest of the group, and suddenly Tony felt even more of an idiot. He had panicked because he thought Julie was asking him back alone, and now he was going to be left to walk home alone. If he kicked himself much more this afternoon he may as well get in the ambulance which was still parked outside. Fortunately Charlotte was on hand and she knew him well enough to realise what had happened and threw him a lifeline.

"Come on, Tony, you may as well come to Julie's and then walk back later with James and me."

"Yes, you are right," he replied almost too hastily.

"Of course," Charlotte smiled as she tugged his arm to join the rest of the group who were already following Julie. Then she leant in closer and whispered, "You are funny sometimes, and Julie is really nice, she won't eat you."

Tony suddenly felt about five years old again, as his face went crimson. "I know."

CHAPTER 7

Growing Challenges

School term started a few days later and Mr Peterson had his usual first-day speech ready and waiting.

"Welcome one and all to my first ever experience as a sixth form year tutor. It is nice to see a few new faces in amongst my familiar family, but for the rest of you, welcome back. I am pleased that you all heeded my advice last year and worked as hard as possible, and now you are no doubt looking forward to a year of rest before you embark on final preparation for your Advanced Levels."

He paused for a moment but continued walking along the rows of desks. Tony, James and Paul all thought that they had already done enough work for a lifetime, and liked the sound of a year off. Charlotte could tell that Mr Peterson was building up to something, and knew full well that she would be working just as hard as last year to get the most out of her sixth form.

"Well, the lower sixth is a very special time for all of you, as you are starting to become young adults and the choice is now up to you. You are all growing up and have to start taking charge of your own destiny. So, you can either take a year off, then make up for it next year by working twice as hard, or work steadily through the two years and undoubtedly achieve far better rewards."

He paused again.

"There are also many new responsibilities that come with sixth form life and I want you all to understand that from now on you are the focal point for the attention of the lower years. The standards that you all set, both inside and outside of the school gates will reflect the standards by which the whole school operates. Please think carefully about this burden of responsibility, and make sure that you are all positive ambassadors for St Thomas school. Many of you will be sampling the pleasures of the opposite sex as well as alcohol over the next year, and this is a dangerous combination. Following the ball last summer the local community is already focusing on many negative aspects of our pupils, so please do not give them any further cause for concern."

There were a few sniggers during the speech but as ever Mr Peterson's words were enough to set the tone for the year. The class almost jumped as the bell interrupted the silence.

"Stay where you are, I haven't finished yet."

Everyone slumped back into their chairs, surprised that they were going to be made late for their first lesson.

"Your first lesson back is with me, and indeed it will be every Monday morning as I try to instil some social awareness into you all this year. The head has decided after the goings on at the ball that we need a more proactive involvement in the social lives of our young adults so I will be here each week to offer guidance and support where necessary."

Silence reigned again. A few people shuffled in their seats, uncertain about how someone so old could possibly give guidance on their lives. Katy, who was sat next to Charlotte, whispered something about periods that started them both giggling.

"Ladies, do you have something to add?"

They both shook their heads and tried to look as innocent as possible. Tony and James who were sat in front of them, had caught the word 'period' but nothing else, but they both turned around and tutted their mock disapproval.

"Okay Katy, if it is alright with you I will continue."

Katy solemnly nodded her approval, and bit her bottom lip to stifle any more giggles.

"The good news that I have for you this year is that a new head boy and head girl will be elected shortly from the lower sixth, and I would very much like at least one of my tutor group to be elected. As I see it there at least four possible candidates in this room, and ideally I would like my class to fill both the role of head boy and head girl. This is a major honour for any pupil so please think carefully about the responsibilities involved, and write the names of your first and second choice boys and girls on the piece of paper that I am handing out. Then turn the paper over and I will collect them when you have all left. Please do not nominate yourself or your best friend simply because they are your best friend. Think carefully about whether the person is capable of fulfilling the role, and would actually want the responsibility.

"I will announce the class results tomorrow morning and the four nominations will then go forward. In total there will be twelve people nominated from the entire year group and you will each have your opportunity to speak at the school assembly next Friday, following which the vote will take place. You now have five minutes to make your choices and leave for your first lesson. I will leave you to make your own decisions as you see fit, and I will be back to pick up the papers in five minutes. Good luck."

After an initial moment of silence, the level of noise gradually built, to the extent where the school bell could hardly be heard. When it did sound everyone jumped up from their seats, turned the papers over and exited the classroom en route to the first lessons of the day.

There was much speculation about who would be nominated, and by registration the following morning the excitement was at fever pitch. Mr Peterson walked in and feigned surprise that everybody was already in their seat waiting for him.

"I hope that you will all be this prompt for registration throughout the year. Now let's get the important jobs over and done with first."

A brief silence followed, before Mr Peterson announced. "The register."

There was a collective sigh from the class, as they were only interested in the nomination results. Once the register was finished he looked up from the list of names and surveyed his pupils, delaying the moment of truth for as long as possible.

"And as they say the results are as follows, and these are in no particular order. Tony, James, Katy and Charlotte."

There was a spontaneous outbreak of applause, interrupted by the bell signifying the start of lessons. As chairs were pushed back and the mass exodus began Mr Peterson raised his hands to demand silence and everyone knew to stop immediately and stand still.

"Your enthusiasm to start work is heart-warming as ever, but please could the four nominees come to see me here at lunchtime, and I will run through the procedures ahead of Friday's elections."

Lessons that morning flew by, and before they knew it Tony, James, Katy and Charlotte were assembled outside of their form room waiting for their teacher to arrive.

"Well you four are unusually quiet this lunchtime, please come in."

They all sat in their seats and waited silently.

"Firstly let me congratulate you all on your nominations, and for my part I think that your classmates have made the right choice, but now the hard part begins I am afraid. At best only two of you will be successful, and at worst none of you."

Charlotte looked across at Katy, and wondered how she would ever be able to beat her friend. Katy was extremely popular with the girls and even more so with most of the boys in the school. In fact Charlotte couldn't ever remember a bad word having been said about her. There were of course four other girls to compete with but Charlotte knew her only real challenge was to do better than her close friend.

Katy sensed Charlotte's stare and looked up to acknowledge her. As their eyes met she smiled and mouthed 'good luck'. Katy knew that Charlotte desperately wanted to be head girl, and in truth she was more than happy for her friend to have the job. With being captain of both the hockey and netball teams as well as making time for James, the weeks already seemed too short as it was. By the same token Katy knew just how much it would mean for Tony to have the position of head boy. He was always supportive of James in everything they did together but in her mind Tony had the most to gain from getting the vote.

Both James and Tony were listening intently to the instructions and guidance being passed their way.

"I will be here if any of you wish to speak to me this week, and as far as possible I will try to give you all the same advice. You should all prepare a short two-minute speech to tell the school why they should elect you, and you will deliver that speech to the assembly on Friday morning. For now, are there any questions?"

James raised his hand and spoke when his teacher nodded in his direction. "Who will speak first, sir?"

"Good question, and this is in fact something that I can control, because I am in charge of proceedings on Friday morning so let me throw it back at you four. How do you think I should plan the agenda?"

Everyone stayed silent, and shrugged their shoulders.

"No volunteers. Okay then, each of you in turn. Katy, Charlotte, James, then Tony."

"Well I would like to go first to make the best impression, and I think we should all have a big placard with our names on, so they know who we are when we are talking, especially some of the younger ones."

"Good thinking, now Charlotte."

"I think Katy is right, talk early on to make a good impression. Plus by the end it will have all been said already and everyone will think that you are just copying the people before you with no new ideas. I think we should also split the assembly into two sections, one for the boys, followed by a vote, then the girls."

"More good ideas. I am pleased to see you thinking this through. Now James."

"I don't think it matters too much about the order, but I think we should write a speech tonight then memorise it so that we can talk without notes. That way we are bound to look more confident than the other nominees."

"Good, good. Now Tony."

Listening to his three friends before him, Tony wished he had their confidence, especially James, but there was no way he would be able to stand up and reel off a memorised speech. He also knew that no one would forget Katy or Charlotte, because they always stood out, but he doubted his own ability to make such a good impression.

"Well I would like to speak last, because I think a lot of the voters will forget who said what after listening to twelve or even six speakers. By speaking last I can incorporate any good points I missed out in my own summing up and everyone will remember them all as mine because I spoke last. That way I should get the most votes."

Mr Peterson sat with a broad grin on his face, moving his gaze slowly along the line of pupils.

"Do you know you are all right, and what pleases me most is that you are all taking the challenge so seriously. The different approaches will each work for you individually, and they reflect the different qualities that you will each bring to the position if elected. It is now up to the other pupils in this school to decide which personality they want as head boy and girl. Think long and hard about how you will sell yourselves, and inspire the others to vote for you. That's all from me for now, but don't forget I will be here if you need me this week."

As the bell went to signify the end of lunch break Mr Peterson pulled his chair back and opened the door for the rest of the class to come in for afternoon registration. With the noise level increasing James sat quietly thinking. He had felt certain in his mind that his approach was right, but Tony had really surprised him, and to be honest knocked his confidence for once. They were great friends, and Tony was the only other boy in the school that James would respect as head boy, but until five minutes ago he had assumed the job was all but his. Now he knew he had a fight on his hands, and from the look on Tony's face he knew it as well.

Over the next few days they all worked hard on their speeches, with James and Katy both deciding to major on their sporting prowess, hoping that it would translate into the same success on Friday. Charlotte refused to write anything down at all until she had read a whole collection of books about successful speech writing, whilst Tony kept pulling a small pad out of his pocket every five minutes and scribbling notes. On Thursday night Katy and James were at her parents' trying desperately to commit their words to memory, and Tony went around to Charlotte's with a whole bundle of scribbled notes and scraps of paper.

They sat at the table writing for the first hour until Charlotte declared her speech as finished.

"I need another few minutes. It is all written, I am just trying to get the right order for the pages." Tony was busy shuffling through his notes trying to demonstrate some sense of order.

"It is only two minutes long, you know, and we do have lessons on Friday as well."

"Very funny."

"Would you like me to get you a drink whilst you finish your masterpiece?" Charlotte was smiling warmly, and clearly hadn't meant anything by her sarcasm a few moments earlier.

"Please, coffee would be nice."

After about five minutes Charlotte walked in with two steaming cups of coffee followed by Janet and Adam.

"Mum and Dad are going to be our audience for tonight, so do you want to go first or last?"

"Last."

"Right then, ladies and gentlemen, I will begin. For those of you who don't know me my name is Charlotte McArthur."

Tony quickly grabbed his notes and started scribbling furiously again. Charlotte allowed herself a brief smile then continued to deliver her two-minute speech.

Janet and Adam both smiled with pride as she finished and clapped. "Two minutes fifteen seconds so that is spot on for time."

"Yes, if your mother had ever stopped after two minutes I think I would feel ten years younger."

"Adam."

"Sorry, love."

Charlotte then moved over to Tony's seat and gestured for him to move. "Your turn."

Tony walked to the other side of the table and nervously cleared his throat. "Hello, for those of you who don't me my name is Tony Alford."

He glanced at Charlotte and could see the smile on her face, but he carried on reading through his speech. He was pleased with what he had done, and enjoyed hearing his own words spoken out aloud for the first time. As he continued his confidence grew, and as he summed up the loud clapping said it all.

"Two minutes dead. That's perfect," called Janet.

Adam meanwhile walked around the table and uncharacteristically threw a supportive arm around Tony's shoulder. "I do believe this young man is coming of age. If you deliver those words that well tomorrow then we will be first to have heard the speeches from the new head boy and head girl."

"Thank you."

"You deserve it Tony, good luck both of you."

Pleased with his own achievements Tony finished his coffee and headed home. He wasn't going to memorise the words by tomorrow, but wanted to tidy up his notes, so he left early, went straight up to his bedroom and finished off the details.

Paula woke him early the next day with coffee, and her usual cheery smile. "This is the big day then. Are you nervous?"

"Yes but not too bad."

"Can I read your speech?"

"Yes but not until tonight. I was happy with it last night so no one is going to read it again until the assembly, otherwise I might start changing bits and ruin it."

"That's fair enough. Breakfast is ready. Don't forget that Graham and Mark are back in the morning as well so hopefully there will be lots to celebrate this weekend."

"Hmm."

Tony showered quickly, dressed and went down for breakfast. Charlotte was already in the kitchen, and after a quick breakfast Paula drove them to school.

"It's very quiet in here today," she remarked as they drove along but neither Charlotte nor Tony were really willing to enter into conversation. As they drove the short distance Charlotte was running through what she perceived as the strengths of all her opponents. She knew that it could go to any of them and strangely enough she was more worried about the other contenders after hearing Tony's speech last night.

Before that she had assumed that James would be head boy, and the girls' choice would be between Katy and herself. Tony's speech had been a real surprise, which was odd coming from her oldest friend of all, but the one thing she did know was that James would be in for a shock later.

The assembly started at nine o'clock, with Mr Peterson taking centre stage at the front, flanked by six boys on his left and six girls on his right. Each had an identical large white board resting against their knees with their names typed onto it.

"Good morning. This year the elections are to be split into two votes, one for the head girl, and one for the head boy. We will hear from the girls first followed by a vote, and then it is the boys' turn. So unless anyone has any questions we will hear from the first girl."

A moment's silence followed, whilst Mr Peterson waited for any questions, then he looked to the end of the line. "Natasha Coles, please." One by one the girls stood up and delivered their speeches. Some were better than others, reflecting very much the degree of effort put in. Katy's name was called forth and she stood up.

Charlotte had noted an increased level of whispering and shuffling during the third speaker, as people were obviously starting to get bored. When Katy's name was called she received the customary round of applause, and a few boys even wolf whistled as she stood up.

"Silence please, we must give everyone a fair chance. Please continue, Katy."

As Mr Peterson finished Katy took off her coat, and laid it down on her chair, to reveal for the first time that she was wearing her sports kit underneath. Charlotte, who was eyeing her friend suspiciously, was sure that her skirt had miraculously shrunk by at least a couple of inches.

"Many of you will know me as captain of the hockey or netball teams over the last couple of years, and I know many of you from training sessions. For the rest of you my name is Katy, and I have stood for election today because I would like to represent the school not only as head of the sports teams but also as head girl. Those of you from years ten and eleven that have played alongside me know that I am fair, and I always play to win which is what I intend to do today.

"Many of you will be taking your year eleven exams in the summer, and I think I speak for the entire sixth form when I say that we will all be here to help and support you through those exams if you need us. For the rest of you, I will take an active part in your sports lesson whenever I can so that we all go to win the Games next summer.

"As head girl and head of the sixth form teams I will be doubly proud to lift the trophy at the end of the year, and all I ask is that you pledge your support to me now. Remember, vote Katy and we will all be winners."

More applause followed and more wolf whistles, until Mr Peterson raised his arms to silence everyone.

Katy meanwhile returned to her seat, and lifted her name placard up to her knees so that everyone could see it.

"Tracy Paxcroft, please."

Charlotte hardly listened to a word of the next speech, as she considered her chances so far. Katy had certainly played to her strengths, but no more than that and as her name was called up Charlotte knew that the contest was still wide open.

"For those of you who don't me my name is Charlotte McArthur. I am proud to be standing today because I would love the opportunity to stand as head girl. When I joined this school I remember just how intimidated I felt at first, and at many stages throughout my time here I have felt uncertain or insecure about the challenges ahead. If elected I would ask that my fellow nominees sat behind me agree to work with me in offering a council of senior students that you can all look to for guidance and support. From my own experience I know how intimidating it can be to speak to a teacher about the many diverse issues facing us all from bullying, to our own physical development or how we deal with the stress of homework and exams. Sixth form students don't have all the answers, but the chances are we have already been through most of what you are now going through, and it was recently enough for us to remember it.

"School is about so much more than what we achieve academically, and in my mind the role of head girl will be to provide a balance. If I am elected today I will do everything I can to provide real support to all of you from year seven upwards, and even if I am unsuccessful I promise that I will always be available to support any of you if needed."

The usual applause started and Charlotte knew she had done enough.

As she turned to her seat she was suddenly aware that her fellow nominees were also stood and applauding her efforts. Everyone continued until Mr Peterson took centre stage again.

"Thank you all very much for your efforts. Now you have five minutes to vote and we will hear from the candidates for head boy. Remember what each individual has said, and pick the one person who in your own mind will do the best for the school."

Tony was surprised to see Charlotte still looking so nervous, especially after her speech had gone down so well. None of the others came close, and he was even having doubts about whether his own words were up to the standard required.

Katy seemed far less concerned by it all, looking around and picking individuals out with a smile or half wave when they caught her eye. It was as though she wasn't really that interested in the vote.

When the boys' time came James did much the same as Katy had, to the point where it was obvious that they had prepared together. As expected he talked freely without notes and actually jumped down off the stage and walked up and down as he spoke. He nearly managed to convince everyone that he was delivering an unrehearsed speech from the heart until he lost his way towards the end. He then carefully slid his hand into his pocket and flicked through his prompt cards before finishing. It was a slick speech, and few people noticed the slight hiccup towards the end.

As his turn got ever closer Tony could feel the butterflies rising, and desperately just wanted it all to be over. He had chosen to go last for good reason though, and patiently waited his turn. To calm his nerves he sat quietly, taking huge deep breaths to try and slow his heart rate. Then finally it was his time.

"And last but by no means least, Tony Alford."

Tony stood up and nervously moved to the front. Everyone sat quietly, although after nearly an hour it was clear that a lot of the younger ones had had enough already. Perhaps going last wasn't such a good idea after all.

"Ready when you are, Tony."

He gave a small cough to clear his throat then looked down at his notes.

"For those of you who don't know me, my name is Tony,

Today all that I ask of you is to follow my simple plea,

Ignore all who have gone before, and cast your vote for me

Then together we will celebrate my unexpected victory.

I won't promise you sporting success,

Nor solve revision problems if your notes are a mess,

But I will do all that I can to impress

And take action to help anyone of you under duress.

My message is aimed at you, one and all,

Vote for me today so that we can all stand tall,

Don't let my campaign falter and fall,

Give me my dream to be head boy at this school.

I will work hard to champion your cause,

Be it anti bullying, teenage acne or worse,

I won't sleep until our dreams are on course,

To make this the best school in the universe.

The outcome today will affect pupils in every year,

So don't ignore my name through idleness or fear,

Your vote matters even if this is your first week here,

So please give me the chance to stand and deliver.

My apologies if this poem doesn't always scan,

But with only one week it's a lot to plan,

At times I feel that I have hardly began,

And now I am lost for words that end with an 'an',

I have said my bit now, and it's time for you to take action,

Remember Tony when making your mark in this election,

I promise to deliver and guarantee you all satisfaction,

So please put a cross by my name when making your selection.

My final verse I promise, so no more yawns from you please,

With everyone's vote I can win this election with ease,

But I won't forget those who answer my pleas,

And give me the first of many victories."

There was a spontaneous outbreak of applause, which brought a huge grin borne out of relief to his face. Tony knew in his heart that whatever the outcome he had done his best, and he was more interested in savouring the moment than the eventual outcome. The same feeling stayed with him, and indeed the others throughout the day. They were all full of praise for each other's efforts and everyone was equally full of hope and expectation at the end of the day when they stood waiting for Mr Peterson's arrival.

"Sorry to keep you all after school, but the voting was closer than I expected. In fact I have had to recount the girls' results twice over because the margin was only seven votes. Before I tell you all who will be the new head boy and girl, may I thank you for the tremendous effort that you put in this morning and during the week. Now for the results.

"Our new head girl is Katy, and you are to be ably assisted by Tony."

There was a moment's silence as the assembled group tried to take on what they had just heard. It seemed so succinct after the hours of planning, and no one wanted to make the first move. Slowly they took turns to move over and congratulate the successful duo.

Charlotte gave Tony a big hug then whispered, "Julie will be proud. She said all day that you were easily the best."

"Thank you. Sorry that you missed out, but there was only one girl's place."

"I know, and my skirts aren't short enough."

As she said the words Katy swung round in front of her, clearly hurt by the remark.

"I am sorry, I guess I am just a bad loser, you will make a fantastic head girl."

"Thanks."

James meanwhile came over to Tony. "Well you outflanked me that time, but it is the last time that I will ever underestimate you."

"We'll see."

From that moment the rest of the year passed with relatively little drama. Graham and Mark returned from their travels, but barely unpacked before setting off for university. Despite constant reminders from their teachers that the lower sixth was not simply a year off, everyone treated it as such. Even Charlotte allowed herself some time off during the year, and put more effort into learning the Highway Code ahead of her driving test than her end of year exams. As ever, her efforts paid off as she was the first person in the year to pass, and she achieved it at the first attempt.

Tony, James, and Paul all followed suit over the next couple of months but all at the second time of trying. Katy was only seventeen in July so she had only just begun lessons by the summer holidays. With some help from her parents Charlotte was also the first person to have a car of her own, when she bought an old Fiesta at the start of the summer holidays. It was only a cheap runabout, but as it turned into another wet summer she loved the freedom that it offered.

Graham and Mark came home for about three days at the start of August but soon departed to Spain to meet up with some friends they had met abroad the previous year. They worked the summer in a Moroccan theme bar, and kept inviting Tony over to see them but in the end he never got round to it. Bob and Paula even offered to pay for his airfare, but in truth he preferred to spend the holidays with his friends. As the holidays drew to a close the Games were once again upon them and everyone saw this as the last chance to secure glory once and for all at St Thomas's. Despite raining most days it was nowhere near as wet as the year before, and when Tony and James cycled up to the school on the day before they were pleased to find the pitches in good order and not at all waterlogged.

"These pitches are in superb condition, and there is no way anyone will call the Games off this year," began Tony.

"Not if we are lucky."

"Come on, James, there is no way they are anything like as wet as last year."

"No, you are right," confirmed James after a brief moment surveying the pitches in front of them.

"It's going to be superb, and we have the best teams at most levels so we should easily make the final."

"Yes."

James continued to walk around testing the ground with the heel of his trainers, before jumping back onto his bike. "Come on, we can't do anything more until tomorrow."

"You do think we can win, don't you?" questioned Tony, almost as if doubting his earlier enthusiasm.

"Yes, we have as good chance as any year, I suppose."

"But you do still want it, don't you?"

"Of course it would be good, but we have blown it for the last few years."

James seemed strangely preoccupied, and lacked his normal enthusiasm. Tony wasn't sure if it was the cumulative effect of the previous disappointments, or whether his friend was simply outgrowing the competition.

"We won't blow it tomorrow." Tony was trying to sound convincing but his tone lacked real conviction.

"Fingers crossed," added James.

"Of course we won't. You and Katy as captains and everyone else really worked up for it." Tony wasn't sure now who it was that he was trying to convince.

"I know, let's hope we don't let them down."

Tony wasn't used to James' lack of enthusiasm, and put it down to nerves, which wasn't like him either.

"Charlotte is taking me tomorrow, and she said to ask if you wanted a lift as well."

"Yeah, what time?" replied James as he instinctively looked at his watch.

"She is picking me up at 8.20, so about 8.30."

"Okay."

They rode back in silence and when James reached his house he turned and waved. "See you at 8.30 tomorrow then."

"Bye."

Tony rode on alone, then finding the house empty he decided to go up to his room, opening a book that he had started about two months previously but ignored for several weeks now. He only managed a few pages before his eyes felt heavy, and he allowed himself to drift off to sleep. Although he only intended to nap for a few minutes it was ten o'clock before he awoke feeling the slight cold of a summer evening. There were voices downstairs now, but Tony decided to ignore them, and without undressing crawled under his duvet and fell asleep again.

Charlotte was her usual punctual self the following morning, but having had a long night's sleep Tony was pleased to meet her at the door as she arrived. As they drove to James house the car was full of anticipation for the day's events.

"This is it then, your last chance to win it for the boys," laughed

Charlotte, trying to hide her own excitement."

"And the girls as well! We have to do the double really."

Charlotte looked across briefly to reveal a large smile then she looked back to the road before speaking. "Was James excited when you saw him yesterday?"

"Not really to be honest... He seemed a bit subdued, nervous even."

"James nervous. Hardly," laughed Charlotte.

"That's what I thought, but he seemed it yesterday."

Charlotte pulled up on the side of the road and they both went up to the front door. Julie answered and invited them in. "He won't be a minute, he is just finishing his breakfast, come in if you like."

"He hasn't overslept again, has he?" quipped Tony.

"No, Katy was on the phone at seven o'clock this morning, and I think it interrupted his beauty sleep because he has been like a bear with a sore head all morning."

As they entered the dining room James pushed his chair back, and gulped down the remains of his orange juice. "Come on then, I am ready. Let's go. Bye Mum."

"Bye James and good luck. Bring back that trophy, and maybe it will put a smile back on your face."

"Bye Mum."

They shut the door behind them and made their way up to Charlotte's car. Tony jumped in the back with the other two in the front.

"Tony thinks you are nervous about today."

"No, it's nothing."

"At least the sun is shining, it should be perfect."

"Yes." James answer was unusually succinct and the other two could tell that he wasn't in the mood for small talk. They continued the short journey to school in silence; arriving at quarter to nine they beat everyone else and sat waiting in the car park.

After a few more minutes of silence Tony spoke up. "So who do you think our biggest challengers will be today then?"

James remained silent so Charlotte answered, "I heard that Chiselton sixth form were quite weak so that should be good for you. Well you can never underestimate them on the day, can you James?" She knew that it sounded lame, but idle small talk was not her strong point.

"No."

Another couple of minutes' silence followed then Charlotte tried again, barely able to hide the frustration in her tone. "What is the matter? This really is not like you, James."

"Nothing."

"Come on, James, we have both known you most of your life and it is not like you to be this uninterested in any sport, let alone the Games."

"It's nothing, really."

Charlotte couldn't understand what the problem was, but wondered if it had anything to with the loss of James' dad the year before. She knew that she couldn't really appreciate what effect it must have on his everyday life and in the circumstances felt it was best left and she decided instead to talk to Katy later on. "Shall we go over to the main hall and wait there?"

"Yes." With that James reached for the handle and pulled open the door.

They all retrieved their bags and started to walk over when Tony spoke. "Tell me to shut up if you like but is it anything to do with your dad?"

"Tony!" shouted Charlotte and James together. After a further pause all three of them threw their arms around each other and huddled together.

"Okay, I give in, but this must not go any further, and I mean any further, not Julie or anyone."

Tony acknowledged the comment "Promise I won't say a word."

"Well the thing is it's Katy. She is late."

Without thinking Tony looked at his watch. "But it is only five to, and no one else is here yet."

Charlotte buried her head in her hands, more at Tony's stupidity than James' shock revelation. Then she turned to James. "How late?"

"Two days."

"That's not a lot I am often up to week late."

"I know but, well, we were a bit worried anyway before she was late, and she never normally is."

"Shit," interrupted Tony, as the realisation dawned. "You mean she is late with her erm…"

"Yes, Tony, keep up please." Charlotte shook her head as she finished. "You need to get this sorted, James, don't let it drag on not knowing for sure."

"I know. The thing is we are barely even talking at the moment, let alone thinking rationally."

Silence prevailed then Charlotte took control. "Look, James, the Games mean everything to you, and you have to concentrate on today. I will go and see Katy, and catch up with both of you later. She needs support at the moment more than you do."

"I know, and I know it should be me but I don't know how to." James sounded lost and hurt, the same boy in fact that she had seen at the Gorge years earlier.

"Leave it to me, I will see you later."

With that Charlotte ran back to her car and sped off just as the first of the opposition coaches came through the school gates. She arrived at Katy's house before she had time to gather her thoughts and ran immediately to the front door. Only as she stood waiting for a reply did it dawn on her that she was totally unprepared for what was about to unfold. Seconds turned into minutes and there was no reply. Charlotte was not going away and pressed the door-bell again. Still nothing.

Third time lucky, she pressed the bell again and held it for a full twenty seconds. Almost instinctively she looked up just as the curtain above twitched. There was some rummaging around inside and then Katy appeared at the front door. Neither of the girls spoke as they stood looking at each other.

Charlotte couldn't help but notice how her friend almost looked ill with red rings under her eyes, no make-up and a generally dishevelled appearance. Katy broke the silence. "You know, don't you?"

"Yes."

It wasn't necessary to say anything more, at least not for the moment, but the girls moved closer and hugged, with Katy sobbing gently into her friend's shoulder.

"Come in," she sniffed, "we cannot stand here all day, and anyway I have to get ready for the Games."

"No you don't, I will tell them all that you are ill or something."

"Like pregnant you mean."

"No, of course not." Charlotte was trying to stay as calm as she could. "Please don't think I am here in judgement, I'm just a friend trying to help."

"I am sorry, this is all my fault, not yours."

"And James."

"Yes, and his, but I shouldn't take it out on you."

"I am not here to give you a hard time, I promise. Not today anyway, even if you did get an A star in biology."

As Katy smiled a bit of colour came back into her cheeks for the first time that morning.

"Are you going to come in for a coffee then?"

"Yes but where are your parents?"

"Away on holiday thankfully."

"So they don't know anything is wrong yet then."

"No, the last thing Mum said was 'look after the house, be good and where James is concerned be careful', but it was already too late for that."

Katy was busying herself about the kitchen as she spoke, and Charlotte sat down at the kitchen table.

"Would you like some toast? I am making myself some." As she lifted out two slices of bread from the packet to put in the toaster, it rolled over and knocked one of the coffee cups onto the hard floor where it broke into a hundred pieces. Katy could do nothing but cry and Charlotte jumped up at once to assist her.

"Look, I am here to help. You sit down at the table and let me sort this lot out. Better still, go and get showered and put some make-up on and I will get your breakfast."

Katy didn't have the energy to argue and trudged out of the kitchen.

Left on her own Charlotte tidied up, made two cups of coffee, as well as some toast then sat at the table. A few moments later Katy reappeared looking slightly better having showered and dressed, but still minus any make-up. "Thank you."

"It's okay."

"How was James this morning?" asked Katy without looking up.

"Worried." Charlotte wanted to say more, and reassure her friend that this was more about her right now than James, but the right words wouldn't come to mind so she said no more.

"I know and I haven't been very fair to him. He says I should just have an abortion if I am pregnant, but that is just so easy for him to say, and I don't know if I can."

"What will you do?"

"I don't know, this whole mess is so unfair. My mum and dad only had me, even though they wanted more children, because they found it so difficult to conceive, and here I am at just 17 and pregnant with my first, and James wants me to get rid of it."

"It's definite then, you are pregnant, I mean for certain like 100%, you have done a test and all?"

"Yes, well no, not absolutely, but I know, believe me."

"Katy, get real. Wallow in self-pity all you like, and I will support you every step of the way, but get the test done now, today."

"Well I was hoping that my period would come, but I am never late." She sounded wounded, and defenceless.

"But you cannot be absolutely sure either. Katy, please take the test. Don't torture yourself."

"No, but if I take the test then I will know for sure and then what? I swear I cannot deal with this on my own, and I think James will just finish with me if I am pregnant."

"Not James, he loves you."

"Yes and he wants to go to university next year, not be tied down with me forever. We will go our separate ways anyway next year if we can. I don't want to hold him back."

Charlotte was a bit taken aback by the last comment, but tried not to show it. She had never really had a serious boyfriend of her own, but imagined romantically that her friends were destined to be together forever. Katy could see at once the shock in her expression and spoke again.

"Don't get me wrong I do love him, but James will never settle down with his first girlfriend. He will be off to university and then he will be spoilt for choice. I cannot deny him that."

"I know, it's just that I always had these dreams about us all getting old as friends, with you and James and your little family all running around."

"And you and Tony happily married as well, with a family of your own."

"Maybe but I think Julie may get there first at the moment. Anyway, Tony is just my oldest friend."

"If any of us stay together I bet it will be you two. You are made for each other, Tony just needs to grow up a bit, that's all. Wait and see, in a few years he will get there."

"Possibly, but this is not about me, it's you we need to get sorted. Why don't I go into Aleton and get a test kit from the chemist?"

"Because Julie works there, and she knows you haven't got a boyfriend, so it won't take her long to work out what is going on."

Charlotte knew Katy was right and tried to think of a plan. "But she was at home this morning, I don't think she is working today."

"We cannot risk it. Would you mind going to Rudbury instead?"

The next big town was a good 45 minutes away which meant a two-hour round trip by the time they had parked and it was nearly ten o'clock already.

"Okay, if we leave now, and you promise to take the test straight away."

"What, in the car?"

Both girls laughed together for the first time that morning, before Charlotte continued. "No not in my car, but straight away when we get back."

"Promise."

"Go and get some make-up on then and I will wash up ready then we can get off."

Back at school everything was going to plan. Paul and Julie had both arrived at about 9.30 and in the absence of Katy, Julie was helping to organise the hockey teams for the lower years. Everything got off to a good start, and St Thomas won seven out of their first eight games.

By midday it looked like the dream final was on the cards, and Paul and Julie came running over to join James and Tony.

"We have just spoken to Mr Peterson, and we only need one more goal to make the final in both the girls' and boys' teams, on goal difference alone."

"Good," chorused Tony and James.

"Show a bit of enthusiasm then, you two."

"Come on, Tony, you can help me round up the Year 10 girls for their match." Julie pulled him gently away from his friends.

"But I promised to help James."

"Paul will, won't you?" Julie was shaking her head, showing her frustration at Tony's constant excuses that were starting to wear a bit thin.

"Yeah sure, whatever."

"Come on then."

"Go on Tony, help Julie, but please remember what I said," added James as he lifted his finger to his lips.

As they wandered off Julie grabbed his arm and pulled him closer. "So are you going to tell me the big secret then or what?"

"I cannot, I promised James."

Secretly Tony wanted to say more and was almost disappointed at Julie's response.

"Never mind then. That's the five-minute whistle. Quick, can you see if you can find Mandy Jones? She is supposed to be team captain."

With that, Julie ran off in the opposite direction, before turning briefly to wave.

Tony found Mandy Jones having a quick cigarette behind the art block, and almost dragged her onto the pitch in time for the whistle. As he stood on the touchline Julie re-joined him. "Where are Charlotte and Katy? Have you seen them today?"

"Only Charlotte. Katy is unwell," he replied without looking at Julie as he tried to conceal his secret.

"Unwell?"

"Yes."

"Nothing to do with James' bad mood then?"

Tony turned to Julie and looked her in the eye. "If I tell you something please promise to keep it a secret for me?"

"She is not pregnant, is she?"

Tony's mouth fell open, and he didn't need to say anything else.

"Bloody hell, is she sure?"

"I don't know the details, but please don't say anything, will you?" Tony knew he had already gone too far, without actually saying anything at all.

"No, of course not, but that's awful, and Charlotte?"

"I am not sure. She went over to see her this morning." Tony had been wondering for some time now what was keeping her, and he was so deep in thought that he didn't even see his best friend walk over.

"Hi James, we are two-nil up in this game already so this is it your dream final." Julie interrupted as she could see James approaching. "I am going to check the other results. I will see you in a minute."

The two boys watched the end of the game then wandered slowly across the pitch.

"Charlotte should be back by now. Where do you think they have got to?" The same thought had been on both of their minds, but it was James asking the question.

"I don't know, have you phoned Katy's house?"

"No, I don't want to pester her."

"Have you thought about what you will do if she is pregnant?"

"Marry her of course, if she won't have an abortion. I have always known we would get married one day, it will just be a bit sooner than I had planned."

"What about uni? I thought we were going to share a flat."

James looked over and smiled. "You will be fine on your own, mate. I will miss uni. if we get married, and I will join the police."

"When did you plan all this?"

"Today really. You have to make contingency plans don't you?"

"Do you really love Katy enough though for marriage and all that?"

"Yeah, of course. Like I said, I have always known we would get married one day."

They walked the rest of the way into the hall in silence, only to be greeted by a jubilant Paul at the doors.

"This is it, big man, your chance to prove just how good you are to the whole school, we are in the final against Chiselton."

*

The journey into town had taken longer than expected and it was nearly 11.00 by the time they parked the car and walked towards the shopping precinct. There were loads of mothers dragging round miserable children as they quickly tried to buy the last bits of school uniform before the start of term. Neither party clearly wanted to be there, and there were frequent tantrums and arguments.

"Is it just me or is someone trying to teach me a lesson by putting all the brats in the world in front of us today?" asked Katy, trying to lift their spirits.

Charlotte smiled, pleased that the fresh air was at least doing something to restore Katy's sense of humour.

"I used to love coming into town just before the new term started to get my things ready."

"Me too, my mum even brought me in a couple of weeks ago because they were going on holiday, just for old time's sake really. We had a really nice day of it." As Katy finished they had already arrived outside the chemist front door and the girls turned to face one another.

"Shall we just walk around a bit first? I am not sure if I can do this."

"You have to, Katy, it won't get easier. Come on, I will come in with you. I will even buy the kit if you like."

"No, I have to do it, just stay really close to me."

Charlotte moved forward and held the door open. Katy took a deep breath, smoothed down her skirt, and with her heart pounding away inside her chest she strode purposefully in.

"Would you like to try our new shades of summer lipstick?"

The sales assistant positioned just inside the door threw her off guard completely, and Katy just stood staring at her.

"Shades of summer? It's our new lipstick range, would you care to try some?"

"Another time, thanks, we are too busy today." Charlotte answered on Katy's behalf, grabbed her friend's arm and marched her into the store. It seemed strangely busy and it took the girls a full ten minutes to find the tester kits, being too afraid to ask for assistance. They both stood in front of the shelf in question, both too afraid to pick up the packet. They were on a quiet aisle, away from the main cosmetics, but even so they tried to look inconspicuous every time somebody walked past, as they shuffled nervously around.

Eventually Katy took charge, and grabbed the packet firmly in both hands. She hoped as she stood in the queue to pay that by holding the box firmly in her hands no one could actually see what it was. Her heart was pounding away furiously in her chest, and her mouth felt drier than she could ever remember. They were at the pharmacy counter, waiting behind an elderly couple, both wishing they could be back at the car as soon as possible. With her racing heart and shortness of breath Katy was sure that she was about to faint.

The elderly gentleman had already taken an age and he was leaning forward to speak to the pharmacist who was obviously struggling to hear his whispers.

"Yes sir, I understand that you want cream but what for? Do you have a prescription?"

The old man leaned closer, and motioned for the lady over the counter to do the same. Then she shook her head again, unable to hear his faint whispers. Clearly agitated by all this his wife pulled him to one side. "Cyril, for goodness' sake just tell the woman you have piles, and get the cream."

Then she turned to Katy and Charlotte as though talking about a five-year-old. "I am sorry, he gets so embarrassed, poor love. Piles, they have been the story of his life ever since I have known him. He used to ride a bike to work back then, but he couldn't get near a saddle anymore."

Cyril was clearly wishing the ground would open up and swallow him whole. As the pharmacist handed him the cream he thanked her and handed over some money.

"No, that is no good, don't you have the bigger tube than that? He will go through that lot in a week, and we will have to go through all this again." Cyril handed back the tube, which was replaced with a much larger one, and he shakily handed the money over again, glancing sideways at his wife hoping she would stay quiet.

"That's better." Then she turned to the girls again. "He says it is a pain in the bottom, well I can tell you it's been a pain in my bottom these last 30 years as well." As she finished she gently touched Katy on her arm and chuckled away to herself at her little joke. Cyril meanwhile put his head down and followed her out of the store.

"Yes ladies, how can I help you? Nothing for piles, I hope?"

Katy looked down at the box in her hand and passed it over the counter.

"Oh, I see, yes £19.95 please. Would you like it in a bag?"

"Yes." A barely audible whisper came out that would have put Cyril to shame. Katy cleared her throat with a small cough, and nearly shouted the next time, "Yes!"

It was so loud that the lady working behind the screen preparing subscriptions stood up and caught her eye. To Katy's absolute horror she recognised James' mother at once.

"Hi girls, why aren't you at the Games? They haven't been called off again have they?"

Katy opened her mouth but nothing came, she daren't look down at the small bag she was being passed, and even contemplated dismissing it as a mistake and running out.

Realising her dilemma Charlotte reached forward and took the package on offer. "No, I just had to get some things for next term, and we are not playing till last thing, so we came over."

"Good luck then, and make sure you give that boy of mine a kiss for luck, won't you Katy?"

"Yes, of course."

With that, the two girls turned and quick marched back up to the front door. It was Katy who got there first, and this time she grabbed the door and swung it open. She hung on to the handle as it burst open and collapsed in a heap outside leaning against the wall and gasping for breath. As she stood there she couldn't help but glance back to the pharmacy counter.

"Look, they are talking."

Charlotte turned and could clearly see the lady who had served them leant against the screen in deep conversation with Julie. "Come on, what's done is done, let's get out of here." Katy knew that either way she was now in this too deep to care about what was being said, and allowed Charlotte to drag her along. They raced back to the car and by midday they were at Katy's house sat at the kitchen table. The instructions were laid out on the kitchen table and with Charlotte stood behind Katy they were both poring over the details. "After all that I don't even feel like I need a wee."

"You must be able to force something out."

"What if it is not enough? There are only two strips here and if I miss or something or I don't wee enough…"

Charlotte walked over to the sink and filled a pint glass with water. "Here, drink this." Katy looked at the glass for a moment then drank it in one. "And another one." Charlotte turned away, refilled the glass and passed it back. Then she pulled out a chair and sat down.

"Here goes then. We will know soon enough now." With that, Katy drank the second glass of water.

"Are you nervous?"

"Like never before. I swear I will never forget this moment whatever. Just like the moment when Julie looked up over that counter. I didn't know whether to laugh or cry. No, in fact all I wanted to do was cry."

"I know. My heart missed at least a beat for you. I think it stopped for about 30 seconds actually."

"What about poor old Cyril though? He seemed like a really sweet old man."

"That's what I was thinking when Julie popped up. You know how we were both really embarrassed to be there and all, and you think that by the time you are his age that nothing will be left to embarrass you again."

"And then your wife tells the world that you have got piles." Katy smiled as she finished, but in truth little could take her mind off the matter in hand.

"Especially telling two young girls in the queue in the chemists, he must have been mortified."

"And then Julie was there. I have to go to the school and warn James. I cannot believe all this is happening for just one moment of stupidity." The pressure was all getting to Katy, and she burst into tears as she finished the sentence.

Charlotte put a comforting arm around her and inclined their heads together. "Come on, you must be ready by now. If I sit around much more today I will need some of Cyril's cream."

"Yes, here goes. This is the moment that determines the rest of my life. I cannot believe that I have been so stupid to bring everything down to this stupid bit of plastic," waving the thin clear strip in front of her friend. "This is it, this strip could change my life forever."

Charlotte didn't know what to say, and as they sat just inches away from each other all she could do was nod slowly.

The chair scraped on the tiled floor as Katy got up and went to the bathroom. As she reached the door she turned and came back, picked up the packet and instructions then went into the toilet. After what seemed like an eternity Charlotte heard the toilet flush and she held her breath.

*

Back at the Games it was all set for the dream final, with both the boys and girls teams from St Thomas to face Chiselton. After winning the toss the boys' team were to play first with the hockey match later. James and Tony were warming up with the rest of the team, whilst Paul and a few of the others were sat on the bench as substitutes.

"Did you get hold of Katy?"

"No, I phoned the house twice during the lunch break, but there was no reply. I just wish I knew what those two girls were up to."

"It's probably for the best, maybe they have gone to the doctors or something."

"You don't go to the doctors to find out. You get a test from the chemists."

"Maybe they have gone around and asked your mum to get a kit then," laughed Tony, unsure whether or not he had overstepped the mark with his comment.

"Very funny. Fortunately she is working in Rudbury today so if they do go to the chemist she won't know at least." The shrill sound of the whistle signified that warmup was over and everyone took their positions on the pitch.

As captain, James went up to the centre circle for the toss to see who would kick off, but lost. Chiselton then started well, nearly scoring in a clever move from the kick-off that was just intercepted at the last minute. The goal kick out was to James, but lacking his usual pace, he was quickly dispossessed. The St Thomas team were defending again, and it went to a corner. Everyone came back, but the man being marked by James managed to out jump him, and took an easy header to score. One-nil down, with just seven minutes gone.

St Thomas then had a brief period of possession, but they were unable to score before James again lost the ball. He knew he was having an awful game and chased his opponent hard, bringing him down recklessly in front of the referee just outside of his own six yard box. There were appeals for a penalty, as well as a red card from Chiselton, but the ref took James to one side instead.

"Look, lad, this is a schoolboy match played in good spirits, don't ruin it for everyone else. You are team captain. If you cannot take the pressure then substitute yourself."

James carried on for the rest of the half, but his contribution was almost non-existent. He was slow to react when passed the ball, passed poorly, and much to the annoyance of the team missed a golden opportunity to level the match with five minutes to go before half time. To make matters worse the resultant goal kick gave Chiselton the opportunity to make it 2-0.

As the whistle blew for half time the whole of the St Thomas team seemed to be affected by James' performance and they all sloped off with their heads hung low. Mr Peterson met Tony on the touchline.

"What is going on out there? This is the last chance for you and James. I thought you both wanted this more than anyone else in the school."

Tony shrugged his shoulders, as if to say, 'I am sorry.'

"Come on, Tony, that's not the attitude that got you elected as head boy. Get out there and show them what you are made of. James clearly has his mind elsewhere so if we are to win it is down to you."

As he finished they were interrupted. "Good day, Mr Peterson. I have to say it is nice to see the sun shining on Chiselton again this year. Don't you think?"

The arrival of Mr MaCauley brought even more wrinkles to the frown on Mr Peterson's brow. "Yes, your lads are doing well, but it's not over yet."

"No, indeed, I see another few goals in this one yet. Oh look, what is this? Have you brought in some cheerleaders to boost your team's morale now? That is all a bit crass, don't you think?"

Tony looked over to see what he was talking about to see

Charlotte and Katy running across the field waving something that he couldn't pick out in their hands. From the look on their faces it was clearly good news though. James had obviously seen them arrive as well and ran up to meet them.

At that moment the ref blew his whistle for the restart, and the teams ran back on to the pitch. Julie caught up with Tony just as he went back on, and shouted good luck. It was a full five minutes into the second half before Tony was able to talk to James, but he knew it was good news from his changed performance alone. "It's okay mate, she has done the test twice, and it is negative."

Just then the ball was passed to Tony and he ran up field with it, passing to James just over the halfway line. James then took it on, weaving through the Chiselton field with his usual turn of speed, and scored a fantastic goal from 25 yards out. From the restart James tackled cleanly, and won possession again, before passing the ball on to another teammate. St Thomas kept the ball, and ran on for another goal to level it at two-two with just eight minutes left on the clock.

From then on it was a fiercely fought contest until Chiselton conceded a corner with only two minutes remaining. James took the kick, and it was kicked in by Paul to the back of the Chiselton net to put them in the lead for the first time. With barely two minutes to go and the lead lost it was now Chiselton's turn to hang their heads, and just as the ref put the whistle in his mouth to blow for full time St Thomas scored again. Four-two was how it finished and the relief on and off the pitch was tangible.

Julie ran up to Tony and gave him a hug. "Well done, now you have to come and watch us do the same in the hockey. And thank you for trusting me earlier with James' secret. It meant a lot that you told me."

Tony didn't know what to say, but before he could answer he felt a huge slap on his back. "Thanks mate, I owe you and Charlotte for today. I won't forget it."

The euphoria amongst the boys was only increased when the girls also ran in four-nil winners, so it was time for a double celebration. After the presentations, everyone packed away and then went back to James' house. Charlotte made two trips, taking the girls back first, and then returning for James, Paul and Tony. When she reached the house for the second time, she saw James' mum going in ahead of them, and quickly warned him about the day's events in the chemists.

As they walked in a few moments later all was surprisingly calm, and Katy was just introducing the two Julies to one another, as they had not met before. "Hi Mum, shall I put the kettle on for everyone?"

"That would be a good idea, but don't you have something to tell me first?"

"Erm. Well, uhh…"

"You did win, I take it."

"Oh, that! Yes. Both trophies are coming to St Thomas this year for the first time ever."

"Well done, let's hope that smile stays on your face now. I hope you have really got something out of today, something more than just winning a game."

No one knew what to say, and Katy and James looked nervously at the floor.

"Enough said, I think, now who wants coffee and who wants tea?"

CHAPTER 8

Into Adulthood

As the class assembled for the start of term a few days later there were some very mixed emotions. The holidays were now well and truly over, a point always emphasised by the sound of the school bell, and what's more this was the last time that they would have to finish the holidays by coming back to school.

Tony sat slumped back in his chair discussing the successful games a few days earlier, and wondering what Mr Peterson would have to say this year. In his mind the speeches were all getting a bit samey, and he knew he could predict what was about to come. "Hey, we should run a sweepstake on how many times we are told that we have to really knuckle down and work this year."

"Yes, I reckon double figures, say 10," laughed James.

"More like 20, I'd say. Here, 20p each and I will put the number down on this piece of paper," ventured Paul, as he quickly scribbled the rules on the top, collected the 20p pieces and walked around the class.

Charlotte thought it was all a bit childish, and told them so but volunteered her money and put down four times. "Don't bother if you think it is below you, four is way too few," laughed Tony.

"Well he is only telling us for our own good, isn't he, and we do know we have to work hard," answered Charlotte with a frown across her face that almost knitted her eyebrows together. Katy was last to put her 20p in, and put down just two times, which caused most of the others to laugh again.

"Well laugh all you like, but I think we have been very lucky to have Mr Peterson all these years, and I have always taken his advice, so I don't think we should even be running this sweepstake either."

"Yes, I know we have, buts it's only a bit of fun," laughed James as he swung back around to face the front at the sound of the door opening.

"Morning all. Settle down please, I only have 30 minutes of your most valuable time, before your final year at St Thomas begins." Mr Peterson paused for a few moments and walked along the front of the classroom.

"Well, it is with great pleasure that I am here today representing a school of champions." A brief cheer accompanied by clapping interrupted him. He nodded in acknowledgement and then continued.

"This is a very important year for you all starting today, and I am sure that many of you are sat there thinking, here we go again, different year same speech." A few of the classmates squirmed uncomfortably in their chairs.

"Well, this year is different. You are all about to become fully-fledged adults in the eyes of the law over the next 12 months, so I don't need to tell you how important it is for you to work hard. You all have your own goals and aspirations for your future lives and from now on you are increasingly going it alone. You will of course always have the support of your friends, family and tutors to help you along the way, but you must focus on what it is you want to achieve in life and gear yourselves up to achieve it. From now on you are all your own responsibility, and I am confident that you have it in you to do well." There was a stunned silence as Mr Peterson walked down the aisles, and Paul tried to conceal the piece of paper he was holding under the desk.

"No doubt Paul has been taking bets on how many times I tell you all to work hard, so sorry to disappoint, but unless anyone said one, which I very much doubt, then he is going to be refunding you all."

Paul turned bright red, and shook his head. Mr Peterson allowed himself a brief smile, and continued before Paul was able to embarrass himself further. "I was already at university, in my second year in fact before I realised that I was the only person who could really make a difference to my results, and that is when I started to apply myself to fulfil my dreams. Surprisingly enough this is where I wanted to be, but I am hoping that if I give you all a head start then you may do far better than I did and maybe even become rich and famous."

He allowed them a few minutes to digest his words in silence, as he took his chair out and sat behind his desk. Rather than look around the pupils he stared down at the register in front of him, running through the list of names with an increasing sense of pride, as he anticipated their potential. Eventually he looked up and picked up a pencil from his desk. "Now as ever the formalities begin, so please answer yes when I call your names." After the register there were a few other formalities to attend to then the bell went for first lesson.

"Off you go then, and remember the two most important things this year are to enjoy it and..." he paused as his face broke into a broad grin, "WORK VERY HARD."

"Yes!" Katy didn't mean to shout so loud, as she also clenched her fist and punched the air in front of her.

Over the next few days the meaning of hard work really hit home, as homework was stacked on top of homework, coursework deadlines were set, and the pressure started to build. At the end of the first week Tony, James and Paul were all discussing how to juggle the workload and still enjoy life when Charlotte and Julie joined them in the common room. As the girls started to get their books out Paul shouted over. "It's three o'clock on Friday afternoon, why don't you two give it a rest? We can go home in 50 minutes."

"You are what you want to be, and some of us want to do well this year. Anyway you three are only moaning about the work to do so why not get on with it instead of moaning?" Charlotte knew her words of wisdom wouldn't go down well, and quickly put her head down into her notes again.

The three boys looked at each other. They all knew deep down that Charlotte was right but that made them more determined than ever to not get their books out. Paul made the first move. "Who wants a coffee? I am going to put the kettle on."

Everyone said yes, and Tony volunteered to help him. As they walked across the room Julie put her hand out to Tony. "Just help me with this English essay a minute, you always understand it quicker than I do."

He looked at Paul, shrugged his shoulders and sat down, as James jumped up. "Don't worry mate, I will give you a hand."

Tony explained the subtle charm of *The Wife of Bath*, as Julie made scribbled notes and Charlotte continued with her chemistry assignment. After a good 20 minutes the door swung open again, this time with Katy, Paul, and James.

"Look, I've passed my test, first time. Now I can drive!" shouted Katie, the joy evident all across her face.

"Well done!" chorused Charlotte and Julie.

"That means the girls have all passed first time, but Tony and James both took two attempts," continued Julie.

"All the best drivers pass second time though," replied James.

"Rubbish, and what happened to the coffee?" teased Charlotte.

"Sorry, we will go and get it now." With that the two boys left again and the silence returned, interrupted only by the flicking of pages and occasional comments. Katy pulled a chair up next to Julie and by the time the coffee arrived Tony had decided he may as well do his English essay at the same time so his books were also sprawled across the desk.

"Look," laughed Paul, "you become what you want to and Tony wants to be a girly swot."

"Leave him alone!" shouted Julie, and put a supportive arm around his shoulders in mock support.

"Aaaahhh don't they make a lovely couple."

"Shush, James," reprimanded Katy, before adding; "We are thinking about going to the pub tonight to celebrate my driving test. Why don't you all come as well, and we could make a night of it?"

"Yes, we could do with break," answered Tony as he stood up and packed away the books that had lain on the table for all of ten minutes.

Julie smiled at him. "What we need is a party or something to really look forward to."

Everyone agreed and then Charlotte joined in. "Well actually it is our 18th birthdays in two weeks, Tony. Mum and Dad wanted to know if we wanted a joint party in The Swan."

"That's an excellent idea. I will ask Bob and Paula tonight." In truth they had suggested a party for his 18th weeks ago, but it was years since anyone had been having birthday parties and he thought the whole idea was a bit uncool. To his amazement everyone had been talking about what to do for their 18th over the last few weeks, and somehow he was going to have to raise the subject at home without looking foolish.

Everyone else confirmed their approval and started to gather their things to leave for the weekend. As they left the common room Julie followed Tony. "So do you and Charlotte have the same birthday exactly then?"

"No, mine is the 20th which is a Saturday, and Charlotte's is the 18th. Why?"

"It's nothing." And with that she went through the door which Tony was holding over. Suddenly he had a sinking feeling in his stomach. "Wait Julie, your birthday is the 21st isn't it? Why don't we make it a threesome?"

Julie stopped where she was and looked at him quizzically.

"Well not a threesome. You know what I mean," spluttered Tony.

"Yes I do, and I think that is what you would like sometimes, a threesome with me you and lovely Charlotte." And with that Julie turned to walk on.

Tony grabbed her arm. "What is that supposed to mean? Anyway you and Charlotte get on really well."

"Forget it." Julie then gently pulled her arm away and ran on to join the others. Tony stared at her for a moment, wondering why he felt so angry. One minute they were discussing Chaucer, the next a party, and now Julie had stormed off in a huff, and she wasn't even his girlfriend or anything anyway. Rather than chase the group he decided to wait till they were well ahead then make his own way home. As he left the building Tony starting kicking an old Coke can in front of him, and slowly dribbled it along the path. As the misshaped canister bobbed along he was desperately trying to keep it in a straight line, but despite his best efforts it jumped and bobbed along a path of its own. He smirked to himself as he considered that the people around him, especially Julie and Charlotte, were about as likely to follow the path he expected as the wayward can. Eventually it rolled into the road, and before he could retrieve it a lorry drove by and the draught sucked it under the rear wheels.

Tony stood at the side of the road, hands in pockets, just staring at the flattened remnants. In truth his brain was not even functioning, no thoughts were there at all, he was just blankly staring at the can, until the whoosh of another passing vehicle brought him back to reality. There was no hurry to get home so with his toy gone he looked around for something else to amuse himself. For once there was very little litter about and instead he sauntered up the small bank at the side of the road and sat alone at the top. He had been feeling very philosophical for the last few weeks, knowing deep down that he was hiding a growing anxiety about the unknown next year. Feelings that he had experienced in the past were resurfacing. He never knew how to react with situations or people that he didn't know, and sadly his instinct always let him down.

The party thing was a classic example. He had said no, thinking that was the right decision, but everyone else in school had seemingly decided that 18th parties were a great idea. Add to this the problems with Julie, and Tony would have happily gone back three years in school to do them all over again rather than move on. James always seemed able to take life on, and make the right decisions. Even Paul had gone further than he had, in fact despite Julie's obvious attraction to or infatuation with him, he had so far managed to get absolutely nowhere.

He kept running the thoughts over in his mind for the next half hour, then with little changed he eventually picked himself up and walked on. Deep down he knew that Mr Peterson had pretty much given him the answers to his questions, and it was time he took greater control and acted with more confidence, even if it was forced.

The night in the pub was spent largely around the pool table, and gave no time for further deliberation. By the following morning the self-doubt was locked away at the back of his mind and after checking with Bob and Paula he went around to Charlotte's and confirmed that the party was on. They sat down for the next three hours deciding whom to invite, and after drawing up a list of 100 names he mentioned the discussion that he had the afternoon before with Julie, expecting some sympathy.

"You bloody idiot, Tony! How could you forget Julie's birthday like that?"

Whoooa, he thought. Once again he had not expected that. Stunned, he sat open mouthed for a minute, his mind spinning at the ferocity of Charlotte's riposte.

"I didn't," he stammered, "but you brought up the party, and I had already thought it would be a good idea so went with it. It's not my fault if she can be so moody sometimes."

"Julie is not moody, but you could think of her once in a while. You will never get anywhere treating her like that, and why didn't you think about having your party with her instead of me?" Charlotte looked angrier as she went on and Tony felt at a complete loss. He wasn't even sure why he needed to be so defensive.

"Well you are my oldest friend, so I naturally thought of you first." Unfortunately his feeble efforts to flatter fell on deaf ears.

"No, Tony, as usual you just didn't think at all. You had better go home now. I am going to speak to Julie to apologise."

"You apologise? Why?" asked Tony incredulously.

"Because thanks to you it's all I can do."

"But we aren't going out or anything. You forget I asked her a couple of times and she always turns me down," answered Tony defensively.

"And why do you think that is?" retorted Charlotte in her most sarcastic voice.

"Because of her exams, and she thinks she has to work really hard."

"Pathetic." Charlotte was shaking her head as if in disgust. "If you showed her you really wanted her then I know she would go out with you." This time she just stood staring at him, hoping that her words were sinking in. For his part Tony couldn't see what the fuss was all about, and anyway he wasn't that bothered about the way things were anyway. Neither of them spoke for several minutes, until the doorbell finally broke their silence. Still neither moved as if it was a battle of wills to reassert superiority.

They could hear voices at the door, growing slightly louder until Janet came in. "Look who I found waiting on the doorstep." Then as she moved to one side James came into the room and smiled uneasily, clearly aware that he was interrupting something.

"Hi there, so is the party set then?" he questioned, treading as carefully as he could.

Charlotte and Tony looked at each other, both frowning heavily, and they left it for Janet to answer on their behalf. "Of course it is, James, they have been planning it all morning making lists of names and the like. I cannot believe that my little girl will be 18 in just a few days and it seems like only yesterday that I was rushing to the maternity hospital in Rudbury. And do you know it wasn't the easiest of births, but she hasn't been any trouble since, have you dear? More than made up for it, haven't you?"

Charlotte opened her mouth to answer, but before she had time to form any words her mother continued.

"And to think you will all be off to university next year and then we will all be left alone in these big houses. You have all grown up so quickly, and you boys can laugh, but I remember when you were running around in short trousers, and now look at you both over six foot tall, you make me feel like a little old lady. Still, when you have all graduated you can come back and look after your parents, can't you?"

Charlotte was prepared this time and spoke as soon as her mother drew breath. "I am off to see Julie, Mum, I will be back around six for tea if that is okay."

"Yes, you carry on, I suppose I have to get used to you not being around, and what about you two boys? Would you like some lunch or are you two off as well?"

"Well I am going into town this afternoon, and I was just calling to see if anyone wanted to come with me," answered James.

Tony took up the offer and after they had said their goodbyes set off in the opposite direction to Charlotte. As they drove along listening to the football on the radio, Tony was brooding over his discussion with Charlotte when James interrupted his thoughts.

"So what was going on between you and Charlotte then?"

Tony explained everything that had happened over the last 24 hours, as James drove on towards town.

"Don't worry about it, mate, it's just women," was his simplistic reply.

"I know," replied Tony, deep in thought.

"The thing is, Katy reckoned that something was going on between you and Julie yesterday afternoon, and last night, but I didn't notice anything myself." As he finished James pulled into a parking space and switched off the engine.

"No, you are right, nothing was wrong last night, she was just in a bit of a mood at the time Charlotte asked about the party."

"Like I said, it's just women. Katy was convinced that Julie wasn't talking to you last night deliberately," laughed James.

"Come to think of it I don't think we did speak last night, but that was because I was playing pool with you and Paul. Anyway, let's hit the shops, I have to get something for Charlotte and Julie for their birthdays." As he finished Tony grabbed the door handle, and got out.

James joined him and a broad smile came across his face.

"What?" asked Tony.

"Why not get them both the same present and see what happens?"

CHAPTER 9

Coming of Age

Fortunately the rest of the planning went much better, and as he awoke at seven o'clock on the morning of his birthday Tony could feel the excitement building already. Julie and Charlotte had not mentioned their disagreements again, and as he lay in bed dozing he was surprised to hear the doorbell ring. Rather than get up and answer it, after all it was his birthday today, Tony sat in bed and turned down his radio to try and hear who was at the door. He could hear muffled greetings but they were obviously whispering so that he couldn't make out who it was until the door burst open, and Graham came in singing, "Happy birthday to you, little bro."

Tony ducked under his duvet. "God, what a racket, you still can't sing then!" he shouted from under the covers. Suddenly he felt the inevitable as Graham jumped on his bed and started gently raining blows on him from above.

"Wakey, wakey, little bro. I have travelled miles to be here for your birthday so the least you can do is get up and greet me."

Tony decided it was safe and lifted back the cover, then the two of them sat chatting and catching up on each other's news as Paula went down to get them both coffees. They talked for about ten minutes before heading down for breakfast. It was always good to see Graham, at least for the first ten minutes. The boys were very different, and not especially close, but they definitely had a unique bond that neither Mark nor anyone else could separate.

Bob and Paula were at the table already and it was all laid out for a full fried breakfast. As they walked in Bob popped the cork on a bottle of champagne and handed it to Tony.

"Here you are, lad, a legal drink at last. Cheers."

Tony took the drink, and hugged Bob, Paula and Graham in turn, before pulling out a chair and sitting at the table. The conversation continued through breakfast as they all caught up on Graham's news, and inevitably talk turned to their childhood as they all reminisced about the good times there had been over the years. Even the accident was talked about in humorous tomes as they glossed over the true horror that they had all felt on the day.

As the post came through the letterbox Bob jumped up to run to the door. "I expect it is the postman with all of your cards, wait there and I will bring them in."

Graham was still laughing about the somersaults he had performed as he went over the handlebars as the kitchen door reopened and Charlotte, Paul, Katie and James came in singing 'Happy Birthday'.

As the racket continued Bob appeared shuffling through a large bunch of multicoloured envelopes. "Ah well, it is good to see someone is popular, and it makes a change from bills. Hey, look at this, someone has written to both of you. And it's an Irish postmark, that's odd." As he finished the sentence his voice trailed away, and Paula jumped up at once to look at the two envelopes.

Graham leant across and grabbed them both, handing Tony his, before they both ripped them open and started to read. An eerie silence fell as the two of them read their identical letters.

Dear Tony/Graham,

This is probably the most difficult letter that I have ever had to write, and I sincerely hope the most difficult one that you ever have to receive.

I have chosen to write now, after all of this time, because Tony, my youngest boy, is 18 years old, and you will both be mature enough to take the news that I have to break. I am not sure exactly what you have both been told about me, but I have always tried as hard as I could to make sure that you were well looked after, and provided for.

Your father died a very tragic death when you were both very young, and to this day I still blame myself for taking the most wonderful father away from you both. I was driving the car back from a party, and because I had been drinking I should never have been behind the wheel. Your father did not know that I was drunk, because I had been secretly drinking to overcome my depression over the previous 3 or 4 years, and I became an expert at hiding it.

I lost control of the car as we rounded a corner and drove straight into the back of a parked lorry, causing your father to take the full brunt of the impact. After the accident my depression became much worse, and I was admitted to a psychiatric unit whilst you were passed to family to be looked after. Everything I had built up to that point in my life literally crashed into the back of that lorry.

It was nearly 7 years before I was able to start rebuilding my life, and to my eternal shame it was only at that time that I found out you had left my aunt and been taken into care, and ultimately placed with another family. I live with the guilt of what I did to this day, but I am not looking for your pity, or forgiveness.

My heart broke when your father died, and you are the only good things to come out of my weakness, but I have never fully recovered, and even now I am too weak to give you the guidance you need as young adults. Do not pity me for it is the two of you, and your dear father, that suffered for my mistakes. I am not a good role model for you and hopefully your new parents have loved you and given you the moral guidance that I so failed to deliver.

Hopefully one day you will accept me back into your lives, and allow me to repair some of the damage that I have caused you both. I will not tell you where I am for the moment but I will write again in the next few months and give us the chance to talk.

In the meantime I cannot say any more to ease the shock of what you must be feeling, but I promise you have never been, and never will be far from my thoughts.

With all of the love in my frail body,

Mum

Neither of the boys even heard the telephone ring, or noticed Charlotte pick up the receiver and answer it in a hushed tone. They had both reread the words several times but each time they reached the bottom of the page they automatically returned to the top, trying to make some sense of what was before them. Tears were welling up in Tony's eyes but he was too numb to blink and the effect was causing a welcome blurring of his vision.

With each reread the anger was building in Graham, and he was trying hard to suppress the shaking building up through his entire body. Tony's stomach was sinking further and further, and he felt the first tear break free and trickle down his face. He let it run until it reached the tip of his nose then sniffed instinctively. He wiped it away with the back of his hand, before another tear welled up and ran down the other side of his face. He wasn't upset about the lies he had been told, but the tragedy of what he was reading.

More than anything he wanted to run away from this place to seek sanctuary, he wanted a cuddle, maybe from the woman who had written the letter. He couldn't bring himself to think of her in terms of being his mother, but he wanted comfort from somewhere. Everyone else in the kitchen stood motionless, uncertain about what was unfolding before their eyes, and uncertain about how to react. Charlotte was holding the telephone to her ear, but focussing on Tony and Graham, almost unaware of the voice on the other end.

"Hello, is anyone there? Tony, is that you messing about, birthday boy? Hello…? Hello?"

Suddenly Charlotte came to, and whispered into the mouthpiece, "Julie, sorry, it's me Charlotte. Look, can Tony phone back? It's not a good time."

"What do you mean not a good time? What is going on, Charlotte?"

"Please Julie, I am really sorry. I will explain." With that Charlotte replaced the receiver and silence returned to the kitchen.

Bob and Paula were exchanging worried glances when Graham eventually looked up and caught their eye. "You knew all along, didn't you, and you lied through your teeth to everyone all these years, didn't you? You have literally kidnapped us and lied to make us the children you could not have."

Paula burst out crying, and grabbed the back of the chair as she stumbled forward. Everyone else in the kitchen recoiled in shock, still unaware of what was unfolding. Tony never said a word but looked at Bob for some sort of explanation.

"Look, I am not entirely sure what is happening, but I can make—
" But before Bob could finish Graham jumped up and waved the letter under his nose.

"Not entirely sure. Not entirely sure. Well the charade is finally over. You have been masquerading as my father for years and all along my mother has been locked away in some home. Take it from me, I am the one who is not entirely sure. Not entirely sure that I can trust anyone anymore. What next, is Tony even my brother for fuck's sake?" Still shaking his head in anger, Graham wiped his mouth with the back of his sleeve and carried on with his rant. "Well I am sure about one thing, I hate you both, and I don't want to ever see you again in my life, and I swear you will both pay for this."

As if to emphasise the final words he slammed the letter onto the table, grabbed the bread knife and pierced the letter with it, leaving the knife stuck upright with the tip firmly embedded in the table. The phone rang again and Charlotte turned to frown at it, frightened about what the impact of the ringing would be on Graham's mood. She didn't have to worry though as he stormed past James, nearly knocking him over, and slammed the front door behind him with as much force as he could muster.

Bob tried to take control. "Charlotte, please answer that, and then I think you had all better leave for now, Tony needs some time on his own."

At the mention of his name, Tony recovered his senses, wiped his face and tried to sniff back any more tears.

"Hello, yes Julie, I am really sorry, but not now, please don't make this hard," but Charlotte didn't get to finish as Tony moved across the kitchen and took the receiver from her.

"It's okay, Charlotte, I can handle this." Then he put the phone to his ear.

"Handle this! What is that supposed to mean? I only phoned to say happy birthday. Well you can stuff your bloody birthday and your bloody party with Charlotte as well for all I care. You don't want me as a friend, all you try to do is exclude me every time I even try and get close to you." Julie was obviously in tears as well, but Tony knew that this was his time to show real strength.

"Julie, Julie, please I need to explain. Give me one minute please."

He took a deep breath and calmly told her about the letter that he and Graham had received. As he finished Julie spoke, trying desperately hard to control the emotion in her own voice and at the same time process what she had been told. It felt strange, but satisfying that Julie was the first one to hear his explanation, with his other friends hearing the details almost second hand.

"I am so sorry, Tony. Really, truly, deeply, sorry… would you like me to come over?"

"Yes but I would like to speak to Bob and Paula, and I promise I will phone you back and I am not trying to exclude you, I promise."

"Sorry, I will talk to you later. I will wait by the phone."

Tony replaced the receiver and looked around the kitchen. James Charlotte and Paul were all obviously extremely uncomfortable with the situation, but it was Bob and Paula that he really felt for. Tony then moved over, and hugged them both as seemingly the most natural thing to do. Tears rolled down his cheeks, and he didn't want to break the firm hold between the three of them. Eventually Bob relaxed slightly and pulled back.

Paula only held on tighter and sobbed into his shoulder, "I am so sorry, Tony, I wasn't sure, I didn't want your birthday ruined like this. I am so sorry."

Feeling uneasy at the intensity of the situation they were intruding, on Charlotte spoke. "I um, think we best leave you to this."

Bob and Paula both acknowledged her with a yes, but it was Tony now who was taking charge. "Look, I need to explain a second. This is a shock to me, and the rest of us, but it is your birthday party tonight as much as it is mine, and I need you all to see this letter so that you can understand Graham. He will be fine later."

With that, Tony smoothed out the letter on the table, and gestured for the others to come and read it. As they did he removed the knife from Graham's copy, and returned it to the breadboard. They all read in a stunned silence and continued staring at the paper on the kitchen table long after they had taken in what was written on it. Nobody wanted to lift their heads for fear of being dragged into a family discussion that was obviously too complex for them to begin to understand. Eventually Paula pushed her chair back, and started to clear up the breakfast things.

"Tony is right, we must not let this ruin today, you all have a wonderful party to celebrate tonight. I am so sorry to have caused all this mess," she sobbed again as she finished the sentence, and turned away from the table towards the kitchen sink.

Tony moved over and put an arm around her shoulder.

"It's not your fault, Paula. I don't really understand what is going on, but I don't blame you for what has happened here."

"But we should have told you more. We didn't know if your mother was still alive, but we knew more about her than we let on, only social services insisted, and I was afraid of losing you both. I lied to you because it was easier than facing the truth and the consequences of that. Bob wanted to tell you but I wouldn't let him." The tears had stopped but Tony could feel Paula shaking as she finished.

"It's okay, you two brought me up and I will never forget that, I promise. Let's clear up the breakfast things and talk about this tomorrow when Graham is back. He will have calmed down by then, knowing him." With that, Tony piled more dishes into the sink, helped by Charlotte and James.

When the clearing up was finished Charlotte, Paul, and James made their excuses and left whilst Tony phoned Julie to explain in more detail what had happened. He then went upstairs to wrap the presents he had brought for her and Charlotte, then lay on his bed studying the letter from his mother. As he read the words over and over his eyes became heavier, and he gradually drifted off to sleep with the letter still in his hand. When he eventually woke Paula was sat on the end of his bed, her eyes ringed red where she had obviously been crying.

"Please don't get upset, I want you to enjoy our party as well," said Tony, fighting through a yawn.

"I will be fine, don't worry. I have just worried all these years about losing you two, and now when you are about to go into the world alone, on what should be our happiest day of all this letter arrives." She was shaking her head slowly as she finished.

Unsure what to say, Tony looked around his bedroom then suddenly caught sight of his alarm clock. "Quick, it is 5.30, you should have woken me up, the party starts in two hours."

"You will be fine, anyway you needed the sleep. Graham hasn't been back, but Mark's mum phoned me about an hour ago to say that he was with them and he had calmed down." With that Paula got up and passed him a fresh towel. "And I put the hot water on for you so you can have a shower."

"What do you mean at Mark's house? Is he home as well then?" questioned Tony, with a frown across his forehead.

"Yes, Charlotte invited him, didn't she tell you?"

"No." Tony almost spat the word out but at least he consoled himself with the thought that the second shock of the day was a lot better than the first. He dressed quickly after his shower, opened the handful of cards that had been missed in the unfolding drama of the morning, and was ready for Charlotte when she called at seven o'clock with her parents.

Charlotte looked stunning in a short black dress, and her long black hair up in a bun. Tony did a mock wolf whistle, and Charlotte feigned embarrassment.

"You two go on, and we will follow you all up in about half an hour. And don't go drinking too much just because you are 18."

Adam was smiling as he said the final words, but Charlotte still shook her head and replied simply with, "Dad, I am not your little girl anymore, you know."

"Oh yes you are."

They both smiled before Charlotte and Tony turned to walk away, just as Bob interrupted them. "I took your bike up earlier, Tony, so that you can take Julie home as promised. Though I can still book a taxi if you prefer."

"No, it's fine thanks, I promised to ride back with her, it's only a mile or so. Bye."

As they walked up the road Charlotte linked her arm through Tony's and inclined her head onto his shoulder. "Happy birthday, are you okay after everything?"

"Yes, fine, it really hasn't bothered me that much to be honest. I was so young when my parents died, or my dad died I should say, that I have just accepted Bob and Paula. Graham has always been more uneasy with it all I suppose."

They walked the last few metres in silence, to be met at the door by Katy, James and Julie. As they walked closer Tony felt Charlotte pull her arm away from his, and noticed the hurt look on Julie's face. He didn't know what to say, but was quite overwhelmed by just how stunning she looked in a short, dark blue, silk dress, with her shoulder-length hair down, but very lightly permed since he had seen her yesterday. As he stood staring he didn't even notice the others going into the hall, until he was aware that it was just the two of them left outside. He also realised that his mouth was hanging open, and he was sure that he had a vacant look on his face. He closed his mouth into a smile and spoke. "You look absolutely beautiful."

It seemed somehow massively inadequate, but when Julie smiled back and mouthed, "Thank you," his heart leapt.

"Will you accompany me into the party, Miss Woods?"

"I would be delighted."

Tony felt weak all over, and his head was swimming as he went into the hall. For the first five minutes he wasn't even sure what was happening as presents were handed over, but he was constantly aware of Julie just at his side. When the music started they took to the dance floor with everyone else. The evening seemed to fly by and before they knew it, it was nine o'clock. James and Paul were at the bar buying drinks, Charlotte was in deep conversation with Mark, and Tony was sat at a table discussing the day's events with Julie.

"I was really sorry that I wasn't there this morning when all that drama was going on," she said, leaning forward so that her forehead was touching Tony.

"It's okay, I should be apologising, over the way I have treated you recently. Charlotte and I are just old friends, you know." Tony wasn't really sure what made him say it but the words were just tumbling out tonight, and he couldn't stop them. It had been an incredible day, but now as Julie shifter ever closer he felt growing warmth enveloping the two of them. "Just friends."

"I know," answered Julie, and moved her head so that she was looking straight into his eyes.

Tony was oblivious to the party going on around him as he

wanted to focus only on the person in front of him. "I saw the look on your face as I walked up with Charlotte tonight."

Julie broke eye contact and looked to the floor. She then touched Tony lightly on the forearm. "Green-eyed monsters, I am afraid. Anyway, it's your birthday I should be getting you a drink."

"No, it's okay, I mean…" He was desperate not to lose the closeness, loved the warmth of the moment that he wanted to last forever. Before he could continue though, events took over as the music stopped suddenly and everyone looked to the front to see Graham staggering about with the DJ's microphone in his hand. Obviously drunk, he was twisting around trying to untangle the curly flex that he had wrapped around his head as he grabbed it.

"So who wants to join me singing Happy Birthday to my little brother? Happy birthday to you…"

No one else joined in and Graham was staggering, trying to stand still and looking around trying to focus in the half light.

"What's the matter with you all? This is more like a wake than an 18th birthday. No one has died, have they?"

Graham almost tripped then recovered himself and spoke into the microphone again. "No, of course they haven't, have they? Just ask the lovely Bob and Paula over there. No one has died, have they?"

The silence was eerie, and no one even turned to look away from Graham. "They can't have kids of their own, so they decide to screw up someone else's life instead."

Paula's hand went to her mouth in shock, as she bit her bottom lip trying to suppress the tears. Tony didn't know what to do, and it was Mark that went over to his best friend. "L-l-l-look, give me the microphone and c-c-come outside. This is not right, mate."

"Piss off back to little Miss Goody Two Shoes, neighbour of the foster parents from hell, why don't you? She might love you one day if you can trust her, if you can trust anyone, that is." Graham was shaking as he finished and fell to his knees. Mark grabbed the microphone off him and threw it back to the DJ, just as James came over and helped him carry Graham out. He fought off their efforts for a brief moment then allowed them to drag him outside with his head staring down at his feet. Tony jumped up to follow them as the music restarted, and Julie grabbed hold of his arm.

"It might be better if you left him a minute."

Tony paused and thought, then put his hands up to either side of Julie's head and looked deep into her eyes again. "I know but I need to speak to him. I am all that he has got," and with that he walked across the dance floor to the exit.

Julie stood staring at his back for a moment before following him. When she reached the outside the coldness took her breath away and it took her a second to focus on the group sitting at the table to her left. James had obviously left them to it, but Mark, Graham and Tony were sat together. She walked over and sat down opposite Tony who was sat beside Graham. After a few moments Tony spoke. "You have to give them a chance, you know. They are the only family we have, and they didn't knowingly try to deceive us."

"We have got our real mother, haven't we? Or didn't you read the letter?" snapped Graham.

"She couldn't cope with us, and Bob and Paula have always loved us like their own, haven't they? We haven't wanted for anything with them."

"You haven't maybe, because they always loved you more, but I have always had to make things happen first," sniffed Graham.

"Rubbish."

"No, it's not. I am on my own like I always have been, with you to support as well, just like when we were kids. You don't help at all, just taking sides against me all the time." Graham looked up with his eyes full of anger.

Tony was shaking his head in disbelief. Mark tried to make light of it all. "Look mate, it is b-b-bloody cold out here, and I think I am on the pull, so come on inside and behave."

"No, you go in. I won't be welcome anyway, I will see you later. It is still okay to stay at yours isn't it?"

"Sure." And with that Mark went back inside.

After a few minutes of further silence Tony squeezed Graham's shoulder. "Come on in, and apologise to Bob and Paula, they really do care for you."

"Bollocks. They have deliberately lied to us for years, and kept us away from our real mother. We don't know what they have been telling her to keep her away, do we?"

Graham was starting to shiver although more from anger than cold.

"We don't know that."

"I do. Anyway, I am on my own from now on and I don't care who I hurt. I was always best on my own anyway. You are 18 now so it is up to you to sort your own life as well."

"Don't be foolish, Graham. Listen to Tony." The sound of Julie's voice shocked them both, as they had hardly noticed her sat there.

"Who the hell asked you to stick your nose in? You don't know the first thing about this." Graham was gesticulating with his hand as he spoke, and Tony wished Julie wouldn't say anymore, but she wasn't about to stop.

"Maybe, but we all have our cross to bear. I have two older stepsisters from my mum's first marriage and they don't even speak to me from one year to the next. Then my mum remarried my dad, and I was the honeymoon accident that ruined their short marriage. So now she's on husband number three, and they haven't even remembered it's my 18th tomorrow. They are always away on holiday without me, and they never show me any love. As far as they are concerned the sooner I leave home the better. So think yourself lucky, you at least have a brother who idolises you, and what's more you have two foster parents who do love you with everything they have to give." Julie stopped for a second as tears started to stream down her face, and the two boys were lost for words.

"So stop feeling bloody sorry for yourself, and get a life." With that, she got up and ran back inside.

Graham looked to Tony, with the merest hint of a smile on his face. "That is one feisty woman you have there, little bro. I am sorry to ruin your party. You go back inside. I will be okay, I think I need to sober up and get my head straight."

Tony's head meanwhile was reeling, and he didn't know where to go first. He stood up from the bench, turned to speak to Graham but no words came so he turned and stumbled blindly into the hall. At the doorway the loud music and bright lights caught him unawares, and he stood transfixed for a few moments.

"Tony, is everything alright? Julie just came in crying. Is Graham okay?" questioned Charlotte.

Almost oblivious to her being there, he scanned the room looking for Julie.

"Tony, talk to me." This time she grabbed his arm, and was shaking him to try and get his attention.

"Yes, Graham, yes he is fine. I think he has gone home or to Mark's to sober up. Where is Julie?" questioned Tony, still trying hard to focus on proceedings around him.

"She is about somewhere. Anyway, they want to do the cake now, and I said we would just say a few words so come on." With that, Charlotte pulled Tony across the room to a table on the far side where Bob, Paula, Janet and Adam were all standing. The music stopped as they walked across, and their guests assembled in a half circle around them. Charlotte took the initiative and thanked everyone for coming to celebrate their birthday, and for all of their presents, then with a special thanks to her parents she passed the microphone over to Tony. He hadn't really listened to anything that had been said, but to his relief Julie pushed her way to the front just as the microphone was handed over. She looked slightly flushed still, but was smiling warmly at Tony, and mouthed, "Happy birthday."

"Erm, thank you Charlotte, for that, I think you have said all the things I was going to say, and we should just enjoy the rest of the party." Tony looked down at his feet hoping he had said enough, but the silence that ensued indicated people wanted more.

Suddenly he heard James voice shout out, "Speech, speech!" and as others joined in it grew into a chant.

Tony looked up again, and couldn't avoid Julie's gaze. To his relief she wasn't chanting, but she had an expectant look in her eye, and clearly she also wanted a bit more from him. He wished he had rehearsed like he did for the head boy job, but it was too late for that now. Deep down he almost thought that James was leading the chanting as an act of revenge, and that thought spurred him into action, as he lifted up the microphone again.

"Today is a very special day, and one that I will never forget for a whole host of reasons. The most important thing about today though is that I am celebrating my 18th birthday surrounded by all the people who care about me, and that I care about most in this world. Without all of you collectively, and individually, I would not be the person that I am today and I am eternally grateful to you all for that.

"It is a real honour to share my party with you all, but I have to pass on my real thanks to just two people – Bob and Paula. Please join me in a toast to them, and then can we please continue with the party, we only have an hour left."

Tony looked around for a glass, as Julie moved forward and handed him the wine she was holding. As she turned to go back Tony slipped his arm around her back and pulled her to his side before he lifted the glass to the assembled crowd, then turned to Bob and Paula. "My parents."

A round of spontaneous applause broke out, and Bob moved across with Paula to embrace him. They both hugged him for what seemed like an eternity, and Paula wiped her eyes as she moved away.

Bob spoke first. "Thank you Tony, it really means a lot to us after today."

"Yes, thank you Tony," continued Paula.

The music had already resumed, and Tony desperately wanted to spend some precious time with Julie. She had been at the front as he spoke, and despite the embrace he could not stop her from slipping back into the crowd as Bob and Paula had been hugging him.

Bob offered to go and get some drinks, and Tony eventually caught sight of Julie again, stood over talking to James, Paul, and Katy. He started to move in their direction when suddenly the music stopped again and this time it was the DJ talking. "For the next record, ladies and gentlemen, a slightly slower pace and you will be led onto the dance floor by your birthday hosts Tony and Charlotte."

Tony smiled, but couldn't believe what was happening. Charlotte came over and walked onto the dance floor with him, as the music started. "Don't you think you should be spending more time with Julie tonight? She really likes you, and you haven't been with her all night."

Tony shook his head in disbelief. "Yes, and whose fault is that?"

"Don't blame me. It's all in your own hands," answered Charlotte indignantly.

Neither of them spoke for a few minutes then Charlotte continued as though she had something to get off her chest. "It is like Mr Peterson said, we are in charge of our destiny from now on. We have to make things happen." The anger was building in Tony. He hated being told what to do, especially when it was Charlotte doing the telling, but he tried to calm himself before replying.

"I have been—" But before he could finish he felt a tap on the shoulder, and he looked around to see Mark.

"D...d...do you mind if I finish this dance?" Tony looked to Charlotte for an answer, and he was surprised to see that her face had broken into a huge smile. "That's what I like, a man who knows how to take control."

Before he knew it Tony was stood alone with a carousel of couples dancing around him. He was looking around for a friendly face, but despite having all of his own guests around him he couldn't spot the one face that he wanted. Eventually he saw Julie over by the bar stood on her own but as their eyes met, she looked away. Without hesitation he pushed his way past the dancing couples, and caught her arm, as she motioned to walk away. "Julie, would you like to dance?"

She looked around at him but didn't answer at first. Tony sensed she was waiting for something more, some sign that he understood what she was feeling. "I am sorry if I upset you earlier, but I wanted to say the right thing for Bob and Paula, and I didn't think. Then I am also sorry for not coming over for a dance earlier but Charlotte grabbed me and I am really sorry. I wanted you to enjoy tonight and I am afraid that I have ruined your evening."

The corners of her mouth lifted into the merest hint of a smile, but it was enough and Tony could feel his heart racing in his chest. He waited this time allowing Julie to speak. "You haven't ruined my evening, it's just that whenever I need you, or want to help you, I always seem to be the most distant person from you."

Tony's mind was a fog; he so wanted to say the right thing, but there was so much he wanted to say right now, and all the time he felt that familiar warm glow rekindling inside his body, threatening again to envelop him completely, but extinguished too often already this evening. He thought for a moment, planned what to say and began. "The problem is everyone thinks Charlotte and I are destined to be together because we have been friends forever, and—"

"I don't," interrupted Julie.

Tony stood with his mouth wide open. Just when he thought he had things set in his own mind Julie had completely thrown him off course. Then to make matters worse she continued before he had to time to collect his thoughts again.

"I don't think you and Charlotte are destined to be together." There followed a long pause as they stood once again staring deep into each other's eyes. If only he could begin to understand what she was thinking behind those beautiful eyes.

"I don't even feel threatened by her, it's just that I would like to share more of my life with you than you allow."

Tony had never felt the emotions that were racing through him before, but the warm glow was burning hotter than ever, and he took a deep breath to try and slow his heart down. He felt like he was drowning in his own emotion, he was breathless, frightened, nervous excited all at once. Julie then spoke for him again. "Are we going to have that dance then? It will be time to finish soon." And she held out her hand for him as she moved to the dance floor.

They held each other close together during the music and continued talking about the day's events and their relationship. Neither of them noticed anyone else on the dance floor, and before they knew it the DJ announced that it was to be the last record. Tony looked around to confirm the time was approaching 11.30, then without any fore thought or planning asked, "Will you go out with me… properly?"

Julie smiled and kissed Tony lightly on the lips before answering. "Not yet, today has been emotional for both of us and I need to know you are doing it for the right reasons. Not this time but maybe next."

It wasn't the answer that he was expecting, but he could hardly believe he had asked the question in the first place, and strangely enough the answer didn't matter at all. They continued to dance together until the music finished then said their goodbyes to everyone who had been at the party. They helped clear away tables and chairs, and packed the presents into the back of Bob's car.

Julie slipped away and changed before coming back to join Tony, who was chatting to Bob and Paula.

"Well it is time you took this young lady home. We can finish clearing up here and we will see you later, try not to be too late." As Paula finished Tony was pleased to see that the day's traumas had no lasting effect, and she was looking pretty much like her usual self.

When they walked outside it was a cool night but not cold, and they jumped on their bikes and cycled away slowly. The cool night air gave Tony time to try and sort out some of what had happened during the day, and he was happy to ride quietly along thinking through the days' events until Julie interrupted his thoughts. "You do understand why I said no don't you. Only you have been a bit quiet since."

Tony slowed to a stop, lay down his bike and walked over to Julie who had also stopped. He motioned to a wooden bench illuminated by the moonlight just a few metres away and they both sat down. Neither noticed the cool evening temperature as Tony put an arm around Julie and pulled her into his side.

"Yes I do, I have just had so much to think about today, that is all, and my head is racing. But right now I want you to tell me about you and your family."

Julie pulled herself in closer than either of them even thought possible. "Do you know that is the first time you have ever asked me about myself? Maybe we are getting somewhere."

"I'm sorry, I don't think I even knew how I felt about you until today, and when you shouted at Graham I was so shocked that I knew so little about you. I feel so immature sometimes despite being 18 and I know that I am not."

"That's okay," Julie interrupted with a finger that she gently placed on his lips before he could finish. "There really is nothing more to add, and you are not immature. It all frightens me too, you know, but I am envious of you for all the close friends and family that you have, and then when I think like this I hate myself for being so selfish."

"You have friends too, as well as Charlotte, Katy and the rest you also have other friends at school."

"I don't feel sorry for myself but I have no real close bonds, not like say Charlotte and Katy, or you for that matter."

"We are just—"

"Don't apologise, please. I have always been happy with my own company, it is not a complaint. In the last year I have wanted something else, and for all of your insensitivity I feel myself drawn to you, but my mum's relationships are something of nightmares and I want the relationships I choose to be stronger than the ones I was given!"

"And is that why you don't want to go out with me, when I asked you earlier?"

"I am not sure."

For what seemed an eternity they sat in silence, their rhythmic breathing in tune with one another. Eventually Tony broke the silence in a near whisper. "How will I know when it is the right time to ask you again?"

"You will, and if you don't it is not the right time."

After another gentle silence it was Julie who broke the silence next. "I know we will both go to uni. next year, and it seems mad to get serious at this stage with exams and all, so maybe we should just enjoy the fruits of a relationship without the pressures. We have so much still to discover about ourselves and right now to be honest the only feeling I know for certain is that it is getting a bit chilly."

The warmth of Julie's embrace was enough for Tony, and he did not want to move apart.

"You cannot believe how I am feeling right now, just sat here it feels like our bodies have fused into one. I hope we do always stay friends, I would hate to lose this." Tony was speaking without planning the rest of his sentences, intoxicated by the joy of the night.

"Me too." Then after a short pause, "Come on, you are supposed to be taking me home, and I have got your present at home as well for you to open."

With that, they walked back over and jumped back on their bikes and rode to Julie's house. They let themselves in and sat talking for a few minutes before Julie went off to get Tony's present. He glanced at the clock as she left the room and noticed it was five to one in the morning. Her present had been in his pocket all evening, so that he could give it to her when it was her birthday. He was pleased with the present he had bought, and glad now that he had taken so much time over choosing it. The gold chain and matching earrings had a teardrop in shape set around a blue stone, and they had cost him more than any other present he had ever bought. At the time Tony didn't know what had possessed him to buy them, and James had even suggested that he split the chain and earrings, giving one to Charlotte and the other to Julie. Thankfully it was only a joke that he had ignored.

As the clock ticked on towards one, he could hear Julie upstairs, probably still wrapping his present, then a footstep on the stairs as she started to descend. Tony got up and walked over to the door of the lounge as she walked in and the sight of her literally took his breath away. Julie had changed into a short white silk dressing gown, through which he could clearly see the outline of the body he had been holding all evening. She walked over to him, put a finger on his lips then held him closely. Tony wrapped his arms around her body, and as they kissed he moved his hands down to take in the full beauty of her shape. Below the silk dressing gown she felt more beautiful than anything he had ever touched before, and he felt the passion rising through his body. As they continued kissing he felt himself melting into her body, and a sense of wellbeing he had never sensed before in his wildest dreams engulfed him.

She felt beautifully soft under his hands, with only the silk gown covering her body, as he experienced an intimacy that he had anticipated for so long. His whole body was pulsing to the rhythm of his heart, and time had seemingly stopped. Tony was trying to let his instincts rule, deliberately not thinking about his next move, trying to let his unconscious side take over. He wanted to give so much, wanted to show just how much the moment meant, yet he was so inexperienced that he was afraid of failure. As they held each other it felt like their two bodies were once again fusing into one. Tony's heart was burning through his chest and the torment from earlier seemed a million miles away.

Julie as ever took control as she slowly let her arms fall to her side before turning and leading Tony upstairs to her bedroom. The room was lit by a solitary candle, giving a warm yellow glow that radiated warmth far beyond the possibilities of the tiny flame. Without speaking they slowly undressed each other, letting their clothes fall to the floor. Neither of them were rushed, merely overwhelmed at the beauty of what they revealed. Julie slid gently under the covers on her bed, and recognising Tony's hesitation encouraged him gently but firmly to lie beside her. Neither spoke as they explored further and slowly progressed to make love for the first time.

They enjoyed the warm afterglow as they lay together in the bed, and neither of them wanted the moment to disappear. For both of them this was the best birthday they knew they would ever have, and it would always be extra special as a moment shared, at a time in their lives that they could never go back to.

The candle slowly burned, flickering away, casting shadows this way and that as the flame danced in celebration of the day, seemingly enjoying the moment as much as the two of them. Time seemingly stood still, but they couldn't ignore forever the reality of the clock in Julie's bedroom as it edged now towards two o'clock. Tony knew he had to make a move, but before he left he reached over and picked up his trousers from the floor to retrieve the present. As he lifted himself back up he whispered, still afraid to break the tranquillity, "Happy birthday."

Julie took the present and unwrapped it with the same unnecessary care that she had had displayed earlier as she undressed Tony. When she finally opened the small box her delight was obvious, and in the light of the dancing candle put on the gifts for Tony to see. She sat up in bed, unfazed as the blankets dropped away from her otherwise naked body, then asked, "How do I look?"

"Absolutely beyond words. You are beautiful, really, really beautiful." He could feel the emotion of the day welling up in him again, and as words failed him a single tear escaped and gently ran down his cheek. Julie waited for it to reach the corner of his mouth then gently leant forward and kissed it away.

"Thank you. You don't have to say anymore, but you really have made today very special." She was deliriously happy, and it showed as her face reflected in the fading glow of the candle.

Tony wanted to stay all night, as he chanced a glance at the clock in the bedroom Julie caught his eye. "I know you have to go, but just five more minutes please." She shrugged her shoulders as she looked over longingly.

Without saying a word Tony reached up and pulled Julie in close to him, they snuggled together and drifted off into a light sleep. After about 20 minutes Tony gently lifted his arm from under her head, which he allowed to gently rest on the pillow. He then dressed quietly and kissed Julie goodbye. As he left her room she snuggled down under the blanket and Tony saw again the beauty of her body draped only in the thin sheet of her bed. He stood leaning against the frame of the door staring at her outline for several moments before tiptoeing downstairs and gently closing the front door behind him.

Once outside he hardly noticed the cool night air as he cycled home, his mind still whirling in a fog of emotions.

He nearly asked Julie to go out with him again before he left but knew it was the wrong moment and now he felt strangely more at ease. If she had said yes he wasn't sure what to do next, or how that would be tomorrow, and he was glad he had left it, which is what he knew Julie wanted for the moment. As he cycled on it started to drizzle, and he pedalled harder to get home quickly, despite the cool air that was making it harder to breathe.

Julie sensed the hesitation as Tony left the room and waited for him to ask her out again before he left. She couldn't and wouldn't say no again tonight, but the question never came. As the door clicked quietly shut she lay in bed dreamily rubbing the pendant between her thumb and forefinger, anticipating the joy of a future shared.

CHAPTER 10

Summer Holidays

The months followed quickly after the party, and even the usual Christmas break passed in a blur as everyone struggled to revise for the mock exams that were scheduled for the first week back in January.

Tony and Julie saw more of each other, but they settled into a friendship that suited them for the moment, and with the coursework deadlines and revision timetables to consider they had little time for anything else. Graham went back to university then claimed he had to work through much of the Christmas holidays to pay off his overdraft, returning home just for Christmas and Boxing Day. Cards arrived from their mother, but there was no further message or explanation, simply a 'Best wishes for Christmas and the New Year. Love Mum'.

They both felt a little cheated, expecting more, but discussed it only very briefly before hiding the cards in amongst all the others from family and friends hanging around the house. Once the New Year began everyone was focussed on exams, job applications, or university places, and before they knew it school was suddenly over. Results were then the big issue, and no one really relaxed until they came out in mid-August. Fortunately the hard work paid off and everyone managed the grades that they needed.

Charlotte excelled with three straight A grades, Katie two As and a

B, Julie two Bs and a C, James an A, B and C, Paul an A and two Cs, and Tony a B and two Cs. After the initial few days and nights of celebration, a wave of anti-climax seemed to slowly spread amongst them. No one had been away on holiday, or indeed made any plans to go away. University didn't start for several weeks and they all seemed at a loss to know what to do. Julie and Katie tried to persuade Tony and James that the four of them should go away on holiday together, but the boys weren't that interested.

With university starting shortly the break from study was now almost over, and the monotony of no daily routine was almost as boring as the final term of school that had preceded it. As usual Tony had been at home alone all morning, and after a snack lunch walked up to see what was going on at James' house. Katie's car was parked, as it had been every other day that week, but he was surprised that Julie was there as well when he walked in.

"Hi, I didn't expect to see you here, I was going to call you later." As Tony finished he realised that he was interrupting something, and looked questioningly at Julie for an answer.

"Katy and I have booked to go to Tenerife for a week. You don't mind, do you, only the travel agent had a good deal on, and we had to say yes... Sorry!" Julie blurted the words out.

"We don't have to apologise. They could have come with us if they had organised themselves." From the look on their faces Tony could tell now that James and Katie had been arguing when he came in.

"That's okay with me. I hope you have a good time." Tony genuinely wasn't bothered, and didn't really think that he was missing out. Plus, he wanted Julie to see that he wasn't going to be immature or jealous or anything. Her reaction was not what he expected.

"Is that it?"

"Um, yeah, sure, have a good time."

This time the angry glances were shared between Julie and Katie as they both stood up and walked towards the door then Katie turned and spoke. "You two are hopeless, and don't deserve us. Have a nice life."

With that they both walked out and forcibly slammed the front door on the way. Tony took a second to gather his thoughts. He had barely been in the room ten seconds, and somehow managed to have an argument with Julie and Katie, without actually realising it.

"What the hell was that all about?"

James shrugged his shoulders in reply and walked towards the kitchen. "Dunno, mate. Fancy a coffee?"

"Yeah I would love one."

They both sat down once the drinks were made, discussing nothing in particular until James suddenly thumped the kitchen table with his fist. "I've got it. We should go back to the Gorge this weekend for our final ever anniversary camp there."

Tony sat back on his chair mulling over the idea for a moment. "But I thought we had the final one a few years ago."

"Yeah, so? This could be the final, final one. I will phone Charlotte and Paul to see if they want to come."

Before Tony could add any more James had gone to the dining room to make the calls. He returned a few minutes later smiling broadly. "Good news, they are both up for it, and M-M-Mark is back this weekend as well so Charlotte thinks he will come."

"Great." The sarcasm in his voice did nothing to hide Tony's' true feelings about Mark.

"He is alright, mate. Anyway, I thought he was in Spain with Graham again," mused James.

"Probably been extradited for some crime or other." They both smiled at Tony's last comment then spent the rest of the afternoon making their plans.

Just as he was leaving the phone rang again, and even from the one sided conversation it was obvious that Katie was the caller. Tony indicated he was leaving and left them to it on the telephone.

Breaking the habit of the last few weeks he woke early on the Saturday morning, ate a massive breakfast prepared by Paula, and left the house by 10.30 to walk to James' house. Paul was already there, and after a quick chat they set off for the Gorge. They had decided to make it an all-day affair, and with no games to worry about tomorrow they intended to enjoy themselves. Tony carried the tents, whilst

James had been put in charge of food, with Paul carrying the alcohol. Charlotte and Mark were expected around 6.00 and they promised to bring more food and wine with them.

It was a dry but dull day, and laden down with their heavy load progress across the fields was slow. They eventually arrived about midday, and Tony set about putting up the two tents with Paul's help whilst James lit one of the disposable barbecues he had packed and put some food on to cook. They picked at the food during the afternoon, drank a couple of beers each, and had a kick about with a football until Paul noticed Charlotte and Mark approaching. He jumped up and cupped his hands together before shouting, "Come on, you two, the beers are getting warm, and the food is getting cold, hurry up!"

"Some help would be nice," answered Charlotte, and the three of them took the hint and ran over to help carry their bags.

Mark had another tent which was quickly erected before the football came out again and the four boys had another kick about whilst Charlotte stayed by the barbecue and opened a bottle of wine. Being late August the light was fading by 7.30, so everyone scouted around to find as much wood as they could, and the barbecue quickly grew into a proper campfire. More food was put on and Paul, who had taken charge of the makeshift bar, sorted out drinks.

"So how come you are back in this country without Graham then? I thought you were working in some bar over in Spain for the summer," asked Paul as he passed another beer to Mark.

"I-I-I had some business to attend to over here so I came back. G-G-Graham wants to buy out the current bar owner next year when he retires, and work there full time after he finishes his degree."

"What?" The way Tony reacted showed that he clearly knew nothing of his brother's plans.

"Th-th-that's it really, he wants to use his inheritance to buy into the bar, that's all."

"So why are you over here? I bet this is your idea and you just want to use Graham's money instead of your own."

"Whatever." Even in the dim glow of the fire everyone could see the resigned shrug of Mark's shoulders.

"Give it a rest, Tony, for once, will you?" It was the first time that

Charlotte had really spoken all afternoon, and she didn't look up but simply raised her glass as she finished and took another sip of her wine.

After a brief uncomfortable silence Paul spoke up. "So is this definitely the last, last Gorge fest then?"

"Definitely," answered James.

"Un-unless we have another one that is," continued Mark. Everyone apart from Charlotte burst out laughing and Paul continued the theme. "We could all be back here with our grandchildren or something in 50 years still talking about the good old days."

"Why not though?" As Tony spoke his thought process was still ongoing. "We should all make a date before we leave tomorrow to meet back here in say five years, promise to be here no matter what happens in our lives. Like a sort of reunion."

Equally lost in thought, Paul carried on. "Where do you think we will all be in five years though?"

"B-b-back here, we just said didn't we?" Even Charlotte smirked this time before Paul carried on almost oblivious to Mark's quip.

"Yeah but five years is a lifetime away. That's like back Year 8 at school. Do you even reckon we will know each then?"

"Of course we will. There is no need to lose touch. My dad's best man came to his funeral and spoke to me afterwards. Apparently they were best mates at school, and they even served in the RAF together, and yet they hadn't been in touch for 15 years. He reckoned that he meant to get in touch over the last year or so but just never got round to it and then it was too late." James paused for thought and then continued. "Anyway, I vowed there and then never to be complacent about friends, and even if we lose touch for a few months or whatever I will always look you lot up, and keep in touch."

Paul raised his bottle "Cheers mate, I will keep you to that. Anyway, you and Tony are sharing a flat at uni. next year so that makes it easier. I will only have to write or phone once and the other one can pass on the message."

"You lot will keep in touch. It isn't that difficult. Graham and I still meet the same people in Spain every year, and carry on like we only saw them yesterday. M-m-most people you meet are friendly and once the initial barriers come down they want to get on. Th-th-the thing is, no matter how many new friends you meet, nothing replaces the bond you have with people that you have known for years and years, it becomes more like a marriage."

As Tony sat taking in what was being said he couldn't help but warm to Mark. He always held this deep routed mistrust of him but perhaps he was wrong and everyone else was right. Charlotte was no fool and she had been telling Tony he was wrong for years.

"So do your mates get on with my brother then?"

Mark looked across and considered the question for a moment before replying. "Yeah, my best mate at uni is a guy called Juan Montez, and Graham is staying at his family's villa with him and a few others at the moment. They are all good mates, but everyone kind of knows the order of things, and Graham will always be my best mate."

"Bloody hell, this is all getting bit heavy for me. Another beer, anyone, before you are all hugging and crying?" Paul jumped to his feet as he finished and threw a bottle to each of them in turn.

"Charlotte, you okay?"

"I will have some more wine if there is some?"

"Yes, coming right up."

As Paul opened another bottle of red he noticed how the rest of the group had moved in closer together, leaving Charlotte almost excluded. He deliberately placed the now open bottle in the centre, and invited Charlotte over. "Come and join the party, you are all on your own out there."

As she shuffled in and sat next to Tony he noticed her wiping her eyes, and it looked like she had been crying. "Are you okay?"

"Yes, it is just the fire glow. It makes my eyes water."

Paul dragged over the carrier bag with the rest of drink inside and placed it in the middle of the group and sat down. "There, that is easier. I won't have to get up again. So anyway, if we do come back in five years can we bring partners as well, you know wives, girlfriends and so on, or is it just us?"

"P-P-Paul, you dark horse, have you got anyone in mind then?" laughed Mark.

"No."

Mark gesticulated to Tony with the bottle in his hand. "It's your call, mate. You have always been the main force behind the Gorge fest so you make the rules. Partners or not?"

Tony hadn't been paying attention, since he noticed the fresh tears on Charlotte's cheek, and was caught unawares by the question. "Sorry, I missed that."

James, who was sat to his left, pushed his shoulder with enough force to knock him over. "Keep up."

Rather than try to sit up again Tony put his hands behind his head and looked up to the sky. "Partners or not, let me think. I reckon we should take a vote. Those in favour raise their right hands."

No one moved but it was an unsatisfactory conclusion and so Tony sat upright and looked around each person individually. "James. Partners or not. Yes or no."

"No."

"Paul."

"Yes."

"Mark."

"No."

"Charlotte."

"Yes."

"Well I say no so my vote carries it, I think. Cheers everyone." For the second time that evening they all clinked their beer bottles in the middle, whilst Charlotte used the back of her hand to wipe her cheeks. When she spoke it took them all by surmise to hear the quiver in her voice "What are you afraid of with partners? All you and James want is a relationship when it suits you with no commitment."

It was clearly directed at both of them but James took it upon himself to answer. "I don't have a problem with commitment, and if this is about me and Katie finishing that was more to do with her than me."

"No, it's not about that but one day you are going to have to grow up, and stop all the matey bit and show someone else some commitment."

Tony could see this conversation was going the wrong way and he felt the tension building in the group as Charlotte spoke, so he tried to change the focus. "You never said that you had split with Katy."

"Yeah, it was the other night when she phoned, as you left the house. She said I was more excited about coming here than her holiday, and I didn't really care about her at all."

"Why did she say that then? She didn't give us chance to be excited about the holiday, did she?"

James was shaking his head, when Charlotte interrupted again. "It's not just the holiday though, is it? And it is not just James. You have never opened up to Julie, and you were never there when she needed you. She told you all about her problems at home, and even slept with you after your party, but it meant nothing to you, and you just carried on as before. You didn't even call her the next day on her birthday, and she was at home alone most of it."

Tony had never told anyone about his birthday night, least of all Charlotte, and he was almost too shocked to reply. The words when they did come were woefully inadequate. "But she never said."

"She shouldn't have to. She gave everything up to you on the night of your birthday, and you never even phoned the next day, let alone ask her out which is what she really wanted." As Charlotte continued there was a stunned and uneasy silence amongst the group. Tony couldn't believe his most intimate secrets were being aired so publicly, but as he opened his mouth to reply no words came out, and he was left slowly shaking his head.

He could see the anger etched on Charlotte's furrowed brow, but he couldn't understand what her problem was. Perhaps it was the alcohol talking, either that or her hormones. He hadn't seen her so angry since the day he soaked her T-shirt, but there was more to it today, a sadness that went far deeper than her anger, but he couldn't pinpoint where the problem lay.

She clearly wasn't finished and without looking up decided to turn her venom elsewhere. "You are as bad as the rest of them, Mark, and I thought you were more grown up than them. You can all tell each other how much your friendship means, with all of your male bonding, but I bet none of you can talk to a girl as honestly, can you?" As she finished she lifted her head and slowly looked at each of the boys in turn.

Tony and Paul both looked away as their eyes met Charlotte's, but James fixed her gaze with his own. He tried to focus into her eyes, refusing to blink despite the temptation that was heightened by the constant flickering glow of the fire. Eventually as the dryness in his eyes was becoming unbearable he spoke, gently shaking his head as he did so. "This isn't about me, is it? Or Tony, Paul or Mark for that matter… Not really… Something else is eating at you, isn't it?"

Charlotte bit her bottom lip as James spoke. She knew suddenly that the red wine had lowered her defences, and rather than being in control felt very vulnerable to the scrutiny of the others. She felt like Alice in Wonderland, shrinking as the world loomed larger than ever around her. She had to get back in control and chose attack as the best form of defence. "Maybe there is hope for you after all. Have you been overdoing the psychology preparation for your degree or what?"

James sat impassively still staring into her eyes, looking for some indication of what was really hurting his friend so much. He hardly noticed Paul get up and walk over to Charlotte and put an arm around her shoulder. "Look, if this is all about you and me, Charlotte, you should have said. I would have asked you out in infants but your mum scared me." As Paul finished everyone watched Charlotte for a reaction, and they were grateful when the corners of her mouth broke into a smile, and she leant over and pushed Paul away.

"Men, I swear you have never really come out of the cave, but I am never going to win this on my own. I need female support, so let's change the subject. Who is going to win the FA cup or whatever it is this year?"

As the mood lightened the conversation returned to less weighty subjects. Everyone joined in the general banter, although Tony was noticeably quieter than the others. The beer gradually ran out and Paul, James and then Mark gradually drifted off to the tents to sleep. Tony and Charlotte were left side by side in the glow of the fire, not talking but just staring into the embers.

After a few minutes of silence Charlotte reached behind her, picked up a glass that had been discarded on the ground and passed it to Tony. "Do you want to finish this bottle off with me?"

"No, I think I will head off to bed myself." Tony put his arm down to push himself up when Charlotte reached out and placed her hand onto his shoulder. She looked over, as he stood motionless half raised off the ground, and Tony could see the longing in her eyes as she said simply, "Please."

After a second's hesitation he allowed himself to sit firmly back on the ground and picked up the glass that Charlotte then proceeded to fill. A sudden crack from the fire made them both jump, and nearly upset their wine glasses. Tony recovered first and raised his glass. "To my best female friend from an emotional dinosaur."

They chinked their glasses together and then Charlotte spoke. "I am sorry about earlier. They didn't know, did they?"

"No."

"Sorry, I thought you boys all boasted about that stuff."

"Maybe I am not like all boys, or maybe you don't know us as well as you thought."

"Maybe not."

"Don't worry, they will be impressed in the morning, they thought I was still a virgin. That is if they even remember given the amount we have all had to drink tonight."

Charlotte took a slow sip of her wine before continuing. "I was out of order though. I am sorry."

"That's okay, like I say it will do me good when James and I share next month. He is always pressuring me to get a proper girlfriend and now I won't get so much pressure from him."

They both sat contemplating all that had been said during the evening before Charlotte spoke again. "So why did you and James decide to go to the same uni? Don't you want to go out and meet new friends and so on?"

Tony rubbed his hand across his chin before replying, trying to avoid a glib answer. "To be honest it just sort of happened. We were doing different courses, but both applied to Bristol University, and it made sense to share when we both got in. We will make new friends and so on but cutting off our current friendship just for the sake of it seems pointless. Anyway, if you weren't going off around the world I might have shared somewhere with you."

Charlotte smirked, and then her reply took Tony by surprise. "I might not be going now anyway."

"But you have planned a year off forever. What has changed all of a sudden?"

"My mum and dad are splitting up... You see my dad has apparently been having an affair for years at work, and they have kept it all hidden. Anyway, his stupid tart wants to move up to Scotland, and my dad has said he will go with her leaving my mum all alone."

"Wow." It was a painfully inadequate response and yet the spontaneity of it summed up the shock so perfectly. The conversation earlier made sense at last and Tony could see where Charlotte's anger had really been aimed.

"But what will your mum do? Who knows about all this?"

"She is going to move as well, so this won't be my home anymore, and no one knows yet except you... and Mark."

"Why Mark? What do you see in him?" The words came out even before Tony had considered what he was saying and he tried to ease off a little, trying to hide his jealousy that he wasn't the person Charlotte had confided in first. "I accept he is getting better with age and I may have been a bit harsh on him but why tell him first?"

"I didn't."

With the emotional strain of the evening, and a large amount of alcohol Tony was in no mood for charades. "You have lost me, I am afraid. Maybe it would be better if we finished this conversation tomorrow."

Before he could stand Charlotte put her arm out to stop him for a second time. "Don't go, I will explain, I promise. Do you remember that story I told you years ago about Mark getting caught taking things from people in the village?"

"Yeah. He tried to get Graham blamed for it, didn't he?"

"Sort of. Well apparently Mark was at the farm one night when he saw my dad with this other woman, and they both saw him. They then apparently concocted this story about the den and everything in case he told anyone in order to discredit him. Anyway, now that his mum knows my parents are splitting up I found out the truth."

"And who told you this? It seems very contrived to me. They were grown adults, and their word would have carried more weight than Mark's so it seems a bit unnecessary. Who told you this version of events?" questioned Tony.

"Mark, of course," Charlotte answered the rhetorical question, incredulous that he was even questioning her at all.

"Well it is all a bit convenient, don't you think? He found out about your dad's predicament and wanted to make the most out of it. There are too many holes in the story for my liking."

Charlotte pushed Tony hard with the palm of her hand onto his shoulder. "You are the most stubborn, awkward bugger I know sometimes... you really can be impossible to reason with."

"And where does this leave you as far as your dad is concerned? Are you as angry as Graham?"

"He is my dad, my protector, my hero for my entire life, and yet now he is suddenly nothing. When he talks it is just words that mean nothing. I cannot believe he has deceived me all these years, deceived my mum. I am angry, disappointed and I will never ever be able to forgive him. And yet through all this I still love him with all my heart because of who he is and what he is."

Although the glow from the fire was fading fast Tony could still make out the tears rolling down Charlotte's cheeks, and knew it was time just to listen. He leant across to embrace her. She snuggled into his shoulder, and for a few minutes sobbed almost uncontrollably. He could do nothing more than hold her until she pulled away slightly raised her arms to Tony's shoulders and they sat staring at each other, with their arms loosely over each other's.

"I am so sorry, and knowing what a mess families can be I can only promise to help all I can. You will always be welcome back here at Bob and Paula's, so your home will be here still."

"Thanks, and I know you have been through far worse, but I am just being a selfish cow as usual."

Tony pulled his head back, and shook it gently, and almost whispered, "No you are not."

In the glow of the fire they continued staring at each other until Charlotte inclined her head slightly and moved forward where their lips met in a passionate embrace. Neither of them wanted the kiss to end but slowly Tony pulled away. "Not now, not like this, not tonight."

Charlotte raised her middle finger and placed it gently on Tony's lips. "Friends forever then, and maybe one day."

Tony kissed her finger then placed it back on Charlotte's own lips. "The caveman in me wants you so badly, but not like this, not tonight."

CHAPTER 11

A New Beginning

Events took over in the next few weeks and with so much going on everyone pretty much went where their individual lives took them. Mark only stayed in England for a couple of days then headed back to Spain to help Graham out before both returned to finish their final year's study. With life at home very difficult Charlotte took the snap decision to start her year of travel straight away, and flew out with Mark to Spain. She met some fellow backpackers whilst out there and continued with them through Europe, America, and Asia. The trip was everything that she had hoped, and moreover it provided a very welcome distraction from her parents splitting up.

Tony and James rented a flat in Bristol and settled quickly into university life, whilst Paul started his degree in IT in Nottingham. Despite the distance everyone made a conscious effort to keep in touch by phone or letter, and had a welcome reunion back at home over the Christmas break. It was strange for Charlotte not to be there, especially as her parents had sold the house and moved out of the village altogether, but for everyone else it felt very much like the old days. Katy and James hardly talked at first but quickly settled their differences and everyone enjoyed the break from uni. Julie went back for New Year to be with her new boyfriend, but everyone else stayed on until early January.

During the Easter break James managed to get jobs for him and Tony at the local sports centre, so they stayed in Bristol for most of the time. Paul stayed with them for a couple of weeks, and then they were into the final term before they knew it. James' mother decided their old house was too big for her on her own, so she sold up and moved to Rudbury where she now worked full time, and gave some of the proceeds to her son. With that money, plus what Tony had inherited they bought a bigger flat to share in Bristol, and spent the first few weeks of the summer holidays decorating it. Then with the bit that they had scraped together during the year they took Paul to see Graham and Mark in Spain.

Surprisingly during the first two weeks they hardly saw them at all. The bar purchase was going through, and they were both busy going through the ropes with the previous owner so that they would be ready to take over. Tony, James and Paul spent most of the time on the beach or sleeping after a late night drinking and clubbing, but towards the end of their break they helped plan the celebration party ahead of the big takeover. Paul spent a couple of days at the bar setting up the computer, and teaching Graham and Mark how to work it, whilst Tony and James walked the streets handing out flyers.

As expected the party was a spectacular affair, with Graham in particular in his element as centre of attention. Unfortunately the plane tickets home had been booked weeks earlier and it couldn't have worked out worse as they had to leave the morning after the party. As it happened the party was still in full swing when their taxi called at 5am. Paul, who hadn't had as much as the other two to drink, bundled them in and they set off for the airport.

Tony and James quickly fell asleep in the back, whilst Paul talked to the driver in the front during the 50-minute trip to the airport. Their flight back was delayed by a couple of hours so they made their way to the tiny restaurant area and used the last money they had to order some breakfasts and coffee. As they sat trying to cope with the tiredness, boredom, and looming hangovers Paul seemed agitated, and even in his half-drunk state Tony picked up on it.

"What's up, mate? Are you sad to be going home?"

"No, it's more what that taxi driver was saying and the club in general. I looked at the books whilst I had access to the computer and none of it adds up."

Tony and James both looked across at each other totally bemused then James asked the question that was bothering them both. "What exactly did the taxi driver say then?"

"You two must have been sleeping. He reckoned the place has been on the market for years and has a really bad reputation. Apparently it is only ever busy when Graham and Mark are there each year, and the locals all reckon the owner just gets all his friends over to make it look busy so that someone would buy it."

"And?" Tony always knew it was a bad idea to fuel this pointless conversation any further. Nothing he had heard so far really surprised him, and to be honest he wasn't really that interested.

"Well when I looked at the computer records nothing made any sense. The banking last year was nearly ten times the takings, and no wages were paid at all, not even to the owner." Paul had more to say but the announcement of their flight boarding interrupted them.

"Look, drink up, we have to board. Anyway, it's up to them, mate. They are big enough and stupid enough to know what they are doing. Just forget about it," yawned Tony.

With that they ran to the departure gate and boarded. Surprisingly none of them really gave the bar another thought as they headed home for a few days before returning to university. Being a fresher, Charlotte had started a week earlier and there was already a letter waiting for Tony at his flat when he opened the front door on his return to Bristol.

James had picked up the massive pile of post as he went in, and sat at the kitchen table sorting through the envelopes and cards as Tony made some drinks.

"Bills, bills, card from Bob and Paula in Tenerife. Look at that, they even have donkeys in Tenerife. More bills, oh, a letter from the delectable Miss Charlotte. Hard luck, mate, no kisses on the back, letter from Julie as well by the look of the handwriting. You are a popular chap."

Tony grabbed the letters from the makeshift pile that James had started and read them all through, before there was a knock at the door and James got up to answer it. He came in few seconds later with a group of their friends all carrying bottles. "Apparently it's time we had a flat-warming party, mate. Here, have a drink."

Tony only knew about half of the group, although with the majority of them being female he felt sure that James would know them all, probably intimately. Sensing that this was going to be the start of a long night he quickly grabbed the various items of post and stuffed them into a cupboard until a more opportune moment and took the first drink on offer.

It was indeed a long night, and Tony couldn't believe it was nearly 2pm when he woke the next day with a storming headache. The flat was full of bodies everywhere and he stepped over them as he made his way to the kitchen and sorted a coffee. As he waited for the kettle to boil he retrieved the pile of post and opened Charlotte's letter to read it through again.

Hi Tony,

Would love to see you soon, it's been a while, and I have missed you.

Uni. is dreadful, and everywhere seems really dull and grey after my year off. Cannot get myself back into the routine of study, and I need to see a friendly face again. Everyone seems to just want to get pissed every night and I am bored with that already.

Please write soon, or better still come to visit.

Sorry to be such a miserable old cow, I know it will get better.

Love always

Charlotte

As Tony folded the letter and put it back in the envelope James walked past the kitchen door with a girl that Tony hadn't even seen at the party the night before, and showed her out, then he came back into the kitchen.

"Cheers mate, I would love a coffee. Bloody good idea this flat, I can tell you. Victoria was well impressed, and I tried all last term to go out with her and she didn't want to know then."

Tony simply smiled in reply and handed over a coffee. Given the number of girls that James had brought back to their flat last year he was surprised he could remember any of them, but he was sure he had never heard Victoria's name before.

Monday morning came around all too soon, and lectures began. With numerous assignments to complete, and plenty of social activities to fill his spare time it was almost a month before Tony made the trip to London to see Charlotte. He managed to schedule a few days off between lectures, and left on a busy commuter train, filled with suits. Rain was teeming against the window pane and all the trees and hedgerows were dancing in the blustery wind. It was a typically miserable autumnal day, but Tony couldn't care less. He had spoken to Charlotte very briefly on the phone a couple of times, but this was the first time they had really got together for over a year now, and he couldn't wait. He knew she wanted a shoulder to cry on, and he was looking forward to giving her that support. In the back of his mind he couldn't help but feel that there was unfinished business from last time, but above all he wanted to just see Charlotte.

Paul was coming down to see them for the weekend, and that meant Tony only had a couple of days, but it was going to have to do for now. With huge anticipation in his mind he closed his eyes and sat back in the seat. It had been a busy month and he could do with catching up on some sleep.

Before he knew it the train was slowing down as it pulled into the station at Paddington. Tony grabbed his bag from the spare seat beside him and jumped off the carriage. He was still half asleep, and the blast of cold air sent a shiver through him as he jumped from the carriage step. With his bag over his shoulder Tony made his way up the platform, looking everywhere for Charlotte, but she was nowhere to be seen. After wandering aimlessly around for a few minutes he dropped his bag onto the floor to use as a makeshift seat under the station clock. He sat watching the people milling around, looking up at the massive journey planner just to his left, then checking their watches and racing off in various directions. Most people looked almost robotic as they fought to keep to tight schedules, whilst there was a tiny minority who appeared to have all the time in the world. A few of them were stopping the busy commuters to ask for change or directions, often eliciting a swift dismissal, whilst others were obviously day-trippers or tourists on the big adventure to London.

The flower seller's stall opposite appeared to be doing brisk trade, and as he studied the queue of mostly men Tony tried to guess their motives. Wife, Lover, Mother, Apology, Anniversary, Funeral; he was enjoying the game as he went through the list to himself, and didn't notice the man he had labelled as Lover approach him.

"Tony, it has to be. Sorry I am late, buying flowers for the girlfriend."

Totally taken aback, Tony jumped to his feet and shook the hand being offered to him. A bemused look had set on his face and all he could think to say was, "I am sorry you are...?"

"I am sorry, I should have introduced myself properly. I am Juan Montez, a friend of—"

"Mark," interrupted Tony before he could finish.

They both stood in silence studying each other for a moment and Tony felt very uneasy as he was obviously at a distinct disadvantage. The man opposite was probably only a couple of years older than he was, with shoulder length jet-black hair. He didn't look at all student like, being immaculately dressed in a long dark coat, dark trousers and dark purple shirt. Despite the appalling weather his hair was propped away from his face with a pair of sunglasses.

"Yes, I am impressed. I heard that you guys didn't get along. I didn't think he would have mentioned me. Anyway I am working in London now, and I met up with Charlie again a few weeks ago, and she asked me to come and meet you because she is in a lecture this morning." As he finished Juan gestured that they walk over to the tube station, and continued ,"Let me get you a pass for the tube, how many days are you here for?"

"Just three including today, I have to get back on Friday to Bristol, but I can get my pass, don't worry." With that, Tony reached into his pocket to pull out his wallet, but Juan stopped him. "No worries, man, you are mates with Mark, and Graham's brother. Let me."

Tony feigned resistance, but knowing he had forgotten to go to the cash point before he left this morning, and his wallet was actually empty, he didn't try too hard. Conversation on the tube was somewhat stilted, not least because no one else seemed to be talking to each other. Every time either Tony or Juan said something eyes would frown at them from the top of a newspaper or book as though they were breaking the law.

Eventually they reached their destination, and they both climbed the escalator, jostling past people as they went. Outside in the semi-fresh London air Juan explained that they would meet Charlotte in a pub around the corner, and Tony managed to draw out some cash on the way. Once inside both ordered some food and drinks before settling at a table opposite the entrance to the bar. It was a quiet pub, being midweek, and the first time that the door opened again was when Charlotte walked in.

Tony hadn't been sure quite what to expect but he was shocked, nonetheless. Far from some sad depressed student Charlotte looked positively radiant with a superb tan, setting off her long dark hair. She looked much taller than he remembered but the radiant smile that came across her face when she saw the two of them was pure vintage Charlotte.

She quickened her pace as she came across the floor, and in response to her outstretched arms Tony stood up, and promptly tripped on the seat that was just in front of him. He gathered himself as quickly as he could and looked up expectantly as Juan swept Charlotte off her feet, with the bunch of flowers that he had bought at the station held in his hand behind her back.

They kissed and Tony could do nothing other than slip as discreetly as possible back into his seat trying to make sense of what was so obvious in front of his eyes. His hands were clenched firmly at his side, with his nails digging deep into his palms. No one was watching in the pub, but if they were Tony was sure that his anger was visible as he felt his whole body physically tremble. He desperately tried to unscramble his foggy mind, and make sense of what was happening. For an eternity he felt like they were the only ones in the whole pub.

Eventually Charlotte pulled away, and turned to Tony, then, as if nothing out of the ordinary was happening she leant over and hugged him as well. "So I take it you two are getting on well? Juan is great, isn't he? And you must like my oldest and best friend in the whole world."

As she looked between them they both indicated their mutual approval of each other, but Tony couldn't help feeling that Juan had deliberately misled him all morning.

The three days went in a blur, as Tony was introduced to all of

Charlotte's new friends, and she even tried to set him up with a couple of them at a party on the Thursday night. Against his original expectations Charlotte had now fully settled into uni. life, and was apparently loving every minute of it. With so much going on the only time they actually had alone was at Paddington on Friday lunchtime. The train was running about 30 minutes late so they went for a snack at the station café.

Tony started the conversation off. "So you seem really happy with Juan. I am pleased," he lied.

"Yes I am, he treats me really well, flowers every week and the like. I fancied him when I first met him last year in Spain with Graham and Mark. Then I couldn't believe it when he got in touch last month."

Thinking carefully about his reply so as not to upset her, Tony tried to move the conversation on. "So is this it, the real thing and all that?"

"Maybe, but I doubt it. It is just good to have someone. You should try it some time." Charlotte hadn't meant to sound patronising but Tony went on the defensive.

"Yeah I will, there have been girls, you know, but just no one worth making a big deal about, and anyway after your mum and dad split up I thought you were off the love thing."

It was a cheap shot, but Charlotte bit her lip and stared out of the window, rather than react. After a few moments she turned back to look Tony in the eye. "The thing is, you look out there and everyone is busy running around in pursuit of some impossible dream, as well as dealing with any personal turmoil they may have going on in their private lives, especially here in London. That is what I found hardest to settle into after my year off when I had basically done what I wanted when I wanted. At first I couldn't get back into it all, and wanted to rebel against the system of exams, pressure jobs, student loans and the rest of it."

She paused to gather her thoughts again then continued. "Then Juan came along and I realised that I really want all of those things, and the pressure that comes with the life I need to pursue as a doctor, and I am working hard to get there. The difference now is that when I am with him I can switch off for whatever time we are together and go into our world, where everything slows down, and his embrace protects me. It may be just ten minutes over lunch, or overnight at his flat, but that time together is so precious, and then I come away fully recharged and ready for the challenge."

Tony was still considering her words when he noticed the clock at the end of the café move to midday, and with more sincerity this time gave his blessing. "I really am pleased for you, but make sure you keep in touch, won't you?"

As he pushed his chair back and picked up his bag Charlotte stretched her arm out and held Tony's hand. "You may not realise it but you were my ring of confidence for years. We will always be there for one another, but I know now that was about true friendship which is far less fickle than love."

Tony smiled in acknowledgement, not sure whether Charlotte was just trying to say the right thing or not, and they left the café, and made for his platform. People were already boarding and they hurried along looking for a relatively empty carriage. Finding one near the front, they hugged and Tony boarded, after promising to phone. The guard blew his whistle almost immediately, and the train pulled out of the station. With a mass of confused thoughts sparring in his head Tony leant against the soft headrest and fell asleep.

It was barely an hour on the train but he instinctively woke as they pulled into Bristol Temple Meads, disembarked and then made his way across town to the flat. It was quiet when he got there, but James had left a note pinned to the kitchen door.

Hope it went well in London.

Paul is arriving at 5.30-ish, and we are

going to the student uni bar for 7.00

I will get Chinese on way back from

Lectures. See you about 6.00

Get ready to party

Tony smiled as he read the note then made some toast and grabbed a beer from the fridge, before settling down in front of the television. He knew there was loads of coursework to write up but it was easier to waste the afternoon vegging out in front of daytime TV, and before he knew it there was a knock at the door, and he checked his watch to see that it was 5.35 already.

It was no surprise to see Paul stood at the door when he opened it, but his appearance since leaving school had changed beyond all recognition. He was by now the tallest of all of them, with long hair that reached part way down his back tied in a ponytail. The black T-shirt and jeans had clearly seen better days, and by the size of his bag Tony doubted whether things would improve much over the weekend. Even so, it was good to see each other and they were quickly sat in the kitchen drinking beer and catching up on things.

James arrived at 6.00 as planned with the Chinese, which they quickly devoured between them. Then whilst Paul sat watching TV the other two washed and changed ready to go out, before they all sat down in the lounge. James threw another can to Paul and Tony before setting the agenda. "We are going in about ten minutes if you want to wash and change, mate."

"No," replied Paul. "I will go like this, I think. I washed this morning before I came down here."

The other two looked bemused then James spoke again, trying to be as tactful as possible. "The thing is, mate, we are all hoping to pull tonight, and Tony needs it after the week he has had, so we all need to make an effort like."

"Don't worry, boys," laughed Paul, "I bet you each a tenner I will pull first, and another tenner each that mine is the best looking."

"Done."

With that, they all drank up and headed up to the bar. It was a party night for the athletics club, of which James was captain, and everyone was determined to get drunk. The plan was to have one last big blow out, and then train hard for the Inter-university Challenge in February. Every member had agreed to abide by the rules, and avoid any more heavy drinking sessions until the challenge cup was back at Bristol Uni. The sense of déjà vu was not lost on any of the friends.

Paul was just along for the party, but quickly entered into the spirit of things, and as ever soon became pretty much the centre of attention. In fairness he came down often enough to be well known with their group of friends and he mixed well with everyone. As the evening wore on James claimed the prize money was his after dancing and chatting with Victoria, but then she left and went into town with some of her girlfriends, and the prize was withheld.

The bar eventually closed at 2.30am, and everyone was forced outside. Tony had lost track of the other two, but James caught up with him as he waited for a kebab with some other friends on the way home.

"Any sign of Paul?" asked Tony.

"No," replied James, "but I saw him in the toilets about an hour ago and he reckoned he was on to a winner. Said he was going to call around in the morning and claim his prize before he went home."

It was raining again when they left the shop, so they wrapped the kebabs, put them in their jacket pockets and ran back to the flat. Once inside James opened more beer and they sat down to eat the food.

For a few minutes they sat in silence eating and drinking until James wiped his lips with a tissue and sat back in his chair. "Best bloody kebabs in the world. I may smell like a cesspit in the morning but that was bloody delicious."

Tony couldn't find a tissue so used the back of his hand then also slumped back in his chair. "Too right, and all the better for having a few pints tonight. Here's to the athletics club." With that, he raised his can into the air before taking a swig. James reached for the remote and started flicking through the channels, but with the volume set low neither was really paying attention to the television. Eventually he threw the control on the floor and looked over to Tony. "So tell me then, how was London and the wonderful Miss Charlotte? I take it you didn't get your leg over?"

Tony shook his head, took another swig of beer and replied, "No, she has a boyfriend, and seems all quite sorted. It was a good couple of days, but I can't see me getting my leg over as you so elegantly put it. Anyhow, I don't think I ever really wanted to."

"Is that why you didn't take advantage that night at the Gorge? Paul and I were watching from the tent willing you on, and you bottled it." James smirked as he finished, knowing that Tony hadn't realised he was being watched.

"You bastard, you never said... But the reality is we are good friends and I suppose deep down that is all I want."

"Bullshit. All blokes want to shag the women they know. There is no such thing as friends unless they are pig ugly, and Charlotte is not pig ugly. I would shag her given the chance, and Paul would."

Tony smiled to himself and thought about what James had said. He agreed with the sentiment but the reality of the situation with Charlotte was different. She was just a friend, but he knew James would never understand that. "Your problem is you would shag any woman, and you got through most of them in the last year. I am a more sensitive kind of guy."

"You shagged Julie."

"Different."

"How?"

"I fancied her, and wanted her, but every time we got close I got scared. I used to think, what if we end up getting married or something and I never go out with another woman? Even after my birthday I wanted to go out with her, but at the same time I didn't in case it got too serious and I couldn't get out without hurting her." As he finished Tony could see that his reasons didn't really register with James, and he decided to say what he knew his friend was thinking for him. "I knew you wouldn't get it. I think too much about these things first, and then it is too late. You just meet them, sleep with them and move on to the next one whilst I am still deciding if I like their personality or just their looks."

"Exactly, you have got to chill out and enjoy it all a bit. Look at Paul, the old dark horse, he is enjoying himself tonight, and we are sat back here with a kebab and a pint." As he finished James jumped up and went to the fridge for more beer. As he returned to his chair Tony could see that he had two brown parcels in his arms.

"What have you got there, mate? It's not my birthday."

"No, I know," replied James. "These came whilst you were away and they are both a bit odd. One is for some guy called Juan Montez, and the other for a Miss Laura Scott."

"Juan Ker you mean," and Tony burst out laughing at his joke. Once James realised what he meant he joined in as well.

"So I take it you know him then. Only I have heard the name somewhere before, I think."

Tony nodded his head in reply then jumped up. "I need a slash, mate. Too much beer. I will tell you in a minute."

When he returned James was again flicking through the TV channels, still with the volume muted, and they both sat watching the ten-second slots before he pressed the next button. Eventually he gave up again hit the red off button and threw the control down again. "So who is Mr. Juan Ker then? I take it he is Spanish, isn't he?"

"Yeah right, about as Spanish as Tesco's paella. I mean he has a Spanish name, but he was made in Birmingham. He is Mark's mate and Graham's as well by all accounts, and now he is living in London and going out with Charlotte, or Charlie as he affectionately calls her."

Even after a few too many beers James knew that he was on delicate ground and decided to tread carefully. "So is he really all that bad then?"

"No," replied Tony, shaking his head and lifting his beer can. "Except he doesn't drink and you know you can't trust a bloke who doesn't drink."

"Too right," answered James, knowing that it was one of his favourite observations on people. "But in his defence he might be super fit or something, that is after all the only reason I know why a bloke should be allowed to be teetotal."

"That is the problem though." Tony was wagging his finger to make his point. "He smokes like a bloody trooper, and, what is more some of it smelt very weird like it was dope or something."

"Aahhh, well," sighed James, "Charlie knows what she is doing," and with that he picked up the remote control for a third time. Again he flicked through the various films and music channels that were still showing before hitting the off button again and tossing it to one side. He then looked at his watch and rubbed his eyes. "So do you think we need to wait up for Paul or what? It is three o'clock and we both said we would go for a run in the morning."

Tony looked at his watch as if to confirm the time. "Let's make it ten o'clock for the run. I will be fine. We can give Paul another hour then and have another beer."

James stretched his arms above his head, and through a half yawn said, "Good plan, I still reckon the dirty bugger will be back soon with his tail between his legs." He then paused for a few minutes whilst he turned the two parcels over in his hands. "So we had better send this one on to your new mate, but who the hell is Laura Scott?"

"Dunno, but the name does kind of ring a bell."

"Here you go then, you can deal with it." With that, James threw the parcel across. Tony tried to catch it but with a beer can in his hand only managed to spill it over himself as the brown box hit the floor with a resounding crash of broken glass. They both looked at each other and laughed nervously. Tony then spoke first. "Let's hope no one wants it then. We had better bin it tomorrow, and I will post the other one off. Just put it down gently on the floor. If anyone asks we will tell them Paul kicked it when he eventually comes home."

James nodded in approval and raised his can again. "Good plan, mate."

"So did you see him actually go off with anyone or do you reckon he is sat outside in the cold just to win the bet?" enquired Tony.

"No, he went off with a couple of girls, probably only into town, but they were all getting on like a house on fire from what I could see," replied James.

"God knows how he does it. He is hardly a real looker, is he?"

"Well Tony, I didn't know you knew what to look for in a guy. Is that your secret after all then?"

"No, you know what I mean. How does he manage it?"

"He is am emig, emigma."

Tony burst out laughing. "Easy for you to say."

James was shaking his can now, trying hard to concentrate. "Enigma, that's the word. He is though isn't he? I mean he is always around us. Always has been, hopefully always will be but we know nothing about him. He is always just there, you know in the nicest sense, but we don't know what he likes or dislikes or anything, what he does, anything. Anything."

Tony had never really thought about it before but James was right.

They didn't know much and he was trying desperately to think of what he did know "He is in a band at uni. Did you know that?"

James shook his head again. "No, you see that is exactly what I mean. Bloody emima thingy. Mind you, with that hair do I am not surprised. Anyway what does he do in a band? He can't sing or play anything, can he?"

Before Tony could answer they both heard a knock on the door and jumped up to answer it. As expected it was Paul, and they let him in before going to the fridge and bringing back three more cans. They all took several swigs in silence before Paul eventually spoke out. "So where is my sixty quid then, boys?" He was grinning broadly having obviously won the bet in style.

James, however, was shaking his head in the chair. "No. No. No. First, Paul, you have to answer ten questions from the list that Tony and I have drawn up. Question one, what is the name of your band, the nature of your music and the role you play in the aforementioned ensemble?"

Obviously enjoying himself, Paul was only too keen to join in. "That's actually three questions but the band is into rock, I write and play bass guitar, and we are called The Gorge."

The other two nodded approvingly, then following the lead set by James, Tony asked, "How many proper girlfriends have you had, and what was the last one called and when did you finish?"

"Well I am currently going out with a girl called Samantha Draper, and have been since I split with my last girlfriend, Michelle Dibley, about eight months ago. I have had about six longer-than-a-week relationships in all."

The mention of a current girlfriend stunned them both, and Paul was really enjoying the attention. He knew that they wanted to know more detail, and deliberately kept it brief.

James was ready with his next question, and swung around to face Paul before he asked it. "So what is your ambition in life, and what team do you follow, or what sport for that matter?"

"No real ambition as such. I want to write more computer games I suppose, and as you know I am not particularly into sport." Paul sat back in his chair as he finished, not returning James' stare. It was as though he was still contemplating his final answer.

Tony spoke next, effectively repeating James' last question. "Look, everyone has an ambition. There must be something you really want in life. You know, your go-to-sleep thoughts, what are they about?"

"My what?" Paul sat up in the chair again and was staring hard at Tony with his eyes screwed up.

This time it was James who answered. "Look, it is just a theory of ours. You can tell a lot about someone if you find out what they think of every night as they go to sleep, you know, the really deep personal stuff that you would only tell people you were close to."

"Nah, I still haven't got a clue what you two are on about."

"Yes you have. Look, when I go to sleep at night I often think about playing football in the park and being spotted by some premiership scout and getting a call up to Man United or something the next day. I know it is nonsense and will never happen, but it sends me to sleep with a happy feeling in my head if I let my imagination run wild, and each night I build up a bit more of the story. Tony, on the other hand, has a dream about some system he is working on to beat the stock market, and one day he starts investing in it properly and it turns the world upside down, and makes him filthy rich. So come on, now you can tell us yours."

"Okay, but you are going to be disappointed. At night I sit in bed and clear my head of everything. I think of the kind of patterns that you get in those kaleidoscopes we had as kids and then I am asleep."

"That's it?" It was Tony's turn to sit forward now in total disbelief.

"Sorry." Paul shrugged his shoulders. "Anyway, I can feel the kaleidoscope coming on and I think you two are in my bedroom."

They all knew he was right, it was now nearly four o'clock in the morning and they were due to go out running at ten o'clock. James went to his room and returned with a sleeping bag which he threw onto the floor. They then cleared the glasses and cans that were lying around before moving the furniture in order to make room for a makeshift bed.

"Night then," said Paul. "See you around midday, I guess."

With the time for the run rearranged for ten o'clock at least Tony meant to reset his alarm when he went to bed, but instead he collapsed on top of the duvet and fell asleep fully clothed. After what seemed like an impossibly short time the alarm went off, and his first reaction was to grab it and throw it across his bedroom. Instead he hit the snooze button to steal his extra nine minutes of precious sleep. Rather than dozing off though, he found himself far more awake than he would have thought. He opened both eyes slowly, and watched the digital display changing as he counted off the minutes. It was bright sunshine outside, and because he hadn't bothered to draw the curtains the whole room was bathed in a warm glow.

He kept going through the night before and in particular Paul's question time and he still couldn't come to terms with the change in his old school friend over the last 18 months. Paul had always been the slightly shy, awkward, and by his own admission geeky one of the group. Now all of a sudden he was in a band, a long-term relationship and apparently God's gift to women as well. Tony wasn't exactly jealous but he still found it hard to believe that he seemed to be the only person who was unable to find a proper girlfriend. Paul wasn't exactly good looking, or trendy for that matter, he wasn't sporty, funny, and he had no real ambition and yet none of it seemed to matter.

As the ninth minute came the radio alarm started up again, and Tony sat up on the bed. He hesitated for a moment to check for any side effects of the beer or kebab, but was pleased that he felt 100%, and decided to shower and get ready for his run. That way he would be more prepared than James, if he could raise his housemate at all, that is. He tiptoed about the house, so as not to wake anyone, showered, drank some coffee and ate some toast as quickly and quietly as he could. It was necessary to climb over Paul to get to the kitchen but he showed no sign of waking at all, in fact the loud snores were his only discernible sign of life.

A toothbrush, flannel and wet razor were all laid out beside the crumpled pile of clothes Paul had been wearing the day before, but he didn't appear to have any other luggage or fresh clothes with him at all. Tony was just contemplating the prospect of his friend wearing the same things again today when the doorbell went.

He put down the remains of his coffee and tiptoed out to the hallway, reacting on autopilot without giving a moment's thought to who would be calling at this early hour. As he opened the door he was pleasantly surprised to find a stunningly beautiful young lady about his age smiling and offering her hand to him as she spoke.

"Hi, my name is Laura Scott, and I think you have something of mine."

Tony was nothing short of awestruck. She was about 5' 10", with very light brown to blonde shoulder-length hair, and a beautiful smiling face. Her face was set off with large dark brown eyes that radiated the warmth of the greeting she was offering.

He hardly took in what she had said, but he knew she must be here for Paul. How the hell did he get such amazing women, and why was she here for him at this time of the morning?

"What, Paul you mean?" was all he could manage to blurt out.

Now it was Laura's turn to look confused as she withdrew the hand she was holding out by way of an introduction. "Oh, I must have the wrong house. I was told it was Tony."

His face broke into a huge smile and almost too eagerly he replied. "Yes, Tony, that's me."

Laura pointedly lifted her left hand to scratch her head before speaking. "Let's start this again. I am Laura Scott."

"Hi, I am Tony Alford. How can I help you?"

They shook hands properly this time and before Laura spoke again the realisation struck home. The broken parcel was for Laura Scott. Tony felt the blood draining from his body and was even starting to feel faint as he tried to think of a way out of this mess without explaining how he dropped it last night.

"Well, I live next door, and my dad sent a parcel to me, but for some reason he put number seven, instead of number nine, and I hope you still have it."

Pretend that everything is fine, thought Tony. *Deny any knowledge.* "Yes, there are a couple of parcels that we got by mistake yesterday and I think that one has your name on it."

As he looked back Tony was instantly aware that this time it was Laura who was stood open mouthed ignoring him. She seemed to be looking at something in the hallway behind him, and fearing that it was her broken parcel he tried hard not to notice, until she spoke.

"Well you must be Paul."

Tony swung around, and couldn't believe what he saw. Paul had wandered out of the lounge and was stood in the hallway stretching his arms above his head in a large yawn, but worse than that, he was stark naked.

"Paul, mate, get some bloody clothes on, there are ladies present."

Without any sense of embarrassment or for that matter urgency he initially raised his arms out above his head then lowered them to cover himself. "Sorry, I heard voices, that's all. I am going back to bed."

Tony turned back to Laura, and was pleased to see that she was smiling at least. "I am really sorry about that. Wait a second and I will get your parcel." He kicked Paul deliberately as he stepped over him to retrieve that package and carried it back, trying not to rattle the broken contents at all as he handed it over.

"Thanks for that, Tony. Do you want me to get rid of the other package for you as well? It might be for one of my flatmates."

"No, it's okay. It's for my brother's mate who lives in London. My brother lives in Spain and he expects me to be a courier for him. I will take it down the post office later on after I have been for a run. But thanks for the offer."

"That's okay. I don't suppose you like running with a partner, only I have been out of practice for a while, and I really want to get back into the athletics team, but I could do with someone for moral support. I put my tracksuit on this morning then came around here to put off starting my training."

Tony couldn't believe his luck. Maybe Paul hadn't blown his chances after all, and he was only too keen to accept. "Yeah, fantastic, I am ready to go now if you are."

Laura lifted the parcel and shook it gently, indicating that she had to do something with it first. Tony winced at the jangling sound it made but she didn't seem to notice. "I will just drop this next door then I will be ready. See you in five minutes."

His heart was pounding even before he started the run, and as they set off together on a gentle run he was fighting to get control of his breathing. The rapid heart rate was making him take small, short breaths and he consciously tried to breathe in slowly without gulping the air down. Slowly but surely he settled into a rhythmic pattern, and found a comfortable speed. Laura was running alongside him, and seemed equally comfortable at the pace as they ran up towards the downs and then around the perimeter of the large open parkland for about 50 minutes without stopping.

Tony was feeling desperately dehydrated, and he had managed to suppress several waves of nausea, cursing himself every time for eating the kebab that kept repeating on him as he ran. He felt sure that his pores were oozing the same smell, and that was why Laura had dropped back a couple of paces. As they passed a bench she called out and Tony turned to see her slumped in the seat with her head bent double between her knees.

"Wow, you are too fit for me. I need to rest, I am sorry." She was breathing heavily and her face had turned bright red with all of the exertion.

Tony took the spare seat on the bench, and shook his head. He too was out of breath and picked up the bottom of his T-shirt to wipe his face and forehead. Eventually he recovered enough to talk. "Trust me, that is about all I can manage for today as well. I was hoping you would stop about ten minutes ago, and I really need a drink badly."

They were both silent for about five minutes and then as they recovered their composure they started to talk. Laura was full of questions, about Tony, James, and Paul, but she was also interested in the fact that he had a brother living out in Spain, which she described as really romantic. In between talking about himself and his family, Tony found out that Laura was actually a year older than him, although she fell ill last year and had a lot of time off so she was now back to do her second year at uni. again.

She was an only child, and her family lived near Reading. It would have been easy to sit talking for hours, but with their clothes covered in sweat they both began to feel the cold and decided to jog gently back to their flat. As they reached Laura's front door Tony mustered all of his nerve and spoke first. "Would you like to go running again tomorrow, and maybe finish the chat? I really enjoyed this morning."

Laura smiled. "I will probably give it a miss tomorrow, but I would like to do it again soon." Then seeing the obvious disappointment on Tony's face, she carried on. "We could always go out for a walk this afternoon if you fancy it, and anyway it will be easier to talk then."

It wasn't a walk that Tony fancied, but he was trying desperately hard to play it cool, without blowing it altogether. "Yeah that sounds good. I will call for you about two o'clock if you like."

"Great, and if you let me have that parcel I will drop it in at the post office before it closes."

Tony thought for a moment before he remembered the package for Juan. "Only if you are sure it is no trouble."

"No trouble, honest."

Grateful for the help, he went home, collected the parcel whilst ignoring the shouts from both Paul and James, then handed it over to Laura. When he returned again a few minutes later the banter resumed and he chose to head straight for the shower ignoring them again. About 20 minutes later he walked casually into the front room where they were both sat eating lunch of sorts.

Without looking at either of them he walked to the kitchen and put some bread in the toaster for himself. Eventually James could contain himself no longer and spoke first. "So is this young lady coming back to see Paul fully clothed then?"

"No, we are going into town later." Tony knew he should have ignored the comment and not told them his plans, but it was already too late.

"I hope you don't disappoint her, after seeing me in my full morning glory like." Paul and James obviously found this highly amusing as they collapsed in laughter.

"We are just going out for a walk, that's all."

"A walk? She did not look like an OAP, are you sure she wants to go for a walk!"

"Yes."

"Tell you what, mate, I think it's your turn to do the ten question thing that you and James did on me last night."

"No way." Tony's response was immediate, knowing that this was dangerous territory.

"Fairs fair, mate. Let's keep it simple, all we need from you is single-word answers, okay?" offered Paul.

Tony wasn't sure but at least this was a compromise that he felt he could accept. He didn't want to look like a spoilsport, but he hated talking about his own life, especially sober. "Okay but that is it, one-word answers is all I am giving."

"Is Laura good looking?"

"Yes."

"Did you get on well?"

"Yes."

"Do you think she fancied you?"

A little more uncomfortable now he answered, "Well I don't—"

"Ah-ah," interrupted James. "One-word answers we all agreed."

"Maybe."

"Do you fancy her?" Paul's questions were coming thick and fast.

"Suppose."

"Would you like a girlfriend if the right girl came along?"

"Yes."

"Is two and a half months a long time?"

The question seemed totally out of context, and Tony screwed up his face to demonstrate his confusion but answered none the less. "Yes."

"Okay then, well, I am coming down again at Christmas for the end-of-year ball that you lot are having, so if you aren't going out with Laura by then can I have a crack at it?"

"Sod off." Tony was smiling as he threw the remains of his toast at Paul, but he could see from the looks exchanged between him and James that the question session had been carefully orchestrated by the two of them.

As it was the two and a half months passed all too quickly, and Tony couldn't believe it as the mid-December deadline approached.

He and Laura ran almost every day after their first meeting, and went out regularly on a social basis, but they had never progressed beyond the stage of being friends. James got on really well with her as well, and apart from warning him occasionally that he was running the risk of doing a Charlotte again, he never interfered at all. Paul, however, took great pleasure in sending a series of postcards throughout December with just a big number on them counting down the days until the end-of-term ball.

The card bearing the ominous number seven on it arrived just as Tony was leaving the flat on the way next door to collect Laura and it weighed on his mind all the time that they were running. It had almost become a ritual now to stop at the same park bench, and as they saw it looming Laura burst into a sprint to race the last few hundred metres. They both reached it together and slumped onto the wooden seat whilst they got their breath back. Tony knew that this was his opportunity and spoke first.

"So are you going to the ball next Saturday?"

Still obviously out of breath, Laura nodded first then spoke a few minutes later. "Yeah, Mike Williams asked me yesterday, and I said I would go with him. I went out with him on few dates last year before I was ill, but I haven't seen him for ages. How about you?"

Tony feigned being short of breath whilst he thought of an answer. The news that Laura was going with someone else affected him more than he expected. It was only then that he realised this wasn't about Paul's challenge at all, he really did want to go out with Laura. The disappointment coupled with cold air made him shiver all over. He stood up to try and get control of his body, but he couldn't fight off the cold. "Come on, I am getting cold. Let's get back."

"Are you okay?"

Tony simply nodded in reply and started slowly jogging back, with Laura at his side. When they reached her front door she reached out and grabbed Tony's arm. "You are going on Saturday, aren't you? James told me that your friend Harriet was coming down with Paul, and you were taking her."

"Charlotte? Well yes, she is coming down, but I wasn't exactly taking her, anyway it doesn't matter. I will see you later." Tony was angry but not with Laura, he couldn't believe James had been interfering. He turned to go back to his front door when she caught his arm again.

"I'm sorry, I may have got the wrong idea. Sorry."

Neither of them said anything more but that single word offered Tony the faint glimmer of hope that he needed.

The night of the ball arrived, and with hired suits, and a new dress for Charlotte, they all got ready in the flat. James had apologised to Tony about messing up his plans, claiming that he was trying to make it easier for him by getting Laura jealous, and it was left at that. Paul had obviously been warned not to push it and didn't mention the challenge all evening. To make matters worse Laura joined the queue immediately behind James and Victoria. Once inside they all sat together on a large table. Tony did the obligatory introductions, and then everyone either sat around drinking or took to the dance floor.

Paul soon reacquainted himself with some past conquests and was off in various directions with various girls, leaving Tony pretty much on his own. Charlotte hit it off immediately with Laura and Mike, but he couldn't be bothered to make any effort and join in that conversation. James spent much of the evening dancing with Victoria, and her younger sister Rachel who had come up for the ball.

By about eleven o'clock he was thoroughly bored and sat at the table alone, whilst everyone else was dancing, when Charlotte came over and pulled him up to the dance floor. "Come on, miserable guts. What's up with you tonight?"

"Sorry, it's nothing." Then after a few moments he asked the question that had been at the back of his mind all night. "So where is Juan?" He only just stopped himself from adding 'Ka'.

Charlotte pretended to look stern but the smile gave away her true mood. "We split up thanks to you! Still, you probably did me a huge favour."

"What?" Tony couldn't believe the accusation, although he was quietly pleased at the outcome.

"Apparently you were supposed to bring some parcel up for him. When it never arrived, he had to go back to Spain to get some stuff, and then he stayed over there with Graham, and dumped me one day by phone."

"I am sorry, really, but I posted the parcel up, well actually Laura did it for me."

"Whatever, it isn't important now." Surprisingly Charlotte seemed genuinely disinterested in the whole matter.

"What about the ring of confidence thing? Have you got a new man?"

"Maybe." Again the smile gave it away but Tony decided not to push for any more info at this stage.

"Laura seems nice, and you two seem close."

Tony nodded in confirmation then added, "She is, but she is going out with Mike now, so that is the end of that."

Charlotte was shaking her head, but as the music was now louder than ever he couldn't make out what she was saying. Then all of a sudden it was silence as the clock moved towards midnight and everyone looked up to see a magnificent display of fireworks from the balcony above. A shower of gold glitter that covered the floor in a thick shimmering blanket followed.

The band then took a short break, and it was announced that a champagne breakfast was available in the entrance hall. Preferring another pint, Tony made his way back to the table to see if anyone else wanted anything. Charlotte elected to go with Victoria and Mike for the champagne whilst the others decided to stay.

Everyone shouted their drinks order and Tony made his way up to the bar, where he joined the back of a long and very slow-moving queue. After standing in line for a few minutes he felt a gentle tap on his shoulder, and turned to see Laura stood there.

"I think your friend is trying to nab my man."

"Charlotte? No, I doubt it, she is not like that," replied Tony.

Laura pulled a grumpy face and pushed out her bottom lip. "That is a shame. I think I came with the wrong man, and I was hoping she might take him off me so that I could leave with the right one."

Tony stood still, wanting to say sorry just so that Laura would repeat the words he had just heard. He opened his mouth but no words were ready, and his mind was in a fog of alcohol and adrenalin.

"Yes mate, what can I get you?"

Tony swung around again to see the bar had cleared and he tried desperately to think of his order. Fortunately Laura remembered them without any hesitation at all. They carried the drinks over between them and handed them out, before Tony realised that they were two short. "We didn't get our own, did we? Come on."

Laura smiled then leant over and whispered, "That was deliberate. I have got a bottle of wine at the flat for us. Let's slip away as I do not think we will be missed. I would like to start my Christmas with just the two of us."

Tony still could not believe how beautiful Laura was and she had an inner strength that she used to take control whenever he was faltering. He had recognised this on their very first meeting, and since that day he had grown to enjoy her company more than that of anyone else he had ever known.

"That sounds perfect to me, let's go."

Once outside Laura linked her arm though his, leant on his shoulder and they walked in a comfortable but all-consuming silence slowly back to the flat. There was no need to dilute their mutual joy with mere words. It was a cold night, and their breath fogged in front of them, but the warmth they shared kept the chill at bay. Once inside the flat Laura opened a bottle and Tony sat down on the sofa. After pouring out two glasses of wine she came over and sat down, nestling in beside him.

Neither of them spoke at first then Laura asked, "This is what you wanted, isn't it?"

A massive grin broke out on his face as he answered, "Absolutely. I was so gutted when you said you were going to go with Mike to the ball. My whole world just sort of collapsed. I didn't even realise before how much it would mean to me but..." Tony was shaking his head, and already conscious that he was blabbering on and talking too much.

Laura sat up and faced Tony. "I am sorry about that. To be honest with you, after I was ill last year I am afraid to commit to anyone, and ever since the first day I met you my heart has been in turmoil. I remember speaking to my dad that night and telling him I had met the man of my dreams."

Tony so wanted to tell Laura he loved her, but how could he so soon, and at the same time he almost wanted to cry with elation. "I am so overwhelmed by my feelings for you I don't know what to say. I am not like James who always has the easy chat, but I have never felt this way about anyone before, and I cannot see me ever beating this again in my whole life."

Neither of them knew what to say to add anything more and they inclined their heads together and kissed for the first time. It was a long, gentle kiss, and as they broke away Tony noticed tears gently falling down Laura's cheeks. He couldn't understand why she was crying, and yet he felt himself welling up at the same time. To stave off his own tears he instinctively kissed her again, gently moving around her mouth like she was a piece of fine, delicate china. He felt the warm salty taste of her tears on his own lips, and wanted more, yet at the same time he wanted to savour every second. As he gently held her it was only the mere tips of his fingers that followed the beautiful soft warm contours of her body. He knew that he was barely touching her at all, yet it was enough to convey his strongest emotions and feelings.

Neither of them spoke again until Laura wiped her eyes. "I am sorry, I don't think I have ever been this happy. Don't you dare ruin this, ever. I want you so badly, I need you, and if I give you my heart don't ever break it."

"I won't, I promise. I cannot find the words I need tonight. I just want to freeze frame this moment forevermore."

The tears had gone now and Laura was smiling again. Tony had seen her every day almost for the last ten weeks, but he couldn't take his eyes off her face. He was studying every detail, falling more in love with her every second. He could feel her breath they were so close, and despite his lack of experience he knew this was the birth of something very special.

They kissed slowly again, then Laura snuggled into his body and spoke. "I really want this so badly, but I need you to let me take things at my pace. I have been fighting my feelings for you, and now I don't want to anymore, but I want it to be special, and I want to take things slowly." Tony knew what she meant, and right now he didn't have to sleep with her. He knew he had something that James and Paul could only dream of, and he wanted this so badly he would do anything that Laura asked. All of a sudden his relationship with

Julie seemed to fall into context, he had liked her but really only as a friend, and she had done all of the running. He fancied her physically, but emotionally it had never felt anything like this. Even on his birthday lust had taken over but he never cared for her in the way he already felt about Laura.

"Is that okay?" Laura twisted around in his arms to look him in the eye as she asked the question.

Tony started to panic. He couldn't believe that he was thinking of Julie at this precise moment, and what was the question? No, the thoughts of Julie and his birthday meant nothing, and he had to clear those thoughts.

"Tony?" There was a nervous hesitation in Laura's voice now.

"I am sorry I was just, well, to be honest with you..." Tony took a deep breath and hoped his gamble was about to pay off. "This may sound really silly but I have only ever had one sort of relationship with a girl before."

"Charlotte?" interrupted Laura.

"No, she is really just a friend. No, it was someone else at school, but it never went anywhere because I never actually felt anything for her as such."

"But you did sleep with her then." Laura shot Tony a disapproving look, before breaking into a smile. "Sorry."

"As I was saying," Tony felt that he was losing momentum, and wasn't sure whether to carry on or not, "I want to go out with you more than anything in the world, and it has only really hit me over the past few days just how badly I want it to work. I won't rush you or anything, and it may be really early days but..."

Before he could finish Laura leant forward and kissed him. "I know, you don't have to say it, and I feel the same."

They both cuddled in closer on the sofa and talked on for hours. The wine slowly disappeared by about four o'clock, and they fell asleep in each other's arms. Tony woke again at about 10am and carried Laura into her bedroom and put her under the duvet. She put her arms up and kissed him and then he tiptoed out of the room. He scribbled a note and pinned it to the door, then left and went back to his flat for some more sleep.

With Christmas almost upon them they saw as much of each other as they could over the next few days, then they phoned whilst apart. Tony went back home to Bob and Paula, and Graham came back on Christmas Eve, spending the next week there as well.

A card was waiting for each of them from their mother, but there was no note or anything else inside. In fact from the few words that had been written it appeared that her health was deteriorating to the extent that someone else had obviously taken it upon themselves to write the address on the envelopes. When Graham saw the writing he declared that it was his intention to visit Ireland and find her over the next twelve months, before it was too late. Tony let the comment go, thinking it was another grand plan that would probably go nowhere at all.

The brothers did spend quite a lot of time together over the holiday period, and talked at length about where they were both going. Graham wanted Tony to finish his degree and join him in Spain, where the bar was apparently prospering but Tony was adamant that he wanted to make his own plans. The best thing about uni. was that no one knew him for anything other than being himself, and he didn't want to go back under Graham and Mark's shadow.

Once the new term started the athletics squad were focussed on the Inter-university Challenge Cup, and they all trained daily for their various pursuits. As usual James took charge of everyone's schedules, motivation, and diets, as well as looking after himself and training up to three times a day. Tony and Laura had the perfect excuse to spend more time together as they were both training for the 1,500 metres.

The Challenge Cup was a weeklong event based at nearby Bath University, followed on the Saturday night by a massive party that had been arranged back at Bristol. Family and friends were invited to be spectators, as well as guests at the party. Nearly all lectures were disrupted in one way or another that week. The idea was to get everything out of the way early in the year so students could then concentrate on their exams and coursework for the rest of the term.

James was entered in five events over the week, starting with freestyle diving then 100 metres front crawl in the pool. Later in the week he then had javelin and discus as well as being part of the 4 x 100 metre relay team. His mum Julie came down every day with Bob and Paula, and Charlotte and Paul joined them later in the week.

James won both of his pool events then came in the silver and bronze positions respectively for javelin and discus. Tony competed on the Thursday morning in the 1,500 metre race and came in a respectable sixth overall, setting a personal best in the process.

Laura was waiting for him as he finished, along with Bob and Paula. They had all met earlier in the week and were sat together during the race.

"Well done, and a personal best. Nothing like piling the pressure on for me this afternoon, is there?" Laura was smiling but the nerves ahead of her run were obviously building, and Tony felt that she actually looked quite pale with the worry.

"You will be fine. Have your parents arrived yet? I am more nervous about meeting them than the run." Tony looked around as he finished but could only see the familiar faces of Bob, Paula, Charlotte and Paul.

"No, not yet, but don't worry, you will be fine, they will love you just as much as I do." As she finished she leant over and kissed Tony, only to be interrupted by Paul.

"Put him down, he is all sweaty and horrible. That's disgusting."

"He is right, you know. I need to get a shower, I will catch up with you all later," answered Tony.

There was a massive queue in the changing rooms, and it was nearly an hour before he returned to the track, where he found Laura already warming up with the other female athletes. She was not looking 100%, and Tony went over to try and settle her nerves.

"Are you okay? You look really nervous, try taking deep breaths and warming up slowly."

Laura nodded as she balanced on one leg, stretching her other one as much as she could. "I know, I am so nervous, this is my first competition in nearly two years, and my dad is here to watch now and he always expects me to do so well."

"You will be fine, really. I had better go and introduce myself. I take it that is your mum sat next to Paula. Wish me luck."

Laura pulled Tony closer, "Wish me luck you mean."

They kissed and then Tony walked slowly up the steps trying to look as calm as he could. Unfortunately he then had to shuffle along the row, asking several bemused people to move bags or clothing so that he could get past. When he eventually reached the group Bob jumped to his feet and did the introductions.

"This is my son Tony, This is Laura's mum Caroline, and her dad Brendan." Everyone said their hellos and shook hands, before Tony looked for somewhere to sit. Unfortunately the only seat available was between Laura's parents and Tony had no option but to sit there.

"So Tony, is Laura okay out there? Only she looks a bit off colour," asked Brendan.

"Stop fussing, dear, she will be fine," interrupted Caroline before Tony could answer. Then he added, "Well to be honest with you I don't think she looks too good, but I asked her and she said it was just nerves."

"See, Tony knows what I am talking about. Women, I swear I will never understand you. Either we don't care or we are fussing."

"Shh. They are about to start." Caroline put her finger to lips as she remonstrated with her husband.

Laura appeared to start well, but Tony was concerned that she went off too fast, and by the 800 metre mark she was starting to fall back from the leading pack. Her pace was slowing all the time, but worse than that she seemed unsteady on her feet. By the time the leading pack reached the 1,200 metre mark both Tony and Brendan were on their feet trying to get a better look at proceedings, then as the final hundred metres approached she stumbled and fell to the trackside clutching her stomach. Without saying a word Brendan jumped down the seats from row to row picking out the vacant spaces as he went. Tony tried to follow but tripped and fell after a couple, then decided to work his way to the steps at the end, which he descended two at a time. He was only 30 seconds behind, but Laura's dad had already lifted his daughter onto a seat where she was being attended to by the trackside medical team.

She looked up as Tony approached still clutching her sides. "I am sorry, Tony."

"Don't be soft, are you okay?"

Nodding her head and still trying to get her breath back. "Yes I am fine I just got it all wrong in the race that is all, and I ended up with an almighty stitch."

"We need to take you back with us tonight, Laura. You will need to see Dr Preston," interrupted Brendan.

He tried to lift Laura and motioned for Caroline to give him a hand. Tony tried to offer his help but his path was blocked with all of the people milling around, and he suddenly felt like a small kid being kept out of the action in the school playground. He briefly considered ducking down and running between everyone's legs when he became aware of Laura motioning everyone away.

"Please just all of you give me some space."

There was a brief silence as everyone looked awkwardly at one another and shuffled back a few paces. Laura then stood shakily to her feet and smiled at Tony. "Not you, come here and give me a hand."

It wasn't a triumphant moment, but it meant a lot that Laura wanted him to help. He looked nervously at Brendan, and was pleased to see the nod of approval that he needed then moved forward and put an arm around her waist. "Are you sure that you are okay?"

Laura nodded then turned to her parents. "Look, we are going back to the flat so that I can get a shower. Pick me up at about eight o'clock and I will go to see Dr Preston tomorrow, but I am coming back on Saturday for the party."

Surprisingly there were no arguments, and with that Laura started walking with Tony in the direction of the exit. Only Bob spoke as they walked away. "We will catch up with you later, Tony, we will call around."

As the others walked away they could hear the concerned mumblings of the group but both chose to ignore them. When they got back to Laura's car she rummaged in her bag to retrieve the keys and handed them to Tony to drive. Then she sat on the passenger seat, with her legs pulled up to her stomach, and they drove quietly back to Bristol. Tony was uneasy at the obvious discomfort that Laura was in, unsure as to what was really going on, but he trusted Laura enough to know she would tell him as soon as she was ready. As they pulled up outside the flat she uncurled her body, and leant across to put her head on Tony's shoulder. "I love you, you know."

"Is everything okay? I am here for you and want to help."

"Come on, take me home and I will explain later."

They walked across the road clutching each other as tightly as they physically could, and then once inside Laura went and showered and changed. When she emerged about 20 minutes later she had recovered a lot of her normal composure, but still looked noticeably paler than usual.

Tony was sat on the sofa in her living room and she sat down across his knees then leant her head back over the arm of the chair. As she lifted her head she ran her fingers through her hair, and spoke. "I owe you an explanation, don't I?"

"Kind of, but it's up to you."

"Aargh… Don't be so bloody nice to me, that is how I got into this mess."

Tony didn't respond but waited for Laura to continue.

She smiled at him then shook her head. "The reason that I have somehow fallen head over heels for you, Mr Alford, is that you let me be me without feeling pity for me. Most people cannot wait to find out all the gory details when I tell them I have been ill, and then they always look at me in a condescending pitiful way for evermore. You have never pitied me at all, and you have allowed me the luxury of being able to tell you things in my own time. You are always keen to know so much about me, and what I want, and what I have done each day. But it is always about me and not my illness and…"

"I knew you would tell me when you were ready, but it somehow didn't seem to be a part of the person that I knew. It was kind of all something in your past," replied Tony, feeling that he had to justify his apparent lack of interest.

"God I hope you are right, for both of our sakes." Laura wiped a small tear away from the corner of her eye before it had time to trickle down her face and all the while Tony was getting an increasing sense of anguish.

"Look, we can do this another time if you would prefer." As he said the words he really didn't know who he was offering comfort to.

In some ways it felt like a cop-out on his part, backing away from the pain of reality, but at the same time he wanted to save Laura from any more.

"No, it's okay, and anyway there is nothing to worry about really. I was diagnosed with leukaemia about 18 months ago, and after a couple of periods in hospital and extensive treatment I recovered, and my blood counts and everything built up again. Then over the last six months with my running and so on I have nearly got back to full strength."

"So are you fully recovered?" Tony knew that his question sounded a bit lame, but he was desperate for her to say yes and at the same time he was only just digesting what he had just been told.

Laura heaved a big sigh, and ran her fingers through her hair again. "That is the problem, it hangs around you like a death sentence. Every time I get a cold, headache or bad stomach I think it has come back, and the doctors won't give me the all clear for another year or so yet... Even then I don't know if it will ever go away."

Tony shook his head, half in disbelief at what he was hearing, and half to give him more time. "I really don't know what to say. I am sorry, but not in a pitiful way, I just don't think you deserve all of this shit. At the same time I am angry with myself for not realising sooner that you were not 100% today. I suppose I feel really shallow and a bit out of my depth."

They sat in silence for a moment then Laura held out her hand. "Hey, we should be out on the town tonight celebrating your sixth place."

Tony took her outstretched hand and spoke again. "Promise me two things: one, you have to tell me everything that is happening from now on."

"Okay."

"And two, I don't want any of this to change the way we are or where we are going. I want to build a life with you, and if I get scared at any point just remind me of this moment here and now, because I want to be there whatever happens, and no matter how difficult our future is."

This time Laura left the tears to trickle down her face as she leant forward to Tony. They embraced and kissed passionately, before she pulled away, smiling at him as though an enormous burden had been lifted from her shoulders. "I don't know where I found you, you know."

"Number seven next door, remember?" They were both smiling now, reflecting the joy that they felt from each other's company. The future was just that, and for now they were both basking in the present knowing that they had each other and a bond that was strong enough to see them through.

Eight o'clock came around all too soon, and Laura went off to pack a few things whilst her parents sat in the lounge discussing the day's events with Tony.

"So are you off out celebrating tonight then, Tony?" asked Brendan, as much to make conversation as anything else.

"No, the big party is Saturday night, and then it's all study unfortunately before our summer exams."

"Ah yes, the party that Laura is determined to get back for. We will do what we can but no promises."

They all sat through a few minutes of awkward silence before Brendan started another conversation. "You must thank Bob and Paula for us, they paid for a wonderful meal."

"Yes, I am sorry we had all planned to eat out, but I hope to take you out next time we meet," replied Tony.

"That's okay." Then after a few moments' silence it was Brendan who made the effort again. "So I understand you have a brother living in Spain, Graham isn't it?"

Before he could reply Caroline interrupted. "Leave the poor boy alone, Brendan, you are not at work now."

Feeling a strange degree of tension in the air, Tony did reply. "Yes I do, he runs a night club out there."

"You see, I am only trying to be polite." Brendan was responding to his wife who had crossed her arms and had a distinctly unimpressed look on her face.

"I am sorry, Tony, My husband can never leave the police behind.

He doesn't mean to interrogate you. He has no real manners, it is his way of trying to be nice."

Fortunately Laura walked in at that moment and sat down on Tony's lap. "Dad, you are not giving Tony the third degree are you? He is not a suspect, just my boyfriend." The broad grin across her face betrayed the obvious closeness between Laura and her father, which was reciprocated as he stood up and walked over to them.

"Well, I am sorry but any man who steals my daughter's heart requires a full interrogation."

"Dad, you are so corny sometimes. Come on, I am going in the car with Mum, and you can drive my car back so that I will be able to bring it back on Saturday."

With that they all said their goodbyes and made their way out to the cars. Tony waved them off and then walked back across the road to his flat. As he walked in the overwhelming temptation was just to head past the living room door and straight for his bedroom. Instead he went and joined the others.

The results had apparently gone well during the afternoon; Bristol had moved up from third to second in the table, and an overall win was now firmly within their grasp. Tony stayed for a while, but with so much more than the outcome of the trials to contend with he retired to his bedroom as soon as he felt he could.

The next 24 hours dragged like no other, and Tony felt very isolated as he dealt with them on his own. He really wanted to share what he was going through with someone, be it Laura, Charlotte, James or Paul, but it wasn't possible. He telephoned Laura's home several times during the day, to no avail, and eventually got a phone call back at about 9pm. He had dozed off in the seat with the telephone in his hand, and was startled by its ringing. "Hello?"

"Tony, is that you?"

"Hi Laura, how are you?"

"Not too bad, we have just got back from the hospital, and I get some of my results tomorrow, but they basically think I am in pretty good shape."

"I could have told them that."

"Thank you. I thought that you would be at the uni. bar tonight. Did we win overall?"

"No, but it was a good second place. Everyone except James seems quite content with that. The rest have gone to the bar but I wanted to speak to you." There was a moment's silence before Tony carried on. "So do you think you will make it back tomorrow?" He didn't want to sound insensitive by asking, but he really was missing Laura and wanted to say so many things that had come into his head over the last day. He knew he should have said a lot of them before but he hadn't realised himself how much she meant to him.

"Yes, I promise. I really missed you today."

"Me too. More than you can possibly imagine," replied Tony. He wanted to continue but Laura interrupted.

"I am sorry to be a pain but Dad has just got back with a takeaway, so I had better go and get something to eat… By the way, Mum and Dad both really liked you yesterday, and want you to come away with us at Easter."

"Yeah, great." Tony couldn't stop the smile on his face, as a lot of the tension from the last day ebbed away. It was daft but it meant a lot that Laura's parents liked him. "Where?"

"Our holiday cottage in Cornwall. I will explain tomorrow. I must go now."

"Okay, see you tomorrow." Tony hesitated then added, "I really love you." He had wanted to say it for so long, planning it all day in his head, and yet he was worried now that it sounded slightly pathetic.

"Aahh… I love you too, and I desperately want to be with you tonight, but it will make tomorrow more special. Just wait and see… I have to go, bye."

It sounded so much better coming from Laura.

"Bye, see you tomorrow."

There was a brief moment's hesitation then Laura spoke. "You haven't put the phone down."

"You first," replied Tony.

"Look, I have to go, my dad is shouting for me downstairs. On the count of three, okay, both phones down together. One… two…

229

Love you… three."

"Hello?"

"Tony, I said put the phone down on three." Laura was giggling now despite the shouts from her parents.

"Okay, this time for real. One… love you too… three." Tony pressed the red button on the handset and snuggled down into the seat. He couldn't wait for Saturday night, but with the exertion, both physically and mentally over the last couple of days suddenly catching up with him he drifted off to sleep.

Laura meanwhile waited for the buzz of the phone to indicate that Tony had rung off then lay back on her bed staring out of the window. She could hear footsteps approaching, and knew from the weight of them that it was her father.

"I didn't think you were ever going to get off that phone, so I brought yours up for you."

"Thanks Dad, I was just talking to Tony," said Laura.

"That's okay. I wanted a quick chat with you on your own anyway. I know we said it earlier but I liked Tony, and his friends. You can tell a lot about a man from his friends, you know."

"Yes Dad," replied Laura with an exaggerated sigh.

"Mind you, I still cannot believe you had to choose him out of all the men at that university." Brendan shook his head as he spoke to feign annoyance.

"Sorry," replied Laura with a half-hearted shrug of her shoulders that belied the apology she had just offered.

"What have you told him?" asked Brendan as he moved over and sat on the edge of her bed.

"That I love him and hopefully it is going to be all right."

"No, you know what I mean."

"Nothing, don't worry," replied Laura. They both sat in silence, deep in their own thoughts, and didn't notice that Caroline was now stood in the doorway. After a few minutes she coughed and broke the silence. "Sorry to interrupt this father and daughter moment."

Laura stretched her arms out, indicating to her mother to come forward for a cuddle. "Thanks to both of you for all of your support again. I still need you, you know, even with Tony."

"We know, and the two of you do seem to have something special there. I just hope Tony can cope with whatever might come over the next few months. I knew straight away with your dad that he was the one for me but I don't know if he was mature enough to cope with all of this back then." Caroline stood in the doorway for a moment longer and then moved over to accept the cuddle on offer from her daughter.

Laura wiped her eyes with the back of her hand. "I will be fine, just wait and see. Anyway, Dr Preston said I am doing fine."

"He also said you have got to slow down and let your body recover properly, and you have a long way to go before he gives you the all clear. So eat up and bed." Brendan was wagging his finger, pretending to be the stern father, but Laura knew better. She stuck her tongue out and blew a loud raspberry before picking up the plate he had brought and starting to eat.

It was nearly one o'clock before she eventually got to bed, and no sooner had her head touched the pillow than she fell into a deep sleep.

Tony was awakened at about the same time as James and Paul crashed into the living room. Charlotte had apparently gone back for the night with Bob and Paula so that she could see her mother and the two lads had been out on a heavy drinking session.

"Where were you, mate? We missed you." James staggered around the room as he tried to open the conversation with Tony then fell into the chair.

"Yeah, you should have been there, mate, you will never believe who has got the hots for you." By the look on his face Paul was bursting to tell him a name, but clearly wanted to play a guessing game first.

Not really in the mood to play games and stone cold sober, Tony feigned disinterest. "What?"

"Mate she is so fit it is unreal, and she fancies you." Paul was obviously far more excited about the whole thing than Tony was. "And they are coming around here in a minute so you had better liven up a bit."

Suddenly his heartbeat was racing away. It was flattering to be told that someone fancied you, but this was the last thing he wanted right now. "Who is coming around?"

"Victoria," replied James as he tried to suppress a yawn, "and she is bringing her little sister Rachel for you, you little stud."

Tony had to admit she was absolutely stunning, and on any other day he would have jumped at the chance to see her, but not today. "But that's ridiculous, and anyway I am going out with Laura."

"Aaahh well while the cat's away," answered Paul, with a broad grin on his face.

James meanwhile leant over and grabbed Tony's arm. "You see, mate," he was slurring his words, and seemed to take an eternity to make his point, "women are like number nine busses, never there when you need them, then queuing round the block to take your money when you have found a taxi."

"He's right," nodded Paul. "And that is the problem with taxis. Too bloody dependable, and who wants dependable when you can just jump on and off a bus at every stop... bit like a bus really, and the taxi need never know."

"Exactly!" agreed James.

Tony had lost the plot ages ago, and was clearly enjoying the whole conversation far less than other two. Deciding that avoidance was definitely the best policy, he stood up and headed for bed.

"You get yourself ready, mate. We will send her in when she gets here, don't worry!" shouted Paul as he left.

Tony quickly got ready for bed and sat propped up against his pillow for a few minutes thinking about all sorts of things. He briefly entertained ideas about Rachel coming into his bedroom, but in all honesty knew he didn't have the bottle for it anyway, even without Laura. He did listen out for the door, but only really to satisfy himself that no one was coming. Then he turned out his light, hoping deep down that it was all part of some elaborate joke they had dreamt up in the pub tonight, which would be long forgotten when they sobered up in the morning.

Fortunately the following morning did cast a fresh prospective on everything, and although there was much talk about the party, Rachel's name didn't come up at all. In fact both James and Paul only surfaced for brief spells in between nursing serious hangovers.

By late afternoon they had recovered fully, and fresh beers were on the go as they all started to get ready for the proper party tonight. Every time the telephone rang Tony rushed to answer it but none of the calls were from Laura.

Charlotte arrived back at about 6.30pm, having caught the train. The plan was to leave by seven o'clock, but with still no word from Laura Tony stayed behind. By nine o'clock there was still no word when the phone went.

"Laura?" questioned Tony.

"Thank God you are in." The shock of hearing Graham's voice sent Tony's heart racing, and as the adrenalin coursed through him his mind was scrabbling to keep up with the conversation. "I am in Ireland and I have tracked down Mum."

"You have what?" Tony could not believe what he was hearing.

"Listen, will you? This is important," continued Graham.

"But why?" interrupted Tony again.

"Because Tony, she is our mother, you little idiot. Don't you get it?"

Tony was about to answer with a definitive no before Graham continued. "The thing is, I have some really bad news. Mum is very ill. She is in a clinic just outside Dublin that treats alcoholics, only she is in a pretty poor state and only likely to survive another few days at most."

Graham paused, as if for dramatic effect, but Tony felt nothing. It wasn't that he didn't care, but he had mourned the death of his parents years ago, and he didn't want to start the whole process over again.

"Are you all right? I know it is a lot to take in." Graham had lowered his voice, and was talking more slowly, more sensitively now.

"Yeah, I am fine, but what am I supposed to do about it?" questioned Tony.

"Don't worry, I have checked the flights, and a plane leaves from Bristol airport for Dublin at 8.30 in the morning. I can buy you a ticket and meet you here in Dublin and take you to the clinic later on tomorrow. Just pack a few things tonight and get there by about 7.00 in the morning."

The anger was building in Tony the more his brother spoke. Above all else he hated being told what to do, and to have Graham running his life like this infuriated him more than anything. "I am not coming." Tony shocked himself after the words had come out. He knew that he said them forcefully by the way that Graham had stopped mid-sentence, and he waited for the backlash.

His hand holding the phone was physically shaking and he forced it against the side of his head to steady both his body and his nerves.

"This is not a matter of choice, you little shit. Our mother is dying, alone in hospital, and you are going to come over and face the truth whether you like it or not. I have had to protect you from the realities of life ever since you were born, and now it is your turn to grow up and face things like a man." Graham waited a few seconds, thinking that Tony was taking it all in and continued. "If you do not come over here straight away I swear I will make sure you pay for it. She is our only family and you don't ever, ever walk away from family when they need you."

"She did." Tony winced as he said the words, knowing it was definitely the wrong thing to say. Unfortunately Graham was the only person in the world who could make him this angry. He never argued with anyone else, but Graham was so single minded, and self-righteous about these things.

"You miserable bastard. Well if that is your attitude don't ever come to me for help no matter what trouble you are in. All I am asking is for you to come over here for one weekend of your life and see your own mother, your real mother, before she dies. Surely you can put your miserable little student life on hold, and miss the pub for two nights for the sake of the woman who was unfortunate enough to bring you into this world."

Realising the futility of the discussion Tony tried one last attempt to reason with Graham. "Look, I am sorry that she is dying, but I don't even remember her as a child. Bob and Paula raised me, and they are my parents. I don't want to go through the grief thing for nothing. I am sorry she is dying, really I am, but she means nothing to me, and that is the reality of the situation."

Rather than appease Graham he was more incensed than ever. "You are such a selfish little shit. All you ever think about is you and your bloody friends. You never have time for me, and—"

Tony knew he was not getting anywhere and slammed the phone down into its cradle. The silence was all around him, interrupted only by his own rapid breathing. The anger in him was boiling over and to vent his frustration he jumped up and started pacing around the room. He wasn't going anywhere in particular and he kicked out at the empty beer cans and anything else that was in his path. He could feel himself perspiring and he tore off his jacket and threw it onto the sofa. Suddenly the phone rang again, and he tentatively picked up the receiver. "Graham?"

"Tony, it's Paul. What are you still there for? You have got to come over here now, mate, Rachel looks absolutely stunning and she keeps asking after you."

"Yeah, I am just waiting for Laura, and anyway I am not interested in Rachel, I have already told you."

Little did he know it but Paul was seriously pushing his luck, and likely to get the brunt of the anger aimed at Graham if he wasn't careful.

"Forget about Laura, mate, she is just stringing you along, the party is—" A succession of quick beeps interrupted Paul, and then the line went dead. Tony was pleased that he had run out of money, and left him in peace. He waited for another quarter of an hour then decided to get some fresh air and went out for a walk. Not sure whether or not he would end up at the party, he just needed fresh air.

Once he was in the cool of the night his head began to clear, and he could think more rationally. He knew he was right to say no to Graham, but he wished he had kept his cool. Suddenly loads of rational things were coming into his head, but at the time he couldn't think of any of them, and then there was the added complication of Rachel, and why hadn't Laura phoned? Tonight was supposed to be all about them, and yet it had all gone so against the plans he had made in his head throughout the day.

He couldn't help shaking his head as he considered the irony of the whole situation. Why was life so complicated like this at the most inopportune of moments? Still deep in thought, he opened the door to the bar and walked in, not knowing what the next twist would be. He felt guilty but he didn't know why. He knew he was right about Ireland, he wasn't interested in Rachel, but this was his second night at home, and there was only so much partying he wanted to miss. Laura could surely have phoned if she had wanted to. By the time he reached the bar everyone around was clearly drunk already, and this did nothing to lift Tony's mood. James walked over and joined him as soon as he walked in.

"Just in time, mate, it is my round. What are you having?"

"Lager please… Where is everyone else?" enquired Tony, looking around.

"Over there, look." As James pointed to the other side of the bar, Tony immediately caught Rachel's eye and she smiled back.

"Look mate, is this thing with Rachel for real, because I am with Laura and all."

"Yeah, yeah, look, you take it all too seriously, I have told you before. She just wants a bit of fun, and you and Laura aren't exactly going anywhere. I am afraid to say you have done another Charlotte there, mate."

Tony sunk the pint that was in front of him in one and gave James the money to buy him another. "Look, you have to tell her that I am not interested. The Laura thing is a bit complicated, but she means a hell of a lot to me, and it is not another Charlotte."

"Really?" questioned James as he picked up his own pint.

"Really, and she has told me that she is really serious about us as well."

James nearly choked on his pint, and spat a mouthful of it out. "You haven't used the love word, have you?"

Tony didn't have to answer as even in the half-light of the bar James could see his friend's face going bright red.

"You really need taking in hand, mate. How many times have I told you? Never tell them that until you have at least slept with them." James was laughing, but seeing the serious expression on Tony's face he put a reassuring arm around his shoulder. "Don't worry Tony, I will square it with Rachel. Anyway, I think it is more Victoria's master plan for us all to go out as a foursome than anything else. Come over and enjoy the party and you will have to tell me what is going on tomorrow."

Tony nodded, wishing in a way that the two of them were back at the flat now so that he could explain everything. He didn't need James' approval, but he wanted to share the burden of what had gone on over the last few days with someone, and his best mate was by far the best person to do that with.

The rest of the evening flew by, and before they knew it the lights were coming on at one o'clock for everyone to go home. Tony had chatted briefly with Rachel, but largely managed to avoid her for most of the evening. In fact he would have stayed away altogether but couldn't resist when Paul started to chat her up. He knew she had been looking over at him all evening so deliberately waited until Paul was in full flow then walked over. Rachel immediately turned her full attention to Tony, and it made him feel good to see the look on his mate's face. As everyone finished their drinks and headed for the bar James put his arm around Tony's shoulder. "Are you coming into town with us? We are going clubbing. The Retro is open 'til 4am now?"

"No, I have had enough for one night, thanks. See you tomorrow."

"Everything is sound isn't it? With Laura and all." The rest of the group were beckoning them to hurry up and James put his hand up to them whilst he waited for a reply.

"Yes mate. Sound, there is just stuff to deal with. I will explain tomorrow."

"Okay, but it is nothing you can't handle is it?"

"No James, you are like an old agony aunt. Just go, will you? We will chat tomorrow."

James didn't wait to be told a second time and ran off to join the others. Tony waited for them to leave then walked back across to the flat on his own. He checked the answer phone, but there were no messages, so he opened a can of beer, flicked on the television and sat down on the sofa. He only intended to stay there for a few minutes but drifted off to sleep without realising it. He was awoken by the sound of the doorbell. He didn't realise what it was at first and stretched out an arm to switch off his alarm clock thinking in his semi-conscious state that he was in his own bed. With his arm outstretched he lost his balance and fell on to the floor, as he rolled off the sofa. He sat there for a few seconds trying to get his bearings then came around as the bell went again. He stood up then went to answer the door.

The bell went again on the way, and Tony noted from the clock that it was only 7am. Who could it be at this time in the morning? As he opened the door, he had a sudden sense of déjà vu, seeing Laura stood there smiling, dressed in a tracksuit just like on the first day that they met.

"Sorry I didn't make it last night, I was stuck at the hospital all day, then my car wouldn't start, and your phone was engaged for ages, and… you aren't mad at me are you?"

Tony couldn't hide the relief at seeing Laura again, and he was smiling as he replied. "No, of course not."

Laura lifted the bag in her hand. "I brought some breakfast, coffee and croissants from the bakers."

"Well you had better come in then."

Laura put her arms around Tony, hugging him as tightly as she could, then reached up and kissed him, before walking into the hallway. Tony closed the front door then turned to follow her. Laura stopped at the living room door and stretched out her arm, pulling the door closed beside her. "I thought we could have breakfast in bed, although it doesn't look like you made it there last night."

Tony looked down at his dishevelled clothes. "No, I uuhh fell asleep on the sofa, hoping you would phone."

Laura smiled a little nervously this time, "Well I am here now," and with that she walked on into Tony's bedroom. Once they were both inside she closed the door behind them then slipped out of her tracksuit and jumped under the covers. Tony undressed and jumped in beside her. "Don't you want your croissants?"

"That's not what I am hungry for right now," replied Laura as she leant across and pulled Tony in close to her naked body.

*

They stayed in bed until six o'clock that evening. It was a beautiful day for both of them, exploring, chatting, sleeping, making love and discovering as much about themselves as each other. They would have both stayed in bed longer, but the reality of the real world dawned as the evening darkness came through the windows. They both had a ton of work to catch up on as well as important lectures on Monday morning and so Laura went back to her flat in the early evening.

It was cold when she walked in but she hardly noticed, and sat down to write up the notes she had prepared a few days earlier. Predictably her parents phoned about nine o'clock to see if everything was okay, then by ten o'clock she had settled down for a long bath. By eleven o'clock she was in bed, warm from the bath, and the inner glow that she had carried with her all day, but she was missing Tony already. She didn't want to seem needy, but after a few minutes' deliberation picked up the telephone and called his flat.

Tony meanwhile had rattled through his work with undue haste then spent the evening discussing everything that had gone on over the past few days with James. As ever he was the perfect listener, and waited whilst Tony explained about Laura, and then the conversation with Graham before saying anything at all.

"I don't honestly know what to say about you and Laura, mate. If you need any support I will be here for you, but I think you have to deal with it as you see best, just make sure it is Laura the person you care for and not her illness. You think more than I do about relationships, and I sometimes wish I was more like you but I know for sure I would have run a mile by now."

"Don't worry, it is not about pity. I like Laura, end of story, and I will deal with her illness as and when," replied Tony. He sounded very matter-of-fact about it, but they both knew deep down that Tony knew little about what he was potentially taking on, and even less about how best to cope with the consequences.

"You don't have to justify it to me of all people, mate. But if you need any support you know where I am. As to Graham and your mum, do you think you said no because it was your brother asking, or should I say telling you what to do, or because you genuinely didn't want to get involved at this late stage?"

Tony hated the way that James always looked at things so differently. If only they were brothers, they would never argue like he did with Graham because you could always have sensible logical discussions with him. Whenever Tony had his mind firmly set on a course James could always give an alternative viewpoint without ever actually being confrontational. On this occasion, however, it was not enough to sway him.

"You are right, and if it had been anyone else asking I would probably have gone. But the point is I still think I have made the right decision on this occasion. Maybe for the wrong reasons, but the right decision nonetheless."

"Just as long as it isn't something that you are going to have around your neck for the rest of your life, and that is even without Graham bringing it up at every opportunity." As he finished James stood up and walked to the kitchen before turning back. "Beer?"

Trying hard to stifle a yawn, Tony shook his head. "No thanks mate, I am going to get an early night." As he stood up the telephone rang and he picked up the receiver. "Hello?"

"Tony, our mum died at 3.52 this afternoon. I have a few things to sort out in Ireland then I will be back over next week sometime. Tell Bob and Paula. They want to arrange a service at the church for us."

Before he could gather his thoughts Graham had put the phone down at the other end and Tony was left holding the receiver completely at a loss as to what to say or do.

"Bloody hell, mate, she hasn't dumped you already, has she? And by phone for that matter," laughed James from the kitchen.

Tony shook his head, still holding onto the receiver as though Graham was about to speak again and fill in all of the blanks. "No, no it was Graham, Mum died this afternoon." His heart was pounding away in his chest, but it was somehow out of shock more than grief. Ever since that letter had arrived on his 18th birthday Tony had been very confused about his feelings towards his mother. Part of him had wanted to find her, but it wasn't a priority, and with so much more to deal with on a daily basis he was happy to leave it until he was older. Now, however, the chance had gone, the finality of death hit hard and yet deep down he was kind of relieved that fate had dealt its hand and defined that part of his life. The chapter was now closed, and apart from the repercussions from Graham he knew he could cope better with the situation now.

Still deep in thought he slowly replaced the receiver and jumped backwards, dropping the entire phone as it immediately rang again. With his blood pulsing through his entire body he scrabbled on the floor and picked it up again. "Hello, sorry I dropped the phone." His throat was desperately dry, and as he waited for the person on the other end to speak.

"Hi Tony, it's me, I wondered if you fancied coming over to spend the night here tonight."

"Uummm." Tony didn't mean to sound hesitant, but he was still thinking about the brief conversation with Graham, and thousands of thoughts were racing through his mind. Would there be a proper funeral, and if so where? Was that what Graham was organising, and would he deliberately exclude Tony after their argument last night? Then when Laura spoke again he could sense the hurt in her voice.

"You don't have to, I just thought..."

Sensing the upset in her voice brought back his focus, and he explained about the phone call from Graham. They talked for a few minutes on the phone then he grabbed a bottle of wine and went around to her flat. As they lay in bed drinking Tony explained all about his past, and although Laura had heard some of it before she listened intently to everything he had to say. They chatted together for several hours before tiredness took over, and Laura drifted off gradually to sleep. Tony knew in his body that he was desperately tired but his heart was still pounding away, and his mind was far too active to allow him to settle.

With Laura in his arms he felt strangely at ease and it was as though in the space of 12 hours one part of his life had achieved fulfilment as another was brewing up into a storm. He knew that when Graham returned later in the week there would be a massive row, and he went over all the possible connotations in his head, trying to ensure that no matter what his brother said he would remain calm.

Above all else he knew that he was right not to go last night. His lasting memory of his mother would have been of a very poorly and frail old lady, and yet as he tried to conjure up a better picture of her he couldn't. Everyone had always said that she had been very pretty, but he could only really remember having seen the one picture of his parents as a young couple, and he couldn't recreate that image in his head, no matter how hard he thought of it. They were often talked about as perfect, with a perfect marriage before alcohol had apparently taken hold of his mother, but he knew very little else about them. And who were the people who had talked about them? Tony was trying to piece together snippets from his past and make sense of it all. Bob and Paula obviously hadn't known his parents, and Tony couldn't remember much about his previous carers, so where were these memories coming from. Were they just the wishful fantasies of a young boy carried into his adult life?

As Laura slept peacefully Tony tried to imagine what his mother went through. How would he feel if one day he were responsible for Laura's death? They had only really been together for a day, but he knew that their bond was something very special. Something he would never recreate if for any reason he lost her. The physical attraction he had that first day had grown into so much more over the last few months, to a point where it was consuming his entire emotions. Every time they were together his heart felt like it was glowing hot in his chest, growing stronger at the same time as it was bonding with Laura's.

As he lay in the half-light of the flat, and almost without realising it he shed a single tear that rolled along the bridge of his nose and dropped gently onto Laura's cheek. Sensing a wave of tiredness taking over his body Tony gently kissed the back of her head, then rested on the pillow and drifted off to sleep. Without opening her eyes Laura carefully lifted her hand and gently wiped the tear away before lowering her hand and pressing it gently against her own lips, kissing the soft pad of her middle finger and savouring the very essence of Tony.

CHAPTER 12

The Truth

As it transpired there was no big confrontation with Graham, because he had to fly straight from Ireland back to Spain on some urgent business. Although partly relieved, there were a great many questions that Tony wanted answered and he felt that he and his brother needed the opportunity to sit down and discuss them. With Easter only a few weeks away Bob and Paula suggested that a memorial service be held at the local church during the break, which Graham agreed to fly back and attend.

Most people had already made their own plans, but Charlotte, James, Paul, and Laura all made sure that they were free to come on the day. Graham arrived back with Mark the night before, and apart from a lot of small talk didn't really get involved in any meaningful conversations at all. He did, however, invite just about everyone over to Spain during the summer holidays for as long as they wanted to stay. Apparently there was plenty of bar work available if needed, but equally there was the offer of free accommodation, and plenty of excitement. Tony sat at the front next to Graham, disappointed to note as he glanced around the congregation that there were only ten people including him in church. Of those, two were his foster parents who didn't even know his mother and four more were his own friends who were there to support him. His whole body was tensed to the point of snapping, and he kept rolling his head to relieve the aches between his shoulder blades. Saddest of all he knew that his stress was born more out of pity than grief. How could a life amount to so little?

Try as he might Tony could not keep his focus on the service, and he found his mind planning the revision that he had to do over the rest of the holiday, rather than grieving for his mother. He kept looking at the pictures that had been placed on the altar, but in truth they could have been anyone in the world and it would have meant nothing less. The eyes had a hint of familiarity about them, and he tried to imagine that they were looking down on him favourably but his thoughts were soon drifting away again…

Laura was taking him down to her parents' cottage in Devon later that day, and they were to spend a week down there enjoying the coast. The thought of a week's holiday, albeit with revision thrown in, relaxed his whole body, and he could slowly feel the tension unwinding. Warm sunshine was filling the church from behind the altar, almost as if his mother's final wish was for him to get away and enjoy the break.

Suddenly without warning Graham stood up and removed some papers from his inside pocket. He turned around to address the small assembled crowd, and looked purposefully from one to another. Tony instinctively pulled himself up and sat rigidly on the pew.

"I have prepared a few words in order to celebrate the good that came from my mother Elizabeth's life," began Graham, before pausing to gauge the reaction.

Tony wanted to look around, but the absolute silence told him that everyone else was as surprised as he was at Graham's action. The entire congregation, small as it was, seemed to be collectively holding its breath, and Tony felt sure they could all hear his heart beat over the stunned silence. If anything the lack of numbers in the audience seemed to heighten everyone's attention level.

"Many of you are here today out of a sense of duty to Tony, and myself, and from the facts that you have heard over the years will find it difficult to spare my mother any emotion at all. Far from being some heartless drunk who was responsible for the death of my father, and then abandoned her children, Elizabeth was a kind, loving and devoted parent."

There was a hushed silence around the church, and Tony could sense that a number of people, including him, were shifting uncomfortably on their pews. What on earth was Graham up to, and what was the point of it all? Sensing the dramatic impact of his opening lines Graham had paused for almost a minute then he purposefully cleared his throat and continued.

"After her death I went through the small suitcase that contained her entire worldly possessions, and found a pile of well-worn love letters written between my parents from the day they met, as well as the diaries that they meticulously kept between them. Many of the pages were stained from the tears that Mum had obviously shed over the years since my father's death, but their entire life together is laid out page by page.

"They met on Mum's first day at university, and to mark their first month together my dad bought a diary that they vowed to keep between them each day. At night they would put an individual entry in about their day, as well as a joint one about the time they had spent together. Any rows they had, and there were very few, were resolved in the joint entry, and they both signed off each day with the words 'Good night my one and only true love'.

They battled against their own families from the outset with Dad coming from a long line of strict Presbyterians, whilst Mum was an Irish Catholic. In a way it is difficult to imagine today they were virtually cut off from their families because of their relationship, but this only strengthened the bond they had. Their only concern, however, was each other, and from the day that they first met they were absolutely devoted, in a way that I imagine very few couples ever achieve. Dad desperately wanted a huge family, mainly to celebrate his absolute devotion to Mum, and when they married after graduating they tried to have children straight away. Unfortunately Mum had a couple of miscarriages and their first child, a girl they named Laura, was stillborn.

"Even through these testing times, their parents never offered them any support at all, and Mum and Dad had to deal with it all alone. Despite all of these difficulties they never once wavered in their love for each other, and carried on trying for a family, but with each setback it is possible to see my mother's joy of life very slightly ebbing away, in the way she wrote in her diary."

As Graham paused for a few moments to gather himself you

could hear a pin drop in the church. The emotion that had been so lacking earlier was literally overpowering the assembled few, and Tony was now so focussed that the tears trickling down his face didn't even register. The mention of a sister called Laura had sent a shiver down his spine. He so desperately wanted to look back and see his own Laura, but his body wouldn't move, and he was so focused on his brother that he had to make a conscious effort just to breathe.

"It was only a year after that when I was born, and the joy that I apparently brought was quite overwhelming. The entries in the diary had dwindled to only a few lines each day, but then after my birth they were each writing two or three pages every night. This carried on for months as Mum in particular charted my progress no matter how minute, in elaborate detail. My grandparents never made any effort to meet me, however Mum did secretly communicate and send photos back to Ireland via her aunt.

Despite that, this period was definitely the happiest in both of their young lives, and their mutual love continued to flourish within their own family unit. A couple of years later they had twins, who they named Tony, and apparently as a means to come to terms with their earlier loss, Laura again."

Tony could sense his heart was about to explode as the blood pumped faster and faster around his body. He had been forcing his breathing for the last few minutes to keep up with his body's demands for oxygen, but it was all getting too much. He tried to slow his breathing down, for fear that everyone would hear him, and as he did so felt the world around him go into soft focus as his eyes then began to close involuntarily. The tranquillity this brought was like a release, and he allowed the moment to linger, as he did so he felt his whole body go limp and slump forwards off the pew. He did not notice the harshness of the stone floor as he lay seemingly asleep for a few minutes of complete tranquillity.

As he came around it felt just like waking in the morning but Tony was also immediately aware of his surroundings and above else felt acutely embarrassed. He looked at his brother, but Graham stood impassively at the front, without even trying to hide his obvious annoyance at being interrupted. Tony lifted his right arm up to the seat in an effort to get back up but his whole body felt like jelly, and Bob who was now beside him laid a hand on his shoulder and whispered for him to wait a moment. Rather than come over Graham had now moved behind the lectern and he waited until Tony was seated, then purposefully coughed, and continued as though nothing had happened. Tony was both embarrassed and annoyed, and at the same time he knew that Graham was milking the moment for all it was worth. He had no doubt that the revelations were factual enough, but the way that Graham was delivering them was his way of getting back at his brother for not going to Ireland when he had told him that their mother was dying. Graham loved controlling events, being the archetypal big brother, which meant that right now he was in his element. Tony had already given him the smug satisfaction that he sought, and tried to look as impassive as possible through the rest of the speech.

"Laura unfortunately did not survive beyond a couple of weeks, although I am not sure of the exact details, but she was unwell from the day she was born. Tony of course did survive, but with the strain now of two children, plus the tragic daughters she had lost, Mum's mental health deteriorated. What was most probably some form of postnatal depression took a hold of her, and at the time there was very little support for women with such conditions. Mum for her part loved both of us as well as Dad, and turned to drink as a means of presenting a relaxed and happy façade to the outside world.

"At the time of the car accident Mum had been drinking, but she did not fail the breath test, and the police did not feel it appropriate to prosecute her in any way. Dad's family, however, dragged her through the courts in a private prosecution, which was eventually thrown out. To them any drink was the route of all evil, and they could never find it in themselves to forgive Mum because of the son they lost."

Graham folded up the papers that were in his hand and put them into his jacket pocket. Tony sensed that his brother knew an awful lot more, but with everyone's minds reeling already it was best that things were left as they were for now.

After leaving the small congregation to contemplate their thoughts for a few minutes the priest stood up, and slowly brought the service to a conclusion. They sang a final hymn, and then most people made their way out of the church. Tony, however, sat quietly at the front staring at the pictures in front of him. The longer that he studied them the more familiar the images became, and yet at the same time the more distant as well. He really resented the way that Graham had told everyone the truth so publicly, without giving him the chance to deal with the turmoil in advance. Tony liked to compartmentalise his feelings, and until today his mother had been in a virtual cold locker marked 'do not disturb'. Graham had not only opened the door, but he had taken in warmth and released curiosity like the opening of Pandora's Box.

Eventually the curiosity lifted him off his pew, and enticed him towards the pictures on the altar. Tony picked them both up and studied them carefully, stroking the sides of his mother's cheeks as though this would help him to communicate with her. Part of him wanted to run out of the church and get as far away as possible, and part of him wanted to stay there alone forever. He didn't notice the tears until they dripped onto the face of his mother. Strangely the drop of water then held a fascination all of its own. At first it sat like a raindrop on the picture glass, but then it swelled as another tear fell, and started to slide effortlessly down, until it rested against the frame at the bottom.

The muffled voices outside had moved away, probably to Bob and Paula's already for the food that they had put on, and the quiet was only broken by the quiet swish of the door as someone came in, and sat on one of the pews at the very back. Tony turned his head to the left side, but not far enough around to actually see who had entered, and then back to the front again as though the pictures were now demanding his attention. He felt the same inner tranquillity he had felt earlier each time he blinked his eyes, but now he was fighting the urge rather than allowing it to take over. He turned his head slightly again, this time to the right. The reluctance to turn back had gone and he gradually turned his whole body until he could see Laura sat alone at the back of the church. She moved the corners of her mouth into a faint smile that conveyed so much more than mere words ever could as Tony turned again to look back at the pictures. His past of which he knew so little was at the front of the church and his future that promised so much was at the back. The two halves of him would never truly meet and yet their influences were so entwined.

After allowing himself a further few minutes of contemplation he moved slowly forward and collected the two frames that he tucked under his arm then walked up the aisle to Laura.

As he approached she turned slightly then they linked arms together, and Laura rested her head on Tony's shoulder but they did not speak as they left the church and walked down through the village. On their way to Bob and Paula's Tony couldn't help but notice how life for everyone else was just proceeding like any other day. He wanted to grab the first person they met and tell them about his day but he knew that there was no point. For them this really was just another day in their lives, and his personal anguish meant nothing. When they reached the front door Laura held his hand and spoke first. "It has been quite a day so far, are you okay?"

Tony smiled and nodded. "Yeah, I am fine, and anyway I have got my one and only true love to support me."

*

The rest of the afternoon passed with surprisingly little incident. But even so, by the time that Tony and Laura got in the car to leave he felt absolutely drained. Fortunately Laura drove, and within minutes of setting off Tony had fallen asleep. When he awoke a couple of hours later, it was nearly dark outside, and they were driving down a pot-holed track, swerving occasionally to miss the worst of the ruts. It was still quite warm in the car, but even so Tony felt an involuntary shiver go through his body as he awoke.

"Hello sleepy head, did I wake you up?" Laura looked across very briefly and smiled, before turning her attention back to the road ahead.

"Sorry if I have not been much company. And where exactly are we?" questioned Tony.

As he looked around he could make out very little about his surroundings. The car headlights were dancing around as they bumped along the track, but they offered little by way of illumination, as the lane was heavily overgrown on both sides. There was no moon tonight, and Tony was sure that they were the only life for miles around. Eventually the hedgerow thinned and a small row of cottages was visible. Laura drove around what looked like a small courtyard area, and pulled up outside the last cottage on the row.

"Home sweet home for the Scott family and of course you this week. Come on."

Before Tony could answer Laura had jumped out of the car and was at the front door opening it. As she turned the key in the lock, she beckoned Tony to hurry up with her other hand. In truth he was still half asleep, and having had no preconceived ideas about what the so-called Scott family holiday home was all about he was trying to get a bearing on his surroundings in the dim half-light. As he opened the car door the sudden smell of sea air, and the sound of lapping waves behind him made him jump.

Tony took a moment then jumped out of the car, and stared into the dark night sky, trying to get some kind of fix on where exactly he was. He squinted with his eyes trying to focus, but the salt in the air was forcing him to blink involuntarily and he was no better off. The wind had a chill edge to it, and he could feel it cutting straight through the thin jacket that he was wearing, then he felt the warmth of Laura snuggling in as she came up from behind and put her arms around him.

"I so want you to love this place. I have loved it all my life and I want to bring my children here one day so that its sheer beauty can mesmerise them. Nothing intrudes on life here except the forces of nature, we are cut off from the turmoil of the outside world, and time becomes irrelevant. This is the best place in the world for you to deal with the loss of your mum, it is like a place of sanctuary, and I am so happy to share it all with you."

As Tony listened to the wind bustling around them, and the gentle lapping of the waves he could sense exactly what Laura meant. He could almost imagine nature whispering in the breeze, "Tony and Laura, Tony and Laura," and with his eyes still straining against the dark, he could feel tears starting to fall gently down his cheeks. After standing for a few minutes Tony gently turned and leant down to kiss Laura. Her cheeks felt moist from her own tears, and they both burst out laughing as they each raised a hand to dry their faces.

"Come on, you, this is a happy place, don't make me cry," and with that she grabbed his hand and ran inside.

Brendan and Caroline had obviously gone to bed already, but there was a note placed prominently on the kitchen table that Laura picked up and read out loud.

"Hope your journey down was good. Dad and I have gone to bed, because we have a lot of driving to do tomorrow. There are some sandwiches in the fridge and a half-empty bottle of wine as well if you fancy it. I have made up the spare room for Tony." Laura looked up from the note, with a frown. "Sorry, Mum is a bit old fashioned, but it will only be for tonight, I promise."

"That's okay." Tony's heart was pounding away in his chest, as the day's varying emotions had taken their toll, and despite the long sleep in the car he was still drained. The love he had for Laura was enormous, and the more they were together the stronger his feelings became. But for all of that he was happy to sleep alone tonight.

"Oh, and she sends her love, and hopes it all went okay today at the service for your mum."

Despite not feeling hungry they quickly demolished the plate of sandwiches and the rest of the wine, then sat quietly in front of the glowing embers of an open fire. It was a large cottage, dominated downstairs by a massive open fireplace that you could literally crawl into. To one side of the fireplace was the dining area, with a soft leather suite at the other end of the room. Around behind the fireplace the kitchen and hallway, as well as a flight of open tread stairs leading to the upstairs.

Laura threw some cushions onto the floor, and they lay down in front of the glowing fire. Apart from the occasional crackle from the embers they sat in silence, both lost in their own thoughts. Tony tried not to dwell on the revelations of the day, and instead thought of the relaxing few days that they would have together over the coming week. The clock above the fire was approaching 1am. He needed more sleep but his whole body felt tense, and his stomach felt like it had been knotted for an eternity. Laura's breathing was deepening, as Tony felt that she was slowly drifting off, but he didn't really have any inclination to go to bed just yet.

The wisps of smoke were winding their way up the chimney, and with every slight draught in the room another part of the fire would glow from amber to red, then slowly flicker and fade away. In the half-light of the fire Tony's gaze drifted up to the clock on the wall, and he counted down the last few seconds to one o'clock. As the second hand swept relentlessly on he convinced himself that he would go up to his room as soon as it reached the hour. Tick tock, tick tock, he was nodding his head to match the rhythm, when suddenly there was a mass of bells from outside that made him jump up. Laura rolled off his lap, and with half closed eyes propped herself onto one hand. She took a moment to come to then smiled at Tony, who had the appearance of a startled rabbit. "It's only the clock tower outside on the square, don't look so scared."

Thankfully she couldn't see his face blush in the dim light, but he still felt the need to explain himself. "Sorry but I thought it was an alarm or something. And anyway the clock says it is one o'clock, and I have counted eleven chimes so far."

"And twelve," chorused Laura as the bell struck again and went silent. "It's all part of our smugglers' heritage, I am afraid. I will explain tomorrow, don't worry. There really is so much for you to see and me to tell you about. I am shattered now though so let me show you your room."

Normally curiosity would have made Tony beg for more details, but for now he was happy to just pick up his holdall of clothes and follow Laura up the stairs. Once in his room he brushed his teeth at the sink stood against the end wall, and jumped into bed. He always felt a little uneasy going to sleep in other people's houses, unsure as to the protocol the following morning, or indeed if he were to need the bathroom in the middle of the night. After the events of the day though such issues were soon forgotten as his mind cleared and he drifted into sleep. There was no time for go-to-sleep thoughts tonight, and in any event Tony had everything he wanted right now in the bedroom across the landing.

*

He woke early the following morning and lay awake for just a few minutes before the clock tower started chiming.

"One, two, three, four, five, six," he counted to himself in a hushed whisper, then on the final chime he slid out of bed and looked out of the bedroom window. It was quite blowy outside, but being at the back of the house he couldn't see any of the coastline at all. He had woken in a very positive frame of mind and wanted to move on from the stresses of the last few weeks. He knew deep down that there were issues relating to his mother and father that emotionally he would need to address at some time, but he wasn't ready yet. Yesterday in particular had been a real shock, and having to re-evaluate the past so publicly had not been easy. Tony knew that

Graham had deliberately dropped his bombshell in the way he did to gain maximum effect, but even so it had effectively altered every value that Tony had established in his past life. He had never hated his mother for what happened, in fact he didn't really think that hatred was an emotion he knew at all, but he had chosen to remain indifferent to her, and until yesterday that was so much easier. The diary had definitely been like opening Pandora's Box in that it had released a real person, who was not only faultless in his father's death, but warm, loving, and caring in her own right.

Now wasn't the time to deal with all this though, and Tony decided that a run along the beach was the best way to blow away the cobwebs and refocus. If this place meant so much to Laura it had to be special and he wanted his senses to soak up all that was on offer so there was no room left to dwell on the past. He pulled his bag from under the bed, dressed in a T-shirt and shorts, donned a pair of trainers and crept quietly downstairs. It was early yet and no one else would be up for a couple of hours at least, so he tiptoed through the lounge towards the front door. Getting up at six in the morning could seriously damage his student credentials, but right now that didn't matter.

"Morning Tony, are you leaving us already?"

"Shit." The sounded of Brendan's voice nearly scared the life out of Tony, and realising he had just sworn in front of Laura's father he put his hand up to his mouth, then mumbled, "Sorry."

Brendan was in the kitchen, and he just smiled back. "Don't worry, I shouldn't have scared you. Do you fancy a partner for your run?"

No was the truthful answer, but Tony knew he couldn't add insult to injury, so he lied instead, "Yes, if you like, but I know it's very early, only I couldn't sleep."

"Don't worry, seven o'clock isn't early, I am not a student, remember. Just give me one minute and I will join you."

Tony was still trying to fathom out the time difference, as something resonated in the fog of his mind from last night, but when Brendan reappeared in running kit, and motioned towards the front door it was quickly forgotten.

"About the time, why did I just hear six chimes if it is seven o'clock?"

"The smuggler's curse. Don't worry, all in good time, Laura will explain," laughed Brendan, obviously delighted at the pun on time, as he opened the front door, and started to limber up.

"I normally do a 5K run if you like from here along the cliff top, then down to the beach, along the shoreline and back, or is that too tame for you?"

"No, that sounds just fine," replied Tony. "You lead and I will follow."

They set off a few moments later and ran for a good 30 minutes. Although virtually in silence Brendan did point out the odd local landmark on the way, then when they were down on the beach he slowed up and put both hands down to his knees, and bent over. "That's me done for I think. Let me get my breath back whilst you take in the beauty of Smuggler's Cove."

The area was indeed beautiful with a high cliff behind them rising up by some 20 to 30 metres, to the grassed area on top with the small group of cottages. They were arranged to reflect the concave shape of the beach below, with the slow-running clock tower in the middle about five metres from the cliff edge. On either side there were well-worn paths down to the small beach cove, and it was down one of these that they had both just run.

As Tony took in the symmetry of the two paths running down each side Brendan interrupted his thoughts. "It's a wonderful place, this, just to relax and unwind. After the stresses that you have had lately it should be the perfect place to relax before your exams start."

"Um yes, it certainly looks pretty amazing. Who else lives here, in the other cottages, and why don't they change the clock?"

"You obviously have a lot to learn, but the cottages are all owned by Laura. Her grandfather left them to her, and they have been in our family for the last 100 years or so. Apparently his grandfather was something of a smuggler, and he won them in a bare-knuckle fight on this beach many years ago. Well, that is the legend anyway." As Brendan finished, Tony could tell that he had told this story a hundred times before, and clearly relished the reaction that it provoked.

"And the clock?" questioned Tony.

"You will have to ask Laura, I am afraid. She will kill me if I tell you everything." Brendan paused for a few minutes then continued in a more serious tone. "If I was you I would take a few days off to spend together then get on with the serious work of revision. Laura thinks the world of you and you both need some time alone together. Caroline and I will be out of your hair later so please make the most of it."

"Thanks," replied Tony, "You and Caroline have been very generous."

"Not at all, as I said these are all Laura's houses... Anyway, I can only imagine that yesterday was really difficult, and you need to get over it in your own time."

Tony wasn't sure why he wanted to blurt out all of his frustrations now, and to Laura's dad of all people, but his mouth was working overtime before he had chance to fully engage his brain. "It would have been okay if Graham hadn't decided to drop several bombshells in the middle of the service. He obviously came across some things in Ireland that he then had to present to everyone in the most dramatic fashion possible."

"I am sorry," replied Brendan with a hint of genuine concern in his voice and that only encouraged Tony to ramble on more.

"The thing is, Mark was there as usual, and he had obviously put Graham up to it. Whenever they both work on something it is guaranteed to spell trouble."

"Mark Richardson?" questioned Brendan.

"Yeah," replied Tony, slightly taken aback. "How did you know that?"

"Oh it's nothing, Laura mentioned him before, and I have a head full of names. Occupational hazard, you know."

For some reason Tony had lost his train of thought completely now, and with the sweat on his body starting to chill in the light sea breeze he decided it was time to head back. "Shouldn't we make a move towards the cottage?"

"Good idea, and with a bit of luck breakfast will be ready when we get there," smiled Brendan, then almost as an afterthought, "Tell you what, I will race you there and the loser has to wash up afterwards."

Tony eyed up his adversary for a moment. There was clearly more to this man than met the eye, and he doubted that the run down here had barely tested him at all, despite his request to stop for a breather. Even so Tony was in good shape, and would take some beating to the top of the cliffs. "Okay then, I will go up the right-hand side of the cliff, you take the left, and I will see you there when you get there."

"Okay then, on three, we both go. One, two, three."

Tony didn't wait to be told again and tore across the sand as fast as he could. He knew better than to look back, and despite the difficult running on the dry sand he made good time across the beach, reaching the far end after about five or six minutes. He jumped over the few rocks at the base of the cliff and then scrabbled to get as good a grip as possible on the steep path leading up to the top. He reckoned that it was ten minutes at most as he reached the top, and without stopping he ran around the clock tower towards the house. As he came into the open there was no sign of Brendan, and he allowed himself a brief smile. Looking toward the house he could see Laura was up, and looked to be putting some breakfast things out on the table. He checked behind several times but still no sign, so he ran on quickly to the house, jumping the low fence on the way. It wasn't a huge distance but at the pace he had run Tony was completely out of breath as he arrived and allowed himself to fall to the floor as he landed.

"Here, you are I thought you might need a cold drink. Took your time though, didn't you?"

Tony blinked a couple of times partly because he was looking up at the bright sun, but more because his brain couldn't reason with what his ears were hearing. The smug look alone confirmed that it was indeed Brendan, but it was impossible. He was hardly even red let alone sweating and there was no way that his route was any quicker. As he tried to fathom the impossible Tony sat up and took the glass on offer without saying anything other than, "Thank you."

Everyone else was clearly in on the joke with Laura and her mother both sat at the patio table drinking glasses of orange juice trying hard not to laugh. Eventually Laura questioned, "Good run then?"

"Not bad." Tony thought for a moment and decided not to give them the pleasure of dwelling on the subject. "I could do with a shower though if you don't mind, before breakfast."

"Sure, carry on," replied Brendan. "Breakfast is nearly ready, I have had my shower but take your time."

Tony hadn't noticed before but Brendan clearly had wet hair, and although hastily he had obviously changed into fresh shorts and T-shirt as well. Without saying any more he stood up and went inside to get a towel from his bedroom. The outburst of sniggering could clearly be heard from the lounge as he walked through, and without intending to instinctively turned around. Brendan caught his eye and looked away just as Laura came running in through the door after him. She was smiling, but in a caring rather than mocking way and Tony could do nothing but smile back. He tried to act nonchalantly, but knew he wasn't the best at having jokes played on him, and wanted so desperately to find out how he had been beaten. "So are you going to let me in on the joke then?"

"Later, I promise." Laura was still smiling broadly, and the intense feelings he had felt last night were resurfacing throughout his body. They were holding each other's waists now and Tony could feel his heart racing away, butterflies dancing in his stomach, and a loving warmth coursing through his veins. They kissed briefly, before Tony pulled away and shook his head. "Sorry, no more of that until you tell me everything."

"Later. We have the place to ourselves for the rest of the holiday, because Mum and Dad are leaving in an hour or so, and I know it is going to be the best time ever." With that Laura stole another quick kiss then turned and walked towards the back, blowing another cheeky kiss and waving before sitting outside amidst further laughing and joking.

Tony showered as quickly as he could then he got dressed and came downstairs. Still trying to show he could accept defeat gracefully, he spoke first. "That was a good run, we will have to do it again some time," and he offered his hand in acknowledgement of defeat. This time though there was no laughter, and almost without looking up Brendan shook hands then motioned to the fried breakfast waiting for him.

The mood had clearly changed over the few minutes it had taken him to get ready, and it was deathly quiet as he sat eating. The other three stayed sat down but were determined not to meet each other's gaze, and Tony got the impression that he was at the centre of the trouble. "I am sorry if I kept you all waiting, I didn't mean to take too long in the shower."

Laura reached across and touched his hand. "It's not that," she volunteered, shaking her head. "Dad is insisting that I come down here this summer to manage the holiday lets, so I won't be able to come to Spain with you, I am afraid."

Before Tony could answer Brendan butted in. "As I said, these cottages are your responsibility now, not ours. They were not left to us, and it is time you took that on board, or sold them."

"No, Brendan, she cannot do that. My father would turn in his grave." It was Caroline's turn to jump in this time.

"I expect he is too busy stoking the fires below to care."

Although he had barely whispered the words, they provoked a strong reaction and Caroline pushed her plate into the middle, spilling a glass of orange all over her husband. "If you had learnt to separate your work and private life years ago the cottages wouldn't have been a burden on Laura anyway, so don't start interfering in her life as well, with your bloody bobby's hat on, and let her go to Spain. The sunshine will do her good."

Tony had never really seen Bob and Paula fight like this, and the tension made him feel extremely ill at ease. The prospect of a holiday in Spain this summer had only really come up at the memorial service a couple of days earlier, and although Charlotte, Paul and James had all made ambitious plans to be there he doubted it would happen. As he went to speak Tony choked, and could only manage a feeble cough. By now though all eyes were on him and for some inexplicable reason he could feel his face going bright red. He gulped down the rest of his orange as quickly as he could, and then cleared his throat. "To be honest Laura and I haven't really decided on Spain, and I would be more than happy to help out here through the summer if that is okay."

Tony looked around waiting for a reaction. Brendan and Caroline were locked in a fierce stare, both mentally daring the other to speak first. Laura had her head bowed slightly and mouthed simply, "I love you."

Eventually Brendan spoke. "Thank you, Tony. At least someone here understands responsibility, and I am sure your brother will be back over in the UK soon enough. And whilst I think of it Laura has to visit her doctor mid-August back at home and we will be away so I trust you can remember that for us as well, can you?"

"Dad," sighed Laura. "I am not a child, you know."

Tony just nodded and smiled to himself. The trip to Spain wasn't about seeing Graham. It was just to get some sunshine. Brendan seemed to think that as brothers they were much closer than they actually were, in fact whenever his name was mentioned Tony felt guilty that they weren't, but this didn't seem like the time or place to discuss it.

"Well perhaps they could go for the last couple of weeks of summer, after Laura has been to the hospital for her check-up." Caroline hadn't moved at all as she spoke, and was still staring intently at her husband.

Brendan was ignoring her though and looked over to Laura. "Maybe that could work, just check with me before you book anything." He paused for a moment before adding, "Promise."

After a brief hesitation Laura spoke. "Promise, Dad-dy." She put added emphasis on the final syllable to show that she was still unhappy at being treated like a baby but said nothing more. After another uncomfortable silence Brendan stood up, still apparently oblivious to his wife's ongoing stare. "I need to change I think," gesticulating to the large orange stain on his T-shirt, "then we can get off."

With that he picked up the empty plates and walked into the cottage, murmuring as he went. "Still, we shouldn't need the air con in the car, looks like it will be frosty enough."

Both Laura and Tony tried not to smile at the final comment but it did break the tension, and even Caroline picked up on it. "I will give him bloody frosty. Just wait till I get him in that car." Then looking to her daughter, "Why does your father have to interfere so? If only he got on with his life and left the rest of us to get on with ours the world would be a far better place for it."

"Yeah but you love him still despite his ways," replied Laura.

"Hummph." Then still shaking her head she turned to Tony. "Sorry about that, I didn't mean to get you dragged in. Brendan hasn't really got anything against you two visiting Graham. I'm sorry."

"That's okay." In truth Tony wasn't bothered about Graham at all, and couldn't understand what all the fuss was about.

Over the next hour they all helped clear away the breakfast things and pack up the car. Then it was time for the goodbyes, and before they knew it Tony and Laura were waving goodbye to her parents as their car sped away in a cloud of dust. Suddenly silence seemed to prevail and all that they could hear was their breathing in time to the gentle breeze, and the lapping of the waves on the seashore. The odd seagull squawked in the distance, but other than that it was as though they were the only two living creatures on the whole planet.

Laura stepped in closer and linked her arm around behind Tony's back. "Now our holiday can really start."

With that they turned and slowly walked back towards the cottage. Tony could again feel the glowing sensation in his body. Never having known such love before, he wondered if he would always feel this way when Laura touched him. How could this feeling ever fade and die? Did the drudge of daily routine gradually sap away the emotion until he would feel as cold meeting Laura as say a stranger in the street? When they reached the front door Laura turned and gently kissed Tony, then held him tightly in her arms for a moment. He could only follow his natural instinct, and moved his head slightly forward to kiss her again. He had only meant it to be a short kiss, but the passion they had for each other took over and they seemed to be locked together for an eternity. It wasn't a rough physical embrace, but wonderfully calm and gentle. Tony ruffled his fingers through her hair as he held Laura firmly, but gently to him. Their kisses were passed with the lightest of touches, each responding with heightened sensitivity, almost sensing what was to come. Tony could feel the warm glow in his body, and his lips and fingertips were glowing red hot. Each time they touched Laura the heat would dissipate for a split second, and then return as his senses demanded more.

They gradually moved back into to the living room and slowly but slowly undressed each other. As Tony lifted Laura's top over her head he let out an audible gasp as he stood back to take in the beauty of what he saw before him. She wasn't wearing a bra, and he could take in at once the full magnificence of her half-naked body. Laura for her part felt unusually at ease with her body, and almost brazen as she stood there allowing Tony's eyes to survey her over again and again. They continued undressing before relaxing on the large rug in the middle of the floor and making love.

Over the last few weeks they had learnt so much more about each other and there was none of the awkwardness or urgency that they had experienced at first. They both took time to explore the others body, pausing unselfishly at times to linger longer with their hands, and kisses, until eventually the time was right and they made love again.

Time seemed so irrelevant, and if anything the hourly chiming of the clock tower cruelly reminded them that there really was another world out there that they belonged to. Tony counted the chimes "One, two, three... ten, eleven, twelve." He had obviously missed at least one set, as though his other senses were demanding so much that his hearing had failed him.

Laura turned her head towards Tony and whispered, "Are you hungry? It's one o'clock already."

About to argue that it was only midday, he was content just to let it go. "Not really, are you?"

"No." With that they both lay in silence and gradually drifted off to sleep again. Tony was awakened briefly by the chimes again on a couple of occasions but didn't even bother to count them. Eventually his mind started to come to life, and although his body was happy to slumber all day long, hunger was niggling away, and he felt it was time to get up. When he looked at Laura she was already wide awake, and had propped herself up on one elbow.

"Hello sleepy head. Did I tire you out?"

Tony smiled before he could think of a reply. "No, I just wasn't sure what time it was, so I thought I would stay asleep. Has that clock outside caught up yet?"

"No, that can never happen, it would bring terror to the family."

Tony raised his eyebrows but said nothing. Knowing full well that the intrigue had been burning on long enough Laura suggested a plan. "Come into the village with me to get some food for a picnic, and we can have it on the beach later, and I will tell you all about the Preddy clan, who ruled these shores many years ago on my mother's side."

"Are you for real?" questioned Tony, looking slightly quizzical.

"Absolutely."

CHAPTER 13

Smuggler's Cove

The afternoon shot by and before long it was nearly six o'clock, as they set out towards the beach with the picnic hamper carried between them both. Walking with the heavy wicker basket along the sandy path, it took over an hour to reach the beach, where Laura carefully selected a secluded spot right up against the cliff looking out to the sea.

She spread out the blanket, placed a few candles around and lit them whilst Tony went in search of some driftwood to light. Much of the wood was tinder dry despite being close to the sea, and a bonfire was soon burning away in front of them as they toasted their day together with the champagne they had bought in the village. They chatted away as they ate from the picnic selection, and Tony couldn't help but draw parallels to his many nights at the Gorge. Life invariably moved on, but then as now it was the simple act of friendship in simple straightforward surroundings that always gave him the most comfort and pleasure.

Laura pulled on her coat and stood up to scan the sea in front of them. "It is an amazing force, don't you think? Relentlessly caressing the beach, changing the coastline year after year bringing so much pleasure, yet potentially so fatal as well."

Tony stood up to join her, and looked out at the sea, as the last of the spring sun gradually slipped effortlessly below the horizon. As he looked along the incoming tide panic gripped him as the realisation struck him that they were stranded. "Look, the tide is coming in, we are stuck here, both of the cliff paths are already blocked off and the sea is still coming in."

Laura turned to face him. "Do you trust me?"

"Of course I do, implicitly."

"Good, then don't panic. Just sit down and let me tell you the history of the Preddy family."

Although still casting a wary eye on the coast Tony was smiling involuntarily, in the knowledge that this was all part of Laura's plan. He felt unbelievably happy as he knew that she had probably never shared the secrets that she was about to impart with anyone else. He raised his glass to Laura, leant over and kissed her gently then leant back against the base of the cliff waiting for her to continue.

"My great-grandfather, or possibly great-great-grandfather, was a bit of a rogue about these parts and the story starts with him. To my dad he was just a criminal, who deserved to be locked up, so I wouldn't ever bring him up if I was you, but a loveable rogue sets a nicer tone. Anyway Great-Grandad Jack Preddy was a major part of local life around here, and he headed up one of two rival gangs of smugglers. They operated along a couple of these coves, luring in the passing ships so that they were wrecked on the rocks just out to sea, then ransacking the load and selling off the wares.

Jack was a young man and he originally worked in partnership with one of the older smugglers called Tyler Wilkes I think. Apparently Tyler was older and wiser, and increasingly worried about the authorities. He urged the locals to curb their activities and only wanted to lure in about one ship every six months or so. Granddad, however, was young and wanted to get more ambitious so he was all for dragging in as many as they could.

Anyway they had a big row and fell out, and then Jack as luck would have it fell in love with Tyler's youngest daughter Sarah. They had a massive row and settled it down on this beach with a fight, which in those days was supposed to be winner takes all."

"To the death you mean?" Tony was intrigued as to where this was going, but in the meantime he loved the story.

"Exactly, Jack beat his rival to within an inch of his life but wouldn't finish him off, and asked just for the hand of his daughter in marriage. Tyler had no option but to agree, and so they were married that night on the beach. Imagine, this very spot is the only bit of beach not to be covered in water so they were married just here.

Jack arranged for Tyler to be carried up to the cottages, and he was slowly nursed back to health, but in truth he never fully recovered." Laura paused for a while, and took a sip of her champagne, before continuing. "Don't think I am making this all sound like a romantic love story, dozens of sailors died each time they crashed the ships, and if the survivors wouldn't cooperate they were beaten to death and thrown to the mercy of the waves."

"Was that bit added by your dad by any chance?" whispered Tony, not sure why he was talking in hushed tones.

Laura simply smiled. "Probably, Mum told me the stories many times as a child, and it was about this point that Dad had enough and stormed out. Anyway where was I? Yes, Tyler was ill, and never fully recovered, but he didn't want Jack to have his business as well as his daughter, so he encouraged his son David to run what he considered to be the family business. Unfortunately his son was weak, and not able to effectively lead the gang of men, many of whom defected to Jack's outfit instead over the following months. He was still bringing in more ships so they saw the rewards as far greater, and they had no respect for David."

As she paused Tony noticed now that the tide was only about ten feet away, and still showed no sign of being fully in. His nerves were telling him to do something but he had promised Laura that he would trust her.

"Come on," she smiled. "We mustn't push it." With that, she removed a large torch from the hamper and packed away the few remaining items on the beach. As she stood up she shone the torch onto a small ledge only about two metres away up the cliff face. It was covered in some rough vegetation growing out from an enormous grey rock. "Come on, that is our way home."

Tony picked up the other side of the hamper, and although anxious about how they would manage the basket up the near-sheer rock face he followed Laura up to the ledge. Once again there was nowhere obvious to go, and Tony wondered if they were going to sit out the high tide and wait for the cliff path to be accessible again. Laura put him out of his misery. "How do you fancy staying here for the night then?"

"Well I suppose it is quite romantic and all, but—"

Before he could finish Laura put her finger to his lips, and then pointed the torch to the top of the large grey rock. At first his eyes couldn't focus on anything, then he realised that there appeared to be a small opening at the very top just large enough for a man to crawl through. "Help me push the hamper through, then I will go and you can follow."

Tony did exactly that, eagerly awaiting his turn to see what was on the other side. He scrabbled up the rock and let himself slip down the other side, where he was amazed to see that it opened up into a large round cavern. Laura was dancing the torch wildly around the walls so that Tony could take in the extent of it.

"So is this where we are staying the night then?"

"If you like," replied Laura, then she held the torch under her chin, illuminating her face in a sinister fashion. "But if you want to hear the rest of the tale of the Preddy family then follow me." As she finished she motioned towards the handle of the hamper which Tony grabbed as he scurried to his feet. Laura walked to the far side of the cave, where a series of steps had been carved into the stone, and she started climbing. Tony counted 165 steps before they came to a halt and they rested the hamper on the top step. Laura reached above her, undid a clasp of sorts, and pushed back the wooded floor over her head, then grabbed the hamper again and they both climbed out into a small square room.

"Where are we now?"

"Inside the Preddy clock tower."

"Didn't you say that Tyler lived here though? Isn't this his clock tower?"

"All in good time but at least you are listening," laughed Laura as she opened the door and then led the way outside.

The breeze was much stronger up here, and even the smell of salt seemed more intoxicating than it was on the beach itself. Laura opened the picnic hamper again to retrieve the blanket then she set the torch down and sat on the blanket. Tony sat beside her before Laura leant over and lay down with her head in Tony's lap.

"Do you want to hear the rest then?" Laura giggled, knowing full well that Tony couldn't wait.

"Well, only if you have the time. It is getting late."

"Of course, we have all the time in the world. Now where was I? Oh yes, both of them were clever men and realised that they couldn't go on as rivals, and Tyler knew his son was losing the battle. The plan was to have a competition to lure in a massive cargo ship that was due in, and whoever succeeded would win the overall title as leader. The two gangs would then come together as one. Jack wanted to do battle in the traditional way, but Tyler knew his son would lose and hoped this way he would have more of a chance.

"On the night in question there was a terrible storm, and Jack positioned himself further along the coast, but they failed to attract the ship, and so they followed its progress along to here on foot.

"Tyler had sent his only grandson to carry the decoy beacon up to the top of the clock tower, so as to mimic the lighthouse by the entrance to the port. The plan worked, because the crew of the ship was having a torrid time of it and desperate to seek refuge in port they headed inshore, and ran aground. The ship started to sink, but because of the weather the smugglers' gang couldn't get to it.

"Jack saw his chance so his gang rounded up their rivals and set off in their boats to reach the ship first. Then at the stroke of midnight disaster struck and the clock tower was hit by lightning, and in the ensuing flash they saw the young boy holding the lantern fall to the top of the cliff."

As Laura paused Tony exhaled the breath which he had seemingly been holding for the last ten minutes. "Are you sure this is for real?"

Laura nodded. "I know, and it gets more unbelievable yet. I am sure it has been romanticised through the telling over many years but much of it does appear to be based on the truth. At this stage Jack was torn between winning the competition, and helping Sarah's nephew. He ran up the cliff as fast as he could. He didn't know about the stone steps, so it took him about 20 minutes to get here, and he found Tyler cradling the boy in his lap, just near to where we are lying now. They both saw the futility of their competition, and rather than carrying on battling tried to help each other. Jack wanted to carry the boy back to the house so that he could be properly cared for but Tyler insisted that some of the other men did that so that the two of them were both left alone up here with Tyler's son David.

"The storm was continuing to rage but the clock above their heads had stopped on the stroke of midnight as the lightning struck it. Neither of them knew what time it was, but in the flashes of lightning they could see the Preddy gang were already ransacking the stricken ship.

"Tyler insisted that they had to give the loot back if they were to save the boy, but Jack just called him a superstitious old fool."

Laura stopped, and allowed herself a brief smile. "I know you probably think I am bonkers but let me read you this account from Tyler's son of the rest of the night. With that, she carefully reached into the back of the hamper and brought out a sheath of well-worn pieces of paper, wrapped in a thin plastic cover. She gently removed them and then leant down in front of the torch to see the words. Tony was sure she could have recited the rest from memory. The tension he felt was so intense that he had to keep unclenching his fingers to avoid them going into spasms of cramp.

She carefully smoothed out the ancient transcript and began to read.

"You always were a superstitious old fool, Tyler, the sea provides and we live off it."

"No, Jack. You have everything in place to be a great leader around here but never underestimate the sea, and nature. She will let us take enough to live on but we have been greedy and we will pay the price if we don't give something back tonight. Otherwise I fear for the life of my grandson and all those men of yours out at sea."

As he finished another flash of lightning lit the night sky and the ship that was stricken on the rocks split into two, taking with it many of the small boats around it. The massive waves continued to lash at the sides of the hull, throwing the men to their deaths as they were smashed into the wooden frame.

I had never seen Jack waver from his cause before but as Sarah came running up to his side I could see the fear in his eyes. "Jack, Dad is right, this is revenge for our past folly. We have to give something back to save Peter. He is only eight years old. Call your men back."

Clearly starting to question his own judgement, Jack reached for the pistol at his side and raised it into the air, knowing that one shot would be enough to bring his men back. As the storm lulled momentarily he fired the shot that echoed around the bay, carried on the torrential winds for a full minute. Again and again I heard the noise carried back to my ears then with relief, in the next flash I could see the small boats turning and making their way back to shore. Still the storm raged on, and with the rain blowing hard against us Sarah fell to her knees. "Jack," she cried, "I am with child. Your child. Do not let my nephew die like this. We have to give more to say sorry. To make your peace with the sea; our provider."

"What more can I give, Sarah, other than myself, and then the child will have no father. How is that good?"

The big man fell to his knees, crying like a baby, holding his wife, my sister, seemingly inconsolable as he realised the consequences of his and my actions. "What more can I give?" he screamed out again.

In the turmoil of the night we hadn't noticed Tyler walk away, but he called down suddenly from the top of the clock tower, and despite the weather and his own frailty we could hear his strong voice as though he was only feet away from us.

"It is not your time, Jack Preddy, it is mine. I am to give myself back to the sea tonight, not you, and all will be at peace. Please look after Sarah and her child, and raise them to respect the sea and all of its power. Look after all these people of our village, and provide for them in a fair way. I am leaving you my cove and all of the cottages to manage as best you can, but it must only be handed down as it was to me and by me. The right successor will make themselves known to you, as you have to me, and I did to my predecessor, and when the time is right you must do what is expected."

No one had chance to reply before the sky lit up again. The fork of lightning seemed to start high up in the sky, and like a pointing finger, slowly descended towards the clock tower. By the time the crack could be heard the weather had suddenly settled, and the men in the boats bobbing around on the waves were all looking up. Tyler fell forwards, his entire body glowing at the tip of the lighting strike as it followed him down, but unlike Peter the cliff top didn't break his fall and as he was carried by the stormy winds he fell to the shore below.

At once the clouds lifted, and the full moon that had until then been hidden illuminated the beach where the men below were now dragging their boats ashore. With the very last efforts that they had in their weary bodies they stumbled and fell across the wet sand on the way over to the body of Tyler Wilkes. Jack and Sarah were on the cliff watching the horror unfold and stood still momentarily. Then they began pulling in opposite directions. Sarah was torn but knew that young life was so precious and ran first to the house where she found Peter had recovered enough to sit up, and give the weakest smile as she entered the house.

In the meantime I ran down the steps, followed closely by Jack who barely seemed in control of his body and despite being the slower man on any other day I reached the body of Tyler first. Blood was already drying on the side of his mouth and across his top lip, as I lifted his head and placed it into my lap. His eyes were open, and for a brief moment I believed he had survived the fall. Then suddenly my attention was taken back to the top of the cliff as the clock started chiming, ringing out twelve times for the midnight that our greed had robbed us of. On the twelfth stroke I lay Tyler's head onto the damp sand, seeing now that his eyes were closed.

The nearest fingers of the next wave came much further than the others and seemed to pick up his body, carrying him out in a single pass to the sea that he had fought with, loved and respected more than anything else for all of his life.

Laura put the papers down then rolled around to look at Tony. All he could do was exhale much as he had earlier in the evening, and shake his head, not in disbelief but to recognise the overwhelming magnitude of the story.

"That really is some story, but it is a bit flawed in places isn't it?"

"No way." Laura realised that she was almost too quick to jump in defence, and so she offered Tony an olive branch. "You have to understand every element of this story or legend, because it profoundly affects everyone who is brought into the secret. Very few people know the whole full extent of it, and locally it is a closely guarded secret. I have never ever told anyone else the story before, and even when I brought friends here as a child they were not told anything."

"Shame, it would have been great for nightmares."

"I know. Mum is effectively the guardian, overseeing my right of passage, and she would only let me involve you in all of this when she was confident of the strength of our bond. I don't want to sound heavy tonight, because nothing has ever given me more pleasure than to share the secret with you, but you are now involved in an almost spiritual part of my life."

If Tony had heard these words from anyone else, at any other time, he would have scoffed, but not tonight. He didn't care for spiritualism, or the like, and he had always paid scant regard to fortune telling and the like as a second-rate circus act but all of a sudden his mindset was changing. Underneath it all he wanted to share Laura's faith, and repay the honour she had bestowed upon him by telling him everything but there were still holes in the story.

"I do believe you, Laura, and I trust your judgment, but will you be offended if I ask some questions?"

"Of course not but I am getting cold so shall we walk back up to the cottage?"

They carried the hamper between them in silence, as Tony tried to prioritise.

Once inside Laura collected two fresh glasses from the kitchen and opened a bottle of wine. They both settled quietly onto the rug, and Laura offered her glass up to Tony, "Cheers. I love you, mister."

Tony smiled back. "I love you too, miss, but your family tree appears somehow flawed."

Laura knew what was coming, because she had been through the same processes over the years, but knew now that the tale was watertight. Even so, it had been fun seeing the look of sheer astonishment on Tony's face earlier, and she couldn't resist leading him on. "How do you mean? It is all on my mother's side, don't forget."

"Exactly, but she wasn't called Preddy, was she? I noticed the family tree thing on the landing earlier and she was..."

As Tony struggled to recall Laura answered for him, "Wilkes, of course."

"But Jack was a Preddy and he would have passed the Cove down to his children, so without a lot of in-breeding how did it end up back with the Tyler family?"

"Well Jack and Sarah did have children, eleven in fact, but I never said it had to be passed down within the same family, and when Jack died he left it to Peter who he always felt should have had the honour in the first place. Remember the line of succession will always be shown to the holder as Jack Tyler had declared, and that is ultimately how it came to me, with mum as my effective guardian."

"So why was your mum overlooked then?"

"Well, her father had always intended that she take it, although to be fair it has never passed directly to descendants like that, but then she met dad, who you may have noticed is a policeman, and a rather officious one at times. Well, my granddad felt it inappropriate for the legacy of smugglers and rogues to end up in his hands so he prayed for some inspiration. Then when I was born he immediately declared that I was the one. At the time everyone felt it a bit strange, but he later died in a car crash when I was only three, and it then transpired that he had been serious enough to leave clear instructions in his will. Dad said it should be contested on the grounds of his obvious insanity but everyone else felt he had made the right choice."

"So what about the clock? How does that fit into the story, apart from the obvious of course?"

"Well after the night's events the clock was running exactly one hour slow. Over the next couple of days they tried to reset it, but it either stopped or ran slow until the hour delay was back to exactly one hour, and it has been the same ever since. I must confess that this is more part of folklore now than the rest of the story. You will see reference to it in the local museum, but they talk of the storm and nothing more. The smugglers' involvement is a tightly guarded secret. Locals now keep the clock and it suits them to keep the hour delay because it brings so many tourists here."

"What about the ship that was dragged into the Cove with the precious cargo?"

"Most of it was left to the sea, and reportedly it vanished within days. Only four gold bars remain, and they are upstairs in a chest with the other documents that pass to the holder in each generation."

"You are joking. There are four gold bars upstairs, and no one has ever sold them?"

"They cannot, that is the whole point. The legacy has been added to over the years, and Jack's wish was that the gold bars be used only as last resort if the holder of the legacy is in mortal danger. If anyone else takes them, then Jack swore on his deathbed that nature would again exact revenge in the way it had on Tyler before him."

Tony smiled acknowledging that he was beaten. "Give up, I have never believed anything so fantastic in my whole life, but I do. I don't know why but I do. I feel like I have been taken into some secret society tonight."

Laura simply smiled back, and stood up. "It is really late, and I would really like you to hold me tonight."

"That would be the perfect end to an amazing day."

CHAPTER 14

Summer Loving

They settled into a daily routine of getting up early, revising all morning and then sightseeing during the afternoon. By the end of the holiday Tony was amazed at how well prepared he was for his end-of-year exams. He knew that in the past he had done just enough to pass exams but Laura had shown him fresh discipline, and he had revised like never before. Before they knew it they were locking up the cottage and heading back up to university. Over the next few weeks they sat various exams, settled back into student life, before breaking up and saying their goodbyes at the end of term. Unbelievably James, Paul and Charlotte did sort out the summer in Spain, and they all left the day after university finished. The whole city seemed quiet as students left, and by the time that Tony and Laura headed back to the cottage it seemed like a ghost town compared to the usual hustle and bustle over the last few weeks.

The summer passed without incident, with Tony and Laura welcoming various guests to the other cove cottages every Friday, then relaxing for much of the rest of the week. At times they both felt that they should really be doing a bit more, but the guilt would only last minutes as they realised how blissfully happy they were with just each other for company. They didn't buy papers, but ventured as far as the village two or three times a week to get provisions, and for the rest of the time they sun bathed, walked the coastline, read books and talked about their plans for the future.

Both were about to enter their final year at uni. and felt a growing sense of responsibility to plan as the holidays neared their conclusion. In reality though, the weeks ticked by and they were no further forward. The odd postcard arrived from Spain indicating that everyone was having a good time; Paul was apparently having a fresh holiday romance most weeks, James had returned to the UK after a couple of weeks to help his mother with some things, then returned at the end of August for the final three weeks before uni. started again. Charlotte didn't put anything on the postcards, but she had written a couple of times, sending long letters, explaining that she had been bored with the constant partying and headed off with some foreign backpackers around Spain. She planned then to return around the time of her birthday for one big party before they all came home.

Laura's parents meanwhile had taken as much leave as they could muster from work and taken a six-week cruise. Apparently they had been planning it for years but with Laura having been ill they had postponed it several times. Now that she was recovered, and with Tony helping her with the cove cottages they decided this was the year to do it. Again, there were occasional postcards but in the main it was a very peaceful and relaxed summer holiday for both Tony and Laura.

By the 18th September the autumnal weather was already heading in, and they spent a quiet day at the cottage. It was lashing down with rain for much of the day, which only added to Tony's frustration. He had dug out Graham's phone number at the bar in order to phone and wish Charlotte happy birthday first thing in the morning, but by six o'clock, he was still pacing around with the piece of paper in his hand. Laura could sense his anxiety, but she was becoming increasingly unsettled herself and pleaded with Tony to phone. "Don't worry about Graham, what will he say, anyway he probably won't even answer the phone. Just get it over and done with and we will open a bottle of wine."

Tony picked up the handset and hesitated a moment before punching in the number. The usual series of clicks sounded as the international exchange sprung into action and then there was life at the other end. The loud music booming down the phone told him it had been answered but Tony couldn't hear any voices. "Hello, is anyone there? It's Tony, Graham's brother."

"Hey everyone, it is Tony, Graham's baby brother. W-w-we

thought you had been taken by aliens. S-s-s-sitting in Devon with your pipe and slippers."

Tony didn't know who was the most obnoxious sometimes, Mark or Graham. "Is my brother around?"

"Si señora, una momento."

That was probably about as far as Mark had got with learning Spanish, thought Tony, then a familiar voice interrupted. "Little bro, how are you?"

"Good thanks, and you?"

"Excellent thanks; I have looked after your little friends all summer waiting for you to come over. They have partied hard, you don't know what you have missed, they have had the best time ever."

Tony sighed and bit his bottom lip trying to calm himself. He didn't like the thought of Graham getting close to his friends all summer. He knew it was irrational, but there were things he liked to keep separate from Graham and Mark. Tony had made these friends himself, and Graham would have been trying to belittle him in front of them all summer. Tony knew he was being stupid but the thoughts would not go away.

"Good, well I knew you would look after them, so I thought it best to leave you to it."

"Like James said this morning, you probably wouldn't have enjoyed it anyway. Still, is that Laura still taking pity on you? I have to say she looked pretty fit when I met her."

This was every bit as bad as he had expected and Tony just wanted to get the ordeal over and done with. "Yes, Laura is fine, is anyone there for me to speak to, only it is Charlotte's birthday."

"Don't I know it? What a day we have had for her, best birthday she has ever had I wouldn't be surprised. So who would you like to talk to first? They are all here, Big J, Charlie and Rampant P."

Tony was cringing as he held the phone to his ear, wishing this would soon be over, and then another familiar voice was on the other end.

"Hi Tony, it's Charlotte, hold on a sec. Yes, a drink please, Graham. Phew, alone at last. Thanks for phoning. We have so, so, missed you this summer. Thanks for remembering my birthday, I was beginning to think you had forgotten."

"Never, it is nice to hear your voice. Has it been good?"

"Yes, in parts, but your brother can be a bit full on, and you were right, Juan is the biggest tosser I have ever met, and Mark – bless him – tries, but he so has to try and impress Graham all the time. None of us can wait to get home."

The relief to Tony was instant, and he couldn't help but laugh. "Sorry, but look have a good day, and we will catch up as soon as possible. And who said I called Juan a tosser?"

"James."

"Oh!"

"Give my love to Laura," was the only reply.

"Will do, bye Charlotte."

Tony was glad that he had made the effort to phone, even if the second or two delays made the conversation extremely stilted. He felt himself willing the phone on as the international exchange clicked away. He even had time to briefly consider whether or not they should have gone to Spain, even for a few days, but the time here had been so good he soon dismissed those thoughts. Right now he would have to rank this as the best summer ever, and he had never felt so relaxed in himself. The sheer indulgence of spending so much time alone with someone he loved so much was an experience beyond equal, and one that he knew would be hard to repeat. They had no commitments other than to each other, and he knew that they had made the most of a near perfect time.

"Bye." The phone system had obviously made its connection as Charlotte's voice brought him back to the present. "Oh, by the way, before I go, how did Laura's tests go? We didn't want to phone in case there was a problem."

Laura had walked back into the room at that moment, and she saw the colour drain instantly from Tony's face. She screwed up her eyes inquisitively and whispered, "What is it?"

Tony felt sick to the pit of his stomach, and was struggling to hold the phone steady. He could feel his whole body starting to break out in a cold sweat. Just two seconds earlier he felt like he was on top of the world. It was like he had been luxuriating in a warm bubble of contentment, and some outside force had just rammed in a massive pin to burst the outer shield, and leave him scraping around defenceless, breathless even, on the floor.

He looked at the phone in his hand, from which he could hear the concern in Charlotte's voice, "Tony, talk to me. Everything is okay, isn't it?" and then back to Laura who was looking increasingly concerned at him.

He knew he had to say something and spoke to Laura first. "Your tests. I forgot them."

Strangely Laura seemed unconcerned, and waved her hand almost dismissively. "We forgot, you mean. Don't panic, I remembered the other day, it will be fine."

He couldn't believe how calm she was being and almost put the phone down until he heard Charlotte again, "Tony are you there?"

"Sorry Charlotte. It's not the best of lines; you were lost for a few minutes," he lied. "Laura says hi! And everything is just fine."

"Thank goodness for that. You had me worried. Anyway, must go, I have someone else here to speak to you."

After a few more seconds' delay he heard James voice on the other end. "Hello mate, thanks for leaving me to the mercy of your brother and his stuttering bloody mate all summer. Luckily I made some excuse up and went home for a few weeks. Hope you have had a good time with Laura."

"Err, yes thanks. Look, I am really sorry about Graham, and all. But you have had a good time haven't you?"

"Yeah it has been good, your brother can be a pain in the arse, but he has his moments as well when he isn't too bad. It was a good holiday. It would have been nice to see you but I can see why you stayed away… Anyway he is making his way back over so I will speak next week. Back to uni. soon! Love to Laura, hope she is keeping you honest."

"Yeah, absolutely."

"Absolutely what?" It was Paul on the other end of the phone now.

"Nothing, how are you mate?"

"Great thanks. It's been good." Then in a whisper, "Please don't grow up to be like your big bro or you will have one friend less, alright?"

Tony smiled again, feeling a sense of smug satisfaction that his earlier fears had proved groundless.

"No problem. See you soon, okay? This call is costing me a fortune, but really good to hear your voice, mate. It has been a while promise to catch up as soon as we can."

"Sure, mate, really missed you as well. Here is big bro for you."

"See what I mean? They have had an awesome time over here, haven't…"

Tony didn't hear the rest as the clock tower struck seven times. He waited for the last peal of the bell, then put the receiver back to his ear.

"What the bloody hell was that? Are you under Big Ben or something?"

"No, it was just the clock tower outside the cottage."

"Ooohh, very nice, Tony has a clock tower outside the cottage, very picture postcard. Still, can't talk now there is a rave in full swing. Bye little bro, and happy birthday for the 20th. I will send a card sometime when all the partying is done."

With that, the phone went dead, but Tony held onto it for a few moments, unsure what to do next. His heart was pounding away, and for a moment he had to take stock of the situation. He had put Laura's missed hospital test out of his mind briefly, but the distraction of conversation had gone now and the nervousness was returning. Laura seemed almost blasé about things, and yet he felt he had let both her and her parents down. She could sense the concern in him, and placed a comforting arm around his middle, as she leant against his back. "I am okay, Tony. I have never felt better. Look, we will contact the hospital tomorrow, and I will make arrangements to see Dr Preston. Now come and have your wine and stop fretting."

True to her word, Laura was up early the next morning and Tony could hear her on the phone to the hospital. She was obviously having the usual struggle to get through to the right department, and frustrated at only hearing one side of the conversation, he decided to go out for a run. It was a glorious morning with a hazy mist all around the beach that was gradually lifting as he ran along the cliff top. The sun was a little subdued at first but its warmth soon started to make its presence felt, and Tony was glad of the gentle breeze rolling in from the sea. The missed appointment had played on his mind all night, and he hadn't slept particularly well as a result, but as so often happened he was able to clear his head whilst running, and felt much happier as he turned to head back in. He had only been out for about 40 minutes but he was pleased to see Laura sat at the front of the cottage reading her book.

"Hi, what did Dr Preston have to say then?"

Laura looked up and smiled. "Go have a shower and I will tell you."

Tony shook his head in frustration, and then with sweat dripping off him bent down to kiss her on the forehead.

"Uggh you are disgusting, get away."

Tony just smiled to himself, then ran in and showered. Laura had put out some breakfast things when he returned, and he sat down at the table, trying to appear nonchalant but desperate to hear the outcome of her phone calls.

"I spoke with Dr Preston eventually, and he was more interested in my holiday than anything else. Apparently he has taken up a new post now at Bristol of all places so I am going to see him there as soon as we get back. He asked the usual questions, and I told him I have been fine, and he said that a restful summer was the best tonic anyway."

"So there is nothing to worry about then?" Tony felt there was a bit more that he wasn't being told.

"Well, he is going to take some blood tests, because I have felt a bit unwell at times, but nothing like the problems before, and he doesn't think it is related. He blamed your cooking actually."

"Charming." They sat in silence for the next few minutes, each deep in thought. Tony had sensed on several occasions that Laura had little or no appetite or seemed strangely lacklustre on certain days, but he had chosen to ignore it. He knew deep down that even he had been happier just to let the world exist around them and for him that epitomised the magic of the Cove. Less than 100 metres from the hustle and bustle of the everyday grind it offered escapism on a scale he had never experienced before.

Laura watched Tony, as he was deep in thought, and wondered about what lay ahead. She knew that she had done well to hide her discomfort from him over the summer, but at the same time she didn't want to ruin the time they had spent together. Deep down she was afraid that the omens were not good, but she knew equally that she was probably just being irrational. So much had been potentially ruined by her illness before, and finding Tony back then had given her the love she so wanted in her life from the most unlikely of coincidences.

Her parents had been extremely reluctant for her to get involved, especially her dad, but Tony had won them over and they could see for themselves just how much he had added to her life. Now it was her turn to repay something to Tony, and she was desperate for her secret plans to come to fruition. Bob and Paula were arriving later for a week in one of the cottages, and assuming that the flights had gone to plan, Charlotte, Paul and James would be arriving around 4.00 as well to help celebrate Tony's birthday the following day.

Laura had wanted to make it special, and had painstakingly made the arrangements whenever Tony went out for a run. At first she hit a slight stumbling block by phoning Victoria to ask if she could make the arrangements, but apparently James had finished with her during his brief return in the summer. Eventually she had found Graham's number in amongst Tony's case and the plans were made.

There was just one issue that she knew she had to address before she could relax and let her plans work through. They had barely mentioned the Cove's history over the past few weeks, but Laura had wanted to bring the subject up herself, and now time was running out. Trying not to sound too obvious, so as not to ruin the surprise for later, she spoke in a whisper. "You know the Cove, and its history and all."

Tony had been looking out to sea, admiring the view, and he swung his chair around as the silence was broken. "Yes."

"Well I know you respect its history as much as I do, but I don't know if I have really stressed how secretive it all is. I have only ever been told the whole story once, and it is not meant to go outside the scope of the few that share in its legacy."

"But I am okay to know the details. You said that your mum was cool with that, didn't you?"

"Yes, but the point is…" Laura hesitated as she didn't want this to sound churlish. "Well I would rather you didn't talk to Graham or anybody else about it. The gold has been known to turn people before, and even James or Charlotte should be protected for their own good really."

Tony didn't know what to say, but the moment was broken by the sound of a car coming up the lane. It pulled up about 200 feet away, but even at that distance he recognised Bob and Paula straight away.

Turning back to Laura, he took hold of her hands that were on top of the table, and leaned in close before speaking. "You paid me the biggest honour ever by telling me about all of this, and I still don't know how to reciprocate with any gesture that can even come close. I don't know what you have been hiding from me, but the warm glow in my heart that is burning away like a furnace right now has been present ever since the day we met. I will never ruin your legacy by betraying your trust, I promise."

Tony kissed Laura quickly then stood up to go, but she didn't release his grip and pulled him back down, then looked him straight in the eye. "Our legacy, Tony, this is OUR legacy now."

Tony just smiled. Inwardly he knew that Laura always had to say so little to say so much. His ramblings were far from eloquent, and he could never think of the right thing to say, but he still knew that Laura understood him.

"Come on, you two, you have had six weeks to get over each other. How about giving us a hand with these bags?" boomed Bob as he got out of the car.

They both ran out to greet their guests, and showed them to their cottage.

"Wow, this is a surprise," ventured Tony.

"You didn't know then?" enquired Bob with his arm around

Laura's shoulders. "You will have to watch this one, she can be a bit sly you know."

Paula had stood back slightly and was eyeing them both up from the other side of the car. "You two look well tanned, and relaxed. Am I going to get a hug as well?"

It was good to see Bob and Paula again, and when Tony learnt that they would be staying for a party on his birthday, as well as the following week, he was overjoyed. The time had been amazing through the summer, but it was equally good to have some new company, as a kind of gentle introduction back to the real world that was only days away. For the rest of the morning he walked around grinning like a Cheshire cat, unable to conceal his natural joy at seeing his parents again. They had some lunch, went for a short walk along the now familiar coast path, before Laura and Bob went into the village for some party things.

Tony went over to the guest cottage and knocked gently. "Come in!" shouted Paula through the open door, and he found her in the kitchen making some coffee.

"You have really grown up more than I could have ever believed in the last few weeks. Laura is obviously good for you, and I am happy to see you both looking so relaxed."

"Thanks," replied Tony. "I have missed you two, but Laura is very special to me."

"I can see that. Call it female intuition if you like, but I always knew you were right for each other."

Tony put a supportive arm around her. "Mother's intuition, you mean."

Paula smiled as she allowed herself to be engulfed in a hefty hug, deeply reassured that despite his feelings for Laura there was still a bit of Tony's heart devoted to her. She discreetly wiped her eyes, as a tear ran down, and coughed to try and steady her voice. "Thank you, Tony. You must think that I am being silly. I think it is the menopause or something."

"No, not at all. Being with Laura this summer has taught me a lot about myself, and without sounding all soft it has made me realise just how much of a debt of gratitude I owe to you two. It was only a stroke of luck that Laura and I ever met in the first place, and in some ways it was only a stroke of luck that I came to be fortunate enough to live with you and Bob."

"You are right in one sense, but life delivers a myriad of twists and turns, that can lead us down any one path or another. Your meeting with Laura may have been one of chance, but it wasn't the meeting that has shaped the outcome, that is purely down to the two of you. From what I have seen you are two like-minded people with a love of life, and you both saw in one another something that was worth pursuing to enhance your lives. Between you it has become the wonderful thing that it is."

Tony knew that only six months ago he would have been too immature to even have this conversation, and yet he felt completely at ease whilst acknowledging fully the gravity of Paula's words. "That was very eloquently put. I forget sometimes just how intuitive you can be."

"You are a good person, Tony, on the threshold of life with a beautiful girl that will help you through. I would never judge you and Graham against one another, but you differ in your approach, and I wish he could see past the knocks that he has endured over the years and look at the greater opportunities that he has been afforded."

Almost instinctively Tony jumped to his brother's defence even before he had fully considered Paula's words. "He isn't so bad, and at least he is making something of himself over in Spain."

"I know but at what cost? He carries such a burden on his shoulders, call it a chip if you like, and I worry about the effect it will have on his future. I just hope that Mark keeps him on the right track."

"Do you really think that Mark is a good influence then?" Tony could hardly hide the incredulity in his voice.

Paula smiled and nodded. "You still have a bit to learn about people, but it will come with experience. You should always judge only on what you see for yourself, not what you hear from others who invariably have their own agenda. I have known Mark since he was a young boy, and I can honestly say that I have never seen anything other than good in him. There has been a degree of mischievousness at times, but nothing any more sinister than that."

Unconvinced, Tony considered his reply for a good minute or more. "Maybe, but I will have to reserve judgement, I am afraid."

Paula didn't reply, she just raised her eyebrows in an exaggerated manner, and smiled at the same time, before sipping on her mug of coffee. They continued chatting away for the next half hour, largely just passing time and catching up on old news and village gossip until Paula mentioned Laura's missed tests, and Tony felt his heart sink.

"To be honest, she spoke to her doctor earlier today, and is seeing him next week in Bristol. She feels fine though."

"Look after her, Tony. She has lost a fair bit of weight through the summer, and beneath the tan, I am not sure that all of her sparkle is there at the moment."

He felt like he was being chastised, and would have struggled to accept this from anyone other than Paula, but at the same time she was only reiterating his own subconscious thoughts. For several minutes he sat contemplating, then jumped up. "Come on, you are on holiday, mid-afternoon is the best time in the Cove. No matter how windy or choppy a day it is, around the water stays dead still like a mirror floating in the sea. I will show you."

As they left the cottage Paula stopped. "Do I need to lock up?"

"No, come on." As he finished the clock struck three times. "Quick it's the next hour, you have to see until 5.00."

They ran as far as the edge of the cliff and sat just in front of the clock tower, with their legs dangled over the edge. Even after six weeks the beauty of the scene before them was breath-taking, and they both sat in silence taking it all in. Several families had driven onto the beach below during low tide, but they were starting to pack their things away as the tide came in.

"So does anyone ever get cut off by the tide then?" enquired Paula.

Tony's mind flicked back to the night that he had felt trapped by the incoming tide. "Not that I know of, but only the locals know of the road to this cove so they know its peculiarities. Lots of walkers venture by but the sea never fully closes off the beach."

"It really is an amazing place. You are so lucky to be able to spend time here." As Paula finished the sound of a car coming down the lane made them both look around. They recognised the vehicle at once, but it appeared to be heavily laden down, and Bob was moving very slowly over the potholes as he came onto the grassed area.

"What on earth have they been buying? The car is almost rubbing the ground," laughed Tony.

Paula knew the answer but didn't reply. Bob saw them and headed the car over in the direction of the tower, stopping about 30 feet away.

"Surprise!" came the shouts as all four car doors flew open, and James, Charlotte, Paul, and Graham fell out of the back and rolled across the grass. Bob and Laura were more elegant as they stepped out, and held off whilst Tony raced forward to greet his new guests.

"Where did you lot come from?" Tony couldn't believe that this was for real, and kept pinching himself to see if he woke up. He was trying desperately to keep his voice calm as he hugged James, Charlotte, Paul and Graham in turn. They all looked to Laura, gesturing that she was the driving force.

"Come on," interjected Bob, "the car is full of frozen stuff, we need to get it all in the freezer we have plenty of time for reunions later." They all unpacked the car, and then Tony arranged drinks, whilst Bob and Paula prepared some food. They rejected all offers of help, and seemed content to get on with it themselves, in their own cottage.

By seven o'clock they served up a mountain of snack food which they brought over on trays and everyone sat around eating and drinking through the evening. Several conversations were going on simultaneously, and each time that anyone moved to get a fresh drink, food or simply to go to the toilet their place was quickly taken and they had to re-join the group elsewhere. It wasn't an intentional shuffle, but it gave everyone the opportunity to circulate, and catch up on events through the summer. Silence eventually fell about two-ish in the morning, as the effects of the day's travelling took their toll and the guests all headed over to their respective cottages.

Tony and Laura cleared up quickly, but both were very tired, and once the lounge area was looking half respectable they also retired to their bed.

"Thank you so much for this. Tomorrow should be great." Tony yawned as he finished, and covered his mouth with his hand. "Sorry,

I really am tired. I think it must be all this company, I am not used to it."

"That's okay." It felt good to have Tony holding her again, to have him all to herself. Laura felt a bit left out as they had all chatted about old times over the evening, isolated even. She hated herself for feeling so selfish, but it was only because it was so strange after their intimacy in recent weeks. Sensing her awkwardness at times Tony had given her reassuring looks, and hugs all night, but it had still felt a bit weird.

"It is good to see everyone, and I hope you get the chance to get to know them a bit better over the next few days," he added through another yawn.

Laura was desperate to change the subject. She was annoyed for being so silly, even more so because Tony had apparently picked up on it. "We will. I already know James really well, and he is always the perfect gentleman, and I have learnt that Charlotte isn't the threat I once thought. Paul makes me laugh, because he is such a womaniser, but so sweet with it."

"Sweet Paul, why do all you women think he is sweet?"

"Oh he is though, for all of his bravado he is quite innocent, and vulnerable. He needs looking after." Laura knew they were teasing each other, but she was happy for the conversation to deviate off down this path. "I can see why women fall for him, you know, he definitely has something about him."

Tony couldn't help laughing out loud. "How does he always get you women so concerned for his welfare? It is all an act, you know, he goes through women quicker than I go through underwear."

"Tut, tut, jealousy is a terrible thing you know, and anyway I was going to ask when you last changed those boxer shorts."

Realising that any kind of reasoned debate was out of the question, Tony just laughed again, and gently kissed Laura. "Goodnight, I am tired. Thanks for all of this. It means a lot."

"No problem." As she finished Laura tried hard to stifle a yawn. Her body was obviously very tired but for her mind at least sleep seemed a long way off. She'd had a strange sensation of butterflies in her stomach all day, and wished that they would go away. Unsure as to whether it was anticipation of the party, ending the holiday and going back to uni. or something that Dr Preston had said. Either way, she was awake for ages after Tony drifted off with a million thoughts going through her head. She wanted to sleep, and tried thinking of anything but herself, but it was a good half hour after the clock tower chimed four times that she eventually drifted off.

When they woke the following morning the butterflies were still there, but Laura decided to just ignore them and get on with things. The day went well, and they lit a barbecue around three-ish, with everyone drinking through the afternoon. Laura felt more involved than the night before, and Charlotte especially took time out for just the two of them to chat. "So Paula seems to think you have finally made a man out of my oldest friend."

"Well I only really rounded off a few rough edges. I think you lot made him who he is."

Charlotte thought for a moment before responding. "That is a really kind thing to say. We have always been very close as a group, and I always wondered how I would feel about Tony especially when he found a partner, but I never thought he would find somebody so special."

The two girls hugged briefly. "Thanks, we are all lucky really. We don't have a lot to complain about, do we, entering our final years at uni. with our real lives just about to start."

After a few moments of contemplation Charlotte replied. "No. I just hope I don't end up like my mother in time."

"I am so sorry," confessed Laura. "I didn't mean to be so insensitive. Tony told me about your dad, and what he did."

Charlotte took a sip of her wine then carried on. "To be honest I barely speak to my dad now; he has a new wife, and new outlook seemingly, but it still hurts. What is worst is the effect it had on my mum. She didn't deserve to be dumped and humiliated in the way she was, and she has never recovered her self-confidence, or self-belief."

"I cannot begin to imagine what it is like, and I am afraid that I cannot offer any real comfort because my family have always been very solid despite their odd arguments."

"It's just nice to talk to someone sensible, to be honest. I have been thinking about Mum a lot this summer, thinking about where I go with my life. Being 21, see, makes you feel you should have some direction. I want to be as happy as you and Tony, and make a start on the next stage of my life. Unfortunately I have not had any female company all summer and chatting with boys, even Tony, is just not the same."

"No man then?" She felt so patronising as soon as the words left her mouth, and wished she could take them back. "I mean, well, to be honest I don't know what I mean. I never really had a relationship before Tony, not like this anyway, and we kind of just got lucky."

Charlotte screwed up her face, and shook her head. "It was more than luck. You are right for each other in a way that I have never seen before. As for me, there is little hope on the horizon, I am afraid. Mark and I have always been close, and away from Graham he is a wonderful caring bloke, dare I say it he even reminds me of Tony. Unfortunately deep down he is still just a boy, and with Graham he is getting mixed up in some very strange things. I don't know that our paths will ever run parallel let alone cross again."

The seed of intrigue had been sewn, and Laura was unsure whether to question her or not. She proceeded very cautiously. "Mixed up in what?"

"Drugs I think, but I am not sure to what extent. They seem to think it is part of the culture where they are but, well, to be honest I would love to get Mark away from it all."

Laura opened her mouth, hesitated and then on reflection said nothing.

"I am sorry, I shouldn't have said anything. Don't tell Tony, will you?" Realising this was a futile request, Charlotte added. "Well not tonight at least."

"Okay. Are you sure though? I mean drugs."

Charlotte nodded in confirmation. "100%, but James and Paul don't know. I found out by overhearing a discussion with my ex one night, and I felt threatened by him afterwards which is why I went off backpacking through the summer. I tried to talk Mark around, but he can only see the pound signs in front of his eyes."

"And what is Graham's involvement?"

"Just between you and me, he is the ringleader. He has to go off somewhere tomorrow to arrange some details that he won't tell me about, and he just won't see sense. He thinks he has to provide for him and Tony. He reckons another season and he will have enough for them to live off for the future." Charlotte frowned as she finished. "He has always had some kind of misguided loyalty or protectiveness towards Tony. That is how he got injured years ago. I am convinced that he has only ever used people like Mark along the way."

"Mark means a lot to you, doesn't he?" Laura knew that she was stating the obvious but couldn't think what else to say.

Charlotte nodded again. She hadn't talked to anyone so freely before, and had never discussed Mark at all, but she was lifting a huge emotional burden as she spoke. "Yes and the silly thing is that Tony and Mark would be good friends if it wasn't for Graham. He brings out the worst in everyone."

Laura felt in her jeans pocket, and brought out her purse. "These are emergency contact details for my flat, my parents, here, anywhere. I carry them because of my illness, so if you ever need to talk you can get me on one of these numbers."

"Thanks." Charlotte put the laminated card into her own pocket. "You know there was a time when I thought Tony and I might get together. We nearly did one night, but I think he would have been wasted on me. He deserves you."

Laura laughed. "Hardly, but I am not surprised. I always sensed a certain something between you two. I was even quite jealous of you last night when I was hearing of your times together in the past, at the Games and all. The one thing that you cannot create in an instant is history. But he is mine now." She tried to look as menacing as possible as she finished.

It was Charlotte's turn to laugh now. "I know, but hopefully we can be close too, you are a good listener, and I have too many male friends like Tony, Paul, Mark and James who hear you but don't listen."

"Definitely but come on, let's join the party." As they made their way into the house Laura noticed Graham alone in the kitchen. He was sat on the worktop refilling his glass with cider, alone as he had been for much of the last 24 hours.

She turned to Charlotte. "You go on, I will catch you up. I want to talk to Graham."

"Just be careful."

With that Laura turned and tapped on the wall by the entrance to the kitchen. "Is this a private party or can anyone join?"

"Private," came the curt reply that she wasn't expecting, "But you are the hostess so come in, and grab a glass." Graham was obviously drunk as he swayed gently on the worktop, waving the cider bottle around.

"Thanks. I have a drink so I am okay."

"Rubbish, you need another." He grabbed a clean glass from the side and filled it with local scrumpy. Laura accepted it happily and placed it on the side, certain that she wouldn't drink any of it.

"Why aren't you joining in with the others then?"

"Kids, playing childish games." He was slurring his words as he spoke. "Bloody cold back over here, isn't it? I can't wait to get back home to Spain. Only came to see when Tony wants to come and work with me next summer."

Laura felt like asking why he bothered at all for all that he added to the party, but she let his rudeness go. "Oh, right."

"Has he mentioned it to you, the family business?"

"Not really, he said you have a club over there, that's all."

"Club, pub, and a restaurant now, quite a little chain. You could come over and waitress if you fancy it, we always need pretty girls."

Laura could see why Tony got irritated so easily by Graham now. "Well I don't really think it is my scene, and to be honest I am not sure if Tony is thinking of joining you."

As the final words left her mouth she felt the mood in the kitchen change. There was silence for several minutes, as they both stood looking, but strangely not staring in the direction of the other. Eventually Graham slid down off the worktop, and moved closer to Laura. Too close for her comfort, but she was in a corner and had nowhere to go.

"You may be my little brother's latest squeeze, but your time will come. If it doesn't happen naturally, which I am sure is only a matter of time, then I will soon finish things off. Don't think there isn't anything I wouldn't do to protect my family." Laura could smell the cider on his breath he was standing so close. She wanted to scream but no one in the other room would hear her over the music, and she tried to gently push Graham to one side instead.

"Excuse me, can I get past?" She was trying to be calm, but knew her voice was trembling as much as her knees.

Graham stood solid, and didn't flinch as she pushed with all her strength on his arm. "You need to learn who Tony respects the most around here. Family is everything for him, not some little tart he picked up at uni."

Desperate not to sink to his level, Laura knew better than to react hastily. She took a deep breath and tried to be rational. She knew she had the advantage of being sober, and needed to retain her superiority. "Your brother is an adult, Graham, and the best thing you can offer him is to start treating him like one."

"Don't push me, missy, because I don't think you would like the consequences."

Laura felt the tears behind her eyes, but she wasn't going to show any sign of weakness. She had never encountered such nastiness before in another human. Why was Graham being such a bully? He had been charming enough earlier on, who was this person?

"Can I go now? I think you have said enough."

Rather than allowing her past, Graham inched forward closing her space even more. She could smell his breath, and the heat from his body was burning through her thin dress wherever his body made unwelcome contact with her own. "You need to show me some manners, missy, now ask nicely." He spat the final words, and with growing repulsion Laura felt the spray on her face. She deliberately resisted the natural inclination to wipe it away, and looked for a means of escaping instead. His physical presence repulsed her but he was much stronger, and he had his arms now outstretched to the work surfaces either side of her slim waist. His right leg was between her legs, burning against them like a branding iron trying to make its mark.

Laura knew what he wanted but she wasn't going to submit easily, another inch and she would aim her knee straight into his groin. She stood her ground, waiting. Her whole body was trembling inwardly, but by clenching her muscles she hoped to remain rock solid. Graham was obviously very threatening and intimidating, and she wouldn't want to be alone with him anywhere else, but here at the cottage she always felt that she could achieve anything. The bravado may have been misplaced, and she was struggling to keep her resolve, but she wasn't about to give up.

"I am going to ask you once more to move, and then I am going to scream. Okay?"

Despite her anxiety she tried to keep her voice as level as possible.

Before she could say anymore though Graham lifted his right hand and clamped it over her mouth, so tight that she struggled to breathe, then he put his left arm behind her and pulled her body in tight to his. "I never thought you were the type to like it rough, but I must have got you wrong. I haven't told you how my brother shares everything with me, have I?"

Laura's heart was pounding away in her chest, and she knew that she was no match for Graham's physical strength. Right now she needed help, and yet she couldn't see where that would come from. Tony was only feet away, but with the party in full swing she knew she was on her own. Graham's mouth was beside her ear and his sweaty brow was against her head, she could even feel his heartbeat and every aspect of him repulsed her, but any sound she tried to make sounded like a pathetic whimper and she did not want to sound defeated.

As her mind started to race with a million terrified thoughts, she was like a caged animal and her senses were on high alert as she heard new voices outside. Not sure if it was just her mind playing cruel tricks, Laura calmed her breathing, opened her eyes and twisted all she could to see beyond Graham's sickly hair.

"Police here, I have had a complaint about the noise."

Graham instinctively spun round and tripped over himself as Laura deliberately entwined his leg that had so offended her moments before. Laura had recognised the voice, and she seized her opportunity and shot past in a split second, throwing her arms around her father's neck. "Hi Dad, I have missed you, and you Mum."

Graham sat dumbfounded, still trying to see how Laura had got past so quickly, and in the drunken fog, trying to work out who these people were. For her part Laura deliberately stood half over Graham so that he could not get to his feet, and took longer than necessary with her greetings. Eventually Brendan saw his plight and motioned Laura across.

"You must be Graham, I recognise you from your photo," said Brendan, "That Tony showed me I mean when I last saw him in Bristol," he added almost unnecessarily. He then put his hand forward in a formal greeting.

"And you are?" questioned Graham, still on the floor without accepting the handshake offered.

"Brendan Scott, Laura's father, and this is my wife Caroline."

Graham nodded his head, wiped his heavily perspiring palms down his sides before pulling himself up and shook hands with both of them. Events were moving a bit fast for him at this stage of the evening. He had snorted too much coke, and drunk too much cider already, but that name was bouncing around his head like a ball on a squash court. Brendan Scott, it meant more than it should to him, but why?

"So where is the party boy then, and Charlotte of course? I hope they are having a joint party. The cake I have here has both of their names on it," questioned Caroline.

"Yes, of course Mum. They are inside. Just go on, I will cut the cake and bring it in." Laura took a deep breath and went back into the kitchen. Graham was still stood where she had passed him earlier, looking pensive. He spoke first. "I should apologise. Too much drink. Only I have always been very protective where Tony is concerned."

Trying to look as relaxed as she possibly could in the circumstances Laura casually leant back against the worktop, and deliberately folded her arms to signify that reconciliation was not an option. "You had better go and join the others." Then just as Graham was about to speak she turned to one side and added, "I would wipe your nose before I go in as well."

Graham sniffed quickly before lifting his arm to rub his face then as he pulled it away he saw the white powder opaque against the sweat on the back of his hand. Panic now seemed to be gripping him, as the balance of power in the kitchen had shifted full circle. His dominance from earlier had totally evaporated, and the startled look on his face resembled that of a rabbit caught in the headlights of an approaching car. "You won't say anything will you?"

Standing up to gain stature Laura spoke in a hushed but equally determined whisper. "You have got six months Graham, to swear to me you are clean… or I will tell Tony. Then we will test where his loyalty lies, and I wouldn't put money on you winning that one, brother or not." She didn't know where the strength was coming from, but as Graham sniffed again and walked away, she saw Charlotte in the doorway.

She waited until Graham had walked past her on his way to the lounge, and then she took his place in the kitchen. "You are one tough cookie, Laura Scott," she said in sheer admiration.

Laura for her part just lifted her hand to show how much she was trembling. "Hardly, but he can be pretty vile can't he?"

Charlotte moved in and embraced Laura in a firm hug as tears filled both of their eyes.

"I am afraid so, but that is not the person that we all grew up with."

"Really, well if that is the case what has changed him? You don't get to be as horrible as that easily."

"No," replied Charlotte. "But I think we both know what is behind it all."

Before Laura had chance to respond the first chords of 'Happy Birthday' could be heard and they both wiped their eyes then ran into the lounge to be a part of the celebrations.

Once the cake was cut the music was turned back on and the party continued. Graham drifted away quickly, and apart from Laura no one seemed to notice his absence. She did briefly entertain the idea of going after him, but fearful of the consequences decided to stay with the others instead. This was Tony's night, and for the rest of the evening she stayed firmly by his side. Charlotte spent much of the time with them as well, that is until Paul put some slower music on around midnight then came over and whisked her off her feet for a dance.

Laura pulled a reluctant Tony up onto the floor as well, and they embraced in a loving shuffle in the cramped space. "You see what I mean now about Paul, he has a certain charm about him, doesn't he?"

"No," replied Tony almost too indignantly.

"But he does, you know, and he is quite cute with it as well."

"I cannot believe we are having this conversation, you know. He is a total womaniser."

Laura smiled inwardly but didn't respond. Instead she leant in closer to Tony, and as so many times over the summer felt their bodies were melting together as one.

The rest of the evening went really well and by 3am most people were starting to flag a little. Brendan and Caroline opted to share with Bob and Paula, leaving Tony and Laura alone in their house. Everyone else was tired from the day's excitement and sloped off to bed at about the same time.

"I can't remember if I have ever told you this before, Tony, but I love you, I love your parents, I love your friends, maybe one day I could love Graham, but the rest of our life is blissfully happy right now."

Tony was surprised to hear Laura criticise Graham, not because he didn't know what a pain he could be, but because she was rarely critical of anyone. Still, they had all had a lot to drink and he decided to just let it go.

"Come on, let's go to bed, I am worn out, and thank you. This is definitely my best birthday ever."

Tony woke around 10.00 the following morning, and made his way downstairs alone. Laura was fast asleep, and though she murmured when he kissed her, he decided she needed the rest and left her to it. Everyone else had beaten him, and they were having breakfast on the lawn when he ventured outside. Surprisingly Graham had left already, electing to walk to the village and hope to get a taxi to the railway station. Laura eventually surfaced around 3.00, just in time to say goodbye to her parents, as well as James, Paul and Charlotte.

Just as they were all leaving Caroline called for hush. "A moment if you don't mind, all of you. It is my, um, 21st again next summer, and I would like to invite you all back here to celebrate. It is a big birthday so start saving, and see you all on the 28th May. I know you all have exams but it will be just one night, and I really want to share it with you all so see you then."

CHAPTER 15

Back to Reality

The return to peace seemed quite eerie at first but it was good for Tony and Laura to share a quiet evening with Bob and Paula before packing themselves and heading back to Bristol. Suddenly life was moving back into the fast lane again after months spent gently strolling along. As they left the Cove they both felt as though they were leaving part of themselves behind, but deep down they knew that ultimately life had to go on as well.

Tony dropped Laura at the hospital on Friday morning, and because she had a number of tests elected to stay in overnight. Back at the flat Tony felt like he was at a bit of loose end, so he was pleased when James announced that he fancied a quiet night in and they started on a mountain of beer that had sat undisturbed in the fridge all summer.

"So what is the story with Victoria then, mate?" Tony had been trying to find the moment ever since his birthday party and now seemed as good a time as any.

James took a slow and deliberate swig of his pint before answering. "I thought it was time to move on, really. Spain gave me the time to think. I have been craving some space for the last six months or so and I decided to set a mental agenda for the next five years."

"And I thought maybe you had found someone else," laughed Tony, surprised at the intensity of his friend's reply.

James contemplated for a moment or two further then shook his head. "No, not this time, but with exams next year I need to concentrate, and revise. Beyond that I think I have missed my chance of a Premiership call-up, so I have decided to join the police next summer."

This time it was Tony who needed time to contemplate. He had always been somewhat in awe of James' maturity. Even before the death of his dad James had been focussed, and once again he had proved himself to be miles ahead of the rest of them. Charlotte had always wanted to be a doctor, but that aside everyone else talked of where to go next year after uni. and yet hardly anyone had done more than pay lip service to it. Tony had put off serious contemplation of the subject all summer, and although he could easily drift into some form of accountancy he really wasn't sure.

"I am impressed mate, so dare I ask what brought this on?"

"In truth I don't know exactly. The relationship that you have with Laura seems very special, and I have been a bit jealous in a bizarre kind of way. I was almost jealous that she spent the summer with you, and we didn't see you, but you are clearly moving on and it made sense to plan myself. Paul is hoping to sign a deal before Christmas with his band and I don't want you two to show me up on all counts."

"Hardly, mate, I was just thinking it is time I started to take my responsibilities more seriously, and take a lead from you." Tony was trying to keep up with the erratic thread of their conversation, whilst battling tiredness and alcohol. "Paul is a dark horse, isn't he? Does he have any chance of hitting the big time?"

"Apparently so," replied James.

"God help us and all the women of the world if he gets fame and fortune as well," laughed Tony. Then they both sat silently for several minutes contemplating the thought of Paul on tour, with some dodgy band, surrounded by a load of groupies.

"So I have told you my plans. What have you decided to do, and are you going to marry Miss Scott?" questioned James eventually.

Tony didn't know whether it was the beer, or just the company of James, but plans were forming in his head where before there had been a massive void. "I am definitely not going over to Spain, but I would like to think that Laura and I have a long-term future. The time down at the Cove was really amazing, and I think it is time for us to make our plans together from now on. I am not saying we get engaged or anything but I think we will plan careers and lives that keep us together."

James carried on at something of a tangent. "I have to say there is something very eerie about the Cove. I almost felt as if the cottage we stayed in was haunted or something." As he finished he could see Tony smiling at him, and decided to carry on in defence. "Look, I know it sounds daft, and I knew you would laugh but it felt odd down there."

"You are right, I am not laughing at you, mate, more in disbelief at your perceptiveness. There is a lot of history about the place, and some of it is kind of ongoing, unresolved." Tony would have loved to go into detail, but knew he couldn't, and before he could carry on James was already changing the subject again.

"So next summer marks the real end of us all being together, it will be new careers, new partners, new families and all that from then on." There was no question, more a rather drink-induced statement of fact.

"And?" added Tony.

"Oh you know, mate. I have had too much time to think over the last few weeks like I said." James put his head back and stared up at the ceiling, apparently seeking inspiration. He then sat up straight again, and looked at Tony. "This may sound strange but while I was home over the summer I helped Mum clear out some of Dad's old stuff, and we threw out loads of his school photos and the like. Anyway I found out he was keen at sports, head boy, captain of the swimming, football and cricket teams."

"That cannot be any great surprise though; it is obviously where you get your talent from," interrupted Tony.

"No," replied James, shaking his head. "You are missing the point. Dad was obviously very popular, and he had notes from everyone when he left school, wishing him luck and all… then nothing." There followed a long pause as they both dwelled on their own thoughts. The evening was forcing them both to take stock, and focus in a way that only their friendship allowed. Tony loved Laura to the ends of the earth, but he was only stimulated to evaluate, and re-evaluate his life when he had these conversations with James. Their friendship was the bedrock around which the rest of his life revolved.

"Mum never met any of his school friends. It was as though that was a closed chapter in his book, and then they all moved on with their new lives," continued James.

Tony was desperate to keep up with the flow of conversation, but with his own thoughts distracting his mind he was struggling to follow the threads offered by James. "And you reckon that will happen with us do you. Lose touch after uni."

"Maybe. I hope not and cannot believe it will happen, but who knows?"

This time it was Tony's turn to shake his head. "Not a chance, mate, and I will make every effort to keep us all in touch. There is no need at all in this day and age."

"Paul is the problem really. He has the habit of going it alone, then reappearing all of sudden with some new persona." James was strangely melancholic, quite alien to his usual pragmatic self.

"I know what you mean," answered Tony, "but that is just him. It won't stop us all from staying in touch though, will it?"

"Maybe," continued James, before raising his glass to Tony. "To a shared future."

"Cheers."

The chat carried on into the night until they both fell asleep on the sofas. James woke around 4am, and shook Tony. "Come on, mate, it's time to get some proper sleep. You have to pick up the future wife in the morning." With that he staggered off to bed.

Tony sat for a few minutes, letting his head clear, and then he went off to bed. He had barely touched the pillow as he fell into a deep sleep. Before he knew it the alarm was blaring away, and he sat upright in bed, continuing the thoughts of the night before. He definitely felt as though a weight had been lifted from his shoulders. Somehow through the alcohol he had found the focus that eluded him all summer. He had made tentative enquiries to a couple of accountancy firms locally, and now was the time to follow one of these up. The most important thing though was to speak with Laura, and make the decision together. He wanted her to see that she was to be part of his life from now on.

Deep down he knew that he had ample opportunity to discuss this all summer, but at least he felt he had got there eventually. Buoyed with enthusiasm Tony showered and made his way to the hospital as arranged, arriving by 9.30. As he walked up to the ward, he was surprised to see Brendan and Caroline stood by Laura's side.

"Hi everyone." Tony bent over to give Laura a kiss then stood back as he saw Dr Preston approaching the bed.

"Hello Tony, Brendan, Caroline." As Dr Preston greeted those assembled Tony felt Laura slip her hand out from under the covers seeking his, which she held firmly.

"I am afraid that the news I have is not the best. Laura here is not as well as we would have hoped, in fact…" As he hesitated for a moment Laura interrupted.

"Do you mind if I explain, Doctor? You can correct me if I get it wrong."

"Of course, Laura."

She gently pulled herself up on the bed then rested back against the pillows. Still holding Tony's hand she squeezed it gently then spoke quietly. "I appear to have bowel cancer, and I need to have an operation in the next couple of days, following which I will need a course of chemotherapy up to Christmas. It doesn't appear to be related to my illness before, but there is no certainty, and like Dr Preston says it doesn't change the future by dwelling too much on the past."

There was a stunned silence, and Laura turned to face Tony, still holding his hand firmly in her own. "I am sorry about this, but I have been there before and I will beat this, I promise."

Tony wanted to say so much, but his head was full of questions that were arriving and being dismissed in quick succession. The gravity of the moment was all too apparent, but why did these massive wrecking balls hit him when they were least expected time and again? He wanted to give Laura strength, and yet he could easily have turned and fled. Something made him stay. An inner strength that he had felt before, a strength that he didn't have to summon, and couldn't call on demand, and yet a strength that he knew would see him through.

Without conscious effort he spoke. "I came here today to plan our future together. I know that you are the person I want to spend the rest of my life with, and this doesn't change my thoughts at all." As he finished Tony felt his whole world was centred around that bed. He had no perception of anyone else present as his total focus was on Laura. The noises from the ward were strangely muted, and even his peripheral vision was obscured. All that he could think about right now was Laura sat in front of him.

"Steady on, Mum will be buying a new hat if you are not careful." Laura laughed, injecting some humour into proceedings, as she tugged on Tony's hand and pulled him in closer to her. "I love you."

Suddenly aware of the others, Tony pulled back and looked around. He had so much to consider and too much to take in. Despite Laura's earlier efforts the general atmosphere remained subdued. They were filled in on some of the detail by Dr Preston over the next hour, before Laura dressed and they were all able to leave. Her operation was scheduled for Tuesday of the following week, and she was then to have chemotherapy for the next six weeks.

Brendan and Caroline stayed with them until about six o'clock, before leaving to head back home, leaving Tony and Laura alone for the first time back in her flat. Both of them had the same question on their minds, and although it seemed strangely inadequate in the circumstances Tony posed it first. "So how are you feeling?"

"Weak, angry, annoyed and above all rather philosophical. How about you?" whispered Laura.

"Much the same really, I have butterflies in my stomach, but all I want is to see you better, so I just want to get on with it all really." Tony answered as honestly as he could. There were some nagging 'What if?' questions at the very back of his mind that had been trying to surface all day but he was happy to leave them where they were.

"Thanks." Laura was smiling, and she looked so healthy and vibrant that Tony couldn't believe any real harm would come to her. "Mum and Dad always dwell on the worst-case scenario, and if I even sneeze when I am on the phone to them they will be on their way down here. Please just treat me like me, like you always have, and if I get down with the chemo then pick me up, or slap me or something. I will be okay."

Tony knew that she was trying to convince herself as much as him, and he knew that her strength would win through. He couldn't think of any more to add, so he simply smiled back and leant forward to hug her as reassuringly as he could.

"And there is one more thing." Laura appeared hesitant. She was sat facing Tony on the sofa, with her legs crossed in front of her, and she leant forward putting her hands down to support herself before continuing. "Given what will be going on, I would like it if you would move in with me here, you know, for moral support." Then as if to justify the request she added, "And that way hopefully Mum won't insist on coming down here to live as well."

Tony immediately thought of his conversation with James the night before, but in the circumstances knew he would understand. He wouldn't be deserting James, but Laura's need was by far the greater right now. He had always imagined that moving in with a partner would be a major moment in his life, but it seemed almost an anti-climax in the present circumstances. "I would love to, but I want us to have a proper party to celebrate in six months when you are better, before our exams start, and then I want us to get somewhere together next year as well if that is okay."

The delight in Laura's face was obvious. "You bet." She leant further forward and kissed Tony before blushing slightly as she continued. "I was more nervous about asking you to move in than I was this morning when I had to tell you about the cancer. I know that sounds weird but it's the truth."

"Don't worry, I am more nervous about telling James than anything."

"Why?"

Realising how out of context his previous comments suddenly seemed Tony backtracked a little. "Nothing, just nothing really."

They chatted for the next couple of hours, largely about very little but they both took comfort from just being able to talk instead of dwelling on Laura's problems. Over the next few weeks they both learnt to focus on the immediate issues rather than the wider picture. Laura had the operation, and started the course of chemotherapy, but kept up her study all the same. Tony would have happily deferred for a year, but followed the inspiration she set and worked harder than he ever had before. Caroline managed to arrange her work so that she could come down two days a week to help out, and Paula also lent them a hand whenever she could.

Christmas was upon them before they knew it, and when term ended James and Tony met up with Paul, when he visited for the weekend. Caroline stayed with Laura for a few days to help keep some hospital appointments, and despite feeling a degree of guilt Tony felt like he was getting a few days off as he spent some time with his friends. It was a classic lads' night out, when all of them could forget about the challenges ahead and focus on getting drunk and having a good time. As ever Paul spent half the evening discussing past conquests, whilst looking out for fresh acquaintances, and once again he stunned the other two with his ability to attract a circle of followers within hours of hitting the uni. bar. The following night they all paid a visit to Charlotte and as usual the conversation followed a familiar path with frequent references to their shared past. Being on home territory she was keen to introduce Tony, James and Paul to her newer friends but then seemed genuinely shocked when she was left alone at the end of the evening with only Tony for company.

"Merry Christmas then, I suppose…" She lifted her glass somewhat half-heartedly in a toast to Tony. "How come my emotional life is such a mess, and yet two of my best friends can desert me for the first two good-looking girls that they meet on a night up here?"

"You introduced them all, so that kind of endorses them really."

"Rubbish, I warned them about Paul and James, and yet they both paid no attention whatsoever to my warnings, did they?" Despite the implied criticism Charlotte was laughing and clearly not upset at all.

"What did you expect? You introduce two good-looking girls to two good-looking guys on the weekend before Christmas and what did you think was going to happen?" replied Tony, taking up the challenge with relish.

"So I am I not a good-looking girl then?"

Tony knew straight away that this was a conversation he couldn't win, and were it not for the drink he would have taken caution and backed off. He had similar conversations with Laura, and the logic simply didn't follow his own. "No, well I mean yes you are a beautiful girl but they weren't going to go off for a night of passion with you were they?" It seemed so obvious that the reply took him totally by surprise.

"And why not? What is wrong with me then?"

"Nothing, I just said you were beautiful didn't I?"

"Well there must be something. I came quite high on your totty list as I remember, but James has never come on to me yet, and nor has Paul for that matter, and that probably makes me fairly unique amongst the female population."

Tony knew he was getting deeper into a conversation he didn't want to be a part of, and started scrambling for survival. "Look Charlotte, you are a nice person, and we all adore you, but we respect you, and that is why they wouldn't take advantage like that."

"NICE?"

Tony closed his eyes, and thought for a second, hoping this time that he could say the right thing. Before he could reply Charlotte shouted the word again.

"NICE? I should have learnt years ago that all you boys want is short skirts and adoration."

"Come on, Charlotte, you are being unreasonable. Paul may be a bit shallow at times, but James isn't. He is a good sincere person who would do anything for any one of us."

"For you maybe, but I am fed up with being the big sensible sister of the group. Why do you all look at me as some kind of androgynous person?"

Rather than speaking Tony leant over and threw a comforting shoulder around his oldest friend. "Look, we all work well as a group because we know our failings and no one has tried to alter the dynamic over the years. I feel sometimes that my relationship with Laura has jeopardised things but I cannot change that. You will find a man who is worthy of you, and if that is Mark then I will accept him for what you believe he is."

"Thank you. I just would like to be the rebel for once rather than the sensible one. Maybe I should just leave my bedroom door open in case one of the others returns in failure."

Tony laughed, but in truth they both knew it wasn't Charlotte, and after a few minutes sat together they both decided it was time to call it a night. They all stayed together for the next couple of days, then on the day before Christmas Eve went their separate ways. Tony made his way down to the Cove where Bob and Paula were to spend Christmas as well, and it was Bob who met Tony at the train station.

"Hi there Tony, had a good journey?"

"Yes, good thanks. A few grumpy old sods on the train that needed a bit of Yuletide spirit, and a few more that have already had a bit too much, but it was fine."

They travelled the few miles to the Cove deep in conversation, each catching up on the others news, and they were met at the end of the drive by Paula and Laura. There were greetings all around, before Laura gently pulled on Tony's arm. "Come on, you, it is my turn now, let's go for a walk. The Cove is at its best in the early afternoon, remember?"

"What, even in winter?"

"Of course, you have so much still to learn about this place, don't you?"

Tony turned briefly to his parents. "Looks like I have my orders. I will catch up with you later." Then he turned and walked off to the clock tower as Laura squeezed his arm and snuggled in close. Tony loved the intoxicating presence of Laura as she held him ever tighter, and as they stopped and looked out at the tranquillity of the Cove, there was no need to talk.

The peal of the bells only inches behind them made Tony jump, and he counted them off in quick succession, one, two, three, four. "Ahh," he said, turning around suddenly. "It's fixed at last. The clock just rang out four times."

Laura burst out laughing, and although it wasn't that funny tears started to roll down her face, and she held her stomach as she tried to control herself. "It is winter now, the clocks have gone back, so it is real time again."

"Yes but if that is all it is, I mean they just don't put the clock on an hour in the summer, then no mystery, no lightning and the whole story falls down."

Still laughing, but trying desperately to keep a straight face Laura continued. "Tony I thought you had accepted the history of the legacy, and remember I told you the clock tower is only a minor part of the whole story, and the clock is now kept by the locals to the same time all year round. No one has even been brave enough to tempt fate again. Remember the clocks did not change time 100 years ago."

Tony was laughing now. "I know I do, but one day I will find a big hole in this story of mystery and hocus pocus."

They were both so happy to be back together that neither wanted to discuss the time that Laura had spent in the hospital, and it wasn't until they were walking back to the house that Tony raised it. "So dare I ask how things went at the hospital?"

"Not great, I am afraid. The chemo was necessary as you know because they couldn't remove all of the cancer, and to contain any further spread, but it doesn't appear to have been very successful. That means I have to go through a course of radiotherapy starting on January the third." Her words hung in the air, as they continued walking slowly back. Tony didn't comment as he tried to comprehend what he had been told, and before he could reply Laura continued.

"Mum and Dad are a bit freaked out by it all, but I only want to focus on getting better if that is alright. Mum is really down, so it would be good if we could carry as normal... Please."

"We will, I promise," The conversation wasn't over, and if Tony could have he would have rewound the clock by at least an hour to give them more time. He stopped just outside the front door. "Look, if I ask you this just the once please answer me, and I promise to only focus on our future after that."

"Of course." Laura knew what was coming, but she waited for the question.

"Will you beat this cancer?"

She pointedly didn't answer, but moved closer and hugged Tony as tightly as she could. They stayed together for an eternity, and it felt like they were two lost souls, under the spotlight in a swirling mass of clouds. Neither wanted to break the embrace for fear of facing the consequences, for a brief moment they were so lost that life itself seemed to be on hold. Eventually they pulled apart slightly, and stood with their foreheads touching as they inclined towards each other. Tony could see the tears behind the veil of her resolute stare, and he didn't want those tears to fall. "Laura you don't have to answer, I shouldn't have asked, I am sorry."

They hugged again, and this time Laura spoke, whispering into his ear. "I want to beat it, and I need your strength to help me do it, but I feel like I am losing the battle if not the war. If I lose then I will go down fighting. That is all I can promise you, I am afraid."

As Laura held him he could feel her tears damp on his neck, and as he did so he started to shiver in her embrace, but he fought the trembling as he was desperate to keep his own emotions at bay. He nodded his head in acknowledgement before they kissed briefly.

"Whatever happens, we are in this for the long haul together, I promise."

"Thank you Tony, but don't give up on me just yet will you?"

"No way, just one day at a time from now on."

"One day at a time," confirmed Laura, and with that they walked slowly back, making their way into the cottage.

Almost immediately they were then caught up in the roller coaster that is Christmas and it took away their time for thought. Christmas Day went well, and after Boxing Day the two sets of parents left for home. Charlotte and James came to stay at the end of the week to see in New Year, and apart from feeling tired and needing a lot of rest Laura was able to carry on as normal.

They had a relatively quiet evening together, before turning on the television at ten to midnight to witness Big Ben strike 12. Laura was exhausted and went to bed shortly afterwards, and as the others sat around James fell asleep on the sofa. Charlotte and Tony chatted about Laura, but it was clear that she had something more focussed on her mind.

"You do realise that Laura is pretty much on her last chance now.

If the radiotherapy doesn't work then there isn't much left for the doctors to try, and what is more it is a very debilitating treatment."

Tony turned to face her in acknowledgement. "Now I know why we invited you down here, it was to help lift the occasion."

"Sorry, but I have known you a long time, and I am not sure that you want to accept the truth sometimes."

"I know what could happen, but Laura is so determined to fight to the end that I have to support her fully. If I let the doubts creep into my mind then I know I will show that inadvertently, and that will knock her confidence. Catch 22, I am afraid, but I do know the possibilities, Dr Charlotte."

"Not a doctor yet! I only wish that I could somehow do more for you both now. Regrettably I don't think I could even if I was fully qualified. I checked Dr Preston out and he is one of the best in the country." Charlotte paused momentarily waiting for a response, but none came and she decided to continue. "I have seen patients similar to Laura before, and their resilience, and sheer determination changes the way you are forever. I just hope that at this stage she is in the successful minority."

Tony didn't know what to say, and elected to remain silent instead. They carried on watching the fire for a while, and sipping their wine before Charlotte spoke again. "So what are your plans for next year then, after you have qualified?"

"This year now," corrected Tony.

Charlotte instinctively looked at her watch and giggled. "So it is."

"Well the plan is to get a job in accountancy if Laura is well. If not we are going to live down here at the Cove for a year or so until she is better. The property here is all hers and it earns more than enough to sustain us both."

"You are not going to help Graham out in Spain then?"

"No chance. I don't need hand-me-down help from him, and I don't think I could work with the two of them anyway."

"This may come as a surprise but I am going over in late summer, and I am going to try and convince Mark to come back to the UK, hopefully to be with me. We have some accommodation booked in

Northern Spain for a two-week holiday where I stayed last year, and I am giving him one last chance."

"So you took my advice then?"

"No," laughed Charlotte, "don't flatter yourself, I am just giving him one last chance like I said."

"One last chance, what do you mean by that?" questioned Tony, trying to sound nonplussed but surprised that he appeared to be out of date somehow.

"Well I know you won't agree but Mark is a great guy, and I have spent time with him off and on over the years, but Graham has always come between us. Now I am going to give him an ultimatum of sorts. He is so different when Graham is not around and together I think that they are both heading for disaster."

Tony looked ahead at the fire, and didn't turn to acknowledge Charlotte, speaking into thin air. "The drugs, you mean."

Charlotte gasped in surprise, and wasn't sure what to say. "My god, I never thought you knew."

"I didn't, but you have just confirmed what I suspected. Paul picked up on some things years ago when we were in Spain, and he found more strange transactions on their computers when he was there last summer, but I have never been 100% certain. James knows more than I do, but he looks to be fast asleep."

"Why didn't you say anything? Does Laura know?" quizzed Charlotte as she leant over and gently shook James to see if there was any chance of him joining in.

"No, and you must not say anything. It would compromise her situation with her dad. The thing is, I am not convinced who is behind it all. Paul claims it is well hidden on the computer system, and under a false set of names and passwords. He isn't sure if it is Mark or Graham, so please be careful how you tackle Mark. You have to remember that deep down I know what Graham is capable of, and I know this isn't him so it leads me to suspect Mark."

Still shocked at this revelation, Charlotte wanted to know more. "So dare I ask whose name the files are hidden under?"

They both paused for a moment as James eventually picked

himself up, and spoke through a stifled yawn. "Yours."

Charlotte could see from the grim expression on his face that he wasn't joking. "Nice of you to join in with that bombshell, but I take it you do actually know what we are talking about."

"I have been listening for the last ten minutes or so, I wasn't really asleep, the files are hidden behind your name."

"Mine... but that doesn't prove a thing. Mark or Graham could have used my name."

"You have to make of it what you want to, we are only giving you the facts, but I have to agree with Tony, it is more likely to be Mark, don't you think? He is the one with the soft spot for you."

They all knew that there was some truth in what he had said, but equally they all thought they were right in their differing suspicions as to who was behind it all. Tony emptied the last drop of wine from the bottle into his own glass and knocked it back before he spoke again. "Drink up, it is getting late."

"Sorry. I am just reeling from the shock of it all. How did they ever get involved in drugs in the first place?" asked Charlotte.

Tony was tired, and he allowed himself a yawn before he replied. "Look, we all have our lives to lead, but be very careful, and don't get mixed up in anything you are not sure about. If you have any doubts at all when you are out there then get back here. Remember, your name is all over the computer linked to some very large money transfers. I have thought about it all lots since Paul told me last summer, and there is one other possibility that might actually be the most plausible of all."

"Go on," replied Charlotte. Rather than feeling tired her heart was pounding so hard that she didn't feel she would sleep for a week.

"You are on your own with this one," interrupted James. "I have to say that you are grasping at straws and using your own bias to cloud your judgement, but it is getting late for me so I am off to bed if you don't mind."

Tony and Charlotte both stood up to hug James before he left, then they slumped back into the sofa that he had just vacated.

"Tell me your theory then," begged Charlotte.

"I am not sure, James may be right, perhaps it would be safer if I kept it to myself."

"Tony I am an adult... remember... so tell before I smother you with this cushion. You cannot leave me in suspense like this."

"Juan, your ex-boyfriend. Maybe he is trying to implicate you for some kind of revenge, and maybe, just maybe, it has nothing to do with Mark or Graham. We are talking about major business here. Paul found over seven transactions in excess of £100,000, and I doubt that either of them could orchestrate something at that level."

"Wow." Charlotte's hand was shaking as she picked up her glass. "Well that is it; I don't think I will go to Spain to see Mark. It is never worth it. Why does it have to be so complicated?"

"Pass." Tony shrugged his shoulders, slumped back into the sofa and sat staring at the fire again. "Remember sixth form, and the time before that, when we only had the Games each year to worry about? That was only a couple of years ago."

They sat chatting for a few minutes longer before Tony insisted that he was too tired and they both decided to call it a night. Charlotte sat awake in bed for several hours despite the mounting wave of tiredness, with her heart beating like mad, and a sick feeling in the pit of her stomach. She was disappointed in Mark, felt anger at him and Juan, but worse still felt a growing hatred towards Graham. She had seen another side to him a few weeks earlier, and she despised the hold he had over Tony. More than anything though, it was the aftermath of another New Year, and she was on her own in bed. The idea of going into James' room for a comforting hug lingered for a while, but the sensible side took over as ever and she stayed in her own bed. With a heavy sigh to herself she rolled over for the hundredth time and whispered to herself, "Become a short skirt girl for a year and see whether it changes your fortunes. Make that your resolution."

Tony meanwhile was equally restless as he tried to get to sleep. Thoughts about their chat earlier kept coming back into focus despite his best efforts to dull his mind and achieve the sleep his body was craving. He felt nervous, but more for Charlotte than himself. Mark had to be at the heart of the drug business, and he was very worried about what impact it would have on her life in the future. Eventually sleep came for both of them, and no one surfaced from either house before 11 the next morning. They all had a shared breakfast, discussed New Year resolutions without actually making any, then despite a great deal of reluctance thoughts turned to the demands of the year ahead.

With heaps of revision and study to do, they all left the Cove on the second of January, before Charlotte and Tony had any chance to discuss Spain again. With so much focus on exams as well as Laura's treatment the month of January flew by, and before they knew it February was upon them. The deterioration in Laura was evident for everyone to see, and despite assurances that it was down to the treatment itself Tony felt as though he was constantly trying to put on a positive facade when in truth he felt bleaker than he ever had.

Fortunately for him, much of his degree work was done through the course, and he only had to sit four exams, but the distraction of revision was almost welcomed by him at times, as a means of avoiding what he could see happening before him. Easter was early, falling at the beginning of March, and he and James planned to stay in Bristol to maximise their preparation time. Charlotte was coming down for a few days, intent on discussing Spain with Tony, and Laura was to go back with her parents for a few days, returning to Bristol for the last two weeks of the Easter break. Paul was dropping in for a few days, but he was unsure as to when, and planned to telephone from the train station when he arrived.

Tony and James told him that they couldn't guarantee transport, but he wasn't bothered, and still wouldn't confirm an exact time or date. The final lectures were on the Wednesday morning, and as Tony crossed the road back to his flat he recognised Brendan and Caroline's car parked outside on the road. The front wheel was just touching the double yellow line, and he would have loved to direct a traffic warden over so that Brendan would be penalised, but thought better of it.

Rather than carry all his notes over to Laura's he decided to drop them off and went to his own flat first. He only intended to be a minute or so, and left the front door ajar as he dropped into his bedroom. He rarely slept there these days, and the bed was covered in scribbled notes, and half open textbooks. Looking at the mess, he quickly grabbed as many of the screwed up bits of paper as he could and rammed them into an overflowing wastepaper bin. They stayed there for a second but the paper gradually sprung back, pushing the bits like molten lava from an erupting volcano onto the floor.

In frustration he kicked the bin, spilling the contents all over the floor, before he heard a gentle knock on his bedroom door.

"Can I come in?" Laura was stood in the doorway, clearly upset, and with very bloodshot eyes that had obviously been crying.

Tony looked up, and swallowed hard. His heart was racing, and he felt a lump jammed into his throat, as the base fell out of the bottom of his stomach. "Of course." His voice squeaked like it had years earlier when it was breaking, and he coughed before trying again. "Of course."

Laura walked over and sat on the bed, placing her hands into her lap.

Tony didn't say a word, but walked over and sat beside her. His hands were clammy and wet, he could feel his whole body sweating profusely, and his heart was pounding away relentlessly in his chest. He felt as sick as he had ever felt, and he kept blinking in the hope that the sweat running into his eyes would go away to stop the stinging. His left leg started to dance uncontrollably until he rested his foot firmly on the floor to stop it, waiting for Laura to say something.

He could see the odd stray tear rolling down her cheek, but still she sat there in absolute silence. Tony wanted to reach out and make everything better, but he feared that it was too late for that. Why didn't she just say something?

Eventually as he felt his own tears running onto his top lip, he shakily lifted his right arm, and tentatively placed it around her shoulders. Laura almost collapsed into him, and the tears that had been trickling down her still beautiful face came now in a torrent between deep sobs. Her whole body was shaking, and all Tony could do was to try and console her until he knew she would be able to communicate with him.

As they sat there Tony had no sense at all of time. Laura couldn't stop herself. He knew she wanted to get some control, could tell from the anguished sobs that she was fighting her own emotions, but she had been fighting so long, and her reserves were so low now. Tony tried to give her strength, he lifted his other arm and cradled her, but Laura had nothing left, she couldn't cuddle back, and it was only her chin resting on his shoulder that was supporting her whole body. As he tried to support them both the reality of how light Laura had become struck him. He felt a vulnerability in her that he had never seen before.

Gradually she recovered her composure, and was able to pull back from Tony slightly, but she didn't want to look him in the eye, instead she lay on her side on the bed. Tony did likewise, but still couldn't get her to make eye contact, and the dread was building in him all the time. He didn't want the truth, he wasn't sure if he was strong enough to handle it, and as he bit his lip in anticipation he could taste blood filling his mouth. The realisation that he was biting too hard brought him around slightly but it did nothing to sway his anger. He wasn't even sure of the purpose of his anger, or for that matter the reason, but he had never felt so bitter in his life before.

"I have lost, Tony. I am so sorry for you, for me, for everything." The words when they came were no less shocking.

Tony couldn't react. He had questions, but despite the tears and blood his mouth was bone dry, and his tongue was stuck to the roof of his mouth. He was shaking all over and tried desperately to get a grip on his body.

"The radiotherapy hasn't worked, and the cancer is taking over. I have maybe six or eight weeks left, that is all, there is nothing left to try. I will get worse each day from now on, and I want you to remember me like this, not some wasted living corpse of skin and bones, so this is goodbye as well."

Still he couldn't speak. His questions were being answered without even asking them, and his worst fears realised, but he didn't know how to react. Laura sat up, pulling strength from somewhere, but Tony couldn't move.

"You need to do your exams, be a top accountant, and make something of our lives for me. Remember me always, please." With that, she leant forward and kissed Tony gently on the forehead. It was an affectionate kiss like a mother to child, and Tony felt like he was the one being comforted. He was taking solace from Laura's strength, but only taking now not giving back. Deep inside it was hurting him more than ever that he couldn't take the lead, but the frustrations of the last months had sapped his strength emotionally as well as physically and he felt washed out.

As she stood up Laura blew one final kiss and said simply, "Thank you," before she walked up the hallway, leaving Tony to wallow in his own self-pity. He heard another woman's voice at the door, and assumed it was Caroline, but he was still lying incapacitated on the bed, and he didn't get up to see what was happening.

Then the door slammed shut and there was a moment's silence before he heard. "Tony, what the hell are you doing?"

The sound of the familiar voice stirred fresh emotions within. Tony had been a million miles away, probably not even on the planet only moments before, focussed on his own plight, cut off from the world he knew. Now suddenly he was racing back to reality, struggling to come to terms with his distress, still not sure if this was a reality he could handle.

"Tony."

The anger in the voice was obvious, and without looking up he knew that Charlotte was staring at him with utter contempt. From the bed he knew that he was vulnerable in the row that was about to follow, but half of him wanted to just roll over and close his eyes. Adrenalin was running through his veins, and bringing focus back to his thoughts, he was not going to be beaten in the argument that was to follow. Distant memories stirred of times long ago, time stuck in the tree, time at the Gorge, and Charlotte was not going to assume superiority as a matter of course again. He raised himself slowly off the bed, aware that his bleary eyes belied the strength he needed to show.

"What?" He almost spat the word back, and hated himself all the more for failing to show his resolve. Why did Charlotte always turn up at these moments?

Her reaction stunned him, and as ever she was able to stay one step ahead of his own thoughts. He wanted a fight, adrenalin was bringing out the animal instinct in him, and he wanted to scream and shout, but without being patronising Charlotte sat beside him on the bed and took his free right hand in hers.

"You are my best friend in the whole world, and I cannot begin to understand what you are going through, but it is because I know you so well that I know your weaknesses. You cannot leave Laura to face this alone. You will live with the consequences for the rest of your life if you do and ultimately it will destroy you. Your grief is understandable, and I love you because of your emotions, but don't let self-pity cloud your judgement. Laura needs you now, and you have to give her 110% of yourself for whatever time she has left. You have an opportunity that your own mother never had. The opportunity to say goodbye to the person you love most in the world. Don't waste it because if you do then it will destroy your life as it did hers."

Tony's mind was a swirl of confused thoughts. He wanted to hate Charlotte but he couldn't. He wanted to blame Laura but he couldn't. He wanted excuses, to justify his actions, but even then he was struggling to find any. "But I am due to start exams in six weeks. My degree is all I have for my future, and this is where I shape the rest of my life."

"Bollocks, Tony. This is not some crummy first-day speech by Mr Peterson. You have a future, Laura doesn't. All she wants is one month of your long life."

"You don't know everything, Charlotte. For once in your life accept that you are wrong. Laura doesn't want me to see her die, she wants to be alone, and she wants me to remember her as she is now."

Tony expected a swift response but Charlotte took her time. She released her grip on his hands and reached inside her jacket pocket. "Here, these are the keys to my car that is parked outside. Take it and keep it as long as you need it. Do what your heart and mind tell you, but don't let me down. You will lose Laura, and that is tragic, but she doesn't have to lose you yet. You can still add a lot to her life, and she still has so much more to give. Stay with her to the end."

With that Charlotte stood up and walked out, leaving Tony all alone in the bedroom. He looked at the keys and threw them onto the floor. He wasn't about to chase after Laura, or Charlotte, and he knew he was right. He walked into the kitchen and put the kettle on; he didn't really want a drink but he was acting almost robotically. As the steam rose he thought about putting his hand into the boiling water. It was a stupid ridiculous thought, but he craved attention, despite the selfishness of it; he wanted to be pitied for once. He held his hand briefly over the steam, but the searing heat brought him back to his senses, and he instinctively withdrew and slumped to the floor, resting his back against the kitchen cabinet doors.

Too scared to even carry out the simple threat to his own body, he hated himself so much at that moment. Partly for wanting to do it in the first place and partly for not being brave enough to go through with it. Tears were running down his face, and he felt himself snivelling like a baby, but he couldn't stop. Not yet at least. He wanted to get all of the hurt out, and then he would refocus and decide who was right. As the tears eventually dried up he felt completely hollow inside, weak and devoid of any substance at all. He knew where Laura would be, the only place in the world where she would want to be at a time like this, and deep down he knew that he had to get there as well. His mind was certain, but his body sat incapacitated, waiting for something to spur him into action.

The same thoughts kept bouncing through his mind time after time and on each circuit the conclusion was exactly the same, but still he couldn't raise himself off the floor. He sat completely motionless, barely even blinking, staring at a small mark on the kitchen unit in front of him. He was still sat there several hours later as night started to fall, and he could sense the natural light beginning to fade. The temperature was falling, and he felt the chill searing into his body. He felt numb from sitting motionless for so long but still he couldn't get up. It was becoming harder to focus on the mark in front of him, as the light failed and this was the cause of fresh frustration. He was angry with the daylight ebbing away, but slowly, slowly he found he was more at peace with himself, and as he raised his hand to run it through his hair it was the first physical movement he had managed for several hours.

Slowly he reached an uneasy equilibrium between his heart and mind; it wasn't a perfect balance by any means but it brought fresh rationale to his thinking. Why had no one been around all afternoon? Where was James? He needed someone to talk to, but Laura was gone, Charlotte had said her piece, and he felt so alone right now. When he eventually heard a key in the door, he stood up unsteadily with eager anticipation. Part of him even hoped it would be Laura, that maybe he had only dreamt his wasted afternoon.

It was James who came in and as he switched the light on Tony had to shield his eyes against the sudden intrusion of brightness.

"Sorry mate, didn't realise you were lurking about in the dark." James was immediately cautious, somehow aware that everything was not as it should be, and he was perceptive enough to bide his time.

When Tony didn't say anything James ventured further. "It is good to get the lectures over with, just study now I suppose."

Again nothing at first, then almost as if the floodgates had suddenly been opened Tony spoke. "Laura has been told that she only has about six weeks left, mate, and she has gone down to the Cove, I think, to stay with her parents. Charlotte has been around, and reckons I am being selfish, running away from it or something. Reckons I should chase after her, but I don't know if I have it in me to face up to what is going to happen. Not at first hand if you know what I mean."

James slumped onto the sofa, trying to comprehend the enormity of what he had been told in those few garbled sentences. Suddenly, choking back tears he cleared his throat and spoke. "I am really sorry, mate, but you will hear that a hundred times from a hundred people and I am afraid it makes no difference at all. No one can make any of it any better, no matter how well intentioned they are, and you will have to deal with it in your own way." He paused for a moment and wiped away a tear from his eyes. "The only advice I can give you for what it is worth is do whatever you believe deep down is the right thing. It doesn't matter what anyone else thinks or does, do what you know is right, and if I can offer any help at all I will, but it is mainly down to you. I found out too much about my own father after he had gone and we never got to share the memories that make me so proud of him now. He was a sporting hero in his own right, a black man well ahead of his time who was admired and respected in a white world back then. I would love to have spent just two weeks learning about his past and yet in the blink of an eye that opportunity was lost. Nothing is more final than death. This isn't a lecture but when someone dies it is too late to say all the things you wanted to, and never found the time or place. There is no going back, nor righting the wrongs, everything stops."

Tony was biting his lip again, and gaining fresh resolve as he did so. Somehow advice from James came much easier. His intentions were identical to Charlotte's, but somehow the words were much easier to receive. He had reached his conclusion hours ago, but some hidden inertia had held him back. Now he had only to acknowledge his friend's contribution, and catch up for lost time.

"That is what mates are for. Thanks James, I think I have to be somewhere." With that he walked into the bedroom, threw a few books into a holdall, then grabbed as many clothes as he could find that were clean, found Charlotte's keys, picked some bits up from the bathroom, and made his way to the lounge again.

"Here, take this with you." James looked almost embarrassed as he passed over the sandwiches and drink that he had made.

"You will make someone a good wife someday."

"Tell me about it." James would have laughed normally, but the time wasn't right, and instead he moved over to give Tony a reassuring hug. "We are all here for you, mate – me, Charlotte, Paul, even Graham and Mark, just call us."

The embrace was so comforting and warming that Tony could have held on forever, but after a long pause he pulled away.

"Thanks," replied Tony before he turned and headed up to find where Charlotte had parked her car. Fortunately it was directly in front of him on the other side of the road, and feeling like he was heading into a black hole he quickly threw his things into the boot and jumped in the driver's seat. He sat for a moment, thinking not about what to do, more which way to go. Tony knew the route of course, but his mind had been so preoccupied for the last few hours that he needed a moment before he started the engine, selected a gear and pulled away.

He didn't want to think any more, so he turned the stereo up as loud as it would go and concentrated on the music and trivial chat from the radio DJs. It was midnight by the time he arrived at the Cove, and he turned the stereo off as he pulled into the track. At first he thought he had guessed wrong because the place was in total darkness. Then as he swung around to face the main cottage his headlights picked up the familiar shape of Brendan's car.

Despite the cold that was already starting to creep into the car he elected to sleep there for the night. If he knocked at the house then Laura's parents would probably answer, and he wasn't ready for the third degree just yet. As it was he had a restless sleep, due to the cramped conditions, and cold, but did manage some rest. He was awoken by the sound of someone tapping on the window, and took a minute to realise where he was. Without thinking he grabbed the handle of the door that he was leaning against and fell out of the car at Brendan's feet. Struggling to regain his composure despite his dishevelled appearance he stood up as quickly as he could. His eyes were barely open, and the cold misty morning air sent a shiver through his body.

"You should have knocked when you got here, Tony. Laura waited up till about 11.30 before giving up on you."

"How did she know I was coming?"

"She didn't, but she would have been disappointed if you hadn't. In fact we all would have been." Brendan was smiling, demonstrating warmth that Tony hadn't expected. "Come in and you can take her breakfast up, she will like that. Mind you, it is more of a cocktail of drugs than food, but she may manage some toast."

They went into the cottage and found Caroline in the kitchen preparing breakfast. Her face showed the strain of the last few days, and as Tony came in she gave him a tearful hug. "Here, take this up would you, and take as much time together as you like. Brendan and I will move into one of the other cottages later, and you can enjoy Easter together".

"You don't have to move out." But his reply seemed almost half-hearted.

"We do." Caroline spoke with a quiet assertion that had a note of finality about it.

Tony took the tray, and carried it up the familiar stairs to Laura's bedroom. He stood for a moment outside her half-open door, looking at the view she loved so much of the Cove, still trying to come to terms with the future that lay ahead. Their times here had been so sublimely happy and now it was all to change. And yet as he looked at Laura she looked okay. Not the perfect picture of health, and she had lost weight of late, but surely the stark prognosis of six to eight weeks couldn't be right. There had to be some kind of mistake.

"Hello Tony, what kept you?"

"I am—" But before he could finish his sentence Laura interrupted him.

"Don't say sorry, you have nothing to be sorry for, just come and sit down, we need to talk. Please don't ever say sorry to me, ever." It was actually Laura who did much of the talking as Tony was happy to just sit and listen.

Over the next three weeks they spent as much time as they could together. Most days followed a similar pattern, with Tony revising each morning, then waking her around midday for anything she could manage to eat. They would then sit watching the mid-afternoon spring sunshine laid on the bed, and chatting about anything and everything. At times Tony would close his eyes, and for a brief moment he could forget the physical deterioration that was apparent before him and imagine Laura how she was barely a year earlier. Despite the slow pace the three weeks passed very quickly, and on the final Friday Brendan and Caroline returned to take over. With Brendan's help they managed to carry Laura down the stairs and out onto the grass area by the clock tower. It was a particularly warm sunny afternoon, but she still needed several thick layers to stop herself from shivering. The sea was its usual tranquil self, and in the warm breeze Tony could easily have drifted off to sleep, before Laura startled him into life.

"I have one last thing to do, you know, one final chance to leave a lasting impression on the world when I am gone."

"How do you mean?" He was sat upright now intrigued as to where this was going.

"The Cove, my legacy. I have decided on its future."

"And?" The question seemed almost rhetorical; as Tony knew full well that Caroline was now about to inherit what was probably rightfully hers in the first place.

Laura took a deep breath. "I am doing this now because I know that I am doing it for the right reasons. Mum is the obvious choice and I almost feel a sense of duty to leave it to her... and yet I cannot."

Thinking he had misheard, Tony blinked in surprise. "Did I just mishear you?"

Without responding directly to his question, Laura raised her right arm and put a finger to Tony's lips. "I am going to leave all of this to you."

Her beautiful radiant smile was still there, despite her thinning cracked lips, and pallid complexion. Nothing could dim the ever present glow from her eyes, and Tony felt almost entranced as he stared in wonder at her awe-inspiring beauty.

"I have a duty to fulfil, and it is you who has proved himself to be a most worthy successor. I have made my decision with the weight of history on my shoulders, and I have tried to pay regard to those who took the responsibility on before me."

Tony was so shocked he could barely speak in reply. "But you can't. I am not even family. Surely your mum deserves the right; she has done so much for you and the cottages over the years."

"She has certainly been an inspiration, but you have to remember the terms of the legacy, the rightful successor will show themselves to me, and you have done that in abundance. I always knew that you would be the one if anything ever happened to me, and I know my decision is right."

"But how can you know?"

"I know in the same way that my grandfather knew, and his predecessor before him. The right choices have always been made. Mum knows that I am leaving it to you, and she is certain that I am right."

Tony was overwhelmed by what had been said, and as he drove home the following day the gravity of Laura's choice was still bearing down heavily on him. Over the next few weeks he visited whenever he could, but as time went on the deterioration became far more pronounced with each return. What was to be his final visit came on the weekend of Caroline's birthday. The big party had long since been called off, and as Tony arrived he was anxious, before he even climbed the stairs to the bedroom.

Laura was fast asleep, and he sat on the end of her bed for several hours before she was even semi-conscious. Her body had wasted away to nothing more than bones, but still her mind was as determined as ever. The original six to eight weeks had passed, and she still clung to the last remnants of life. There really was nothing left now apart from her mind and soul, but as Tony stared he could still see the crucial elements that made Laura so special. Her breathing was laboured, and erratic, and each time a breath was delayed Tony's own heart raced in dreadful anticipation. Her lips had paled against her taught skin, and her once glorious hair had thinned and greyed, so that she looked like an old lady.

She awoke for the briefest of conversations a couple of times over the weekend, but even speech was becoming difficult for her, and though she was long past caring now she had little control of her body at all. Even taking a sip of water from the straw he offered was laboured and painful to watch, as her thinning lips could not keep the liquid in and Tony had to hold a tissue beneath the mouth he had kissed so passionately just months before. The whole process was a truly dreadful thing to witness, but Laura never showed any self-pity or anger. She always carried herself with dignity, and although Tony knew she had to be in great discomfort at times she never once complained to him.

The journey home was especially arduous, and he nearly stopped on several occasions just to book into the nearest hotel until it was all over. There was an exam the following morning, his final one, but his tutors had already told him he did not need to sit it, and yet it was his own need to finish the process properly that spurred him on.

For three hours the following morning he put up the mental blockade that had got him through the recent weeks and focussed on the paper in front of him. For that brief period nothing else mattered, and his entire world consisted of the four brick walls of the lecture theatre. There were butterflies before the exam, and during it, but for once they intensified the moment the final buzzer indicated his time was up.

His fellow students left him sat in his chair as they vacated the room, and Tony could hear the whoops of delight drifting back along the corridor. People were already analysing their answers, trying to second guess their shortcomings, but to him it meant nothing. Life was about to change, and he didn't want to walk out of this inner sanctuary into a world that he didn't much care for right now, to fight his battles alone. It was worse than that he even felt like he was losing part of himself.

The scraping of a chair behind him made him swing around, to see the familiar face of James sat behind. "Joe said you had stayed behind when they all left. I thought you might need some company, but tell me to bugger off if you would prefer."

"No, you are okay. I have to phone Brendan and I just have a bad feeling." Tony was sat looking impassively ahead.

"Come on, I will come with you. There is a phone just outside here."

Tony still wanted to stay within the temporary sanctuary but James was at the door holding it open. He almost dragged his feet as he walked up the few steps to the pay phone.

He fished in his pocket, and then turned them out when he found nothing, but the relief was short lived as James put two coins into the slot He dialled the number and waited for ring tones.

Brendan answered as expected.

"Hi. It is Tony, I was err just…"

"Tony I am sorry, but we lost her about ten minutes ago. The doctor is upstairs."

He didn't know how to react. He had shed enough tears, and there weren't any more left. James put his arm around him to provide what little comfort he could, but the moment seemed to just hang there.

*

"Tony, it is Caroline, I know this probably isn't the time, but I have to thank you so much for all that you gave to Laura. You fulfilled one part of her life, and showed her happiness that many people three times her age never achieve. I will never ever forget what you have done."

The tears at the other end of the phone were filled with grief, and Tony felt his own voice wavering as he responded. "I feel so totally empty Caroline that I cannot begin to pay sufficient tribute to Laura right now, but I will call you both back later." With that he slowly replaced the handset, and slumped to the floor underneath it. James sat beside his friend but said nothing. Both sat enveloped by the void that Laura had left, in a world within a world.

CHAPTER 16

Life Without Purpose

Tony felt completely lost, with no direction or purpose in life, and it was a feeling that would linger for weeks. The funeral came, and went, then the summer started but he could barely muster any enthusiasm for any of it. Caroline took control of the Cove, because he couldn't face visiting it alone, although he promised to be more responsible the following year.

Bob and Paula stayed in Bristol for a few days, but nothing seemed to raise his spirits at all. Eventually with relentless pressure from all sides he agreed to visit Graham in Spain for a short break at the end of August, and he flew out on the bank holiday Monday. Mark met him at the airport, and helped him with his bags to the car.

"G-g-glad to see you only packed a few things; they don't give you a lot of luggage space in these." Mark indicated the shiny Porsche Boxster across the car park.

"Wow, business cannot be bad."

"S-s-sorry, I wasn't trying to brag, it is Graham's car actually I have just borrowed it. I will pack your bags, jump in."

Tony climbed in and relaxed in the leather seat. He hadn't slept at all on the plane, and tiredness was starting to catch up on him.

"Is it far to drive?"

"A good hour, you can have a snooze if you like." The roof was open, and Mark was shouting from outside, then he dropped the bonnet and joined Tony.

"There you go, plenty of luggage space if you know where to look." There was a moment's silence as he looked for the right key, then before putting it into the ignition Mark looked across at Tony. "I was really sorry to hear about Laura. She was quite a lady from what I hear, and no one deserves what happened to her."

A little taken aback at this generosity of spirit, Tony wasn't sure how to respond. "That is good of you. Thank you."

"The strange thing is it has made me realise that I have to refocus my life and sort myself out. I am going to northern Spain tomorrow with Charlotte and if it all goes well I am taking my share of the business and getting out of here."

"What about Graham?"

"Please don't tell him. I know you two are brothers, but please don't tell him yet. I promise to sort it out but he could do anything right now. He is a bit erratic at times to say the least, and he has to be handled carefully."

"You are not the Mark I remember." Tony knew it sounded feeble, but he was shocked at his former adversary.

"We all have to grow up at some point. I just wish Graham would, because he is mixing in some dangerous games."

"Drugs?" Tony was staring straight ahead and did not turn to face Mark as he spoke.

"What do you know?"

"Enough."

"There is no such thing as enough where these people are concerned. If you know nothing make sure you keep it that way and keep out of the way. If you know a little then be very, very careful who you share that information with because you will be putting your life and theirs at risk." Mark was talking impassively, with no sign of his usual stutter. His hands were firmly gripping the top of the steering wheel, and he was also staring intently ahead.

"Is that a threat?"

"No, not at all. I am clean, I always have been, but it is a very mixed up world. Just being Graham's brother out here puts a spotlight on you, and possibly even a price on your head, so be careful about who you talk to. I want out completely, before I get implicated any more."

"So where does Charlotte fit in, or are you just using her?"

"No way." The denial was firm and instant, but the old doubts about Mark were already surfacing.

"Charlotte is the life I want, not the one I have."

Why was he telling Tony all this? After all, he had never looked out for him before, or was it a double bluff of some type? How had the two of them got mixed up in whatever it was? Tony wasn't in the mood for these games, and had a good mind just to board the next flight back home.

"Thanks for the advice. I think it would be best for me to see Graham, and head home in a couple of days, but in the meantime we had better get going hadn't we?"

Mark nodded his head, and fired the car into life. As they raced along the Spanish roads with the engine howling away Tony forgot his worries about Graham, and gradually drifted off into an uneasy slumber. When the car eventually drew to a stop, they were in a small village, and Mark jumped out, grabbed a parcel and wandered off, leaving Tony alone in the car. Although he had been feigning sleep for the last 20 minutes or so he was wide awake, and as soon as Mark was out of sight he jumped out to follow him, still suspicious about his motives.

As it was, the surveillance was a waste of time as he merely walked to the local post office, before realising it was shut and making his return to the car. Tony raced ahead, and was slumped in the seat again as he returned. Mark mumbled something about crazy siestas, and then continued to the club.

Graham was there to meet them as they drew up, and apart from looking a bit tired everything seemed to be pretty much business as normal. They all had a few drinks in the bar that night before Graham had to go off on business, and Mark ran the bar through the night. Tony watched for any signs of trouble, but nothing seemed out of place, and he retired to his room about 3am, with the club still in full swing. He was awoken the following morning by a gentle tap on the door, and as soon as he came to his senses he called out, "Come in."

It was Mark who entered with a cup of coffee, and parcel similar to the one he was carrying yesterday. "Morning, I brought you this, I am about to leave to meet Charlotte."

Tony took the coffee, and waited, sensing that there was more to come.

"W-w-would you mind doing me a favour today?"

"Sure, what do you need?"

Mark thrust the parcel forward. "These are some flyers we need printing for the end of summer party, and I was supposed to post them yesterday. An old mate of ours does them cheap for us in the UK, only the post office was shut, so... if you wouldn't mind."

Tony leant forward and picked up the parcel. "Yeah, no problem."

"O-o-only Graham will go mad if he sees you so don't let him know if you can avoid it, okay."

Mark seemed genuinely scared of Graham these days, which was a little bizarre, but all the same Tony agreed and put the parcel to one side. "Right then, have a good time with Charlotte and I guess I will see you around."

"Sure, only put the parcel away I r-r-really don't want Graham to see it, if you don't mind." As he finished Mark retrieved the package, and slid it under the lid of Tony's suitcase that was lying on the floor, before turning and leaving.

Still tired from the travelling and late night Tony pulled the duvet back over himself, despite the growing heat in the room, and drifted back off to sleep. Over the next couple of days, he caught the odd hour with Graham, but was mainly just bored around the apartment, or club, and decided to head back to the Cove instead to see out the rest of the summer. He managed to get a cancellation flight, and explained to his brother before dragging his case out from under the bed to pack up and leave.

As soon as he opened the lid, he saw the parcel still lying there, and couldn't believe he had forgotten it. He wasn't bothered about letting Mark down in general, but he hated forgetting to carry out a promise. Fortunately the label was for someone in Nottingham, so he decided to pack it and post it first thing from the airport. He was still turning it over in his hands as he heard footsteps approaching and hurriedly threw it into his case with a load of clothes on top.

"You ready then, little bro, only I have an important deal on this evening that I have to get back for. Mark should have sorted it, but he can be bloody unreliable at times."

Thinking about the parcel he had just thrown in his case he could only agree. "Yeah, I can imagine. I am nearly ready, just five minutes."

Tony finished packing his case then carried it back downstairs, and put it into another Porsche Boxster that he hadn't seen before. "So whose car is this then?"

"Mine, you fool. You didn't think I nicked them both, did you? Come and work with me when you have got Laura out of your system and I will get you one too."

No thanks, thought Tony, but he knew better than to say anything. As they drove to the airport they talked more than they had all summer, more than they had for years. Graham appeared to relax the further they went, and as they arrived about 30 minutes before check-in they sat talking in the car.

"I was deadly serious about what I said earlier, you know. We have a big business out here now, of which you have only seen a tiny fraction, so there will always be a job for you if you want one."

"Thanks," replied Tony, unsure how to let his brother down gently. "I need to pursue a career on my own for now though." Then he added slightly hesitantly, "I am sure that you understand."

"Yes," nodded Graham. "And when you find your next woman try to find one who is a bit less feisty. The last two both had a go at me as soon as I met them."

The mere mention of Laura brought back fresh anxiety, and images that Tony had been trying to suppress of late. He knew that he was still far from over her death, and wondered when the pain would ever go away. Feeling strangely melancholy, and lost, much as he had done for weeks now, he leant over and offered his hand to Graham. "My plane is due so I had better be getting off."

They shook hands, hugged briefly before Tony wandered across the car park with his case in tow. He desperately wanted to raise his mood, but felt down all afternoon, and as he sat on the plane he was pleased to see that no one took the seat next to him. He wasn't in the mood for small talk, and just sat there allowing his mind to be a complete blank on the flight.

When they landed at Heathrow the airport terminal was the usual heavy bustle of people, and he just wandered along in his own little world as excited travellers pushed him this way and that in their eagerness to reach their chosen destinations. He reclaimed his bag, stood for passport control, then wandered through the nothing to declare channel. The guard had his usual disinterested look, that met most holiday flights from Europe, but Tony couldn't help staring at him, wondering how he ever motivated himself to get up each morning.

As the guard suddenly spoke Tony jumped in startled amazement. It was as though a shop mannequin had suddenly come to life in front of his very own eyes, and he missed what was said the first time.

"I am sorry. What was that?"

"You understand English then, sonny. I said is this your case, and did you pack it yourself?"

For some unknown reason he looked at the label before replying. "Yes it is mine, and yes I packed it."

Expecting that to be the last of it he picked up the bag ready to leave, but the man clearly wanted to justify his existence today.

"Wait there a second." The guard didn't move, but merely shouted across the corridor to a colleague. "Here George, can you help me check this one?"

Tony looked around to see an equally glum guard walking across to join them. The new arrival indicated a small room just off to one side, and the three of them walked in.

"So then is this your bag, and did you pack it yourself?"

"Yes." Tony was trying hard to hide his frustration, but knew there was at least a hint of it in his voice.

"Well this is just a routine security check. If you could unpack the contents of your case, and let us go through it all, dirty washing and all, we have gloves." Both men laughed at this unfunny line that they clearly used every day.

Tony lifted his case onto the table, and unzipped the lid before unpacking the contents. He couldn't understand the butterflies in his stomach, but carried on regardless desperate to get the ordeal over and done with. As his fingers hit the brown paper parcel the butterflies intensified, and he suddenly had a terrible sick feeling, that was taking all the strength out of his legs.

The guards clearly noted his hesitation, and George picked up the package to examine it, before throwing it across to his mate. "Present for Granny I presume?"

Tony could feel the sweat running down his forehead, although he didn't really know why his heart was thumping away in his chest. With a mouth suddenly bone dry he tried to speak as confidently as he could. "No it is some printing I have to get done for someone."

"Printing eh?" questioned George, nodding in a very purposeful, but somehow doubting way. "You won't mind then if we just nick the little corner here, and have just a little tiny eentsy weentsy peek inside, will you?"

Tony knew that there was no need for his silly baby voice, and so wanted this charade to be over. At the same time his deep rooted distrust of Mark was clattering enormous alarm bells inside his head. As he heard the paper slowly start to rip his worst fears were recognised. George had taken control, and he was making a great drama of tearing the paper. He started in one corner, but as the packaging unravelled the tear opened out in a broad triangular sheet of paper. Eventually with the slowest of tearing there was a small sheet of paper hanging down, and George tipped the packet until four large sealed clear bags of white powder dropped one at a time.

"Well I think that you printer is going to be a bit disappointed with this, don't you?"

"But I—"

George was beaming, clearly delighted that his day had suddenly come to life, as he put his finger up to his lips. "Shhh, keep it for my boss. I am just going to get her, and I suggest that you think long and hard about what you tell her when we come back, or you may be very, very late for your printing."

Tony knew that he was an enormous amount of trouble, and yet part of him really didn't care anymore. After the year he had had so far he was all for giving up anyway, and above all else he didn't want to give these patronising couple of no hopers the job satisfaction from other people's misery that they so craved.

The rest of the afternoon was a bit of a blur. He was bustled from room to room, shown to fresh people then passed to others until eventually he was sat in front of two officers with a tape running being read his rights. They looked like Laurel and Hardy sat together. The older man was hugely overweight, balding, with glasses, whilst his colleague was a small dark haired thin man. Apparently their real names were Bill and Dave, but Tony thought Laurel and Hardy more apt. His personal possessions like his wallet and keys were spread out on the desk, along with the packets of white powder and he had already been subjected to endless questions.

As he sat looking at the meagre pile of possessions on the desk in front of him, he couldn't believe how pitiful it looked, surely not the tools of an international drug smuggler.

"Now then Tony, are you sure that you don't want a solicitor, because it is going to be in your best interests to get one. And do you have anyone that we should contact?" asked Dave, in an apparently caring friendly manner.

Still staring just at the desk and his possessions on it he didn't really feel like saying anything at all. There wasn't even a lot to look at but his focus switched between the few items periodically. The wallet had about £10, a few credit cards and that was it. As he imagined the contents the realisation of a way out of this mess suddenly hit him, and he sat upright. Both the policemen moved back instinctively as he gestured towards the wallet. "Yes in there, a number for Brendan Scott, he will sort all this out. Phone him please."

The two men looked at each other, and both furrowed their brows in concentration as Dave asked; "The Brendan Scott. You know the Brendan Scott."

"Yes, his number is in there. Take a look yourselves."

Bill picked up the black wallet, flicked it open then tipped the contents out on the desk. Tony could see with relief the words he had seen a hundred times before, on the small scrap of paper in front of him.

Call me any time if you need me

01254 896532

Brendan

Bill then picked up the note, looked quizzically at Dave, before speaking; "For the benefit of the tape. Interview suspended 19.42." Then he left the room.

Absolute silence prevailed thereafter, so much so that Tony could only hear the gentle click of the wall clock behind him. The time passed slowly, and the boredom was excruciating. He wanted to remain in control and tried anything he could. He counted the ticks of the clock as they echoed through the otherwise silent room then next he tried to suppress his blinks as he sat motionless staring at the desk in front of him. Eventually Dave returned with another officer who stood to the side of the desk with his back to the wall. Tony knew that this was his moment so he didn't look up, or even acknowledge the returning policeman. He just continued to sit impassively waiting to be told that this particular nightmare was over.

"I have spoken to Brendan Scott."

The smile was starting to come, and Tony concentrated hard to remain expressionless for as long as possible.

"And he vaguely remembers you as being a friend of his daughter, but nothing more, and even if his daughter was still alive he doubts he could intervene in a matter as serious as this. Basically this is your mess, and you have to deal with it."

The officers exchanged a brief look before turning their attention once again to Tony. Rather than being the end of the nightmare, this was only the beginning. Over the next few days he was repeatedly interviewed, then locked back into a cell, where he remained awaiting further questions, and ultimately a trial.

He had no answers, and very little fight, being almost resigned to accept whatever life threw at him. The only bright light on the horizon came when a hurried visit was arranged from Bob and Paula. By now Tony knew better than to build his hopes up, but even so he was ill prepared for the next shock.

His parents looked dreadful when they arrived, and Paula was so obviously distraught that it was left to Bob to deliver the devastating news that Graham had been killed in a car crash, apparently on his way back to help out with the police. In the meantime the real culprit Mark had disappeared off the face of the earth after leaving Charlotte hurriedly in northern Spain.

Tony could barely go on from day to day, and felt no inclination to help his own defence the prosecution or anyone else. He contemplated suicide on several occasions, but didn't have the energy or focus to carry it out. Only one enduring thought stayed clear throughout, the desire to get revenge, and it sat glowing like a red hot poker in the swirl of his otherwise muddled and confused mind. Through every waking hour, and many a restless night the image of Mark was etched into his brain. As time went on he slowly turned those thoughts of pure hatred into a plan of action.

CHAPTER 17

Re-awakening the Past

The telephone started ringing away for the third time in only five minutes and Charlotte knew that there must be some kind of emergency or the caller would have given up by now. Life as a junior doctor certainly had its up and downs, but right now she needed sleep. The last 72 hours had taken their toll, and when she caught a glimpse of her face in the mirror at the end of her mammoth shift she felt certain it had aged a full ten years.

That was six-ish yesterday evening, and she had been promised a whole five days off to recover. After the short walk back to her flat she had fallen asleep on her bed fully clothed around 7pm. Now barely 12 hours later the phone was ringing incessantly, as someone was no doubt trying to drag her back to work.

She grabbed the receiver and tried to emphasise her annoyance with the curt tone of her voice. "Hello."

"Charlotte, thank God it is you. I was just about to give up and call you at work."

The male voice on the other end had a familiar sound to it, but her brain was still half asleep, and as the numbed cells inside slowly came to life she couldn't put a name to it.

"I am sorry, am I needed at work."

"No, Charlotte, I should have introduced myself. It is Brendan

Scott, Laura's father."

The last few words brought her mind up to speed as quickly as if someone had thrown a bucket of cold water on her. She had been trying to contact this man for years to help Tony, but he wouldn't return calls, and had proved very elusive indeed. Now all of a sudden he was waking her up from a long awaited and much deserved sleep. Something had obviously happened, but why now of all times when Tony was due out in a few weeks.

"I... err wasn't expecting to ever hear from you. What has happened?"

"Look, Charlotte, have you got a pen and paper?"

"Yes somewhere." She stretched her phone across the flat, and was still only just able to grab a pad left by the door. "Yes I do, why?"

"Take down this number, it is my mobile, and I will answer it anytime you call... promise. I don't have time to explain everything now, but Tony failed to return to jail yesterday, and we believe he is out looking for Mark."

There was a brief pause, and Charlotte felt like saying, 'Big deal, let me go back to sleep,' but she resisted sensing the obvious alarm – or was it concern? – in Brendan's voice.

"The problem is that Mark is under surveillance and Tony could easily jeopardise years of hard work, let alone his own life. You have Mark's address so can you go there and see if you can find Tony for us? If I send anyone else he may panic and run away, putting his life in real danger."

Questions were building up in Charlotte's mind, and she needed answers before she would do anything at all, let alone help this man who had so cruelly abandoned Tony in his hour of need. "How do you know I have Mark's address, and why have you been watching him for years?"

"Charlotte you have to trust me on this, time is absolutely of the essence if we are to avoid more bloodshed. I will answer the questions you have asked so far, but no more at this stage. We know Tony was given Mark's address from his defence team, when Mark refused to stand as a witness, and we know he put it in a letter to you.

We also know that you both distrusted him, and his extent of involvement with the drug scene was never clear which is presumably why you have never made contact with him."

This was all proving a bit too much. Who exactly was the 'we' that he kept referring to, and had they been monitoring her as well as Mark, and even worse Tony's letters from jail? "This all seems a bit too farfetched for me, you will have to explain more."

"Charlotte I can't, not today. If you value Tony's life you must go to the house now, and see if you can track him down. I will phone back in ten minutes to see if you are ready to leave." Without even a goodbye the click of the phone indicated he had hung up.

Reluctantly she put the handset down and showered as quickly as she could. By the time the phone rang again, she was halfway through a piece of toast, and blowing a mug of coffee trying to cool it down.

"Hello."

"Charlotte, what is your decision?"

There was obviously no time now for pleasantries, and the almost patronising way that he kept using her name was starting to really grate on her tired and weary nerves.

"Yes, I will go, but that is it. I am doing this only for Tony, not you, and after I visit the house I want nothing more to do with the affair. Understood?"

"Charlotte you can walk away at any time, but your services will be invaluable to me. Please ring back as soon you have any information."

As she drove the 30 miles or so to the house the events so far that morning kept going through her mind, and she tried desperately to place them in the context of what had happened to Tony and Graham over the past four years. She had to ask a couple of times for directions, and eventually found that the property was situated at the end of a long track past a school, although the postman who gave her the final directions reckoned it had been empty for years.

There was a lay-by on the main road just before the turning and Charlotte pulled in to think about a plan of action. She was going to go along with Brendan for now, but she could sense that Tony was being used somehow like a pawn in larger game, and he had to be warned. Unsure how to do that for the best she quickly scribbled her own phone number on a piece of paper with the words CALL ME CAVEMAN C, and placed it on the passenger seat. It was a bit cryptic but she hoped it would make sense, and it had to be encoded somehow if it wasn't to alert the wrong people.

After a few deep breaths, she turned the ignition key, and nervously headed down the lane, turning up into the last property, before the track was blocked by a five-bar gate that led into open fields. Looking around the property seemed immaculate, yet eerily quiet and empty, with no lived-in feel about it. The area strangely gave her the creeps so Charlotte grabbed the note and looked quickly about for somewhere to leave it. The gate at the side had some split panels that she could stuff it through, but on second thoughts it may go unnoticed there. No, the letter box was the best place. She would leave it hanging down, and hopefully if Tony visited the house he would read it out of curiosity.

As she gently trapped it in the flap, a sudden noise from behind startled her, and she accidentally pushed the note further in than she had intended. People were approaching fast, definitely more than one, but she couldn't see where from. Fortunately she had left her engine running, and without appearing flustered she returned to her vehicle as quickly as she could.

Before driving off she backed up slightly then turned to look at the note from her half open door, annoyed that she had pushed it so far through. The footsteps stopped and she looked around to see an odd couple who were apparently returning from their picnic lunch in something of a hurry. Trying to not look out of place she completed her swing back into the drive then sped off back up the lane as fast as she could.

She wasn't really sure why but her heart was pounding away as adrenalin raced through her body, and she could feel herself sweating all over. Her hands were the worst and she took them off the steering to wipe against her clothes at the end of the lane. On the journey back she couldn't help wondering what Tony was up to, and why he was risking everything at this late stage of his sentence. In his last letter he had told her that he accepted his punishment, and although everyone knew he had been set up by Mark or Graham he now only blamed his own stupidity. Unfortunately when she most wanted to talk to Tony she wasn't able to, and this had been the case for the last four years now. James and Paul kept in regular contact, but it wasn't the same. She had split with her boyfriend a month or so ago and had wanted Tony to talk to them as well, but she had learnt to just get on with things on her own.

As she drove back towards Bristol she remembered the times that they had all spent there when Tony and James shared the flat, and it brought back a lot of happy memories. The tiredness that had been with her earlier had evaporated, so she drove back to a small café that they had frequented years ago, and stopped for a coffee, and early lunch. As she sat at the table the need to talk to someone was overwhelming, and eventually she scrambled around in her handbag, picking out the piece of paper with Brendan's number on it.

Just as she dialled the number into her mobile, the young waitress arrived with her food, and Charlotte placed the phone down on the table, weighing down the scrap of paper underneath it. The rolls took her mind off the morning's events momentarily, but with her mobile phone display indicating the number that she had already punched in she eventually picked it up and pushed the green button to make the call.

It barely rang at the other end before a clearly agitated voice answered.

"Charlotte?"

"Yes, it's me."

"Thank God, we lost you. Where are you?"

Alarm bells were ringing again; some force far greater than she understood was at work here and Charlotte didn't like the tone of these brief chats. What did he mean by 'lost her'? Was she being followed herself?

"Charlotte, are you still there, are you okay?"

"Yes, I am fine. Brendan, what is going on here?"

She used his name deliberately as a kind of empowerment, to show she was as much in charge as he was.

"Charlotte I cannot explain everything, but if Tony is at the house he may be in real danger. What did you put on the note that you left?"

The revelation that she was indeed under surveillance made her very wary, and she decided to be deliberately cagey.

"Nothing, I just dropped the paper through the door as a ploy, you know, to give me a pretext for being there if anyone asked."

"Well done, Charlotte. That was good thinking. All I can tell you now is that we have information that Mark is about to complete a major drugs deal tonight that will tie him and one of the biggest players in this country together. Charlotte, we have never had such a perfect opportunity to close this whole operation down, but Tony will be in real danger if he shows up. These are major players and I doubt either party would hesitate to eliminate him if necessary."

Not for the first time today Charlotte had to check that this wasn't some elaborate dream brought on by overtiredness. How had Mark ever got into this? Her old school friend, and one of the only men she had ever let herself fall head over heels in love with. She still to this day thought they would eventually share a future together. None of it made any sense. Mark had his faults but her judgement had always proved more reliable than this. Only her own father had let her down so spectacularly.

"What do you want me to do?"

"Charlotte stay away from Mark's house, go home, and I will arrange for the local police to send someone to meet you there. We will bring you in, and you may be needed later depending on how this all works out. I have to go now, but call me when you get to your house. It is 2.30 now so how far from home are you?"

Surprised that time had passed so quickly Charlotte instinctively checked her watch. Home was barely ten minutes away, but she wasn't sure if that was where she was heading. More than anything else in the whole world she hated being told what to do, and was likely to do the opposite even if it meant putting herself in danger.

"Forty-five minutes I would say, with traffic. I will call you."

She pressed the red button to end the call immediately, so that she wasn't able to give herself away. Lying wasn't her forte, and she didn't want her voice to betray her true intentions. The bill had been brought over during the phone call, so she carefully tucked £20 under the plate and ran over to her car. The waitress was getting a generous tip, but time was of the essence right now. There was only the briefest of hesitation, before she turned the car around and retraced her earlier steps.

The school bell sounding in the distant was an unnatural intrusion in the countryside and it stirred Tony from his slumber on the top of the hill. It must be just after three, he thought as he watched the last of the mothers pack children into their cars and head off home. Eventually he stood up, and suddenly noticed how hungry he felt. With a massive stretch he was seriously having second thoughts about what to do next. He had missed the chance to get anything from the cars up the lane, and as far as he could see the house still looked deserted. The thought of handing himself in seemed somehow to be gaining credence. He would get a telling off but little else, and that would be it. What would another month or two inside mean anyway?

As the hustle and bustle up the lane subsided Tony slowly became aware of two other voices nearby, but he couldn't see anybody. The hill had Mark's house in front of him, then the wall and hedge that marked out the lane ran on the other side to the five-bar gate that he had noted earlier, before opening out onto open fields. He could see the very top of a car parked away in the distance at the end of the lane, and decided to make his way along to it under cover of the hedge to see if there was any food he might pinch.

The voices grew louder towards the end of the lane, but it was difficult to make out the conversation. As a precaution he sat down at the end to plan his next move. He had learnt in jail that a strong, confident approach was very often all he needed to ward off problems. If you look awkward and weak then other people see that straight away and act accordingly with an air of supremacy. Take a confident, strong approach on the other hand, and you look neither out of place nor nervous. Tony stood upright, took a deep breath to puff his chest out then ventured out from the cover of the hedgerow, trying to look as though he was on a daily leisurely stroll.

As he saw the couple sat in their car at the end of lane, just inside the gate his plans took an unexpected twist. He raised his head back intending to acknowledge them with a friendly hello, but something was very out of place, and he stood there open mouthed. The odd couple who had been out for a picnic earlier were facing him, and they appeared equally taken aback, but it was the large man who spoke first of the group. "Tony, don't run away, you are not in trouble."

Primeval instinct took over, and like a caged animal Tony looked left and right for a way out. His brain was working faster than any computer ever could, readying his whole body for action yet at the same time formulating an escape plan, weighing up the various alternatives. The car would easily outrun him over the fields so the only way was back up the lane, and to use the element of surprise in his favour.

Without further hesitation he raced forward, jumped onto the bonnet of the car, then with a single step he was then on the roof, and from there he jumped over the closed gate and into the lane. He didn't know where to go next but ran as fast as he could up towards the school, with the sound of their engine bursting into life behind him.

As a police siren then screamed from behind he knew his instinct had been right, and a brief smile crossed his face as he saw another car turn into the lane ahead. He quickly dived to the side, expecting backup for the first pair to arrive, but was immensely relieved as he recognised the friendly face he had seen earlier. The car crunched to a stop on the loose shingle just feet in front of him, and Charlotte leant over to throw the passenger door open.

Tony raced around, just squeezing between the open door, and wall, before he jumped in the passenger seat. Surprisingly Charlotte didn't need instruction, and had already thrown the gears into reverse and was heading back up the lane as fast as she safely could. Looking forward through the clouds of dust Tony could see the pursuing police car had now negotiated the gate, and the thin woman officer was talking hurriedly into her radio. Suddenly and quite unexpectedly Charlotte braked hard and nearly span the car as she struggled to control its slide. Without hesitation she had thrown it back into first and was once more racing forwards back up the lane risking a head-on collision with the unmarked police car.

"What are you doing? We need to get out of here!" shouted Tony in disbelief.

"I cannot. Look behind, there are two more cars racing towards us, we have to get back the other way. The open fields are just ahead, if we can get past the police car we will be okay."

Tony glanced behind, then forwards again just as the unmarked car inexplicably turned off their siren and started reversing, apparently desperate to avoid a crash with Charlotte who appeared in no mood to take any prisoners. It felt like a scene from the keystone cops, and with half a smile on his face Tony asked, "Do you have any idea what is going here? Because I don't."

Before Charlotte could answer the smiles were wiped off both their faces. The already shattered silence of this quiet country lane was blown apart by the sudden sound of rapid gunfire. They both looked around back in stunned silence as the car immediately behind slewed sideways, blocking the lane completely, and the driver lay slumped forward against the wheel. The passenger kicked his door open, then rolled out of the car and ran forward bent double. He fell to the ground and opened fire on the car he had just left. A massive explosion came next as the car burst into flames, and then the man was back up and running but a second explosion caught him unawares and he was again thrown to the ground. Charlotte stopped in her tracks, and looked aghast at the scene of complete devastation behind her. She was fighting her natural instinct to help out, and at the same time preserve her best friend. The running man was up on his feet, and hobbling awkwardly now, but she didn't want to wait around anymore, and rammed the gear stick forwards.

There were more police sirens now, but further away, at the top of the lane, and with the thick acrid smoke billowing from the burning vehicle they couldn't see them. Suddenly Tony put his own trembling hand onto Charlotte's and shouted, "Stop the car. Quickly, you must stop!"

With fear she had never known before racing through her she was happy to leave the decision to Tony and robotically did as she was told, bringing the car to an immediate stop. As soon as they were at rest he jumped out, and opened the rear door, bundling the running man into the back seat, before shouting fresh instructions. "Go, go, go, across the fields as fast as you can, we need to get out of here."

As their new passenger scrambled to sit upright Charlotte caught a glimpse of him in the rear-view mirror and her mouth dropped open in shock. She nearly ran over the policewoman who had jumped out of her car and was standing by the gate to the field in a vain attempt to block the lane.

"Graham?" was all she could say. Her throat was dry, drained by the sweat that was pouring from her other pores.

Before anyone could answer the passenger opened fire on the unmarked police car, blowing out both side windows on Charlotte's vehicle as glass flew everywhere. He fired until a resonant click indicated the ammo was exhausted and for good measure tossed the gun away.

Tony dragged Charlotte down under cover until the noise stopped then twisted around in his seat, staring at the man behind them. He had obviously had surgery to change his appearance, and to many a casual observer it was someone else, but their passenger was unmistakably Graham. "What the hell is happening? You are supposed to be dead."

"I nearly was thanks to you two bumbling halfwits." Then without hesitation he slipped his hand inside his jacket and removed a small handgun, which he used to wave instructions.

"See that barn over there, take me to it as fast as you can."

Charlotte followed the order, and headed towards a derelict-looking building that was situated as far across the open countryside as she could see. Tony pushed the gun aside, as though it was no more dangerous than a rolled up newspaper. "You don't need that in here, now what is happening? We were told that you were dead."

Graham slumped back in his seat, and a sickly smile spread across his face. "Bumbling Spanish police, I am afraid. Mark had my car, and they assumed it was me who died. In the circumstances it suited me to let them believe that so I never challenged them. Now if you don't want two more deaths today then do exactly as I say."

Charlotte was accustomed to trauma but could not stop herself as the sudden realisation of Mark's death twisted her heart and caused a wave of nausea to take over. Without slowing the car at all she turned and threw up out of the broken window. Despite what she had thought of Mark earlier that day the loss of him came as an even greater shock, and she had no thought whatsoever of the danger to her own life right now.

Tony was equally in shock, but self-preservation was taking over, and he tried to relate to his brother's better nature. "Look, you are not going to kill us, are you? So put the gun away, and let's get this mess sorted."

Still leaning back in his seat, Graham moved his gun across until the barrel was against his brother's temple. "Get the picture, little bro. You nearly got me killed, and certainly brought my life into huge danger by turning up here with the bloody police today. I nearly had everything sorted for the rest of my life, and now I don't have any options left, so just sit there and be quiet or I swear I will pull this trigger."

Stunned by the words he could barely comprehend Tony twisted around and sat facing the front, willing the car to reach the barn as quickly as it could. When they got there it was evident that the building was nowhere near as tumbledown as it first looked and Graham jumped out, skirting around the front of the car, pointing the gun between the two of them. He fumbled in his pocket with his free hand to retrieve a key, which undid the heavy doors, and swung them open to reveal a four-wheel-drive Range Rover. Motioning the other two forward with the gun, Charlotte was ushered into the driver's seat and they set off across fields, eventually hitting the road nearly an hour later. This was obviously all part of a carefully rehearsed escape plan, and although the route appeared confused it had clearly been set up as a means of losing any would-be pursuers.

They drove in virtual silence but all the time Tony was trying to plan his own escape. He had spent the last four years planning a different kind of getaway, but this time he had to plan quickly, and make no mistakes whatsoever. As they approached the first town he was desperately trying to get his bearings, and sensing this Graham forced him to lie down in the rear foot well, all but obscuring his view of the outside world. After about 20 minutes he felt his body getting stiffer, and was relieved when he heard the barked instructions for Charlotte to pull the car over to the side.

"I am taking you to a safe house that I have, but we may need to stay there for days. If you co-operate I will feed you, and clothe you, but I am under no illusions that my survival is paramount, and I will not hesitate to use this." Graham was waving the gun around again as he finished.

Neither hostage spoke, so he continued. "We need provisions, and there is a large supermarket up ahead, and I need to get some things. We may be holed up for a few weeks yet so no silly games." They drove on for about a mile, before slowing and parking up. Graham grabbed the back of Tony's hair, and pulled him up. Still waving the gun around threateningly, he spoke to Charlotte. "Don't think I won't use this because he is my brother. Stay here and don't move until I come back."

Then he bundled Tony out of the car and they picked up a trolley that Graham filled with essential food and provisions. Afraid to do anything, but frightened not to as well, Tony was desperately looking for a plan. He knew his options were limited but he also knew he was in a no-win situation. Distraction of some order was his only hope, and he was desperate to get back to the freedom he had barely tasted in the last four years. As they passed a rack of CDs he grabbed a couple and tucked them covertly out of sight behind his back, tucked into the top of his jeans. He only had half a plan in mind, but hoped it would be enough.

Trying not to drop them he stood rigidly behind the trolley until Graham approached and forced the gun into his ribs. "Act natural, you idiot, and don't bring attention to us. You look like a bloody stuffed parrot. Relax and look normal."

Tony wanted to complain, but realised the futility of it, and instead wandered a couple of feet away from the trolley trying to look like a normal shopper. This seemed to appease Graham, and they slowly made their way around to the checkout. Once through the till area, he waited for his opportunity as he walked alongside the trolley, and deliberately pushed it into an elderly couple coming the other way. In the confusion and apologies that followed he took his chance and dropped the CDs on top of the paid for shopping.

"Walk ahead of me, and look natural, or I might sort you out quicker rather than later. Remember, I only really need one of you," sneered Graham.

Tony didn't need telling twice as his plan started falling into place, and he happily walked six paces or so ahead of his brother who was pushing the heavily laden trolley. As he went through the final security bollards he counted slowly to himself, *One, two, three, four, five, six,* then before he could reach seven the stores klaxon went off.

He could hear the commotion behind as the security guards moved over to Graham, "Excuse me, sir, have you forgotten to pay for something?"

Tony quickened his pace, half expecting a shot to tear through his worn out body at any moment, but it didn't come. He was still counting, and on twenty broke into a run to the car. Charlotte saw him approach and turned the ignition key, but as he reached the passenger door the engine was turning over without any sign of life.

"Quick Charlotte, he must have immobilised it somehow. Get out, we have about two minutes, we need to run."

Without any further thought they made their way to the back of the car, and looked for cover of some sort. There was nothing about, but the taxi rank opposite offered hope, and they ran across and jumped in the nearest available car.

Attempting a terrible American accent Charlotte said, "Can you take us to the nearest motel? We need somewhere to stay for the night."

Having seen most things before he wasn't easily fooled and when the driver caught Tony's eye in the rear-view mirror he winked. "Sure thing. Tourists eh?"

CHAPTER 18

Who to Trust?

They drove on for a couple of miles before booking into a Travelodge. Once in their room they had so much to discuss but barely spoke as they both collapsed on either side of the double bed.

"Do you think this will all go away if we lie down here and go to sleep?" asked Tony without any real conviction.

"No," replied Charlotte. "I have checked several times today already and this is no dream."

"Nightmare, you mean."

She just nodded in reply, and with fear starting to take over she started to feel physically sick inside again. Her hands were shaking, and she wearily asked the obvious. "What now?"

Tony pinched his top lip and shook his head slowly. "I don't know. Remember that day when I was stuck in the tree? Well I have never felt so scared and alone in my life since. The difference is you saved me back then, and this time you are stuck in the middle of it with me."

Rather hesitantly she ventured an option. "I have a telephone number here for Brendan Scott, or if you would rather I could phone James."

"Brendan was no use before, so why today? I think James is a much better option."

Still wary of divulging too much she was at first reluctant, then remembering that it was Tony she blurted out the sequence of events that had led her this far from the early morning phone call, to her own defiance of Brendan's instructions.

After listening intently, he let out a long slow whistle. "We may have to give him one last chance but I still say we phone James first. He has never ever let me down in the past."

Tony took the phone as Charlotte offered it to him, and saw that James' name was already displayed onscreen.

"Just press the green button, and it will dial for you."

He did as he was told then he held the phone to his ear. After a single ring he heard a familiar voice on the other end.

"Charlotte, is that you? Where the hell are you?"

"James, it is me, Tony. What do you know?"

"Enough, I know enough to know that your lives are in real danger. Brendan has brought me into the case because I know Mark, as well as you two, but these are very nasty people who have little regard for human life. I wanted in on the investigation weeks ago, but he said his team could handle it. Thankfully he relented today after they screwed up and nearly got you both killed."

"What should we do, James? Please tell me as a friend first and copper second. It is fair to say we both realise the gravity of the situation we are in."

"Phone Brendan, plain and simple, then move to safety. Look after each other, but please do as I say." Then as an afterthought to emphasise the point he almost shouted, "Now."

"Okay mate, point taken. I will call you later." Tony ended the call, and looked across for help. "Do you have a problem with me contacting Brendan? It looks like our last chance."

"No," then she added, "but be careful. I know he is Laura's dad, but don't tell him everything until he tells us all he knows."

Tony nodded his agreement, and picked up the piece of paper that he was being offered. His brain was still trying to dissect all that had happened over the last few hours, and before he pressed the green button to make the call he looked at Charlotte.

"We are in a position of strength here."

"Really? I don't see how," shrugged Charlotte.

"Think about it. Only we know about Brendan's involvement, and the fact that he was waiting to catch the drugs gang. Graham thinks it was an unlucky coincidence as they tried to get me. And… Brendan doesn't know that Mark is in fact Graham."

"True, but how does that help us?"

"I don't know yet," admitted Tony, then with a shrug of his shoulders he let the phone dial the number that was already up on the display.

"Charlotte?" came the all too familiar sound of Brendan Scott.

"No, it is Tony, but Charlotte is here with me."

"Thank God you are safe. Caroline would have killed me if anything had happened to you."

"You haven't been much help over the last four years, so why care now?"

Ignoring the bitterness in Tony's voice Brendan took a moment then replied, "I promise you I care, and I have been looking out for you all along. You were always safest in jail, I just forgot about your ability to surprise me."

Still unconvinced, Tony didn't want to go any further with this conversation, but equally he knew that Brendan could offer the lifeline they needed. "Can you get us out of here?"

"Yes, where are you?"

Charlotte had been listening to the conversation with her head closely against Tony's as they shared the handset, but at this point she pulled away and shook her head violently.

"We are safe at the moment. Make transport available, we are about an hour or so from Gr- Mark's house. I will call you in 20 minutes." With that, he pressed the red button to end the call and threw the phone down onto the bed. "I cannot believe I nearly said Graham, I am sorry."

Charlotte didn't say anything, preferring instead to lift her arms indicating she wanted a cuddle. They wrapped their arms around each other and sat in silence for what seemed like an eternity. Tony felt a sudden surge of sexual chemistry replacing the fear that had been controlling his entire body for the last hour, and he felt suddenly overwhelmed and confused by his feelings for Charlotte. It felt strangely reminiscent of a night long ago at the Gorge, as they kissed, gently at first then more feverishly.

This time it was Charlotte who pulled away, indicating it was time to stop. "We mustn't do this. I am sorry, but this is the trauma and shock taking over."

Tony smiled back in acknowledgement. "I know, I am sorry."

"Don't be, I feel the same as you do right now, and it would be so easy to say yes, but not today. Let's phone Brendan, and get picked up."

Tony made the call, and half an hour later there was a knock at the door. Tony opened it to be greeted by the large half of the odd-looking picnic couple from earlier. "You must be our escort then, I presume."

"Not exactly, we have brought you a car to use, and you are to drive to the Cove, where Caroline will meet you. We are following down tomorrow, so try not to get us into any more trouble meanwhile, please."

Mention of the Cove and its pure tranquillity seemed strangely alien on a day like today, but the mere mention of it brought back floods of memories. "No problem. See you again then."

"No doubt," replied the officer before he shuffled off back to a waiting patrol car.

The familiar red car that he had vaulted over earlier was parked about 20 metres away, and Tony could see the dent on the roof which had resulted from his acrobatics. Turning back to the room he called to Charlotte. "Come on, let's get out of here, our transport has arrived. You can drive, I am a bit rusty."

"Coming."

As they slammed the door behind them they both shared a sense that they were leaving a sanctuary of sorts, and they linked arms as they crossed the car park, trying to provide whatever comfort they could to one another. Tony opened the passenger door and jumped in then passed the key over to Charlotte. Before starting the engine she pulled a small black book out of her back pocket and held it aloft in her left hand.

"What is this, your little black book? I hope I am in there somewhere," laughed Tony.

"Not mine," teased Charlotte as she shook her head, and tapped the book on the dashboard.

"And?" begged Tony, enjoying the moment despite the immense tension that was tying his insides up in knots.

"Well I couldn't help having a good root around in Graham's car when he went into the shop, could I?"

"So what is inside then?"

"Names, phone numbers, bank accounts from what I could see. Here, have a look whilst I drive." With that, she passed the book over and turned the ignition key.

Tony settled into his seat and started studying the book page by page. He was so involved in the detail that he didn't notice the time passing, and before he knew it they were pulling off the main road onto the track up to the Cove. Looking up for the first time in nearly three hours he spoke in a quiet whisper. "Just pull up here a second, you need to see this before we get out."

Charlotte pulled to a stop, and with dusk already starting to fall she put on the interior light. "What's up?"

"Look, this book is filled with names and bank account numbers, but it is all very odd when you look at the names that have been chosen."

"Why?"

"Look here, on this page it is Tony, with four or five bank numbers alongside, and my phone number in Bristol, then Bob, and Paula on separate pages with different account numbers."

"So what is so strange about that? He just uses names he knows to set up accounts."

"Yes but look here." As Tony flicked through page after page all bearing the same name, with up to a hundred bank account details a chill went through them both.

"I don't get it, why is he using my name on all of these pages?"

"He is obsessed with you, isn't he? It is obvious now. You said before that he always got in the way of you and Mark."

"But what does this all mean now? How can it help us?" questioned Charlotte, barely able to hide the growing fear in her voice.

"I don't know but he also lists a couple of numbers in his own name. For now we should just keep this between us, and then try to use it to our advantage."

Charlotte shivered involuntarily, not because of the cold, but the uneasy feeling that the latest revelations sent through her. "Come on, I need to get some sleep, let's get to the cottage, we will talk about this tomorrow."

With that, she put the car in gear again and drove the remaining few hundred metres. Caroline had obviously been waiting at the window and rushed out to meet them both. After a prolonged hug with Tony, she embraced Charlotte and motioned towards the house.

"Come in, you two. I have been worried sick. I made some supper for you both. Come in and eat up, you must be starving."

Tony hesitated at the doorway as Charlotte followed Caroline in. This house was so important to him, and the memories of Laura were always strongest here. It had been a long time and he needed to compose himself before he brought the trauma of the last few years into the tranquillity of the Cove.

After a few deep breaths he went inside and they both ate the food that had been prepared before retiring to bed, completely exhausted from the day's events. Tony felt strange being in Laura's old room, and somehow even worse when he looked in her wardrobe to see some of his old clothes still hanging there. He went to go downstairs and ask Caroline about them, but thought better of it and climbed into bed instead. The familiar sound of the waves gently lapping onto the shoreline below brought comfort, but his mind was too busy to settle properly.

After a disturbed night of half-sleep he was awoken by the sound of voices from across the landing, and although he couldn't make out what was being said, he knew that Caroline and Charlotte were deep in conversation. Rather than getting up he flicked through Graham's address book again to see if there were any more clues inside. As he turned page after page, he felt increasingly uneasy about what he was seeing before him.

Bob, Charlotte, Graham, James, Juan, Julie, Laura, Mark, Paul, Paula, Tony, The circle of people that had been the focus of his last 20 years were an odd reference point, and the mystery was, why had Graham used so many of Tony's acquaintances to cover his tracks? And why were so many pages devoted to Laura, and Charlotte?

The familiar ring of the clock tower outside broke into his concentration, and on the seventh strike of the bell Tony decided to dress and wander downstairs for breakfast. As he slowly made his way down the steps he could hear a bustle of voices and was surprised to see just how packed the lounge was when he entered. Charlotte and Caroline had been joined by Brendan, as well as the picnic couple from yesterday. James had arrived too and appeared to be standing guard at the door.

"Morning Tony, come and join us so that I can update you both." Brendan indicated that Tony should take the vacant seat next to Charlotte as he finished.

He then took a quick swig from his cup, which he handed over to Caroline before continuing. "You have of course met the intrepid duo of Sergeants Dave and Jenny. They were assigned to protect you yesterday if you turned up at the house but unfortunately it all went a bit wrong." As he finished the sentence Tony noted the disdainful look that he shot in the direction of his officers.

"James is here to protect you for the next couple of days, so don't please try to lose him." Brendan stared hard at Tony as he finished before standing up, and removing some papers from his inside pocket. "We are not sure about Mark's next movements, but fortunately we did pick up some very nasty individuals yesterday, and even after the explosion in the car we have enough to prosecute them. Mark unfortunately got away, and we have his parents under surveillance in case he goes to them for help. They haven't heard from him for years, and don't want to but desperate people and all that."

Tony tried not to look at Charlotte but from the corner of his eye knew that she was thinking the same as him. It was Bob and Paula that they should be watching, and maybe this was the time to tell all.

"You two need to stay here for the time being, because you are relatively safe, and I need to return to London in the next hour or so, but I would ask one favour before I go." Brendan paused and looked between Tony and Charlotte, both of whom sat impassively, showing no reaction whatsoever.

"I have a phone number here that was recovered from the people we arrested, and I believe it is Mark's phone. If one of you two, preferably Charlotte, could ring the number, we need about two minutes to get a fix on the location."

Tony turned slightly to see her head nod in acknowledgement, before Brendan continued.

"Okay you two, grab some breakfast and I will sort the necessary details."

They ate in virtual silence, desperate to talk, in particular with James, but afraid to discuss their knowledge in public. Eventually Brendan walked into the kitchen offering a phone and scrap of paper with the number on it to Charlotte. "We are ready if you are."

"Yes, let's get it over with, but what should I discuss with him?"

"Anything, only don't tell him where you are for your own safety, he is most probably armed and extremely dangerous right now, and Tony if you could wait out in the lounge or garden we do need absolute silence. Everyone else is outside."

Tony took the hint and wandered out to find Caroline sat alone on a chair by the patio table. "Hi, mind if I join you?"

"Of course not."

They sat in silence for a minute or two before Caroline spoke again. "This is all a bit of a mess, isn't it? I am sorry you had to get dragged into all of this."

A little confused by her comments Tony stared at the familiar face of the clock tower, and reflected on how different he felt to the summer spent here with Laura. "It is not your fault, it was my brother who got us all into this."

"Your brother and my husband in a way. I just wish it would all go away. Laura would be turning in her grave if she knew what you had been through."

"Yes, I am sorry."

Caroline leant in, and spoke in a hushed tone even though no one else was within earshot. "Tony, don't be sorry, none of this is your fault. Blame me, Brendan or Graham and Mark, but never yourself."

She paused for a brief second, then took Tony's hand in her own, as though she was about to divulge some very important information. Looking into her eyes he could sense that her mind was struggling to put her thoughts into words, and it was a feeling he knew well. To relieve the obvious pressure on her Tony looked away and glanced up at the clock tower as the hand swept gently towards nine o'clock local time.

Reacting as soon as the realisation hit him, he jumped up as the first strike of the bell sounded out, flew past a shocked and bewildered James then raced into the kitchen, grabbed the receiver from a startled Charlotte, and stabbed at the red button, then when it wouldn't disconnect he threw it with all the force he could muster onto the floor where it smashed into a handful of pieces. As the bell continued to strike another eight times there was a stunned silence in the kitchen, and as Tony glanced around he could see that everyone was staring at him in complete shock. Silence prevailed until Dave walked in with a set of headphones half-cocked over one ear. "Sorry, Guv, lost the signal just too soon, barely another ten seconds. Can we try again?"

Brendan was on the floor now picking up the broken pieces of the phone whilst still staring up at Tony, apparently more in disgust now than alarm. By way of apology and explanation Tony knew he had to come clean, and he looked at Charlotte for approval as he began. "You have to understand something, Brendan. Something we haven't had chance to explain before."

As if to lend her support Charlotte nodded her approval and Tony continued. "The person you are hunting isn't Mark, it is Graham, he has had surgery or whatever but it is definitely my brother."

Of the people now assembled in the room, only Caroline let out an audible gasp of surprise. Brendan either knew or suspected beforehand, and equally James appeared to accept the revelation all too easily.

"He knows this place, he knows the clock tower, and…" At this moment Tony wanted someone to help him out. Had his overreaction ruined the police operation for the second time in two days? Was Brendan about to have him arrested?

"You were right to stop the call, Tony, but we don't know what Graham heard. You must tell me anything else that you know regardless of how insignificant it may seem before I go back to London."

Again Tony looked to Charlotte for guidance, and with a reluctant shrug of her shoulders she conveyed what she was thinking. They had no choice but to share the book, and he reached into his back pocket and handed it over. Brendan had a cursory glance through the pages then went into the lounge with David.

Over the next few hours the police officers sat in a small huddle, radioing or telephoning various colleagues before Brendan announced that he had to leave with James for a few hours and suddenly calm was restored. Caroline was clearly increasingly anxious as she prepared lunch, and Tony felt that she was deliberately avoiding eye contact with him after their aborted conversation from earlier. When the food was ready they all sat out on the patio to enjoy the beautiful warm sunshine as they ate. Conversation between the five of them was very stilted, and basically revolved around the views of the Cove, and the sounds of the sea.

By one o'clock Tony felt that the tension was unbearable, and so he stood up and stretched his arms behind his head. "Would anyone like a walk along the cliff top? I fancy a bit of fresh air."

"Sorry but we have orders to stay here, and you shouldn't wander off too far either," replied Dave, spitting crumbs from his mouth as he chewed through a half-eaten baguette.

"Caroline?" questioned Tony in response.

"No, I er, have to clear these things away, and you really mustn't go too far for your own safety." Clearly still quite flustered, Caroline grabbed a few dirty plates and hurried into the kitchen.

"I will come if you like, just let me get changed a minute, you cannot go alone." As Charlotte finished she pushed her chair back and ran indoors.

True to her word she was back almost as quickly, and with a promise not to be gone too long they set off, with Tony pointing out as many local landmarks as he could remember from his visits of four years ago. After walking for nearly an hour they were still able to hear the clock strike twice, despite the distance, and instinctively Tony looked down at his watch. "Three o'clock, we had better head back in case the others are getting worried about us."

"Do we have to? It seems a million miles away from yesterday out here, can't we just stay a bit longer?"

"That is why Laura loved this whole place so much. It is only just off the beaten track but you leave the pressures and stresses of the outside world at the end of the lane. There is no fear, no crime, no malice or anything here, and I don't think anyone could fail to be over awed by this place."

"Thanks for the sermon. So can we stay a bit longer then?" pleaded Charlotte.

"No, I want to show you the beach under the clock tower at its very best. It will be incredibly still right now, and the water reflects the sun like a vast shimmering mirror, as though it is luxuriating in the warmth of the suns glow, relaxing before our very eyes."

"Come on then, I will race you." With that, Charlotte turned and started to jog back gently. Tony ran at her side, but as they approached the stone tower he was dismayed to see that the sea was actually quite choppy. So much so in fact that a couple down below were struggling to load up their boat as it bobbed up and down, just a few metres from the shoreline.

They were carrying supplies from their van that was on the sand but already the tide was fast approaching the front wheels, and they kept dropping their load as they rushed to carry it to the boat.

"So who uses this place then? Doesn't it all belong to Laura's parents?" asked Charlotte.

Tony smiled at the question, and answered as honestly as he could. "I cannot tell you the whole story but this all actually belongs to me now. It was Laura's and she left it to me. Those people down there are probably just locals, and they have free use of area, but it is owned by me now. I will only ever be a sort of custodian though, because it is really a shared ownership with the families that live

359

around here."

Obviously taken aback Charlotte couldn't help but look stunned. "Wow, you are a bit of a dark horse as well, aren't you?"

Before he could reply, Tony heard a car crunching up the track, and turned to see Brendan and James returning. Hoping that they would be bringing some positive news at last, they ran the short distance back towards the cottage.

"What has happened? Why is no one answering the telephone or radios? Where are the others?" Brendan had dispensed with any pleasantries as he jumped from the car almost before it had stopped.

Sensing the urgency in his voice Tony swung around to look at the cottage, and realised at once that something was seriously amiss. The front door was no longer just open, but hanging across the door frame, supported only by its bottom hinge. He didn't wait to think of his own safety but raced over, vaulting the lopsided door and running into the lounge where the evidence of a violent struggle was everywhere. The sight of blood spattered by the stairs to the upper floor was an ominous warning of what might lay ahead, but Tony didn't hesitate, and jumped the steps two at a time. James was just behind, shouting for him to be careful, and wait for backup, but acting just as recklessly himself. They reached the landing and could hear muffled cries from inside Laura's old room.

The door was open, and blankets and pillows were strewn around everywhere. Tony crept forward, until he could see Jenny's head with her back to the bed. He raced around to see her, but stopped in shock as he reached the other side of the bed, and saw for the first time the body of Dave laid across her legs, with dried blood matting his hair. James was only just behind him, and as his training took over he shoved Tony aside, and rolled Dave on to his back. Then he pulled the tape off Jenny's mouth before turning his attention again to his injured colleague.

Dave was still obviously alive but had clearly lost a lot of blood, and was only semi-conscious at best.

"Tony run down to the car, and call for an ambulance. Use the radio then get yourself back here."

With a terrible sense of déjà vu evoking memories of his race for help at the Gorge years before, he span around and jumped down the stairs barely touching the steps at all, then he flew past Charlotte and ran to the car. Tony put the call in then headed back to the cottage, barely able to comprehend what was happening. As he reached the bedroom Charlotte had taken control, and was shouting instructions as she tried to treat Dave's wounds, and stabilise him as much as she could.

"We have to move him downstairs, the ambulance could be ages yet, and we cannot care for him all crumpled up here beside the bed. Try to make him as comfortable as possible and—"

"Is that safe? Shouldn't we wait for the ambulance?" questioned Brendan.

Clearly not impressed at having her judgement questioned Charlotte stared back for a brief moment, then as if to reaffirm her control she replied instead to James. "Quick, grab hold of his leg, he isn't badly injured, and there are no broken bones, but he is concussed, and he is dehydrated so we need to get him to have some water."

Without any more discussion they gently lifted Dave, and carried him gently down to the sofa downstairs. Brendan then ushered Jenny into the kitchen.

As Charlotte attended to her patients she looked up at Tony and whispered, "What the hell happened?"

"Graham, I guess."

"Where is he now?"

"No idea. Is Dave going to be alright?"

"Yes, he will be fine." She nodded in confirmation. "Have you seen Caroline?"

"Graham took her with him," interrupted Brendan as he walked in looking grim. "You two need to stay with me. He has an accomplice with him, and probably a boat."

As he finished they heard the distant sound of sirens approaching, then Brendan raced outside to meet the ambulance. They quickly assessed the situation, with Charlotte's help, and brought in a stretcher to take Dave away. He was taken on board and driven away at full speed, although with no sirens this time. The lovely sunny day from earlier had completely vanished to be replaced by a chill breeze and damp fine drizzle. As they all stood outside the dampness went right through their clothes and the chill wind almost cut into their bodies.

"What now?" questioned Tony, hoping that they could get back into the warmth of the cottage.

"I really don't know. We have to find Graham, preferably before he finds us, or gets away altogether," replied Brendan, clearly frustrated that he was being outwitted and outmanoeuvred.

"What about the boat we saw on the beach, Tony? Could that have been Graham?" shouted Charlotte.

"What boat?"

"Down on the beach earlier there was a boat and van, but I think they were just locals." Tony was angry with himself that he had forgotten to mention this earlier. As he finished the clock started striking and they all looked up as they counted the four strikes. The drizzle was increasingly heavy, and with the light fading visibility wasn't great, but to Tony's dismay he immediately recognised the walk of the person approaching them. With increasing anxiety he also knew that it was a gun being pointed in his direction. In an instant the fear from yesterday that he had managed to quell for almost 24 hours resurfaced, and he felt his body lose all of its strength as suddenly his mouth was bone dry, and his hands clammy and wet.

From some misplaced sense of duty or sheer recklessness he walked forward, totally disregarding the gun that was pointed in his direction.

"Stay where you are, Tony. You other three, over beside him now," barked Graham as he stood still now about five metres away.

They followed their orders, and waited.

"Is there anyone else in that house?"

"No," came the reply from all three of them in unison.

"Right then, I don't have time to check but if you are lying I will not hesitate to use this gun, and if you take me out then you will never see Caroline, Bob or Paula again. Understood?"

They all nodded in confirmation, but only Tony spoke. "Graham this has to stop. Get on your boat and go, but this cannot carry on. What are you trying to do?"

Moving very slowly he raised the gun again, and pointed it just at Tony now. "You have ruined everything all my life, and all I ever did was for you. You have never had to struggle like I did just to live and still you are an ungrateful little bastard. Tell me one good reason why I don't pull this trigger right now."

As he finished Tony could see his fingers loosen and adjust the grip on the gun. He closed his eyes waiting for the shot to ring out.

"No, Graham." Charlotte's voice suddenly shifted the focus. "You cannot kill Tony, or any of us. You are a good person. I always liked you as a friend and I know you haven't changed that much. Put the gun down and walk away. You can still make amends, you know."

"You never liked me at all. You tolerated me because I was Mark's friend and Tony's brother but you never liked me. None of you did, you had your closed little group and I was always the outsider."

"That's rubbish, Graham, I liked you always, and I never shut you out. Mark was your friend, but James and Paul liked you as well."

James had been strangely quiet but he knew his input was essential now. "She is right, Graham, it is time to move on."

"Mark was a waster as well. He ruined my life by letting me ride a dangerous bike then he tried to take my position within school. I was stuck in a wheelchair for months when I should have been racing around playing sport, and without the drugs the pain would have been unbearable at first. Why do you think I stopped him being the hero at the Games? I had a hold over Mark until you stuck your oar in and tried to drag him back to your bosom, but he never made it, did he?" sneered Graham.

He was shouting at Charlotte, and appeared increasingly desperate. The implications of his words sent a chill through the little group, but remarkably she kept her composure, and continued the dialogue. "Compared to a lot of people you have had it easy, and you know it deep down. You don't have to prove anything to me, Graham. I know this isn't you. You are a naturally generous, caring person. You cared for your mother, and you love Tony, Bob and Paula. They are your family, and family means more than anything to you."

"Shut it, I said. You don't know anything. I have always been on my own. I tried to help Tony but he always knew best and ended up ruining my life as well. Now all of you get over to that clock tower, and keep your distance from me."

As they walked around in a large arc, both Tony and Charlotte picked up on the emotion evident in Graham's last response.

"Now listen to me, and I might just let you live. There is a van on the beach with Bob, Paula, and Caroline all tied up in the back. The way that tide is coming in I reckon you have about an hour to save them. I am going to get on the boat moored over there, and if I get away you can free them. If I get stopped I will press this and blow the van sky high."

Only Brendan recognised the radio-activated detonator as being authentic, but it didn't matter. They all knew that Graham was clearly very desperate and very dangerous.

"Where will you go, Graham? Charlotte is right, you are family. You cannot leave us all and disappear like this. It isn't like when you were a little boy stealing food to survive."

Graham smiled, and shook his head. "For once one of your little sad girlfriends has done me some good. That house up there was loaded with gold bars, would you believe? And seeing as Laura doesn't need them I have taken them. It was a struggle, but with some help from Juan I got them onto the boat, so you see lovely Laura is looking after me. I always thought that she fancied me deep down, you know, and Julie for that matter. They just stayed with you out of pity."

"You cannot take that gold, Graham. You are about to make the biggest mistake of your life. The gold belongs here, it cannot be taken away. Please give it over and hand yourself in, this is your last chance!" shouted Tony against the torrential wind and rain.

"Enough!" shouted Graham in reply, with a determination that made everyone stop. "I am going to run down to the Cove. It is 4.30 by that clock so I reckon it will take me half an hour to reach the boat. You can make a move at 5.00, but when I reach the beach I want you all to stand at the cliff edge so that I can see you otherwise I will blow the van." As he finished Graham swung a heavily laden rucksack awkwardly onto his left shoulder.

This time it was James who replied. "Look, Graham, why don't you leave that bag behind? You must have the other gold already and it will only slow you down. If you don't get to your boat soon it will be too dark to get away."

"Don't push me, James. I liked you, always have, but don't push me, if I have to use this gun I will."

"Graham please hand me the gun and turn yourself in. You can still sort this mess out. With the information you have I can minimise your sentence," interrupted Brendan, although the sense of desperation in his voice was apparent to everyone present.

"Brendan Scott you don't know how much I would love to see you rot to death. If only I had more time I would make sure you had a slow and painful death that would make Laura's look like a picnic in the park."

"Leave Laura out of this, Graham, she is nothing to do with this. You are a murdering lowlife drug trafficker so stop with all the self-pity. You made your own life and screwed it up all on your own. I have listened to all the crap you have been spouting but the only person you have to blame is yourself. You are a nothing compared to Tony. He showed my daughter respect for human life that you couldn't even imagine." The desperation from a moment ago had now been replaced with anger. Brendan was gambling with Graham's emotions, but it was a risky business and everyone around held their breath.

Tony could see his brother tense up and tried to intervene. "Graham, please listen, you need to take stock of this mess. It is not too late to—"

The shot rang out as if in slow motion, against a backdrop of high winds, swirling rain thunder and lightning. The whole cove lit up, and the assembled group felt as though they were in freeze frame. Brendan was the only person to move a muscle as he fell to the floor holding on to his thigh. Graham stood breathing heavily, biting his lower lip, waving the gun between the other four then returned its aim to Brendan. "Now tell them the truth. You have persecuted me for years for nothing. You had a vendetta against me even when I was only small time, and you had to use your own daughter to haul me in, didn't you? She didn't care about Tony, you used her to entrap me, you don't care about anything apart from getting a result. Tell them the truth. You are lower than anything I have become. You are vile police scum at its worst."

In spite of his obvious pain Brendan felt the need to respond in defence but turned to Tony, not his accuser. "It is not true, Tony, he is trying to play with your mind."

Trying to take in everything was impossible. His thoughts were spinning in all different directions, but his brain put up barriers every time he ventured down different paths. "What is he saying about Laura? How was she involved in all of this?"

"See, little brother, this is why I have always tried to protect you from the world. But you could never see it, could you? No, you had to make your own way, and look what you have done."

"What? What have I done? I loved Laura, that's all."

"She used you, Tony, to help her dad catch me. I don't know how it happened but I sent a drug consignment over to Juan, then you gave it to her, and it never reached him. That caused a load of strife and he had to race back to Spain to make amends with our contacts. That packet was worth nearly £100,000."

As the wind and rain lashed against their backs, Tony started to edge backwards. His world was collapsing around him, and he couldn't cope anymore. It would be easier to end it all now, he just wanted to walk backwards off the cliff, but Charlotte realised what was happening and grabbed him back.

"Tony, see sense please. Laura loved you more than life itself. You know that in your heart, and you have to trust your own judgement. You have to stay alive for her sake. She gave you everything she had, and your love prolonged her life beyond any reasonable expectations, and she is still protecting you now. Don't throw it away. She may have had a loyalty to her dad as well, but only in the pursuit of good. As soon as she met Graham she warned him to get off the drugs, and when he threatened her she stood up to him. I was in awe of her then, and I still am today. If we had stood up to Graham when we had the chance years ago we could have stopped all this back in our schooldays. I have always loved you because you make good judgements, independently of Graham. You are your own person, you always were so believe in yourself."

"Shut it," responded Graham, desperately fighting against the billowing wind and rain.

Charlotte saw the gun pointed directly at her now, but she didn't show any sense of fear whatsoever. Graham continued with pure venom, but still she stared back unflinching.

"Your time is running out, and this chatter is getting us nowhere. You can come with me if you want, Tony. The rest of you stay put. Make a decision." The sheer hatred in his voice was threatening, but it made Tony see some sense. Charlotte was right. He took inspiration from the strength Laura had shown in him and knew it was time he took control again.

"Go if you are going, but I am staying. You don't deserve my love or support, and I swear if anything happens to anyone else then I will track you down and exact my own revenge. Laura obviously had you sussed the moment she met you, because she was worth a thousand of you." As he finished Tony could feel the relief running through his body. He needed to be rid of Graham, and the demons associated with him once and for all. Maybe this was the fresh start he had needed since Laura died.

"You loser. Well don't expect to hear from me again. I will be spending the money she left for me." With that, he turned and hobbled off into the dusky evening. His bag was clearly a real burden, and the weather was not helping at all. The wind was blowing so hard now that it was almost impossible to stand on the cliff top, and as Tony glanced up he realised that the rhythmic tick from the clock tower had stopped.

"What is it, Tony? What is up?" shouted Charlotte struggling to be heard above the inclement weather. She knew instinctively that something important had caught his attention.

"The clock has stopped. It is sending a message. It is telling us how to win."

"What are you on about?" replied James. "What is happening here?"

"Tony, it is old superstition, nothing more. Get to my car and radio for help!" screamed Brendan, his hands now covered in blood as they cradled his wounded leg. "and get us another ambulance."

"No. Brendan you don't get it, do you?" He bent down now, but still had to shout to be heard. "This is history repeating itself. The forces of nature are helping us. Laura is helping us. History is helping us."

Tony stood up and despite the harrowing weather he could see the sense of complete bewilderment on everyone's face. No one wanted to speak so Tony carried on, keen to stay in control. "Jenny, you and Charlotte take Brendan to the house. James, you follow me."

"Tony it won't work. You need real backup. Real people, not spooks." Brendan sounded desperate, but maybe it was the lack of conviction in what he was saying that drove Tony on.

"Brendan you must trust me, trust your daughter. This is Laura's cove. She is doing this, and if you believe in your daughter you will trust me." With that, he raced over to the clock tower, opened the door and lifted the false floor.

He heard a distant, "Be careful," as James shone his torch down the narrow steps and they raced down to the cliff face.

In the half light of the torch Tony climbed down by feel as much as anything else, and counted the steps as he went. Thankfully James followed dutifully without questioning where they were going or what they were doing. He had absolute faith in his best friend, and knew better than to delay their progress with unnecessary questioning.

"One hundred and sixty," as he moved on around the next curve natural light, albeit a half light was flooding in ,and Tony jumped the last few steps and ran over to the boulder masking the entrance to the tunnel. He had an excellent vantage point from here but he couldn't make out where his brother was through the blustery rain that was lashing all around them. The water level had risen considerably, and the van was starting to shift position each time the tide came in and receded.

They clambered over the rock together, slid down to the beach and raced over to the van. With the water now around waist height it was slow progress, but by using their hands as paddles they managed to reach the back doors. At first Tony feared that they were locked, but then as the tide went back again the water level fell, and he was able to wrench the door open. Before he could speak someone floored him with a flying tackle, and he was being held underwater.

All the air went from his lungs, and all that he could see was a white swirling mass of bubbles. He was flailing his arms about, trying to strike his attacker, but his chest was screaming out in pain, desperate for oxygen.

Suddenly, just as he was starting to lose the battle for his life the attacker dragged him up out of the water, and through bleary eyes his focus was gradually restored to reveal Bob's familiar face. "Sorry Tony, I thought you were Graham. Thank God you had James with you or I would have drowned you."

The apology seemed totally inadequate, but they knew that it would have to suffice for now.

"Forget it... Are you okay?" Tony was bent double still spluttering for breath, but desperate to beat Graham back to the cliff.

"Yes, we managed to work ourselves free, and then I wanted to surprise Graham. The van is rigged with explosives, and I didn't open the door in case it was wired."

Tony had never even considered the possibility when he pulled on the handle moments earlier, but thankfully they had all survived. "All of you follow James, back up to the cliff as fast as you can. I will close the van and follow."

He watched them disappear for just a second before wading closer to the van. Unfortunately with the water now swirling inside it was far harder to shut the door than he had imagined, and the blustery wind wasn't helping at all either. He leant against the door panel putting every ounce of strength he had left, but the sand under his feet simply shifted away sapping his energy, and negating his efforts. Try as he might he couldn't close it the final few inches that were required for the latch to click, and eventually he had no option but to give up. The weather was worsening all the time, and now it looked more like midnight than late afternoon.

Tony trudged slowly back through the water, using what little strength he had left, but very conscious that Graham would be upon him any minute. Maybe they would miss each other in the darkness, but he held out little hope of that happening. As he finally broke free of the water he moved a little faster, but he was freezing cold, soaking wet, and battling a severe wind that seemed to be bouncing off the cliff face and forcing him back. At the bottom of the cliff he glanced up at the rock above him that was to provide sanctuary. He knew it was only a matter of metres to climb, but it seemed like the summit of a mountain right now. The rest of the group were just clambering to safety, and with sheer determination forcing his wrecked body on he started the climb. It was by no means easy and even finding a foothold in the pouring rain was difficult. He slipped back several times, and could see streams of blood running from his torn nails, back down his hands and arms. Suddenly a bright flash lit the sky, but the loud bang which followed from behind indicated that this wasn't lightning.

As Tony struggled to twist his head around, a smaller bang coincided with a flash glancing off the rock ahead. He recognised the shot from the cliff top earlier, and this time he turned his whole body over and allowed himself to slide down to the sand. There was unfinished business to attend to, and despite his lack of a weapon he knew that he had to take Graham on face to face. They both stood staring at each other, Tony at the base of the cliff where he had enjoyed a picnic with Laura many years before and his brother some 20 metres to his left side. The natural shape of the Cove was sheltering them now, and they were in a basin of relative calm, whilst the storm continued to range all around and above them.

"This is it, Graham, judgement time. Everyone is safe, so you have nothing left to bargain with."

"Wrong, I have this. So it is advantage me." He waved the gun about as though daring Tony to come and get it.

"That may represent the currency by which you live your life but it counts for nothing here and now. Kill me but the police will pick you up sooner or later. You may as well quit now."

"You really don't get it, do you little bro? I am in control of everything right now. Juan is in the boat ready to go and I am taking you with me as security, dead or alive."

"Why, Graham? Where does all this hatred come from? What can it possibly achieve? You have ruined your life enough and it is time to stop running now."

"Far from it. I have money, and I will have freedom not only from the police but you as well. All my life has been tainted since you were born. Mum and Dad were happy before then, happy and loving until you came in the way of their happiness and spoilt everything. I wish you had died along with your wretched little sister."

Tony could barely muster the strength to respond at all, and with the toils of the last few days taking their toll he slumped forward onto his knees, and joined his hands behind the back of his head. "Shoot me then, because I am not going anywhere with you."

He stayed rock still with water gently lapping around his knees waiting for the shot. To pass the last few moments he started counting to himself and reached ten as the sound came, but as he felt the searing pain hit his left shoulder he was already aware of a far greater force. The sound of the sea was roaring now like a distant jet engine, but getting closer every second.

His left arm felt limp, and he could feel the warm blood running down inside his shirt, but this wasn't the end. He wasn't ready to die, and in sheer defiance he scrambled to his feet and looked over at Graham. The roar was almost deafening now, and as Tony looked out to the sea he could see a massive wall of water approaching from the distance. Strangely his brother had stood transfixed ever since the shot left his gun, whether from shock at what he had done or some other force it wasn't clear. Despite his injuries Tony knew he had to make it to safety, and he scrambled as quickly as he could up the rock face using only his uninjured right arm. Progress was slow, and with the rumble growing ever louder he turned to look back.

Juan's boat was being carried on the crest of the massive wave that was now only feet away then as it moved relentlessly on it picked up Graham as well and in the next moment Tony was also under the swell. He could feel the water dragging him backwards, but he was completely helpless, as any effort to swim was completely wasted. His lungs had barely recovered from earlier, but now they were desperately seeking air again, and then suddenly the water was carrying him forwards back towards the cliff face. He was on the surface now riding the wave, as though suddenly the sea was lifting him up. He sucked in gulps of air at every opportunity, spitting the salt water back, trying to suppress the rising nausea.

Once at the base of the cliff he felt the sea lower him, almost serenely, before it receded out into the Cove. Then the waves returned just the once and barely kissed his feet before receding completely. Totally drained, Tony couldn't move and allowed his eyes to close. Sleep wasn't an option but he needed time to rebuild his strength. Within minutes he felt the warmth of late afternoon sunlight on his back, and he could hear approaching voices. He opened his eyes and saw James followed by Charlotte, Bob, Paula, and Caroline, as they were all scrabbling down the cliff face.

At his feet lay Graham's rucksack and another larger black holdall that was half submerged in the wet sand already. The van was on its side, barely ten feet away, still being tossed around by the ebbing tide. The remains of the boat were strewn everywhere, and Graham's lifeless body lay about 50 metres away, bent double in an impossible way with another lifeless form sprawled across him.

Caroline reached Tony first, and threw her jacket around his injured shoulder. "Thank God you are okay. Brendan has gone to the hospital, and there is another ambulance on its way." She took a moment to survey the devastation around then tried to pick up the black holdall, but it was too heavy so she unzipped it to peer inside before looking back to Tony.

"Just as I thought. Laura chose well. The legacy of the Cove has saved mortal man from the folly of his ways again, and I know you will pass it on wisely."

Sheer exhaustion took over and Tony closed his eyes. The pain in his shoulder was excruciating, but he mustered enough strength to pull his weary body up into a sitting position, and Caroline slumped down beside him. Both ignored the wet sand and lapping waves as they looked out to sea, with Caroline's head inclined into Tony's shoulder much as her daughter had done on many occasions before.

Printed in Poland
by Amazon Fulfillment
Poland Sp. z o.o., Wrocław

53957153R00215